Stephen Clegg was born in Stockport in 1947. He is retired and living happily on the south coast of England with his wife. Since the publication of his first novel 'Maria's Papers' in 2012, he has been nominated for three prestigious book prizes and was a finalist in 'The People's Book Prize 2013/14'.

This book is dedicated to my beautiful grandchildren,
Eleanor, Francesca, Vincent, and Sebastian.

I love you all more than words can convey.

I am eternally grateful to my wife Jay, my daughter Nicola, my loyal test readers Jayne Miles, Jean Dickens, Lorraine and Kevin Middleton, and Michele Norton, who all helped me through the writing of this novel.

Additionally I owe special debts of gratitude to Staff Sergeant Ted Wylie REME for his invaluable help and advice about the suggested development of The Halo, and to ex-British Telecom Technical Officer Peter Milnes for his expertise on the workings of telecommunications.

Thank you, you all know how much you mean to me.

Stephen F. Clegg

The
Hallenbeck Echo

AUSTIN MACAULEY
PUBLISHERS LTD.

A CIP catalogue record for this title is available from the British Library.

ISBN 9781786299178 (Paperback)
ISBN 9781786299185 (E-book)

www.austinmacauley.com

First Published (2017)
Austin Macauley Publishers Ltd.
25 Canada Square
Canary Wharf
London
E14 5LQ

Preface

Friday 26th January 2007. The deserted St
Mary Cross Animal Research Unit,
Skelmersdale, Lancashire

A horrific and tortured squeal erupted from within the building. Every last drop of blood drained out of Naomi's face. She snatched her mobile from her ear, wheeled around, and stared wild-eyed at the locked doors and mirrored windows.

A second screech followed by an agonised wail launched her heart rate to stratospheric levels, and she started to back away. And then something big and heavy slammed into the inside wall, opposite her.

Not daring to take her eyes off the building, she lifted the mobile phone back to her ear and said, "Holy Christ Helen, did you hear that? They told me that this place was deserted." She waited for a response but heard nothing. She looked at the phone and saw that she'd lost the signal. She gasped and said, "Right – just what I need…"

Deep in the trees at the end of the facility, the man with the gun was just as shocked; he too couldn't take his eyes off the rear elevation in case something smashed its way out.

Naomi heard the sound of an approaching vehicle and began to run towards the gates. She heard the engine slow, and realised that the security guard had returned. As he appeared at the top of the drive, she charged up to him and half-yelled, "I thought you said this place was deserted!"

The guard looked up and said, "It is."

"It bloody well isn't!"

The shocked guard said, "It is, I assure you. Nobody's occupied the place for at least five years."

"Then how the hell do you explain a God-awful, tortured screech coming from within the building?"

"What?"

"A screech, a gut-wrenching wail, and then something big slamming into an inside wall?"

The guard frowned, looked at the building and said, "*What*, in there?"

"Yes in there!"

The guard looked back at Naomi and said, "That can't be; show me where."

Naomi led the guard to the rear of the building.

The man in the trees watched their approach and removed a silenced pistol from his jacket pocket.

Naomi reached the place where she'd heard the sound and pointed to a window. She said, "It was in there."

The man in the trees lifted the pistol and took aim.

The guard said, "No way! Inside there are just old labs filled with junk. They're completely empty."

Naomi said, "I am not lying, and I was not hallucinating! Something *is* inside there and it let out a horrible shriek!"

The guard looked back at the building, and didn't know what to say.

Minutes later, as Naomi and the guard walked back to the entrance, the man in the trees pocketed his pistol and took out a mobile phone. He dialled a number and said, "Something's seriously wrong here boss, the weirdest thing just happened…"

Chapter 1

Rain, rain, rain: Harry Appleton cursed the never-ending deluge that cascaded down the windscreen of his van as he turned off the narrow country road and pulled up at the security gate of the Slaidburn coal-fired power station.

The security guard put his raincoat on, walked out to the car and said, "Evening sir, filthy night isn't it?"

Appleton flashed his pass and said, "You can say that again."

The guard pulled his peaked cap lower down and bent to the driver's window. He said, "We were expecting you earlier Mr Appleton."

Appleton peered out of the small opening and said, "Yes, I'm sorry about that; this bloody awful rain hasn't made it easy to see where I was going – and I was held up at Ferrybridge C before coming here."

"Ferrybridge? Good grief, you haven't driven from there have you, sir?"

"Yes, and when I finish here I have to get home to Manchester."

The security guard expelled a long breath, "Rather you than me, sir." He shook his head and then said, "Right, best not to keep you chit-chatting," he touched the peak of his cap, returned to his hut and pressed the switch that opened the barrier.

Appleton smiled, nodded, and drove through to the station.

It had been four days since the catastrophic lightning bolt had shut down the enormous Drax Power station in North Yorkshire, and the torrential rain still hadn't abated.

Massive pressure had been applied by the public and Government to get the power restored, but the engineers still hadn't fixed it. As a result, Drax Power had had to fall back onto its emergency contingency plan.

Some power had been restored to commercial enterprises and a few homes with the aid of the Ferrybridge C power station in West Yorkshire, but, and much against the advice of the senior engineers of Drax, an executive decision had been taken to re-fire the standby Slaidburn station until the repairs had been completed, and all the safety tests had been run.

Malcolm Ridyard, the engineer first despatched to Slaidburn, stared at the computer printout given to him by Appleton and then looked back at the bank of switches on the dull, grey, fifties-style console. He said, "This doesn't match."

Appleton didn't respond. He continued to scrutinise the banks of old-fashioned dials and switches until he heard Ridyard speak again.

"Harry, did you hear what I just said?"

Appleton turned and said, "No, sorry, what was it again?"

Ridyard pointed to the computer printout and said, "This doesn't match what we've got here."

Appleton frowned and said, "What doesn't match what?"

"This," said Ridyard, "come and see."

Appleton cast a last cursory look over the array of dials and then walked across to Ridyard. He glanced at the printout and then said, "Sorry, I've had a long day, what am I supposed to be looking at?"

"According to this printout, we have six switches to throw to restore power to all areas of the station's capability but, here we have seven switches."

Appleton looked up and saw where Ridyard was indicating. He looked down at it and then back up. He said, "Bugger ..." He turned the bulky printout to face him and then said, "This is all we need. The instruction says to throw the six switches, but it doesn't enumerate, and there aren't any numbers or letters on the actual switches telling us which ones are the right ones."

"Exactly," said Ridyard.

Appleton expelled a long breath, stared at the switches again, and repeated, "Bugger!" He looked at his watch, saw that it was 12:35 a.m., and he knew that his boss would be in bed. He looked back at the switches and then turned to Ridyard.

"Do you live far from here Mal?"

"Miles – in Lancaster."

"Me too, Manchester."

"Blimey, I thought I had it bad, why?"

"Because we're both miles from home, tired, hungry, pissed off, and we've been given a bloody printout that's incorrect. That's why."

"And your point is?"

Appleton looked at the array and then turned to Ridyard. He said, "We have a decision to make. Do we pick six random switches, throw them, and hope that we've got the right ones, or do we throw all seven?"

Ridyard looked back at the switches and then down at the printout. He said, "I don't know Harry …"

Appleton pondered and then said, "What harm would it do if we threw all seven? Each of the switches turns on a specific area of Lancashire and West Yorkshire so it's not as though we'll overload anywhere. When these controls were designed they all had fail-safe systems built into them, so even if we were to double the output to any given location, we couldn't overload the system because one or the other would shut down."

"So what are you suggesting?"

"That we throw all seven, wait half-an-hour, and then if no red lights start flashing and we get no panicky calls, we go home and get some well-earned rest."

Ridyard thought for a few seconds and then raised his eyebrows. He said, "It sounds like a plan to me."

Appleton nodded, double-checked that they hadn't missed anything in the printout, and then watched the white lights turn on one-by-one as he threw the switches.

They waited for the prescribed half hour.

They saw no indication that anything was amiss, they didn't receive any telephone calls, and they concluded that everything was running smoothly.

At 1:35 a.m. they bid the Slaidburn security guard a 'good night' and returned to their individual homes.

Chapter 2

Michael Werm or 'Bookie' to his friends and colleagues – had gained his nickname through his love of reading and the obvious connection to his surname. He was a painter and decorator by trade and though he always got on well with his fellow tradesmen, he never joined in any of their sporting lunchtime games. Every day he would take his food and drink along with a good book to a quiet place and immerse himself in whatever took his fancy at the time.

The contract at McCready House had commenced in September 2006, when the property had been purchased by a private developer from one Lady Jocelyn Fitton-Kearns who had relocated to a luxurious, cliff-top apartment overlooking Bournemouth's seven miles of sandy beaches.

McCready House was a brick-built, three-storey, terraced, Georgian-style property. On the façade, the front door was situated between two reception rooms, whilst to the far left, was a small integral garage. A garage that may have housed cars up until the 1960s, but as the design of cars had widened, it had become a storeroom for all of those unwanted or redundant items that 'may have come in handy' whilst Lady

Jocelyn's husband, Lord Frank of Godley, had been alive, but in the end they had not.

Two rear reception rooms mirrored the front rooms on the ground floor, and to the rear of the small garage lay the kitchen, scullery, and pantry. Running up from the front door to the top of the house was the staircase and landings that led to the first and second floor bedrooms and bathrooms.

One-by-one the contractors had moved in, moved out, and made way for the next skill, until it had been the turn of 'Masters & Lowe, Painters & Decorators Ltd'.

The proprietors, Richard Masters and Dan Lowe had been friends and business partners for many years, and whilst Dan's acerbic tongue kept the staff well and truly motivated, Richard kept his accountant's eye on the finances often to the disdain of those feeling the results of his financial restraints.

Bookie had waited until his co-workers had finished their lunches and had moved outside to kick a football around, and then he'd picked up his beloved lightweight cane chair and taken it into the front room at the far end of the central hall.

As soon as he walked in to the unpainted room, he was beset by the same odd feeling that he'd had each time he'd been there. He looked all around, up and down, but as per each of his previous visits, he couldn't see anything out of the ordinary

He set the cane chair down by the front window, looked around, and wondered if it might be something to do with the internal dimension. He walked back to his toolbox, removed his tape measure, and measured the room's length, breadth, and height. He then walked up the stairs and did the same to the two rooms directly above. They were identical in size.

With a resigned sigh, he walked back downstairs, sat in his chair, and put the thought out of his mind. Minutes later he was lost in the fictive realm of his novel.

His allotted half hour passed too soon, he closed the book, stuffed it into the voluminous pocket of his white overalls, and bent over to pick up the chair. As he did so, he heard a sound. He stood up, remained stock still, and listened. Seconds later he heard it again. It sounded like a bleep; a faint distant bleep. He looked around and wondered if somebody had walked down the hall towards him. He ambled over to the door and peered outside. Nobody was there. With a puzzled expression on his face he turned to go back, but stopped when he heard the familiar voice of Dan Lowe.

"Time's up Bookie – we want this room done before four o' clock so that Bronzy John can get away." Dan was about to turn away when he saw the look of puzzlement on Bookie's face. He said, "Anything up?"

"I thought that…" he looked into the room, realised that he hadn't heard the sound again, and then said, "…never mind, it's nothing."

Dan said, "Okay, come on then." He turned to head back to the kitchen and then heard a voice say, "Oh for Christ's sake – tell me that this isn't happening!" He leaned around the door of the other front reception room and saw Basil, Bookie's mate, holding up a box of rolled wallpapers. He said, "What's the problem?"

"Who ordered these?"

"Richard."

"Typical! Why is he always trying to cut back? When I say I want twenty rolls of paper, why do I always get eighteen? Doesn't he think that I can count? And what the fuck is he doing ordering the paper anyway? He knows…"

"Alright, alright," said Dan, "calm down, I'll give him a call." He turned back and saw Bookie looking into the far room and said, "Bookie! Come on! We haven't got all day!"

Bookie walked back into the unpainted room, picked up his cane chair and got half way to the door when he heard it again. He stopped, listened, and was about to put the chair down when he heard Dan call, *Bookie – get your ass in gear and come on!*

He frowned, cast one last glance around, and then walked back to the other front room.

Chapter 3

Naomi Wilkes, the head of Walmsfield's Historic Research Department, put the phone down on her desk and looked across to her friend and colleague, Helen Milner. Technically she was Helen's boss, but neither of them saw it that way.

Helen said, "What?"

"Bob Crowthorne's just reported in to reception and he's on his way to see us."

Bob Crowthorne, a Superintendent who'd transferred from the Lancashire Constabulary to the Greater Manchester Police, had developed not only an excellent working relationship with Naomi and Helen, but a friendship, too. He was a serious bachelor by design and nature, but since Helen had commenced work in the Walmsfield Historic Research Department his crusty and professional exterior had begun to dissolve and he'd enjoyed more than a few bouts of good-humoured banter with her.

"Were you expecting him?" said Helen.

"No, but I…"

There was a knock on the door, and in that instant, a pressure, similar to a thumb pressing down on Naomi's left shoulder manifested itself, and she knew that it heralded the start of one of her psychic episodes.

She'd first become aware of her unusual capabilities in 2002 when she'd been investigating the mysterious goings-on at the nearby Whitewall Farm. It was an investigation that had meant much more to her than just professional interest, because it had been connected to her own great great great Aunt Maria Chance; and since that time she'd learned that the feeling either preceded hearing something, or that somebody from an unknown dimension was close by and paying attention.

Her psychic help had been invaluable, too, and though she was reluctant to speak about it to most people, Bob Crowthorne, who at first had been dismissive, had been somebody who had benefitted from it, and had secretly started to hope that it could help wherever he needed it.

"Come in Bob," called Helen.

The door opened and Crowthorne stepped inside. He took off his cap and said, "Good morning, ladies."

Helen knew that he was in his mid-forties; not by his ruggedly handsome, clean-shaven face and square jaw line, but by his staid and well-mannered character.

"Morning Bob," replied Naomi, pointing to a chair, "this is a pleasant surprise."

Crowthorne sat down and placed his cap on Naomi's desk.

"Can I get you a cup of anything while you're here?" said Helen.

Crowthorne shot a sideways playful glance across to Helen and said, "Yes, a tea please, ataxi."

Naomi looked at Helen with an inquisitive look upon her face.

Helen smiled at Crowthorne, nodded in a knowing-way, and said, "Uh huh! My fault," she turned to Naomi and said, "After talking to Bob on the phone a few times, he invited me to call him by his Christian name. He then asked what he should call me, and I said 'a taxi'."

Naomi smiled and said, "Ah, I get it now."

"Yes," said Crowthorne feeling a bit awkward at showing his softer side, "and I shouldn't have…er…" he looked down at his feet unsure of what to say and then looked back up and saw Naomi smiling.

"Bob Crowthorne," said Naomi, "whatever next? First you start to believe in my hocus-pocus psychic side…"

Crowthorne made a harrumphing sound and said, "I wouldn't go that far, *believe* is a bit…"

"…and now I find out that you have sense of humour!" She saw the faintest flush of embarrassment spread across Crowthorne's face and then turned to Helen. She said, "So go on then, ataxi, go and get the teas."

Helen grinned and said, "Give him a break N, he's positively squirming."

Crowthorne looked at the two girls and found that he was enjoying the banter; something that was often in short supply at the police station. He turned to Naomi and said, "Hen? That's your nickname? How did you come by that? Was it thought up by your mum and dad whilst you were still an egg?"

Naomi's mouth dropped open. She'd never heard Crowthorne joke before. She turned to Helen and said, "Give him a break? Does that sound like he needs a break?"

Helen laughed and said, "Nope, I guess not! I'll get the teas."

Naomi looked at Crowthorne and said, "And it's not Hen, it's N. Helen calls me N and I call her H."

Crowthorne nodded and said, "Ah – I see – N." He smiled and looked down once more.

Naomi saw, and said, "What?"

Crowthorne smiled again and then looked back at Naomi. He said, "Since I heard that your nickname was N, I've said, I see." He looked up and saw the look of puzzlement on Naomi's face. He said, "N – then I C – get it?"

"Oh now I see too…"

Crowthorne grinned again and said, "Don't start with numbers as well!"

Both friends were still laughing as Helen walked back in with the teas. She said, "Okay what have I missed?"

Crowthorne and Naomi exchanged glances and laughed again at Helen saying, 'OK.'

Naomi shot a last chiding glance at Crowthorne, turned to Helen and said, "I'll explain later." She then turned back to Crowthorne and said, "Now, all fun aside, to what do we owe this honour?"

For the first time since entering, Crowthorne's demeanour changed. He said, "It's our old friend Adrian Darke."

He turned to face Naomi and said, "We think that he's up to his tricks again."

Adrian Darke had first crossed swords with Naomi in 2002 when she had been investigating the mystery surrounding the Chance family and Whitewall Farm. In an attempt to conceal his family's historic involvement in illegal proceedings there, he had unnecessarily lost fifty thousand pounds which he attributed to her. Then in 2006, after Naomi had received more information about the Chance family, she had been complicit in exposing his underground drug manufacturing facility within his own Cragg Vale Estate. This had led to him having to flee the Country and go into hiding. But within weeks, he had been found in America and extradited to the UK. Thereafter Naomi had received a series of cryptic one-word notes that led her to Ralph Waldo Emerson's poem *'Brahma'* and the threat that it implied.

In November 2006, he had been found on the floor of his prison cell. He had been pronounced dead on the scene and his body had been taken to a mortuary pending a post mortem examination. Two days later it had gone missing. One day after that the attendant who'd transported the body had been found strapped into the front seat of his car at the bottom of Dunsteth Reservoir.

Following that, neither Darke nor the doctor who'd pronounced him dead had been seen again.

"So he's definitely alive then?" said Helen.

"Yes we believe so," said Crowthorne, "two days ago a known drug dealer was arrested in Manchester City Centre, and because he'd been arrested for the same offence twice before, he tried to cut a deal by offering to name his suppliers in exchange for a reduced sentence."

"And was one Adrian Darke?" said Helen.

"No, Darke isn't stupid enough to get involved in any of the front line dealing, but," Crowthorne turned to look at Naomi, "one of the names given was a character that you've encountered before – Hayley Gillorton."

Naomi shuddered and said, "Ugh, yes, I remember her alright."

"Isn't she the objectionable woman who pretended to be an archaeologist at Cragg Vale?" said Helen.

"Objectionable would have been on a good day," said Naomi, "and she's not a woman, she's an animal." She turned to Crowthorne and said, "Have you arrested her?"

"No."

"Then how do you know that Adrian Darke is involved?" interrupted Helen.

"Because Gillorton, who had a brass neck the size of Battersea Power Station, had the gall to send a message to Manchester Police saying that in exchange for her freedom, she'd be willing to shop the entire upper echelon of Darke's businesses, and say where we could find him."

"*Had* a brass neck?" said Naomi.

"Yes, her body was discovered yesterday, impaled on the metal fence of a scrap dealer's yard in Birmingham."

Helen was shocked. She said, "Oh my God, that's awful!"

Crowthorne looked at Naomi's face and guessed what she was going to ask.

Naomi said, "How was Gillorton's message received?"

"By phone."

Naomi raised here eyebrows and said, "So somebody in the Force conveyed the message to Darke or his people, and she paid the price?"

"It would seem so, yes."

"So you have an informant in Greater Manchester Police?"

"Yes, I'm afraid it appears that way."

"And how many people could have had access to that message?"

"Hmm," said Crowthorne, "therein lies the rub. We believe that it was a maximum of six right now, but we could be way out. When the message was phoned through, the officer who took the call wrote it down and passed it on to his desk sergeant. The message lay on his desk for more than twenty minutes before being passed to CID. It was then lying in an in-tray in the CID general office for another forty minutes before somebody had the chance to look at it.

"Even then it wasn't dealt with as a matter of urgency, because we frequently receive messages like that, and none of them ever state that if they don't receive a response within a given period of time, the deal will be off." He looked at Naomi and Helen and said, "So in a nutshell, any number of people could have looked at the message and passed it on."

"And knowing that you have an informant in your camp, is what brought you here in person?" said Helen.

"Yes, correct." Crowthorne turned to Naomi and said, "I know that it's been a while since you received those weird one-word messages that led you to Emerson's 'Brahma', but now that we have definitive proof that Darke is alive…"

"Unless Gillorton was lying to save her own skin?" said Helen.

Crowthorne turned to Helen and said, "That's not likely. Look at the response."

Helen thought about the situation for a few seconds and then said, "Yes, I suppose so."

"If Darke hadn't been vulnerable, what would have been the point of killing her like that? And in such a public way? In my opinion, he is alive, and he ordered Gillorton's execution as a blunt and brutal warning to anybody considering turning him in."

"So what about me?" said Naomi. "Do you think that I'm in danger?"

Crowthorne looked down and said, "Not in the short term, no. I do believe that he still wants revenge for the loss of his facility at Cragg Vale, but the sending of those notes speaks volumes to me. I think that he intends savouring his revenge, and not rushing it."

25

"Well that's a comfort," said Naomi.

Crowthorne nodded and said, "Having said that, we can't be sure of an exact time frame, so under the circumstances, I think that it would be better if you went to stay with some relatives in a different part of the country until we've caught Darke and his cronies."

Naomi was shocked. She said, "Leave Walmsfield?"

"Yes."

Naomi glanced at Helen's shocked face. A diamond hard edge to her character surfaced and she turned to face Crowthorne. She said, "No, I'm sorry Bob, I'm not going. I'm a Chance. Our family motto is 'Qui Potest Capere Capiat' – 'Let him Take What He Will Take' and we don't give to our enemies, we take from them." She looked straight into his deep blue eyes and added, "And I'm sick and tired of that creep trying to hurt and intimidate me and my friends, so if he wants trouble, he can bloody well have it!"

Chapter 4

"The pessimist sees difficulty in every opportunity. The optimist sees the opportunity in every difficulty."
Sir Winston Churchill 1874 - 1965

On the 17th of November, 1932, Churchill wrote an article that was published in the *Daily Mail*. It stated:

"Do not delude yourselves. Do not let His Majesty's government believe—I am sure they do believe—that all that Germany is asking for is equal status. I believe the refined term now is equal qualitative status by indefinitely deferred stages. That is not what Germany is seeking. All these bands of sturdy Teutonic youths, marching through the streets and roads of Germany, with the light of desire in the eyes to suffer for their Fatherland, are not looking for status. They are looking for weapons, and, when they have the weapons, believe me they will then ask for the return of lost territories and lost colonies, and when that demand is made it cannot fail to shake and possibly shatter to the foundations every one of the countries I have mentioned, and some other countries I have not mentioned"

The British Parliament wouldn't listen to Churchill and his repeated warnings about the build-up of power in

Germany and Italy, but certain factions within the Ministry of Defence had.

They had known that they wouldn't have the support of the government with its pacifistic and placating ministers and policies, so under instruction from one enlightened, ex-military, minister, and supported by several high-ranking officers from all three British armed forces, a special unit had been set up.

Its location was at an underground facility near Keasden Beck, in The Forest of Bowland, West Yorkshire, and it had one simple instruction. *"To develop and manufacture a devastating and demoralising weapon, deliverable by air, hitherto unknown by mankind."*

The unit, referred to as 'K1' had been set up in May 1933, four months after Hitler had become the German Chancellor, and for its first eighteen months it hadn't had any success.

On the 15th of September 1935 the 'Nürnberger Gesetze' or Nuremberg Laws, came into power defining who was Jewish in Germany and one month later, Professor Karl Hallenbeck of the 'Deutscher Waffenforschungseinheit', or 'German Weapons Research Unit' arrived at K1, with a promise that he and his entire Jewish-born family could relocate to England in exchange for his help.

Wednesday 6th October, 1937. MOD Weapons Research Facility,
K1, Keasden Beck, Yorkshire

Two locked steel gates, four feet high, sporting a white, mud splattered sign with red words, warned,

Ministry of Defence
KEEP OUT

They were the only things that prevented intruders from entering at that point. There was no electrification, no barbed wire, and because it was at the end of a long and winding road in the back of beyond, not many people knew about the place. And those who did, didn't take much notice of it. To the observant, tyre tracks could have been seen in the mud going through the gates, but nobody ever saw a vehicle entering or leaving, because nobody ever ventured that far into the fell, that late at night.

Through the gates and over the slight incline was a different matter however. There, those who had ignored the warning would have been faced with a fifteen feet high, electrified fence, an imposing gate, and three armed soldiers.

Inside the unit were seventy-five personnel, and they'd had a breakthrough: *The Halo.*

It was a devastating air-burst bomb filled with an accelerant, an early derivative of napalm, and hydrogen. Once detonated a massive burst of burning accelerant hovered like a brilliant white halo before floating down to earth in a deadly mist. A scorching, skin-stripping mist that couldn't be extinguished until it had burnt itself out. Additionally, the more the accelerant burned, the lighter it became, which resulted in it being able to be carried huge distances on the slightest of breezes.

Early tests on animals with small versions of *The Halo* had been so horrific and shocking that most of the personnel had been unable to purge their minds of the sounds of the poor creatures screeching in agony as the fuel seared through their bodies. And following those tests, a hardcore group of personnel had become averse to the research programme, believing that a nation such as Great Britain should never sanction the use of something so horrific.

Leading the protesters was a research biologist named Doctor Eleanor Drake who had been given the task of discovering ways to overcome gas attacks by enemy countries. She'd been given samples of nerve agents from foreign powers and had been asked to analyse and grade them, and then set about discovering ways to prepare the British Armed Forces in the event of such an assault.

What she hadn't learnt until the results of *The Halo's* tests had been revealed, was that she and her team had been duped.

The group responsible for constructing *The Halo* had taken the results of her team's research and had incorporated the most devastating nerve agent that they'd found, into the weapon.

Eleanor and six leading physicists had lodged their opposition to the future use of the agent but their objections had been ignored. Thereafter she'd tried to rally quiet support to halt the progress of the weapon but she'd known that their hands had been tied.

Apart from being bound by the Official Secrets Act 1911, where they were not allowed to disclose information *"For any purpose prejudicial to the safety or interests of the State"* they were aware too, of the clandestine, and watchful eye of SIS, the Secret Intelligence Service, sometimes referred to as MI5 or Military Intelligence, Section 5.

The Director General, known to all as 'C', was Admiral Sir Iain Vincent KCB. Rumours abounded that he might have been one of the original founders of K1 and the protesters had no doubt that if they attempted to divulge any information to outsiders about their horrifying weapon, they might suddenly disappear from the face of the earth.

This impossible state of affairs had led the protestors into a secretive war of attrition and they missed no opportunity to undermine the progress of *The Halo* even by the tiniest of actions; actions that would be unnoticeable to all who were unaware, but that had constantly hampered and delayed the proceedings on an irregular basis.

On the other side of the fence was Professor Karl Hallenbeck and his leading assistant, fellow German physicist, Doktor Axel Klossner.

Hallenbeck, tall, slim, athletic, blond, and handsome, aged 33, was aware of the effects of *The Halo*, but he was also aware that he was in England courtesy of the leaders of K1, and that should he waver in his duty to achieve his given objectives, he and his family could be transported back to Germany at the drop of a hat. That made him aware of the horrific results, but unmoved and impersonal.

Klossner however was a different kettle of fish. He was medium height, dark-haired, and had a rugged handsomeness that hid a ruthless and ice-cold interior. He was a bachelor, 26 years old, and despite his degree in Physics, had become overtaken by a burning desire to become a member of Heinrich Himmler's *Schutzstaffel*, or *'SS'*. But his ambition had been thwarted because of his grandparents' Jewish ancestry. He protested and pestered the SS authorities about his rejection to such an extent that earlier in 1937, he had been sent to the Oranienburg Concentration Camp north of Berlin, whilst they considered whether or not he had been 'a subversive'.

His degree in physics had been his saviour. He had been recruited by Professor Hallenbeck to work alongside him in the German Weapons Research Unit, but thereafter Klossner had harboured a deep-seated hatred of his fellow Germans, and his Jewish ancestry, and when he cold-heartedly

31

witnessed the suffering of the animals during *The Halo* tests, he imagined it to be those people that he hated the most. Stripped, strapped to a bed, and screaming in agony.

Hallenbeck looked across the double-desk inside the small, one-window office that overlooked the main workshop. He saw Klossner studying a map and said, "You need to ask a local Axel, we are German and we can't tell what the actual ground looks like from paper maps."

Klossner looked up from the Ordnance Survey map of Lincoln and said, "I can accept that, but I can work out the kind of terrain we want. I shall locate two possible sites, and then visit them for myself."

Hallenbeck frowned and said, "My friend, you are a physicist, not a ranger. Why are you even bothering yourself with such a task?"

Klossner made a sweeping gesture with his left hand and said, "Look around you Karl – and then ask me again why I am bothering myself with it."

Hallenbeck looked at the uninspiring grey-painted, wooden walls of the tiny office strung about with plans, diagrams and blueprints.

Klossner said, "You see? It is because I enjoy it. Every day I work here with figures and calculus, and this to me is a pleasant distraction – and now that you have forced me to say it, it also offers me the chance to escape from your watchful eye!"

Hallenbeck smiled and said, "Okay, but please don't take all day about it. The test is in four weeks' time and we don't want to delay it because of your intransigence and desire to keep from under my eye!"

Klossner smiled and made the Nazi salute. He said, "Ja, ja, mein Kommandant!"

Hallenbeck winced and said, "Not funny Axel, not funny."

Klossner looked down at the map and kept on being drawn to an area south of Boston named Sandholme. To the east of it, three distinct marshes were shown on the map, Wyberton, Frampton, and Kirton. To the east of them was The Wash with its extensive tidal flood plains which could prove useful if anything should go amiss with the detonation sequence. He knew then, that if they were careful to choose a time and date with an ebbing Spring tide, all the peripheral evidence of the experiment stood a good chance of being washed away too. The fields to the east of Sandholme looked perfect. They would be able to transport in the cows, sheep and pigs under cover of darkness so that that part of the test wouldn't alert any curious locals, and set up the temporary pens in which they'd all be sacrificed. Finally he studied the rudimentary road detail, and circled the whole area with his pencil.

Wind direction was a huge factor in their experiments and he knew that *The Halo* was uncontrollable once detonated, therefore he needed a similar location on the west coast of England. His eyes were drawn to Morecambe Sands because of the extensive tidal bay, but he soon dismissed the area because it was so overlooked from most locations. Then he spotted Duddon Sands and nearby Sandscale Haws to the west of Dalton in Furness in Lancashire.

The road infrastructure was in place and there were tidal flood plains either side of the Duddon Channel. There were no nearby dwellings, and room for the cattle pens.

Then he saw that some abandoned iron mines were located within one-and-a-half kilometres of his chosen location, and the sight of them set his mind working ten-to-the-dozen.

He had struck up a homosexual relationship with a young private responsible for transporting men and equipment to K1, named Ronnie Bowers, and during their most intimate moments they had speculated what it would be like to witness a naked young man suffer the effects of *The Halo*. And the more they'd thought about it, the more they'd wanted to see it. That made Duddon Sands perfect. The abandoned iron mines would be an ideal place to conceal somebody if they were ever going to live-out their cruel and perverse fantasy.

He picked up his pencil and circled it. He wrote the number one on that location, and number two on the Sandholme site. He then put the pencil back on his desk, got up and walked around the desk to Hallenbeck.

"Karl," he said, "I've located two potential sites, might I be permitted to visit them within the next week?"

"Would you like me to come with you?"

"No, that won't be necessary on this occasion, but if they're as good as they look on paper, it would be worth you looking then."

"And where are the sites?"

"One is in Lincoln if we have a westerly wind blowing, and the other is in Lancashire if the wind is blowing from the east."

Hallenbeck mulled things over for a second and then said, "Very well. I expect that you'll need a couple of days, so I'll arrange a driver for you. When would you like to go?"

Klossner needed time to plan if he was going to propose the kidnapping aspect to Bowers. He said, "Next Tuesday would be good, and don't worry about the driver, I can arrange that."

Chapter 5

Bookie Werm looked out of the window and groaned. The rain was coming down sideways and he knew that his workmates wouldn't be going outside for their usual football kick-about. Instead they would be playing some diverse form of basketball with the makeshift equipment they'd set up in the integral garage. It didn't mean that they'd be close to him when they played, but the thudding and thumping about and the raucous yelling once they'd started playing, echoed throughout the whole building, disturbing his lunchtime read, regardless of whichever room he tried to shut himself in, and them out.

He finished his ham and cheese 'sub' roll and heard one of his mates' say, "Basketball it is then!" He nodded to the room, got hold of the back of his cane chair and dragged it down to the end of the corridor.

"Fancy a game today, Bookie?"

Bookie turned and saw one of the apprentice painters looking at him from the other end of the hall.

"No thanks, buddy," he said, "it's not really my thing."

"Okay, suit yourself."

Bookie nodded and smiled, and walked into the unpainted room. He placed the chair by the window and then shut the door. He sat down, opened his book, and frowned. He looked and listened for a few seconds and then heard a faint 'bleep'. He closed the book and stared at the right-hand wall.

"Bleep" – it sounded again.

It was the same sound that he'd heard on the previous Friday. He got up, walked to the wall and put his ear against it. Seconds later, he heard it bleep again. He knew that the wall in question was the party wall to the adjoining property, and that the sound must have been coming from in there, but if whatever it was had been bleeping throughout the whole weekend, he wondered if something might have been amiss.

He walked across to the sash window, lifted it and looked left along the pavement. Nothing seemed out of the ordinary. He closed the window, walked back to the wall, and placed his ear against it again.

"Bleep".

He looked at his watch and counted away the seconds.

"Bleep".

It was thirty seconds from bleep to bleep. He tried to localise the sound. He placed his ear against the wall in several locations, but the volume sounded the same wherever he went. He stepped back, stared at the wall with a frown on his face for few seconds, and then sat down. It was 1:43 p.m. and his break finished at 1:50 p.m. If he was going to take the matter further, he'd do it in works' time, not his own.

He attempted to read, but couldn't. He became obsessed by the bleeping. He counted fifteen of them, looked at his watch and saw that it was 1:50 p.m.

"Time's up, Bookie!"

Bookie heard the familiar call from Dan. He stood up, went into the corridor and called, "Boss, you'd better come here and check this out."

Fifteen minutes later four men stood with their ears to the wall. They could all hear the bleeps, but none of them could localise it.

"What do you think it is?" said Bookie.

Dan frowned and said, "Dunno. It sounds like some kind of alarm, but I couldn't vouch for that." He scratched the back of his head and then said, "And you first heard this last Friday?"

"Yes."

"Why didn't you say anything then?"

Bookie raised his eyebrows and wanted to say that it was because he'd been yelled at by Dan. Instead, he said, "I didn't think it was important."

One of the other men said, "It's definitely coming from next door."

Dan looked at him and said, "Thanks Einstein. I think we all got that."

"Only if it is," said the man, unabashed by Dan's comment, "and it's been going since last Friday, shouldn't we at least knock and see if everything's okay?"

Dan pursed his lips and said, "I suppose…"

"I'll go if you want?" said the man.

"No, you carry on with your work. I'll go."

Minutes later Dan walked to the front of the house next door and studied its layout. From top to bottom and from side to side it appeared to be identical to McCready House except for the balustrade at roof level. That was several feet lower.

He walked to the front door and rang the bell. The door opened and an old lady answered. An old lady whose face had been moulded by time and Mother Nature to reflect her disposition and life; and by the look of it, she'd suffered with haemorrhoids, sitting on an unpeeled pineapple, without underwear, for most of it.

37

Dan recoiled at the sight of her unwelcoming countenance but then recovered and said, "Good morning, er, Madam, I wondered…"

"What? What did you say?" said the old lady.

"I said good morning, Madam, I…"

"It isn't you dopey bas…"

Dan frowned as the old lady's voice trailed off before he'd heard what she'd fully said. He said, "I beg your pardon I…"

"I said *it isn't,* you dog-eared twat."

Dan was shocked. He said, "Did you just call me a twat?"

"You heard that then?"

Dan wasn't behind the door when it came to trading insults, but he attempted to retain some civility. He said, "Yes I did – regrettably – now, what do you mean, 'it isn't?'"

"It isn't morning, brain-of-Britain."

Dan frowned again and then looked at his watch. He saw that it was after 2 p.m. He said, "Yes, sorry, I…"

"And so you should be coming round here disturbing an old lady, you selfish shit."

Dan had had enough. He said, "Old lady? You're more like an old fishwife with that mouth!"

"That's right – go on – take advantage of a vulnerable old lady. You come round here disturbing me when I'm supposed to be having my afternoon nap and then you insult me! What do you want to do now, smash me in the face and nick my handbag, you ugly fuckwit?"

Dan couldn't believe his ears. He stared in dismay at the old battle-axe and didn't know what to say.

The old lady took the initiative and said, "Well, make your mind up, or am I going to stand here and die of old age while you get that bonehead brain of yours going."

The gloves were off. Dan said, "Listen you mealy-mouthed old trout, I only came round to see if you were alright."

"What for? Do you know me?"

"No I don't, and after listening to you, I don't want to either."

"Well that makes two of us, so fuck off and leave me alone." The old lady then stuck the middle finger of her right hand up in front of Dan's face, turned around, and slammed the door in his face.

Dan was shocked. He stared at the closed door in disbelief. He'd never met such a bad-tempered, foul-mouthed old lady. He decided that he needed back-up.

As if the gods had heard his call, he saw Richard pull up outside of McCready House. He walked across to him, explained about the bleeping, told him about the old lady, and then asked him if he would accompany him back to see her.

Richard smiled and said, "I can't wait!"

The friends walked to the old lady's house and rang the doorbell again.

The door opened, the old lady saw Dan, and then caught sight of Richard. She said, "Yes?"

"Good afternoon, Madam," said Richard, "we're sorry to disturb you, but could we have a quick word?"

The old lady looked Richard up and down and then said, "What about?"

"Would it be easier if we came in?" said Richard.

"Who for?"

Richard faltered and then said, "Please ignore that. We came because we've heard a bleeping coming from your house, and we wondered if you'd heard it too."

"A bleeping? From my house?"

"Yes."

"What kind of bleeping?"

Dan was waiting for an outburst at any moment.

"The sort you get from an electrical appliance or something," said Richard.

"No I haven't." The old lady stepped back in and started to close the door.

"Wait," said Richard, "just one moment."

The old lady hesitated and then stepped forwards again.

"We, that is my colleague here, and his workmen can hear a distinct bleeping coming from your house, so we've assumed that something must be amiss."

The old lady frowned and said, "Like what?"

"I don't know – maybe you've left a phone off the hook or something?"

The old lady looked puzzled for a couple of seconds and then said, "Alright, you'd better come in." She stepped to one side and held the door open.

Richard entered, but as Dan attempted to go in, the old lady held her hand up and said, "Not him, he's an arsehole, and his eyebrows are too close together."

Dan frowned and looked at Richard who just shrugged.

The old lady slammed the front door shut and said, "Which room?"

Richard said, "It's the party wall to McCready House."

The old lady nodded and led the way into the room. She said, "So what's bleeping?"

Richard stood stock still and listened. He couldn't hear anything. He looked at the old lady and then pointed to the wall. He said, "Do you mind?"

The old lady shrugged.

Richard walked across to the wall and listened. He couldn't hear anything. He then placed his ear against the wall in several places, but again, he heard nothing. He turned to the old lady, saw that she was wearing a wedding ring and said, "I'm sorry Mrs…?"

"Pilchard – Esme Pilchard."

Richard didn't know how he contained his smile, but whatever minor contortion his face made, gave the game away.

"That's right, go on, take the piss out of an old lady!"

Richard said, "No, no, no, I wouldn't do such a thing. I've never heard the name Esme before; is it a contraction of something?"

Esme stared at Richard for a few seconds and then said, "It's short for Esmeralda."

"Ah," said Richard, "a beautiful British name."

"British?" said Esme, "it's Spanish, and it means 'emerald', you tit."

Richard nodded and said, "Right, I stand corrected. Well, Mrs Pilchard…" – he still couldn't get the sound of *"it's me pilchard"* out of his head and was glad that Dan wasn't there right then – "I can't hear any bleeping from in here, so whatever it is must be coming from our side."

Esme nodded and led the way back to her front door. She opened it and saw Dan waiting outside. She turned to Richard and said, "And tell monkey features there to keep away from me in future." She glared at Dan one last time and then slammed the door shut.

Dan was shocked at the vehemence of the old lady again; he looked at Richard and said, "Fuck knows what I've done to rattle her cage."

"And I doubt that you'll be getting an invite to her next birthday party either."

"Yeah, like I'd want to go!"

Richard smiled and said, "Poor old Esme Pilchard, and such a vulnerable old dear."

"Esme Pilchard?" blurted out Dan. "That's her name – 'it's me fucking pilchard'?"

"That's what she said."

"Pah! No wonder she's permanently bad-tempered!" He glanced back at the house but didn't see any sign of her. He turned back to Richard and said, "So, did you find out what was bleeping?"

"Nope. And I couldn't hear anything when I put my ear against the wall either."

"Did you try…?"

"Several locations? Yes I did, but I still heard nothing."

Dan frowned and then said, "So, whatever it is, it's coming from our side…"

Chapter 6

In the bare and functional lounge of a basement flat, in one of the redbrick terraces in Nevern Square, Chelsea, the dapper, but dangerous Adrian Darke presided over a meeting of his closest generals and associates. He still retained his Mediterranean-style, clean-shaven, good looks, with his square jaw line, full head of dark hair, and striking blue eyes, but those who knew him could see that he had been withered by the calamitous business events of the last few years. Some of which, including his once mega-successful drugs-supply business, had been lost thanks to the interference of Naomi Wilkes.

Sitting before his scornful looks were Dominic Sheldon the former MD of his estranged wife's Christadar Property Holdings, his Chief Operations Manager Garrett Hinchcliffe, his personal bodyguard the huge and imposing Leander Pike, known to all as FA Cup because of his protruding ears, Deangelo Constantin the shady Acquisitions Manager and 'fixer' of his even shadier company Darke Desires, and Ajax, his number one assassin.

Adrian quelled the light conversation around the table by raising his right hand and saying, "Right, down to business; who killed Gillorton?"

Silence reigned. All those present looked from face to face.

Adrian remained silent for a few seconds longer and then repeated, "Who killed Gillorton?"

Silence.

Adrian looked into the eyes of each person in turn, and lingered before passing on to the next. He didn't see anything furtive about anybody. He sat back in his seat and said, "I can understand if her demise was some kind of misplaced loyalty to me, and if somebody in this room did do it, I will forgive them, but for the last fucking time – who killed Gillorton?"

More silence.

"Right – then if it was nobody here, who could it have been?" He looked at Hinchcliffe and said, "Garrett?"

"I don't know, AD, and that's the honest truth. And if you'll forgive me for saying, it's not as though you're treading on anybody's toes at the moment because you've been out of the loop for the past few months."

Adrian felt his top lip curl; he said, "Yes, and mostly thanks to that Wilkes bitch, but I'll deal with her in good time."

Two pairs of enquiring eyes looked at Adrian, those of FA Cup and Ajax. He saw them both look and said, "Later – I have something special planned for her." He looked back at Hinchcliffe and said, "So, Garrett, do you have any ideas?"

Hinchcliffe looked down and shook his head; he said, "None, AD."

"Dominic?" Adrian turned to Sheldon.

"I'm at a complete loss too – sorry."

Adrian felt his frustration level rising; he looked sideways at Constantin, and said, "Deangelo?"

Constantin shook his head too.

"Has *'Desires'* been making waves with any unstable foreigners lately?"

"None that I'm aware of AD."

"What about that psycho twat from Chad?"

"Njomo? No, he was killed by his own tribesmen two months ago."

"Did he have any kids?

"He did, but they were all killed too."

"Some good news then?"

"I suppose."

Adrian surveyed his so-called 'top management'; they were sitting around the curved beech table that once dominated his penthouse boardroom off Piccadilly Gardens in the centre of Manchester. It reminded him of the times when he was the untouchable supremo of his huge and thriving companies, and how he had now descended to the status of a rat trapped in a cellar. Inside, he seethed.

In front of everybody was a bottle of Perrier water, a plastic tumbler, and an envelope. He poured himself a drink, took a sip and said, "So we're completely in the dark?"

Hinchcliffe took a sip of water, picked up the sealed envelope, looked at it, and then put it down. He made a sound, and all eyes turned to him.

"Garrett?" said Adrian.

"It's clutching at straws maybe, but we aren't completely in the dark."

"How do you figure?"

Hinchcliffe turned his chair to address everybody. He said, "What was that death all about? It was obvious that she'd been executed because there was nothing above those railings – and none of us are stupid enough to think that she was attempting to jump a ten foot spiked fence and just landed on her back halfway across. And why Birmingham? What was she doing there? Had she gone there on business?" He looked from face to face but saw only blank looks. "So," he reiterated, "what was she doing in Birmingham?"

"Private business, or visiting a relative maybe?" said Sheldon.

Hinchcliffe turned and said, "You think?"

Adrian said, "What point are you trying to make Garrett?"

Hinchcliffe turned to Adrian and said, "From Hayley's death we can assume two things. One was that somebody was sending us a clear message that we're now under attack…"

"Whoa, wait a minute, Garrett," said Sheldon, "that's too big a leap. You can't assume that we, as an organisation, are under attack because of the death of one of us. What if she upset somebody personally?"

"Not likely," Hinchcliffe paused and then said, "Maybe I should have stated that either we as an organisation, or AD himself, is under attack."

"What?" said Sheldon. "And how did you make that assumption?"

Hinchcliffe picked up the envelope again, squeezed it to see how thick it was, and then placed it back on the boardroom table. He turned to Sheldon and said, "Because if Hayley had been killed for personal reasons it wouldn't have been like that. She could have been bumped-off on impulse, or it may have been a planned event, but it would not have been done so publicly."

The room remained silent.

Adrian turned to Ajax and saw him nod in agreement. He turned back to Hinchcliffe and said, "You said that we could assume two things. What was the second?"

"That two, maybe three people were involved in Hayley's death."

"Two or three people?"

"Yes," Hinchcliffe looked at everybody's face and then said, "There's no way that one person could have impaled a lump like her on her back on top of a ten foot fence on their own. Remember the size of her?"

Ajax looked down but kept silent.

"Do we know the extent of her injuries?" said the middle-aged, but still attractive Italian, Constantin.

"Why do you ask?" said Adrian.

"Because it wouldn't be easy to impale somebody on a fence, there are a lot of factors to consider. Her clothing, the number of spikes and how sharp they were. Was she placed on the fence and then yanked down, or was she dropped onto it?"

"What was the road surface like near the fence?"

Everybody turned and looked at the taciturn and mysterious Ajax; they were fascinated by him. He was tall and good-looking, his slim, muscular body was dressed in an immaculate, light grey suit, and nobody had ever seen him in the flesh before, not even Adrian.

"I don't know," said Adrian, "the first we learned of her death was when the news broke."

Ajax nodded and lapsed back into silence.

Adrian continued to stare at Ajax for a while and then realised that he wasn't going to elucidate. He turned to face the others and said, "So what now, anybody *any* ideas?"

Hinchcliffe looked around the room and then said, "We send out feelers. We make discreet enquiries," he turned to Sheldon and said, "You can contact your man inside Greater Manchester Police and put in a call to Gabriel Ffitch maybe?" He turned to look at Adrian for approval.

Gabriel Ffitch was the Town Clerk of Walmsfield and both he and his mega-prickly PA, Morag Beech, had been wormed into their positions within the Council through the devious machinations of Adrian. They'd been placed there as his eyes and ears, and in return they'd been paid handsome annual gratuities. What Adrian didn't know, was that once Ffitch and Beech had heard of his death, they'd been glad to be rid of their connection. And neither of them knew that he was still alive.

"No," said Adrian, "leave them be for the moment. They think that I'm dead so they'll be innocent of anything we may conjure up."

Sheldon said, "Talking of them, you don't think that Gillorton's death could have anything to do with the Wilkes woman do you?"

"No, no way," said Adrian shaking his head, "no way at all."

"You're not forgetting how she dealt with that last security guard at Cragg Vale are you? She had him shot and hog-tied to a quad bike quick enough…"

Adrian faltered for a second and then repeated, "No – no way – the way that she got him was pure luck."

Ajax listened to the exchange with a renewed interest, and decided to learn more about Naomi after the meeting.

"Okay," said Hinchcliffe, "we'll leave Ffitch and Beech alone for now, but the rest of you have all got contacts. I suggest that we make some discreet enquiries and then meet back here in a week's time; that sound okay?"

Nods of approval came from everybody.

"Right," said Adrian, "then that's settled; in your envelopes you'll find a thousand pounds spending money. When we meet next week, there'll be five thousand pounds for the person who discovers Gillorton's murderer. Now, leave one-at-a-time, don't make it obvious, and I'll see you all as arranged."

Everybody stood up except Adrian and Pike.

As the group was leaving, Adrian said, "Ajax, a word please." He waited until the three of them were alone and then said, "Today is the sixteenth of January. It is my birthday on April the first. After our meeting next week I don't want to see you again until my celebration dinner. At that dinner I want you to present me with a gift; a gift that I'll pay you one hundred thousand pounds for."

Ajax didn't reply – he nodded.

Adrian leaned forwards in his chair and said, "I want Naomi Wilkes' head. I want her to have no warnings, no threats, and no hint of what's coming to her."

Ajax looked into Adrian's cold eyes for a second, nodded, and said, "Okay…"

Chapter 7

"There we are, sir," said the Dick Scrivenor, the engineer from the General Post Office Telephone Exchange in Settle, "all ship-shape and Bristol-fashion."

Hallenbeck looked at the new installation on the wall of the central laboratory next to his office, and said, "And what do I have to do again?"

"It's simplicity itself, sir – in the event of an emergency take hold of this red handle, push it up, and make sure that it won't go any further."

"And it will do what?"

"It'll let those who need to know, that you are in trouble and unable to contact them in any other way."

"And who will it connect to?"

"I'm sorry, sir – that I don't know. I'm a humble engineer sent to make sure that the installation is in working order. And according to all of my tests, it is."

Hallenbeck frowned and said, "I am a humble research physicist, and these modern communications systems intrigue me."

"Me, too, sir."

"Well not you I hope…"

"That," said Scrivenor, "is because this is my line of work, and I doubt that I'd be able to understand anything that you're involved in."

Hallenbeck nodded and said, "Yes, I suppose so." He looked at the large metal switch again, and said, "Wouldn't it have been easier to fit a special telephone?"

"You have plenty of telephones Professor, and you can dial whoever you want at any time, but this system will still operate in the event of a breakdown of all standard communications systems. The pushing up of that handle will send an electrical signal that says, 'we're in the doo-doo, come and help."

"The doo-doo?"

Scrivenor recalled that the Professor was German and said, "I think that you German gents call it, 'die Scheisse'."

"Ah, yes, of course," said Hallenbeck. "So if all else fails we throw that switch and help will arrive without us having to say a word?"

"You have it in a nut-shell, sir."

"A nut-shell? What does a nut-shell have to do with it?"

Scrivenor drew in a deep breath and said, "Forget the nut-shell comment, sir – you are right, help will come without you having to speak to anybody."

"Good. And you want me to educate everybody else about its use?"

"Yes, sir."

"Very well, I will do that. Now you may go because I have a lot of work to do."

"There's one other thing, sir, you need to sign my paperwork." Scrivenor reached into his leather briefcase, extracted several sheets of paper, and handed them over. He saw Hallenbeck begin to read the copious amount of small print and then said, "They are all pretty standard stuff, sir – if you want to skip the trivia you can sign the back two pages."

Hallenbeck flicked through the paperwork and saw where he had to sign. He removed his fountain pen from his coat pocket, signed the first, and was about to sign the second, when he noticed a Ministry of Defence stamp on it. He looked at the engineer and said, "This is a Ministry of Defence document, what is it referring to?"

"You can read it if you like, Professor, but since this is an MOD establishment, we are required to send a copy of any documentation we create, to them."

"And within all of this small print, it states what exactly?"

"That we have installed the fail-safe unit, that you are aware of its existence, what it's for, and how to operate it."

Hallenbeck said, "Ah, I see." He scanned his eyes across the small print and didn't see anything that made him look twice. He signed the document and handed it back.

Scrivenor stuffed the paperwork into his briefcase and extended his right hand. "It's been a pleasure to meet you, sir," he said, "and good luck with whatever you are doing, especially if it's going to poke a finger into Herr Schicklgruber's eye."

Hallenbeck shook the offered hand and said, "Yes – thank you." He looked at the switch and said, "But one moment please – how do *I* know that it's working properly?"

"You don't, sir, but I do." Scrivenor hesitated as he saw the look of doubt remain on Hallenbeck's face. He said, "You are of course at liberty to throw the switch if you doubt its functionality, but given its unique purpose, I doubt that those extreme professionals who might respond to such a call would take kindly to nothing more than a curious try-out."

Hallenbeck nodded and said, "Yes, perhaps you're right." He looked at the innocuous-looking switch and then back at the engineer. "I will make sure that everybody here knows what to do. Now you may go."

Scrivenor said, "Thank you, sir," touched his forehead, and departed.

One hour later, Scrivenor sat in the lacklustre canteen of the telephone exchange opposite his dull and boring works manager, with the equally uninspiring name of Alf Plum. He looked at Plum's lacklustre features and wondered if it was ever possible to have a normal, everyday conversation with him. But, as per usual, and following several failed attempts, he reverted to work-related topics and said, "So let me get this straight, Alf, "You know where that K1-type signal is going to, but you don't know where it's coming from?"

"That's correct, lad," said Plum.

"Unless it is coming to you direct from K1?"

"Even then I wouldn't know that," said Plum.

"Why?"

"Because all of those red-phone-type systems are routed through dedicated lines, and through several exchanges."

Scrivenor stared at his manager for a few seconds and tried to fathom the conundrum.

Plum said, "And I'm not the only one who'd be in the dark. Every other exchange manager would be too."

"But why?"

"Security, plain and simple; we know that we have four dedicated lines running through this exchange and it's up to us to maintain and repair them in the event of a fault occurring. But because of their nature we are only ever allowed to know where the signal is going to from here, but not where it's come from."

"So," said Scrivenor, "if somebody makes a call from a red phone, anywhere, or uses one of those high security lines, it doesn't go direct from the user to the receiver?"

"That's right, lad; let's say that somebody from an MOD office, in for example, Liverpool, makes a call to his HQ in London, or wants to contact somebody in MI5 or MI6. He would pick up the phone, press the button and somebody would answer. But the call wouldn't be routed from Liverpool to London. It could be routed through all sorts of variables dependent upon how secure the line was. The call could initiate in Liverpool, be routed to Glasgow, then to Lincoln, from Lincoln to Cardiff, and then onto London."

"Ah, I see now," said Scrivenor, "and the manager of the exchange in Glasgow would know that the call was being routed to Lincoln, but he wouldn't know that it had come from Liverpool."

"Precisely," said Plum, who was never more animated than when talking about phone systems, "and the manager of the exchange in Lincoln would know that the call was being routed to Cardiff, but he wouldn't know that it had come from Glasgow. Get it?"

"Yes, and it's up to each exchange manager to maintain his section of those lines."

"Right," said Plum.

Scrivenor pondered for a few seconds and then said, "But who would know the layout of that line from end-to-end?"

"Somebody in one of the upstairs offices of the MOD or whatever government department that type of system was installed in."

"And if the line failed somewhere along its length – do we have a secret book somewhere under lock and key in case we need to know where to look?"

"No we don't. We make sure that our part of the line is regularly inspected and tested, as do all of the other exchanges. Then in the event of a failure, the man with the overall plan can contact individual exchanges to establish if anything is amiss at their end."

"And have you ever received such a call?"

"Never – we're fastidious in making sure that our individual parts of the line are working properly, because we know that it could be our country's security at stake." Plum paused and then added, "And if Mr Churchill is right – we don't want any of it compromised if that bloody lunatic Hitler is sabre-rattling as much as he says he is."

Scrivenor said, "Thanks, Alf, I understand now." He looked at his watch, nodded his head in the direction of the Switch Room, and said, "Right, I'd better get back and check on the lads, there's more than a few sticky relays in bank three, and I want them sorted out by tonight."

Chapter 8

James Garrison walked into the room at the far end of the hall and said, "You have me enthralled, Dan. Please explain."

"Over there, Mr Garrison, go and listen."

James Garrison was the Project Director of Garrison-Lane Plc, the company that had purchased McCready House. He was forty-six years old, slim, handsome, well-dressed, rich, and recently divorced.

His ex-wife had complained that he'd spent far too much time with his work projects, but his major 'project' had been his stunning-looking, blonde PA, Ariel Lindstrom, and he'd made endless time for her.

He'd been on his way to his private jet with Ariel when he'd received the call via his car phone, and had diverted to McCready House out of pure interest.

Garrison walked towards the wall and placed his ear against it. Within seconds he heard the bleep. He remained where he was until he'd heard another two bleeps, and then turned to Dan. He said, "You're right, how intriguing." He looked at Bookie Werm and said, "And you were the first to hear it?"

"Yes, Mr Garrison."

"Last Friday you say?"

"Yes."

"How come nobody heard it before you?"

Dan tried to ease some of Bookie's obvious discomfort and said, "Michael's a book-reader, sir, and doesn't tend to join in any of our lunchtime games. He usually finds a quiet room and reads."

Garrison turned to Bookie and said, "I can understand that. Now, Michael, Had you been alone in this room at any time before last Friday?"

"Yes I had, the best part of two weeks I'd say."

"And you'd never heard the bleeping before?"

"No, sir."

Garrison said, "Hmm," and then turned back to Dan. He said, "And you're sure that the sound isn't coming from next door?"

"My partner Richard went to see the old trout..." he hesitated and then quickly said, "...er old lady, I meant..."

Garrison raised his eyebrows in question.

Dan saw the look and said, "I'm sorry, Mr Garrison, but she's a right one. She must be at least eighty; she has a really bad disposition and she swears like a trooper."

Garrison smiled and said, "She sounds like fun."

Dan raised his eyebrows and said, "Not when you're on the end of it!"

Garrison continued smiling and said, "Okay, please carry on."

Dan nodded and said, "Richard went round, had a listen at the other side of the wall but couldn't hear a thing."

"Curiouser and curiouser," said Garrison. He looked at the wall, then turned back to Dan and said, "How about you – could you hear anything?"

"She wouldn't let me in."

Garrison smiled again and said, "Wouldn't let you in?"

"No, she made me wait outside."

"And what had you done to rouse the old lady's ire like that?"

"That's just it – I've no idea. The bloody old trout's taken an instant dislike to me and swears at me at every opportunity."

Garrison couldn't help himself. He laughed out loud, and said, "Now you've made me want to meet her. Perhaps I'll knock and see if she'll give me permission to listen too."

"Yeah? Well good luck with that…sir."

"Did Richard listen at different locations on the party wall?"

"He said so."

"In that case, I think that I'd better go and listen for myself. What's her name?"

"Mrs Pilchard – Mrs Esme Pilchard."

Garrison wanted to smile and say something, but he realised that it would be inappropriate.

Minutes later he knocked on Esme's door and waited.

Nobody answered.

Garrison knocked again, but to no avail. He turned to Dan and said, "She must be out."

Dan was about to respond when he saw movement through one of the net curtains. He said, "Somebody's in, I just saw some movement. Why don't you try the bell?"

Garrison turned, saw the old-fashioned bell-push on the wall next to the door, and pushed it.

The door opened and Esme stepped into the doorway wearing a white and red rose-print dress, and a back-to-front baseball cap. She said, "Yes, what do you want?"

Garrison said, "Good afternoon, Madam, I'm…"

"Cut the crap and get to the point," said Esme, "and before you start – I'm not interested if you're selling anything."

Garrison was shocked by the old lady's bluntness. He said, "I'm not selling anything, I'm…"

"Well what *do* you want? Spit it out butterballs, I'm busy!"

Garrison had never received a reception like it before and didn't know how to respond. He wanted to be indignant, but he was oddly fascinated and amused by the experience. He drew in a deep breath and said, "I'm from next door and I've come about the bleeping."

"So you've not fixed it yet?"

"We don't know what it is, or where it's coming from."

"In that case, stop buggering me about, and get on with it." Esme stepped back and shut the door.

Garrison was stunned; he stared at the door for a couple of seconds and then turned and looked at Dan.

"Told you," said Dan.

"I can't believe it – what an old harridan. She didn't give me a chance!"

"Are you going to ring again?"

"Too right I am." Garrison turned and pushed the bell again.

The door opened and Esme said, "What now?" She caught sight of Dan standing in the background and added, "And what have you brought monkey-features for, back-up?"

Garrison frowned and said, "Madam, please – I want to come in and listen to the bleeping for myself?"

Esme let out an exasperated gasp and said, "Alright, but be sharp about it. I've got some girlfriends round and you're disturbing our afternoon."

Garrison raised his eyebrows, shot a quick glance at Dan and then went in. He said, "Can my…"

"No!" said Esme, and slammed the door in Dan's face. She led Garrison to the room with the party wall and opened the door.

Garrison couldn't believe his eyes. The room was in virtual darkness except for a long white light similar to those seen over snooker tables, shining over a poker table surrounded by old ladies. The atmosphere was thick with cigarette smoke and whisky fumes, and he thought that he could distinguish the faint smell of cannabis too.

He coughed, waved his hand in front of his face in a futile effort to clear the air, and then looked around the table. The five seated ladies all sported similar baseball caps to Esme's – with the peaks to the rear, and they all appeared to be between seventy and eighty years old. Not one of them had a friendly countenance, and all appeared aggravated by his disruption of their game. He said, "I'm sorry to interrupt your game, ladies, I won't be long."

"What's he here for Esme?" said one lady.

"Not the filth is he?" said another.

"No," said Esme, "he's one of the workers from next door."

"He looks a bit 'toffee' for a workman," said another.

"Maybe," said Esme, "but if you quit your yacking and let him get on, we can get back to our game."

"And that would suit you right now, wouldn't it, Esme Pilchard?"

Esme glared across the table and said, "What do you mean by that, *Ada Burrows*?"

"Handy him calling round when he did."

"What are you talking about?"

"Still got your cards in your hand I see – are you sure they're the same ones you went out with?"

Esme was furious. She said, "You cheeky mare! I ought to bitch-slap you for that."

"Yeah?" said Ada rising to her feet, "you wanna try that do you?"

Garrison was stunned. He said, "Ladies, ladies, calm yourselves; I'm not the police and I'm sorry if I've messed-up your game. I just want to put my ear up against that wall, and then I'll be out of your hair."

"And probably signal to fish-face what I've got in me hand too," said Ada.

Esme said, "Fish-face? You cheeky cow, I'll…"

"Ladies!" said Garrison, *"Please!"*

Another old lady stood up and said, "Don't you go calling Esme fish-face Ada Burrows or I'll plant me brogue up your arse! You're no…"

Garrison felt as though he was caught up in some sort of bizarre world full of aggressive old ladies. In a loud voice, he said, *"Ladies! Stop!"*

A deathly silence followed.

Garrison looked around the smoky room and saw the half-dozen old ladies complete with eyeshades and baseball caps staring back at him. He said, "Thank you – now, I need you all to be quiet whilst I listen."

He continued looking from face to face for a few seconds longer, then walked to the wall, placed his ear against it, and listened. He heard nothing. He moved to another spot and listened again.

Nothing.

He tried three more places, but heard nothing at all. He then walked across to the door, turned, and said, "Thank you ladies, I'll see myself out." He closed the lounge door, walked towards the front door, and was about to depart when he heard a voice say, "Cheeky sod, coming in here disturbing our game…" He shook his head and stepped outside.

"How did you get on?" said Dan.

"I don't know what to say – I've never encountered such an aggressive bunch of old women."

"There were more than just Ma Pilchard?"

"Yes there were, and all as bad as one-another."

"Bloody hell; and did you hear the bleeping?"

"No, not a thing."

Dan looked at Garrison for a couple of seconds and then said, "Bugger – and I don't suppose that we can ignore it?"

Garrison raised his eyebrows.

Dan said, "Bugger," again and then added, "there goes the schedules."

Chapter 9

Naomi and Helen looked up when they heard an unexpected knock on their office door.

"Come in," called Naomi.

The door opened and Postcard Percy walked in with an older, but well-dressed lady.

Postcard Percy was a local amateur historian and had been a close friend of Naomi's since she'd started work for Walmsfield Borough Council in 2000. He and his eccentric band of friends had proved invaluable to her - and latterly to Helen - with their wealth of local knowledge. Percy also had copious amounts of old literature, books, newspaper clippings and the hundreds of local, old postcards that had given him his nickname.

"Percy!" said Naomi. "What a lovely surprise. What brings you here today, and who do you have with you?"

"Good morning, ladies," said Percy, "may I introduce you to a new friend of mine, Mrs Valerie Lockyer."

Naomi stood up and extended her hand. She said, "Hello Mrs Lockyer, this is my friend and colleague Helen Milner."

Helen stood up and shook hands with the lady too.

"Please call me Val, Mrs Lockyer sounds so stuffy."

Naomi said, "Okay, Val, I'm Naomi, and that's Helen. Are you here on business, or just visiting with Percy?"

"Percy suggested that I come here today."

Naomi turned to Percy and said, "Why?"

"It's an unusual story," said Percy, "and one that would be better told with a cuppa – if that's okay with you ladies?"

Helen smiled and said, "Sounds like my cue! Percy you're tea, milk, no sugar because you're sweet enough…"

Percy smiled and said, "You've got it!"

"And Val?" said Helen.

"Coffee, white, no sugar please."

Five minutes later Naomi waited until everybody was comfortable and then said, "Okay Val, if your story's got Percy fascinated it must be good. What is it?"

Val put down her plastic cup and said, "It's a bit protracted, and I don't want to take up too much of your time, especially if I'm distracting you from anything else."

Naomi pointed to her in-tray and said, "Paperwork is the bane of mine and Helen's life down here, and Friday's the main day for it, so we would welcome any distraction."

"I'll second that," said Helen.

Val smiled and said, "Okay – my goal is to find out what happened to my daughter when she went looking for my mother."

Naomi said, "Whoa, good start; how long has she been missing?"

"For the last two months."

"And your mother?"

"Since 1973, but she was born in 1915, and may have died by now."

"And the police are aware of both missing persons?" said Helen.

Val turned to Helen and said, "Yes, and trust me, I've pestered the life out of them, but with no result."

Naomi turned to Percy and said, "Does Bob Crowthorne know about this?"

"Bob Crowthorne," said Val, "who's he?"

"He's a Superintendent with the Greater Manchester Police," said Percy, "and he's a good friend. We've worked together on numerous cases." He turned to Naomi and said, "Val only moved to the area from London at the end of last year so she's been dealing with the Metropolitan Police up until now."

"So Bob isn't aware of this at the moment?" said Helen.

"He must be indirectly," said Percy, "but Val's story never made it to TV or Radio, so it wouldn't have been 'in his face' if you take my meaning."

"Never made it to TV or Radio?" said Naomi, "What about the 'Crime Watch' type programmes that appeal to the public for help. Surely they were interested?"

"My story mustn't have been important enough," said Val, "because nobody even interviewed me."

"Hence me advising Val to come and see you ladies," said Percy.

Naomi took a drink of tea, and then pulled a notebook out of her desk drawer. She said, "Okay, you've got me hooked, let's have all of it."

"It started in 1972. My mother, Violet Burgess, was fifty-seven years old and worked in the pharmaceutical industry for a company named Ascensis. They were based in Skelmersdale, Lancashire and she had been working for them since 1970. She never spoke to my sister and me about her work, and whenever we asked her, she would say that she was a research scientist helping to develop safe ingredients for use in cosmetic products.

"Then sometime in 1973, we started to notice things. She would come home from work in an agitated state, or sometimes disappear up to the bathroom, where we would hear her crying. But, if we ever asked her what was wrong she would become evasive or dismissive and say that it was nothing for us to worry about. Some nights we could hear mum and dad arguing in the dining room, and on one occasion we heard dad storm out and shout, '... *well forgive me for wanting the best for this family ...'*

"Janet, my younger sister, and I, went downstairs and found mum weeping in the lounge. We asked her what was wrong and she told us that it she had discovered some stuff at work that she didn't agree with, and that somebody had begun to make her life unbearable. We told her that if she was unhappy, she should leave and get another job, but she said that leaving wasn't an option."

Naomi shot a quick glance in Helen's direction, and saw her troubled face. Animal testing had popped into her mind, and she wondered if Helen had picked up on it too.

"We told her that it was 1973," continued Val, unaware of the exchange, "and that nobody could force her to stay where she was, but at that point, she suddenly seemed to gather resolve. She became calm and determined looking, and said, "Girls, I want you to remember something. If anything unusual ever happens where I work..." she then faltered, as though she wasn't sure what to say. I went to speak, but she put her hand in the air and said, '...wait, I know that this won't make sense to you, but you need to check out pipeline PL3.' We asked her what that was, but then she stood up, made us promise to say nothing about it to dad, and ushered us back up to bed.

"Over the next few days we pushed her for more info on 'PL3' but she told us that we'd understand if we ever needed to. We asked why we couldn't mention it to dad, but she clammed up and refused to say any more about it. Within a few weeks, it was as though the whole episode had never occurred. We weren't aware of her coming home upset anymore, and in fact, she looked as though she'd become more focussed and determined; but, whatever was going on, she never, ever, spoke about her work again."

Naomi said, "Sorry to interrupt you, Val, but did she ever say what product she was working on?"

"No – do you think that it was important?"

The feeling of the thumb pressed down on Naomi's shoulder; she lifted up her right hand and began to rub it.

Helen noticed the action and knew what was going on.

Naomi said, "I'm not sure, but it would have been useful to know."

Val shrugged and said, "It was the seventies, we were young, and we didn't give it much thought. It was mum's job, and that was it."

Helen said, "Then what happened?"

"On the evening of Sunday, the twelfth of August – I'll never forget it – my sister and I were in our back garden with our boyfriends whilst mum was inside doing stuff. Dad had gone to the local pub to play darts with his mate, and we were enjoying being alone because we'd all had a few wines and we were feeling a bit er, playful, if you take my drift?"

Naomi smiled and nodded.

"Then, about eight o'clock, mum came out to us and announced that she'd received an urgent call from work, and that she had to go out for a couple of hours. She told us to behave ourselves, by which, we took to mean 'don't go upstairs', and said that she'd be back when she could.

"At the time, we were both delighted because we had the house to ourselves – but, from that night to this day, we never saw her again."

Naomi stopped taking notes and said, "Obviously you went to the police?"

"Yes: they went to her workplace and were told that nobody had called her. They checked the company's outgoing calls with the telephone exchange, but saw nothing recorded for that night. They then checked our incoming calls and got the same result.

Helen frowned and said, "Did the police carry out a house-to-house search?"

"They did," said Val, "and nobody had seen her that night."

"How did she get to work?" said Naomi.

"By car, but that wasn't ever found either."

"Did the police check the breaker's yards?" said Helen.

"They checked everywhere."

Naomi looked at Helen and said, "Intriguing."

"The investigation went on for months without success. Occasionally a police detective would turn up at the house with what he thought might be a new bit of evidence, but nothing ever came of it. In the end the months and years passed by, the raw pain of Mum's loss subsided, and we all moved on."

"And what about the PL3 comment," said Naomi, "did you mention that to the police?"

"Yes, but nothing ever came of that either."

"And what about your daughter?" said Helen

"Denise. On her twenty-sixth birthday in November last year, she asked her dad, my late husband Peter, about my mum. He told her the story that I just conveyed to you, and she became captivated by it.

68

"We were living in Hillingdon, London, at the time, because Pete was a pest control officer there, but Denise was a travelling merchandiser for Cadbury's Chocolate, and when she found out that she was going to have to attend a sales conference in Preston, she said that she was going to try to find the place where my mum had worked. We told her that the company had long-since shut down, but she said that she would go and look anyway.

"Frankly, we didn't give it much more thought; but, before she went, Denise spent some time researching Ascensis on the internet, she printed some stuff out, and then left two days earlier so that she could go to Skelmersdale and do some poking about."

She looked down as she felt her throat tighten. She stopped speaking for a few seconds and then gathered resolve. She lifted up her head, and said, "And we never saw her again either."

A deathly silence followed.

Percy was the first to speak. He said, "How awful?"

Naomi said, "Is the investigation still going on?"

"As far as I know."

"And have the police been able to offer any kind of theory about what happened to your daughter?" said Helen.

"No. We didn't find out that she'd gone missing until the Monday after the conference when somebody called from Cadbury's to ask why she hadn't attended."

Helen said, "My God, how bad is that?"

"So she disappeared before the conference?" said Naomi.

"Yes."

"And it was *you* who called the police?"

"Yes. I told them about Denise's plans to visit the old Ascensis site, and that it was like history repeating itself. They investigated – for weeks – but no sign of her was ever found."

"And wasn't she caught on any security cameras anywhere?"

"No."

"Did you apply to have an appeal put on TV and radio?" said Helen.

"Of course we did. We begged them, but despite promises to do so, nothing materialised."

"And what about your sister Janet – did she get involved in any of the investigations?

"Or did she ever try to find your mother?" added Naomi.

Val looked at Helen and then Naomi and said, "She tried, but then she was killed in a motorcycling accident in 1975, which of course was like a double-blow to family."

"And what about your dad," said Naomi, "did he ever voice any suspicions or tell you about the private conversations that he'd had with your mum?"

"We asked him, but he said that it had been private stuff and nothing to do with her disappearance. The police questioned him extensively, too, but he wasn't able to shed any light on anything."

"And did the police ever consider that your dad might have had something to do with your mum's disappearance?" said Helen.

Val turned to Helen, frowned, and said, "Of course not, he was as distraught as the rest of us."

Helen nodded and sat back in her seat. She didn't want to stick her fingers too far into the open wound, but she pushed some more. She said, "What did your dad do for a living?"

Val looked at Helen with furrowed eyebrows and said, "Why?"

Naomi realised where Helen was going. She opened her mouth to cut in, but the thumb pressed down on her shoulder, and she held her tongue.

"No reason in particular," said Helen, "it's just that being a professional researcher, I like to have as many facts as possible to hand."

Val said, "Oh, I see. He was an animal keeper in Ormskirk Zoo."

Two sets of alarm bells went off, one in Naomi's mind, and the other in Helen's. They cast a glance at one-another.

"I wasn't aware that there was a zoo in Ormskirk," said Naomi trying to sound more light-hearted than she felt. "I take it that he's retired now?"

Val looked down and said, "No. The zoo closed down years ago, long before I moved to Hillingdon, and dad died in 1977, bless him."

"Your dad died in the seventies, too?"

"Of natural causes?" said Helen.

"No, he committed suicide on January the third."

"Good Lord," said Percy, "I wasn't aware of that. You've certainly had more than your fair share of grief to deal with."

"Yes," said Val, "but it was years ago with Mum and Dad, so I've had time to get used to it."

Helen wrestled with her conscience, and then couldn't help herself. She said, "Were you the one who found him?"

"No, he was found by a passer-by at the base of the Beachy Head cliffs."

"*In East Sussex?* Was he there on business or something?"

"No – apparently it had all become too much for him and he'd driven down there just for that."

Naomi's alarm bells were ringing full-tilt by now, but she decided to call a halt to the grilling. She said, "That is some story." She shot a *'no-more-questions'* glance at Helen and saw her acknowledge.

"And that is why I brought Val to see you," said Percy.

71

Val turned to Percy, smiled, and then looked at Naomi. She said, "Do you think that you can you help me?"

Naomi looked at Helen, saw her nod, and then turned back to Val. She said, "I don't know how far we'll be able to go with this …"

"Or given the previous circumstances how tricky it could get," added Percy.

"… But I promise you this," continued Naomi, "we will exhaust every avenue to help you find out what happened to your daughter – and to your mum."

Half-an-hour later, Percy sat at home mulling over the meeting. He thought about everything that had happened, and everything that had happened to Naomi over the last few months. He picked up his mobile phone and rang Bob Crowthorne.

Chapter 10

Hallenbeck pushed the pile of paperwork on his desk to one side and looked up. The tiny office was thick with cigarette smoke, and a pall of it hung over their desks. He wasn't a smoker, but he was used to it. He glanced down at the yellowing maps that normally hung from a bulldog clip on the office notice board, and half-wondered whether the smoke was adding to their discolouration. He looked at Klossner and said, "They were good choices of location Axel, I approve of them both."

Klossner smiled and said, "Good, we have the logistics to sort out, and we will be subject to the weather conditions on the day…"

"That is my biggest concern," said Hallenbeck interrupting Klossner's flow, "we have all the money we need to complete this project, but there are unanswered questions about some of the other equipment."

Klossner frowned and said, "Everything appears to be well catered for; we have the manpower, spares, tools, money in reserve – what's the problem?"

"It's the potential for disaster launching an unmanned dirigible."

"And that is your concern? Not the weapon exploding or somebody seeing it?"

"No, that could be explained away as another airship disaster. Between the LZ-4 exploding in Echterdingen in 1908, and the Hindenburg at Lakehurst last May, there have been twenty other airship disasters, so one more wouldn't be beyond belief.

"My worry is that once we launch the dirigible with the pre-set timer, we will have no control over it. What if the wind blows it off course, or some mechanical failure sends it the wrong way? It could be disastrous in the extreme."

Klossner thought about the disused iron mines at his preferred Sandscale Haws site in Lancashire, and his, and Bowers' desire to see a young man suffer the effects of *The Halo*, and realised that he had the sudden opportunity to swing things his way. He looked at Hallenbeck and said, "True; and what if the timer suffered a malfunction and the weapon didn't detonate. We could end up sending it to God knows where." He paused and then added what he hoped would be the clincher, "Perhaps we shouldn't even consider the Lincolnshire site; we wouldn't want it to end up in Hitler's hands would we?"

Hallenbeck was horrified; he sat back in his chair and lapsed into his native tongue. He said, "Mein Gott im Himmel, nein…"

"And my field trips revealed that there were numerous RAF Stations in Lincolnshire, but almost none in Lancashire. Yet another reason for choosing there."

Hallenbeck looked at his friend and shook his head. He said, "This project is a lot more dangerous than I thought it would be, Axel, and I don't mind admitting that it causes me to lose a lot of sleep."

"Then we must adopt our German principles. We must make sure that nothing can go wrong before we even consider launching. We will stick with Lancashire, we will make sure that the timer has a double fail-safe operation, and we will only launch when we are sure that the wind conditions are perfect."

Hallenbeck nodded and said, "Yes, good. It's comforting to know that you are watching my back, my old friend." He sat in silence for a few seconds and then added, "And then I suppose, all we have to do is to transport, inflate, and launch a hydrogen-filled dirigible in the middle of the night, from a remote field in the north west of England, and do it without the local police or RAF Station noticing."

Seconds later there was a tap on the office door. He looked up and called, "Come in."

Doctor Eleanor Drake walked in and said, "Professor, might I have a word?"

"Of course, would you like Axel to leave?"

Eleanor looked at the cold Teutonic features of Klossner and said, "No, thank you, what I have to say should be heard by both of you."

"Then," said Hallenbeck, "please proceed."

Klossner sat back in his seat and looked at Eleanor; she typified everything that the Führer had proposed the true German peoples should look like. She had blue eyes, straight, shoulder-length blonde hair tied back in a ponytail; she was slim, athletic-looking and had a shapely figure above a perfect pair of legs. And he detested her.

Unaware of Klossner's thoughts, Eleanor announced, "I want you to stop developing *The Halo*."

Hallenbeck was stunned; he raised his eyebrows and said, "Stop developing *The Halo*? Why would you ask me to do such a thing?"

"Because it is barbarous in the extreme and everybody involved in its development will live to regret it."

Klossner's lip all-but curled; he said, "That sounds like a threat *Fraulein* Doctor."

Eleanor turned to Klossner with pure contempt in her eyes and said, "It is a statement of fact, *Herr* Doktor."

Hallenbeck felt the air begin to sizzle between them and cut in, "Wait, wait," he said, "what do you mean we will all live to regret it?"

Eleanor took her steely gaze off Klossner and turned to face Hallenbeck. She said, "I mean that if *The Halo* completes its development and is ever deployed, not only would it be the cruellest and most barbaric weapon ever used against fellow humans, it would also prompt anybody we use it against to develop a similar weapon for use against us." She looked from face to face and then added, "And we, we three people in this room right now, have the ability to put a dead stop to all that potential suffering and misery."

"But that is our brief," said Hallenbeck, "that is our reason for being here."

"No it is not," said Eleanor, "we are here, according to our brief, 'to develop and manufacture a devastating and demoralising weapon, deliverable by air, hitherto unknown by mankind.' We are not here to develop an uncontrollable, unstable weapon that would deliver the most brutal of deaths and injuries to our enemies!"

Hallenbeck was stunned into temporary silence.

Klossner stared at Eleanor with unadulterated malice.

"We," continued Eleanor, "can develop a weapon that would be devastating and demoralising, and deliverable by air, but it could at least be humane." She looked at Hallenbeck's impassive face and then spoke before thinking. She said, "I'm not stupid, nor are my colleagues, and we…" she faltered, and could have spit for making a reference to colleagues, but it was too late.

Hallenbeck saw Klossner glaring at his desktop.

Eleanor quickly gathered her composure and continued "…we know that we are here to develop a weapon to kill our enemies, and no doubt lots of innocent people will die besides, but present company excepted, we should be British about it and deliver something that will do the job quickly and efficiently without causing unnecessary suffering."

Hallenbeck didn't know what to say. The 'colleague' statement had thrown him. He was alarmed that he could be sitting on a top-secret project with a growing number of dissidents who could disrupt progress by antagonism alone. He looked at Klossner, and saw him glaring at Eleanor with ill-concealed malevolence. He opened his mouth to speak, but was cut off.

"Your attitude and naivety offends me Doctor Drake, and if we were in the Fatherland, you and your *'colleagues'* would be arrested for such cowardly dissent."

Hallenbeck's head whipped around; he couldn't believe that Klossner had made such an insensitive remark. Once again he opened his mouth to speak, but was cut off.

"The Fatherland?" gasped Eleanor, *"Das fucking Vaterland?* You arrogant son-of-a-bitch! Who the hell do you think you're talking to?"

Hallenbeck leapt to his feet and said, "Stop, stop!"

Klossner stood up and towered over Eleanor. He said, "Don't you dare talk to me like that or I'll…"

Hallenbeck slammed his fist onto the desktop and shouted, *"Stop! This instant – both of you!"*

Eleanor and Klossner turned to face him.

"We are supposed to be on the same team! Axel – sit down! Doctor Drake – calm yourself and please sit down too."

He waited until Eleanor and Klossner had sat down, and despite them eyeing each other in a vehement way, said, "This is intolerable and it cannot be allowed to carry on. We are all members of a top-secret research facility and if we can't trust each other, who can we trust?" He looked from face to face, but drew no response.

"Doctor Drake, Eleanor," he said, "I can understand your sentiments about *The Halo* and I sympathise with them. And if you doubt that, look at who I am; a German national working for the British Government overseeing the development of a weapon that could be used against my own people."

"The same people who wanted to send you to a concentration camp," said Eleanor.

"That is not true! The Jews have lived in peace for hundreds of years with the German people. We constitute respectable German-born families, doctors, politicians, bankers, artists, and musicians. We are not just the snout-nosed *'Jude'* portrayed in the Nazi Party depictions! It is the National Socialists under Adolf Hitler who would want to segregate and demean us, not the German people."

Eleanor looked down at her feet, and then back up again. She said, "Yes, of course, that was insensitive; I apologise."

Hallenbeck nodded and then said, "So you can see – I too have the same misgivings about the type of weapon we are developing."

Klossner stared at Hallenbeck with suspicion. He recalled being taken to one side and being given a card with a contact number on by one of the upper echelon of the founding group, and of being advised to "report any misgivings about individual members' conviction to the programme."

Hallenbeck was unaware of his colleague's dispassionate study of him and said, "And that is why I want us to develop such a weapon as *The Halo*. I want it to be so fearsome, so appalling, that those who could be on the receiving end would wither and retreat from even the threat of us deploying such a thing."

Klossner relaxed – to a degree…

Eleanor wasn't convinced; she said, "And how would those people know what to be afraid of, without somebody letting it slip that we have such a terrifying weapon?"

"Because we would keep it a secret until it is too late for them to respond. That is why secrecy is vital to the project."

Eleanor said, "That is a dream, an ideal, but it's poppycock. It won't happen in real life and you know it. Other nations, especially Germany, or maybe even Italy under the rule of that other fanatic, Mussolini, will soon learn of *The Halo,* and they *will* produce a version of their own to use on our people."

"And I re-iterate; that is why we must keep this project top-secret, and not have pockets of insurrectionists likely to reveal or undermine it." He paused and then added, "And one shouldn't forget the consequences of breaching the Official Secrets Act, to which we are all subject."

Eleanor sat back in her seat and looked at Hallenbeck. She wasn't sure whether he was truly naïve, or believed in his own lunacy, but either way, she realised that if she and her colleagues were to succeed with their intentions, it would have to be without his or Klossner's knowledge. She recalled being told by her father that the Willow was better equipped to handle a storm than an Oak, by being supple instead of rigid.

She decided to switch tack and said, "I must admit that I hadn't given any thought to your ethical dilemma Professor, and I can kind of understand your logic, so I will not oppose your plans to continue with the development of *The Halo*, but I warn you, if you ever attempt to deploy this horrific weapon against anybody, including the Nazis, you will lose my loyalty, and I will do everything in my power to stop you."

Hallenbeck said, "That is frank and honest, and I appreciate your reasoning, but do not assume that my empathy is a sign of weakness. I am passionate about this project and if I think for one minute that you are trying to undermine me, I will do everything in *my* power to neutralise you."

Eleanor's right eyebrow raised a fraction. She looked from Teutonic face to Teutonic face and realised that these weren't such reasonable men after all; and that maybe, she shouldn't have aired her opinion. With as much dispassionate dignity that she could muster, she said, "In that case we have an understanding."

She stood up, nodded at both men, and left the office.

Klossner waited until Eleanor had departed and said, "She is going to be trouble."

"I agree."

"Then would you like me to do something about that?"

Hallenbeck pondered for a few seconds and then said, "Not yet; first we need to establish who her colleagues are, and then we'll deal with all of them."

Chapter 11

Bookie Werm was working his way to the corner of the room, applying a coat of white undercoat to the skirting board, and listening to the intermittent bleeps from the opposite wall getting louder, the closer he got to it.

The whole weekend had gone by since James Garrison had been on site, and still nothing had been resolved about where it was coming from.

He shuffled along to the corner where the front wall met the wall with the bleep behind it. He dipped his paintbrush in the paint and carefully cut in the top edge of the skirting board. Next he leaned down and cut in the bottom, making sure that no paint went on the expensive parquet flooring. Once satisfied with that, he turned his attention to the corner itself. He dipped his paintbrush in the paint, dabbed the excess off, and was about to apply it when he noticed that the contours on the top of the skirting on the 'bleeping wall' didn't meet those of the front wall as perfectly as they should have. He put the paintbrush down, got up and walked to the corner that he'd previously finished. He dropped down, examined the profiling and saw that those boards did match up. He walked to the corner by the entrance door, the one that he'd painted first, and found the same thing. Next, he walked across the room to the corner at the other end of the 'bleeping wall, and examined that. It, too, looked wrong. As though somebody had …

He said, "No, it can't be." He went to the front door, stepped out onto the pavement and looked at the party wall between McCready House and that of Esme Pilchard's. He followed the line up from the pavement to the edge of the balustrade and saw nothing unusual. The two terraced properties were clearly delineated by it, because Esme's was at least one metre lower along its full length.

"What are you doing out here?"

Bookie turned and saw Dan staring at him. He said, "Checking something out."

Dan sauntered over and said, "What?"

"I saw something in the room with the bleeping, and it got me thinking, so I came out here to check it out."

"Okay, you've lost me. What did you see, and what are you checking out?"

"I was painting the skirting and noticed that the two corners under that wall appeared to have been cut at some time."

Dan said, "Obviously it was cut – the chippies couldn't just bend it round the bloody corner."

"I know that," said Bookie, "but I mean recently."

Dan frowned and said, "How recently?"

"I don't know – it could've been years I suppose."

"That's not recently!"

"Okay, sorry, I should have said that they'd been cut later than the other two."

"And how do you know that?"

Bookie turned to face Dan and explained, "When professional painters do a proper job, they always strip the old paint off first. But, when it comes to corners, especially

82

corners such as skirting's and architraves you can't remove all of the paint from the joints. It only ever gets reduced back to surface level. Therefore, if any of those joints had ever had a tiny gap, over time they would have been filled up."

"Go on," said Dan.

"And that's the case with two of the corners in that room, but not the corners adjacent to the wall with the bleeps. They have gaps and the contours don't marry up."

"Oh," said Dan, "I see what you mean – you think that the skirting's been cut away and then replaced because there's no excess paint between the joints?"

"Right," said Bookie, "but it wasn't to stick some kind of bleeper behind it because the sound doesn't come from floor level."

"So now you're out here, trying to figure out if the wall line is right with the building?"

"Spot on." Bookie pointed up to the balustrade and said, "But it looks fine to me, it ends directly in line with the party wall next door."

"So we're still no closer to figuring it out?" said Dan.

Bookie felt foolish and said, "No, sorry, boss."

Dan looked at the two properties once more and then said, "Okay, you'd better get back to work in case Garrison shows up again and thinks that we're shirking."

The workmates started to walk towards the front door of McCready House when they heard a violent banging on the window of the Pilchard property. They turned and saw Esme pointing at them through the window. They stopped and looked as she made it plain that she was pointing towards Dan.

Dan pointed to his chest and mouthed, "What? Me?"

Esme nodded, then stuck two fingers up at him, and pulled the curtain back in place.

Bookie burst out laughing and said, "Shit boss, what was that all about?"

"I don't know! The old witch has taken a dislike to me for some reason."

"And you have to put up with that every day do you?"

Dan was about to nod and walk away, but then had a change of heart. He turned around, walked back to Esme's house and banged on the same window.

Esme pulled the curtain to one side and saw Dan glaring at her.

Dan pointed to her and mouthed "Go fuck yourself!"

Esme understood and shouted back, "Up yours monkey-boy!"

Dan shouted back, "You can talk, you withered old twat."

Esme stuck the middle finger of her right hand up and pulled the curtain back.

Bookie couldn't believe his eyes and ears. He'd never experienced such an aggressive old woman before, and he loved seeing the exchange. He grinned at Dan and said, "Unbelievable – truly unbelievable!"

They started to head for McCready House when they heard a window open behind them.

Esme shouted, "Shitbag!" and then slammed the window shut.

Bookie burst out laughing again and continued to walk towards McCready House when out-of-the-blue something registered. He said, "Hey, wait a minute." He stopped walking and said, "That room's not right."

"Which room?"

"The old lady's."

"What do you mean?"

"Let's go back and I'll show you, but…" Bookie hesitated unsure of the response he'd receive from Dan, "…we could do with going in."

Dan groaned and said, "Oh Christ…"

They walked back to Esme's house and Bookie knocked on the door. Seconds later it opened.

Esme saw Dan, blanked him and turned to Bookie. She said, "What do you want?"

"My name's Michael Werm and I work next door…"

"Yes, yes, I gathered that, get on with it."

"It's about the bleeping. I think that I've figured out where it's coming from, but it would help if one of us could come in and stand next to your party wall."

Esme pondered for a second and then said, "Alright, you can come in, but monkey-boy stays put."

Bookie turned to Dan and said, "If you stand where we were a few minutes ago, I'll stand next to the wall in Mrs Pilchard's place. See if it lines up with our party wall and the balustrade."

Dan frowned, but nodded and walked back to where they'd been.

Bookie walked into the room, pulled back the net curtain, and stood next to the wall. A few seconds later he saw Dan give him the thumbs up. He thanked Esme and walked with her to her front door. Before she opened it, he said, "Why don't you like Dan?"

Esme looked up at Bookie and said, "What are you talking about?"

"You, and your obvious dislike of Dan."

"But I do like him, he's got balls. It's been ages since I've had a good swear at a man, and it's been even longer since anybody swore at me – I enjoy it. It's good fun."

Bookie smiled and said, "Right, in that case I'd better not tell him how you feel."

"No," said Esme, "don't you dare or you'll spoil it."

Bookie made the gesture of zipping his lips from left to right, and opened up the front door.

The moment Esme saw Dan she said, "You still here, chimp features? Shouldn't you be at that Fred Carnot's circus you call a workplace and be getting this bleeping sorted out instead of coming round here and disturbing a helpless old lady's sleep?"

"You a helpless old lady? You're neither helpless nor a lady, you fucking old trout," Dan paused as he realised what he'd just said, and then added, "Or should I say fucking old pilchard?"

"That's right shit-for-brains, take advantage; I expect you'll be wanting to knock me down and steal my handbag next?"

"No," said Dan, "I'd like to knock you down and drive ten ton truck over your face!"

"Yeah?" said Esme, "well any time you'd care to try it, bring it on!" She stuck her middle finger up in front of Dan's face, and then slammed the door shut.

Bookie grinned from ear to ear and said, "Looks like you have an admirer."

"And it looks like you need specs," said Dan. He paused for a second and then said, "And it pains me to say it, but you were right about that party wall. Where were you standing when I saw you through the window – a couple of feet from it?"

"No, I was right up against it."

Dan raised his eyebrows and said, "Oh that is a surprise," he looked back at the two properties and added, "because if that's right, the difference between our two walls must be at least six feet."

Bookie frowned and said, "*At least six feet?* Are you sure?"

"At least," confirmed Dan.

Bookie looked at the façade once again. He said, "Then there's a false wall in McCready House, and it must go from top to bottom because all of those right-hand rooms are uniform."

"No," said Dan pointing up to the roof, "it's not possible. If there is a false wall it must be on the old trout's side, look at the line of the building. Our property drops straight down in line with the end of the balustrade."

Bookie looked at the balustrade, and then said, "Just wait here one minute."

Dan watched as Bookie walked over to Esme's house and knocked on her door. He saw her answer, say something, then close the door. He waited until Bookie had returned and said, "What was that all about?"

"I asked her how long she'd lived here."

"And what did she say?"

"Most of her life; which goes to prove that the false wall is on our side."

"How do you figure that out?"

"For two reasons; One, there's the recently cut skirting, and two, if she'd been aware that a false wall had been constructed in her house, she wouldn't be as mystified as we are about where the bleeping could be coming from. She'd have known that there was a void there, and maybe what was behind it."

Dan raised his eyebrows and said, "Blimey, good thinking, Spock." He looked back at the balustrade and then said, "I think that we'd better get Garrison back here and have a good look at that roof."

Chapter 12

Crowthorne looked up as he heard a tap on his office door and called, "Come in."

The door opened and Detective Sergeant Brandon Chance stepped in with Postcard Percy.

In April 2006, Brandon Talion Chance, known to all as 'Leo' – a distant relative of Naomi's – had been an undercover officer codenamed Phobos who had helped her to escape from an underground drugs facility, owned and run by Adrian Darke in the grounds of his Cragg Vale Estate. But in July 2006, whilst in his protective care, Naomi had been kidnapped by a man named John Hess and held to ransom in exchange for his freedom. In the end, Hess had relented, and whilst attempting to return Naomi from the confines of the disused grain mill in which she'd been held, he'd fallen down a two-hundred foot silo whilst being attached to her by a length of rope. The trauma caused to her stomach by Hess's fall and ultimate death, caused her to lose her unborn son.

Subsequently, Carlton had never forgiven Leo for what he considered his lapse in duty, and held him responsible for his son's death.

Crowthorne stood up, extended his hand, and said, "Mr Johns, nice to meet you in person at last."

Percy shook the offered hand and said, "The pleasure's all mine, sir."

"Please," said Crowthorne, "there's no need to be so formal, call me Bob."

"Then you should call me Percy."

The men nodded and smiled at each other.

Crowthorne pointed to the chair in front of his desk and said, "Before we start, can I offer you a cup of tea?"

Percy sat down and said, "Yes please, milk, no sugar, I'm…" He faltered and then refrained from making his usual remark about being sweet enough.

Crowthorne looked at Leo, saw him nod, and pressed an intercom on his desk. He ordered tea for four.

Leo opened his mouth to question the number but was cut off.

"So," said Crowthorne turning to Percy, "I take it that Naomi went for it?"

"She did."

Leo frowned and looked at the two men.

Crowthorne looked at his watch, turned to Leo and said, "I'll explain in a minute, because I'm expecting…"

There was another tap on the door.

"Come in," called Crowthorne.

The door opened and Carlton stepped inside. He nodded and smiled at Crowthorne and Percy, and then caught sight of Leo. He said, "Why is he here?"

"Please, sit down and let me explain," said Crowthorne. He waited until Carlton had perched down on one of the chairs in front of his desk, and then passed him a cup of tea. "Now," he said, "Leo is with us because I ordered him to be here, but he doesn't yet know why." He looked from curious face to curious face and then said, "We believe that Adrian Darke is alive, and that he could be planning some sort of revenge against Naomi."

"Alive?" said a shocked Carlton, "and on what do you base that assumption?"

"Intelligence – his disappearance from the morgue – the death of the attendant who moved his body, and the death of one of his close associates who'd offered to shop him and his top bods in return for immunity."

"Good grief," said Carlton, he glanced at Leo and then added, "and what has any of this got to do with Detective Sergeant Chance?"

"This has everything to do with him because he's been in charge of Naomi's protection."

Carlton nearly exploded. He said, "*What? Him?* He's the reason she was abducted from Dunsteth Reservoir, and for losing our baby!"

Leo looked down, but didn't respond.

"That is not true, Carlton," said Crowthorne. "I appreciate that Naomi was under his protection when she was kidnapped by Hess, but Leo wasn't responsible for Naomi losing the baby."

"Pah! So you say. If he hadn't been so lax in his duty…"

"Now wait just one moment!" said Crowthorne, "I haven't said this to you before because of the pain you had to endure, but whoever would have been in charge of Naomi's protection that day, would have done exactly what Leo did; he played it right by the book…"

"Then the book needs rewriting!" said Carlton.

"I don't dispute that; and lessons were learnt that day, but I stood by my choice of Naomi's protection back then, and I stand by it now. He is the best, and I mean the best, that we've got, and apart from that regrettable incident at Dunsteth, he has an exemplary record of success." Crowthorne paused as he let his words sink in, and then continued, "And a lot of people, including your wife, owe him their lives."

Carlton looked at Leo and saw him staring in humility at the floor. He looked back at Crowthorne and didn't know what to say. For several seconds silence reigned, and then his cold, hard, dislike of Leo retreated a few notches. He said, "Okay, maybe I have been a bit harsh, and I know that I owe the Sergeant a huge debt of gratitude, but…"

Leo looked up and said, "There's no need to explain sir, I understand; and for the record, I've gone over and over that scenario until I'm blue in the face – but how to react given the same circumstances? I hope that I'm now better prepared."

Carlton stared at Leo for a few seconds, and then turned to face Crowthorne. He said, "You said that Sergeant Chance was in charge of Naomi's protection? Since when?"

"Since she returned from America last December."

Carlton was shocked. He said, "Last December? But…" he didn't know which question to ask first, "…but, why? When? And Naomi's been watched since the beginning of December?"

"For the most part Naomi, but we've watched you both when you've been together."

Carlton couldn't believe his ears. He said, "What, every day?"

"Yes."

"But what about the cost? Naomi's not royalty."

"No, but there are several aspects to her clandestine protection. First and foremost is her welfare, and second is the level of apparent hatred that she has generated in Adrian Darke. He's already wanted for questioning about numerous deaths, here in the UK, and in America, and we understand that more than a couple of African countries have applied for his extradition too, but, we don't have any treaties with them, and whenever he's been wanted for questioning in the USA, he's been at large.

"Naomi seems to be his Achilles' heel. We believe that his desire to get revenge on her, justifies the level of protection we're providing, whilst also offering us the best opportunity to draw him out and arrest him."

Carlton let out a gasp and said, "My God, you're not saying that Naomi's being used as bait are you?"

"Not in the slightest. That is why we are giving her the level of protection that she has."

Carlton cast his mind back to all of those occasions since Naomi had returned from America where they were together. Out alone, with friends, with family, and the rest, and he couldn't recall a single instance where he felt that they were being watched. He said, "And she, we, have been watched twenty-four hours a day, seven days a week?"

"You have."

"Even at home?"

"Even at home."

"And Sergeant Chance has been in charge of all that?"

"He has."

Carlton turned and looked at Leo once again. He said, "Well, I'm amazed. I had no idea."

"You weren't meant to," said Crowthorne.

Carlton looked at Leo again, and shook his head. He extended his hand and waited until a surprised Leo took hold of it. He said, "Thank you Sergeant. From me, and from Naomi, you've done an outstanding job."

"Thank you sir," said Leo, "given our past history that means a lot to me."

Carlton's ice-cold dislike of Leo disappeared and he said, "You're welcome, and given our new level of intimacy, I think that you should call me Carlton."

"Thank you Carlton, and I'm Leo."

The two men nodded and new understanding was forged.

"Now," said Crowthorne, "the reason for this get-together. Following my meeting with Naomi and her colleague Helen in her office last Monday, Naomi made it plain to me that she had no intention of going into hiding until we'd apprehended Adrian Darke. That was going to be a problem for us until Percy called and informed me that he'd introduced them to a lady whose mother had gone missing in the 1970's, and that they were interested in following up her story.

"That on its own wouldn't be of more than the usual professional interest to us because of its historic nature, but when Percy told me that the lady's daughter had also gone missing, and in the same place as her mother, that was something else.

"I put out a request for more info from the Met. Police in Hillingdon, London, because that's where Mrs Lockyer lived and had instigated the enquiry, and somebody told me that an officer had been sent up to liaise with a member of the Lancashire CID in Skelmersdale, where both of the women had gone missing." He stopped and looked at each face to make sure that they were following, and then said, "Only that wasn't the case at all."

Leo sat up and began making notes in his pocket book.

"Because," continued Crowthorne, "when I made enquiries into who had been liaising with the Met officer, nobody could be found. Indeed nobody at Skelmersdale knew what I was talking about.

"I then re-contacted the police at Hillingdon and tried to establish who had been sent up to Lancashire, and by whom, and not only did they deny any knowledge of such an event, they also had no record of me contacting them the day before either."

A deep frown cut into Leo's face.

"And where does Naomi fit into this?" said Carlton.

Crowthorne sat back in his seat and said, "Clearly something's not right. But, because I can find no reference to either of the women going missing, I can find nobody from the Lancashire force who dealt with a police officer from the Met, and nor can I find an officer who knows anything about this case in Hillingdon, I am at a complete loss.

"Of course I'm curious about these events, and I shall be making further enquiries, but in the meantime, I thought that I might give Naomi and Helen free-reign to investigate this mystery."

"What? When at least two people have already disappeared?" said Carlton, "I don't think so!"

Crowthorne looked at Carlton; his ex-military bearing was still evident, and despite him being middle-aged and working in an office, he still appeared to be fit and strong. As usual, his dark pinstripe business suit and white shirt with matching tie were in impeccable taste, and the set of his square, clean-shaven jaw below his handsome, but business-like face, made him look imposing. He considered his answer for a second and then said, "Let's not be too hasty about this Carlton. First off, you know that Naomi, and of course Helen, would be watched at all times …" He saw Carlton raise an eyebrow and said, "… yes I know what you're thinking, but the level of protection is now significantly increased …" He saw Carlton nod in acceptance, and then continued, "… and we know how effective those two ladies have been in the past at solving historical mysteries. And, best of all, it would take them out of Walmsfield for periods at a time."

"But they'd have no jurisdiction to work in Skelmersdale being employees of Walmsfield Borough Council," said Carlton.

"Unless their services were requested by Lancashire Police, and Walmsfield Borough agreed to let them do it," said Crowthorne.

Carlton pondered for a few seconds and then said, "Can you get such a request now that you've transferred to the Manchester force?"

"I can."

Carlton nodded and said, "Okay, but I'd have to run it past the Town Clerk first."

"May I ask a question?" said Percy, "would you have any objection to me or any of my friends assisting Naomi with this venture?"

Crowthorne looked at Leo and saw him nod in agreement. He looked at Percy and said, "We wouldn't have any objection, but please bear in mind that she and Helen will be being watched by the police at all times whilst they're together."

Percy took Crowthorne's drift and said, "Ah, yes, right, I know that some of my acquaintances can be er…"

"Odd? Questionable?" proffered Crowthorne.

"Yes," said Percy, "but they are well-intentioned, and they would guard Naomi and Helen's welfare with equal diligence."

Crowthorne said, "Alright – did you have anybody particular in mind?"

Percy raised his eyebrows and said, "EM?"

Crowthorne said, "EMDW? – Are you sure?"

"He'd be perfect."

Carlton and Leo sat with frowns upon their faces, completely oblivious to what had been said.

"Okay," said Crowthorne, "but keep him away from the Smarties."

Carlton and Leo's confusion increased.

"I'll try," said Percy, "but you know what he's like when he's on a case…"

"Er, can I ask what just went on?" said Leo.

"I'm sure that Percy will explain later, but for now let's just wrap this up.

"Are we all agreed that in order to confuse any possible plans by Darke, that Naomi and Helen can look into the Lockyer case?"

Nods all round.

"In the knowledge that they will be being monitored by us of course," added Crowthorne. "And that they will be allowed to work in Skelmersdale?"

"With the Town Clerk's permission," said Carlton.

"Then it's settled, Leo will liaise with you both at all times, and give you special numbers to ring if you need him."

"One last thing," said Carlton, "do you think it possible that Naomi and Helen will discover anything?"

"And solve two historical cases that no police know about, with no clues, no evidence, and in an unfamiliar town?" he looked from face to face and then turned back to Carlton and said, "Not likely is it?"

Chapter 13

In an unassuming house in North Mall, on the north bank of the River Lee, in Cork, Robert Somersby, a high-ranking British Government negotiator, and Neil Askew, an undercover MI5 agent, posing as an under-secretary, entered a darkened room. They were ushered to two chairs, plonked down, and had their blindfolds removed. Once their eyes had become accustomed to the low level of light, they made out five hooded figures sitting facing them from behind a table. On the table was a single pad of writing paper, a pencil and a Beretta M1934 semi-automatic pistol.

With customary cool-headedness, Somersby said, "Good morning gentlemen."

Askew remained silent and kept his eyes peeled for any movement towards the gun.

Patrick Boyle, the man in the middle said, "Say your piece."

Somersby cast a glance at Askew then turned back to face the hooded figures. "Alright," he said, "British Intelligence is aware that Sean Russell's right-hand man Declan Keane, has been involved in negotiations with Oscar Pfaus, an agent of the Abwehr, or German Intelligence to try to persuade the Nazi Government under Herr Hitler to plan a bombing

campaign against Great Britain in conjunction with the IRA."
He stopped speaking for a few seconds, but when nobody
responded he continued. "We believe that he is doing this for
two reasons. First his abject hatred of Great Britain and our
partitioning of Northern Ireland, and second to try to regain
his status within the IRA following his Court Martial for
misappropriating funds in January this year."

Boyle said, "You appear to be well-informed."

"It is our business to be," said Somersby.

"And your point is?"

"His Majesty's Government wants to put a proposition to
you."

"What kind of proposition?"

"That Ireland sides with Great Britain in any potential
conflict with Germany."

Boyle let out an involuntary gasp. He said, "And why in
God's name would we do that?"

Somersby looked down for a second and then back up
again. He said, "What I am about to say would be so
contentious and sensitive that if it ever leaked out, the
proposition would be off. We would disavow anything to do
with this meeting and vigorously deny any connection with
the IRA. Is that understood?"

Boyle said, "Go on."

"No, sir," said Somersby, "before I proceed I need to
know that we have an understanding on this issue."

"Okay," said Boyle, "we have an understanding. What is
your proposition?"

"In the event of an armed conflict with Germany, and our
victorious emergence from such a conflict, if Ireland sides
with Great Britain, we will give up our claim on Northern
Ireland and return to you, a single united Eire."

Five mouths behind five hoods fell open. The men looked at each other in disbelief.

Boyle tried to remain calm and said, "That is one hell of a proposition, Mr Somersby."

"It is."

"And it has the *full* backing of His Majesty's Government?"

"It has the full backing of those whose influence could make this happen."

"In both Houses of Parliament?"

"Yes."

"And the Joint Chiefs of Staff?"

"Of the British Armed Forces, yes."

Boyle looked at his companions. He gathered that they would be bursting with excitement and enthusiasm, but in the case of one of them, he was wrong.

Michael Duffy, a staunch Irish patriot, was horrified. He didn't want a united Ireland; he wanted revenge for all of the hateful and sadistic things that the English had done to his family, friends, and countrymen over the last fifty years. He wanted to kill, to disfigure, and to revel in the suffering and anguish that he would cause, and it was his greatest desire to have the IRA side with Germany in a war with the English.

But he also realised that his feelings weren't shared by some of the older men in the upper ranks. They had done their share of fighting in the struggle to unite Ireland, and he knew that they would be thrilled at the prospect of that struggle now being on the verge of bearing fruit.

He opted to keep quiet for the rest of the meeting – and about his personal feelings – in case it brought him into direct conflict with his superior officers.

Boyle was still reeling from the shock of the proposal. He looked into Somersby's eyes for a second and then said, "If what you say is true, then we have the basis for further negotiations." He looked from left to right and saw his companions nod. He then turned back to Somersby and said, "How would you like us to proceed?"

"Naturally we appreciate that you will need time to acquaint, and no doubt convince your colleagues about the veracity of this proposal, so we would like to invite whomever you feel most able to represent you in these pivotal negotiations to London, to meet with our top people."

Boyle nodded. His head was spinning with the implications of such a consequence. He knew that he could be on the verge of making history; be one of the founding fathers of a new united Ireland; a modern hero who would be revered for generations to come. It was intoxicating in the extreme, and he had difficulty in thinking straight without heading off on a whirlwind of potential heroic outcomes.

Somersby said, "Might I suggest..." he reached up to retrieve his diary from the inside pocket of his jacket and saw the man next to Boyle grab the Beretta and point it at him. "It is my diary," he said, "and your man was thorough in checking my clothing for firearms before we entered ..."

Boyle reached across and placed his right hand over the top of the Beretta and pushed it back down on the table. He said, "Old habits ..."

"So I see," said Somersby. "Let's hope therefore, that we can achieve a successful outcome from this meeting so that we can all return to a more civilised way of life."

Boyle wanted to snap an acerbic response back, but he was still immersed in the enormity of the occasion. Instead he said, "Indeed, Mr Somersby, indeed."

Somersby looked at the man who had grabbed the gun, raised his eyebrows, and said, "May I?"

The man nodded.

Somersby reached into the inside pocket of his coat and took out his diary. He flicked through it and then said, "Might I suggest that you come to England on Friday, the fifth of November?"

"The fifth of November? The night that Guy Fawkes tried to blow up your Parliament?" said Boyle. "Now there's an interesting choice."

"I am a lover of irony," said Somersby.

"You don't say?" said Boyle. He paused and then said, "I'm sure that you are aware that not all of my companions would be made welcome through your border controls in order to attend this meeting."

Somersby realised that some, if not all, could be wanted by the British Authorities. He said, "Yes, I understand." He paused for thought, and then said, "We have several Royal Navy vessels patrolling the Irish Sea, I will arrange for one to pick you and your delegation up from Belfast and transport you to Fleetwood."

"Fleetwood?" said Boyle.

"Yes, it has less prying eyes than Liverpool. There you can stay overnight at our expense, and the following morning we will escort you First Class by railway train to London. Does that sound acceptable?"

Boyle looked left and right once more, saw nods of acceptance, and then said, "It does."

"In that case I shall make the arrangements and convey the finer details to you via the normal channels. We look forward to seeing you and your representatives in London on the sixth."

Boyle nodded, and said, "I never thought that I'd say this to a member of the British Government, but it has been a pleasure meeting you today."

Three of Boyle's companions nodded, but not Duffy.

Somersby nodded back and said, "Thank you, I reciprocate. It has been a rewarding experience."

Seconds later the blindfolds were put back on, and Somersby and Askew were led away.

In the basement room, the men removed their hoods, stood up, and one put on the light.

Boyle hugged each man in turn amidst a cascade of plaudits and back-slapping. He said, "In my wildest dreams I never thought I'd see the day that a member of the British Government would come to a lowly Irishman and offer him such a deal! This calls for a celebration."

As Boyle led the men to a nearby bar, the last thing that Duffy wanted to do was to celebrate. He was going to stop it, and nothing was going to get in his way.

Three-quarters of an hour later and back in the confines of Somersby's hotel room, Askew completed his search for any sign of a listening device.

"All clear," he said.

Somersby nodded for Askew to follow him into the adjoining bathroom. Once inside he turned on the bathtub's cold water tap and said, "Can't be too careful."

Askew nodded and said, "It seemed to have gone well."

"Yes," said Somersby, "my feeling too."

"Do you think that they'll go for it?"

"I don't know, but the proof of the pudding will be if they board HM Spartan."

Askew looked at Somersby and said, "My job has taught me to keep a cool head and a steady nerve, but I have to hand it to you sir, you did a magnificent job."

"Hmm," said Somersby, "considering how few of our own people know about this venture just yet, including Chamberlain himself no less, let's hope that nothing goes wrong. It would be just the catalyst needed to drive the IRA into bed with Hitler and his pack of psychotic warmongers – and we would be the fall guys to pay the price."

Chapter 14

James Garrison, Dan, and the Site Foreman, an irascible and abrasive character named Pete Bully, stepped into the cage of a sixteen metre hydraulic boom lift in front of McCready House.

Bully closed the cage door, made sure that the safety block was in place and then pulled the operating lever back. He waited until the three arms of the boom had lifted the cage above the level of the balustrade, swung it over the top of the roof, and then dropped it as low as he could without making contact.

"Good Lord," said Garrison, "I don't profess to be a building tradesman, but even I can see that that's not right." He pointed to the end of the balustrade adjacent to Esme Pilchard's property.

Bully frowned and said, "Bugger me."

Everybody could see that the line of the roof from McCready House extended at least another six feet beyond the end of the balustrade, before stepping down onto Esme Pilchard's roof.

Bully swung the cage across to the end of the balustrade and saw that it had been deconstructed in such a way as to give the impression that McCready House ended at that point, and the Pilchard property began.

Garrison said, "I'm not being stupid here am I? McCready House does actually end at the roof line, and not the balustrade?"

"That's correct Mr G," said Bully, "which means that somebody has erected a false interior wall from top-to-bottom."

"But why?" said Garrison.

Silence ensued until Dan said, "Maybe it has something to do with that bleeping."

Garrison and Bully looked at Dan, and then back at the roof line.

"I still don't get it," said Garrison, "if somebody wanted to erect a false wall inside McCready House that would be up to them. But why try to conceal it from the exterior by shortening the balustrade?"

Dan and Bully didn't answer.

"The only possible explanation," continued Garrison, "would be an attempt to deceive whoever owned McCready House in the years after the concealment that nothing was there."

"That sounds a bit cloak and dagger to me," said Dan, "and a bit spooky too." He paused for a second and then said, "And it makes you wonder what's behind that wall."

Garrison shrugged and said, "There's only one way to find out."

Bully said, "You're not suggesting that we open it up are you?"

"Aren't you curious why the false wall is there?"

Bully shrugged and said, "We have a deadline to keep to, and as contactors, none of that stuff is our business."

"But my company owns that house, and I am curious," said Garrison.

"Okay," said Bully, "but isn't the building Grade Two listed?"

"Not at the moment. It is being considered for listing, but right now we have carte blanche."

"In that case we could remove a couple of bricks from each level and see what's behind with a fibre-optic camera," said Dan.

"That sounds like a plan," said Garrison, and we'll start with the ground floor." He turned to Bully and said, "I'm leaving the country tomorrow, how soon could you arrange it?"

Bully pondered for a few minutes and then said, "By mid-afternoon today."

"Right," said Garrison, "take me back down. I'll leave you alone for now but I'll be back at 2:30 p.m."

At 3:30 p.m. Bully, Dan, Bookie, and Garrison were in the ground floor room of McCready House. Three bricks had been removed from the centre of the wall and the fibre-optic camera was ready to use. The air of anticipation and level of curiosity was at an all-time high, and the sound of the bleeping was much louder.

Bully turned to Garrison and said, "Ready, Mr G – do you want to look first?"

Garrison looked at Bookie and said, "Weren't you the guy who first heard the bleeping?"

"Yes, sir."

"Then I think that you should look first."

Bookie said, "Thank you, Mr Garrison, that's very kind of you." He looked at the fibre-optic camera and said, "What do I have to do?"

The camera was a hand-held plumbing endoscope similar in shape to a plastic pistol with a small, full-colour screen connected to the back of it. Attached to the 'barrel end' was a metre-long high-density, polyethylene cable with the camera lens and two small high-output LED illuminators in the tip.

Bully switched on the unit, waited until the screen resolution had focussed, and then said, "Okay, poke the cable through the hole, and let's see what's there."

Bookie inserted the fibre optic cable and swivelled it to the right, towards the window elevation. At first he thought that he was seeing things, and then he exclaimed, "Blimey, look at this!"

Everybody gathered around the small digital screen and saw an old-fashioned high-backed, winged armchair.

"Bloody hell," said Bully. "Why would anybody want to wall up an armchair?"

"Move it up and down," said Dan.

Bookie twisted the cable until the camera crept up the old cream wallpaper with a faded chromatic pattern upon it, until the print of a portrait came into view.

"Hold it steady and adjust the focus," said Garrison.

Bookie did as instructed and everybody saw that it was a framed portrait of King George the Sixth in his naval uniform.

"That dates things," said Garrison. "King George died in 1952 so this must be from the late forties or early fifties."

Bookie panned the camera up and then down but saw nothing more of note. He then moved it slowly around to the left.

A few more gasps erupted when a desk came into view. They saw a large blotter pad, a two-tier document tray containing sheets of paper, an ink pot, a glass ashtray, and a ceramic or china container holding several pencils.

Bookie swivelled the camera further left, and before he could stop himself, said, "Fucking hell – look!"

Perched on the right-hand side of the desk was a red telephone from which, every thirty seconds, a bleep emitted. There was no rotary dial wheel, but where one should have been a small red light illuminated every time the phone bleeped.

"Good grief," said Garrison.

Everybody started to talk at once.

Bully said, "What was this place, a government office or something?"

"I've no idea," said Garrison.

Dan said, "Who did you buy it from, Mr Garrison?"

"A private owner…"

"And why did he or she wall up part of an office?"

Garrison shrugged and said, "Maybe it was walled up when the last owners bought it."

"So who owned it before them?" said Bully.

"I don't know."

"How long had the previous owners had it?" said Dan.

And then Bookie spoke, and stopped everybody dead. He said, "Who's calling?"

All four heads looked down at the digital monitor as Bookie swivelled the camera onto the phone once more. It bleeped and the light flashed again. They all looked at one-another in silence.

Garrison turned to Bookie and said, "Now that is a good question, Mr Werm" He turned to Bully and said, "You need to open up a void large enough to let somebody in."

"Shouldn't we call the police or something?" proffered Dan.

Once again the chatter stopped.

"Or maybe MI5?"

"MI fucking 5?" said Bully, "What are you talking about?"

Garrison looked at the hole and heard the phone bleep again. He said, "Dan has a point you know. Those weren't ordinary phones they were usually something to do with national security and the like."

"But it's been walled up for God knows how long."

"Maybe," said Garrison, "but it only started bleeping two weeks' ago."

"That's weird," said Dan. "Think about it, why would anybody wall a live phone up?"

"And why would anybody wall up half an office?" said Bully.

"To preserve it for posterity or something?" said Bookie.

"With a live phone in it?"

"Maybe the people who walled it up, never expected it to ring again," said Garrison.

"Then how come it is, and like Bookie said, who's calling?" said Dan.

Garrison was filled with uncertainty. He saw everybody looking at him and then gathered resolve. "Right," he said, "Peter, you open up enough of that wall to allow access, and then check every other room with a false wall. I'll call the local police."

"No, wait," said Bookie.

All eyes turned to him.

"This is your house, Mr Garrison. Whoever walled up that bit of old office never expected that phone to ring again, so it can't be a matter of national importance, can it?"

"And your point is?" said Garrison.

"An opportunity to experience a once-in-a-lifetime event. Wouldn't you always be able to tell your grandkids that you were the one who answered that phone if it was from somebody historically important? Or would you forever kick yourself if you let somebody else take that call if it was a voice, or maybe an old recording, from the past?"

Garrison looked from face to face and then nodded. He said, "Mr Werm's right – I'll do it."

Within half an hour, Garrison and Bully had stepped through the hole and into the walled up section of the old office. Bully's men had set up arc lamps that illuminated everywhere.

The new section of wall had been decorated on its interior to match the existing wallpaper so that anybody sitting in the old office chair may have seen the same view as they had in the years before. A single framed picture of an old Dreadnought class battleship from the World War one era hung on the wall they'd stepped through, and the carpet was cut off at the skirting board.

Garrison picked up one or two pieces of paper from the in-tray and saw that they were non-descript items that had been placed there for effect.

Apart from the intriguing phone, the most startling thing was the lack of dust or cobwebs. Everywhere looked as though it had been dusted and vacuumed just days before.

The phone bleeped and flashed again.

Garrison looked at Bully and saw him nod. He drew in a deep breath and said, "Right, here goes…"

He waited until the phone bleeped and flashed again, then picked it up and said, "Hello…"

Chapter 15

"There are none so blind
As those who will not see"
John Heywood 1546.

Gabriel Ffitch the Town Clerk looked across his uncluttered desk at the dapper figure of Carlton Wilkes. He noted Carlton's expensive-looking clothes and for a second, speculated how much it had all cost. He also knew how determined Carlton could be and, as per his previous meetings with him, he felt mildly intimidated.

Carlton looked straight into the eyes of Ffitch and said, "Well?"

Ffitch cleared his throat and said, "This is most unusual and I don't know whether it's within my remit to be able to sanction such a thing."

"Of course it's unusual," said Carlton, "and under normal circumstances I wouldn't ask such a thing, but Naomi is my wife, and my top priority is her safety."

"Her safety?" exclaimed a surprised Ffitch, "What do you mean her safety? Is somebody threatening her or something?"

"Yes, her old adversary Adrian Darke."

The sound of Darke's name hit Ffitch like a hammer blow. He said, *"Adrian Darke?* I thought he was dead."

"So do most other people," said Carlton, "but not the police. They think that he's alive and well, and planning some sort of retribution against Naomi for exposing his drugs set-up at Cragg Vale."

Ffitch was mortified. Both he and Morag Beech, his PA, had been convinced that they'd been rid of Darke for good, but Carlton's revelation made him feel as though an invisible tether had been replaced around his neck.

A massive conflict of interests raged in his mind. On the one hand he was being paid an annual stipend by Darke to spy for him within the Council, and on the other, his greatest desire was to sever all connections to him. But, and it was a big but, he also knew that untoward behaviour against Walmsfield Borough Council could lead to the sack, whereas disloyalty to Darke meant certain, and for-the-most-part, painful death.

He looked at Carlton and said, "And you think that by me sanctioning your wife and Ms Milner to work in Skelmersdale, it will somehow throw Darke off their scent?"

Carlton realised how pathetic his request sounded and said, "I don't know; maybe, maybe not. I expect that Darke has all sorts of moles planted around the place …"

Ffitch felt an involuntary shiver run up his spine.

"… and I'm not naïve enough to think that he wouldn't be able to track them down if he was trying, but what I am suggesting is that by Naomi and Helen breaking away from the confines of their usual Walmsfield District boundaries on sporadic occasions, it might at least add to Darke's logistical difficulties, if he was attempting to er, er …" Carlton couldn't bring himself to say it.

"Attempting to what?" said Ffitch.

"You know, take them or …"

"Take *them*?" interrupted Ffitch. "You think that Ms Milner might be on Darke's hit list as well do you?"

"No – maybe, I …" Carlton felt that he was slipping out of his comfort zone and knew that he'd be a lot more objective if it wasn't his wife and Helen that he was talking about. He tried to settle his nagging doubts by re-asserting himself and said, "Look, let's stop beating about the bush, Gabriel. It's the opinion of Greater Manchester Police, and me, as Naomi's husband, that she'd be safer working outside of Walmsfield; and now that Lancashire Police have requested her help in solving a legitimate historical enquiry, it could all come together. All we'd require is your endorsement."

Ffitch needed to talk to Beech. He said, "It sounds okay in principle, but please give me thirty minutes to mull things over."

"Thirty minutes?"

"Yes, that's all I'm asking, and I'll give you my definitive answer."

Carlton said, "That's fair I suppose, I'll be back in thirty minutes." He got up, walked across to the door and said, "Thank you Gabriel – this means a lot to me, and to Naomi."

Ffitch nodded and waited until the door had closed. He reached across to his intercom, pressed it, and said, "Mo, I need you now."

Seconds later Beech walked in, shut the door, and perched her heavy frame on the chair in front of Ffitch's desk. She said, "Christ, babe, you look like you've been put through the ringer, what's up?"

Beech and Ffitch weren't in a personal relationship but they'd spent a lot of time together in, and, out of work, and though both suspected that something might happen between them one day, to date, it had not.

He'd tried over and over to stop her calling him 'babe' whilst at work, but as the time had passed he'd become accustomed to it.

Because Morag's surname was Beech, she'd always referred to the two of them as 'Ffitch and his bitch.' She dressed in black, was overweight, and plain looking. She had a ruddy complexion, a diamond stud in her nose, and she gave the impression of being imposing and unapproachable, but, she was an excellent and mega-loyal PA.

In appearance Ffitch was the total opposite. He was a spruce dresser; he was good-looking, one inch shorter than Beech, and he was slim and elegant; but something gelled between them. He loved being in her company, and he loved sharing the inexhaustible supply of cream cakes that appeared on a daily basis, on her desk.

"Darke's alive."

Beech was as shocked as Ffitch. She said, "Bloody hell. How do you …?"

"I've just had Carlton Wilkes asking me to sanction his missus working in Skelmersdale."

Beech frowned and said, "What? What has that got to do with Darke?"

"According to Superintendent Crowthorne, Darke is planning some sort of vendetta against Naomi Wilkes and now Lancashire Police have requested her help with some historical enquiry in Skelmersdale."

"Hang on, slow down, babe," said Beech. "You're not making sense. What's Skelmersdale got to do with anything?"

"It's a ruse by the police to get her, and her buddy, out of Walmsfield in case Darke comes looking for them."

Beech paused for a second as she digested the info, and then said, "So what? If he does, he does. What's your problem?"

"The problem is – do I tell Darke what the police are planning?"

Beech drew in a deep breath and said, "Ooh yeah, shit ..." she hesitated and then jumped to her feet. She looked sideways at Ffitch and said, "... cake time."

She disappeared out of the office and returned seconds later with the box of cakes and two paper serviettes. She pushed a serviette and the box across Ffitch's desk, watched him extract a dark chocolate éclair and then took one herself. She took a big bite, wiped the corners of her mouth and said, "We say sod all."

"But what if he finds out at a later date that we knew what the police were planning and we didn't tell him?"

"Did he tell you that he wasn't dead?"

"No."

"Then it's problem solved. If he couldn't be bothered to tell you that he was alive, why should we presume that he was? Especially since he took such elaborate measures to fake his own death."

"But ..."

"But nothing, hun; if at some time in the future it becomes public knowledge that he's alive, we can re-think things and plan accordingly."

Ffitch took a bite of the chocolate éclair and sat back in his chair. He stared at Beech for a couple of seconds and then said, "You're right. We've been that guy's eyes and ears for five years now and I think that he's had his money's worth."

Beech nodded and said, "Spot on."

They sat in silence mulling over scenarios until they'd finished their éclairs, and then Beech looked at her watch and said, "They were nice; they're from that new bakers on the corner of the High Street. Want a coffee?"

Ffitch nodded and said, "Yes please." He looked up at Beech and said, "I'm going to let Carlton Wilkes's missus and her sidekick work in Skelmersdale; and we'll continue to assume that Darke's dead."

"Sounds like a plan. I'll get your coffee, and if you're on the phone when I get back I'll put it on your desk and leave you be."

Ten minutes later Carlton phoned Crowthorne. He heard him answer, and said, "Ffitch has agreed. Naomi and Helen can work in Skelmersdale."

There was a pause.

Carlton said, "Did you hear me Bob. Ffitch has agreed to let Naomi …"

"Yes, I did hear," interrupted Crowthorne, "but something's happened at my end. I'll call you back in a few minutes."

Carlton was shocked to hear the phone go dead. He frowned and was about dial Naomi's number to tell her the good news, but something stopped him. He sat back and put his left hand up to his mouth and waited.

The phone rang. He picked it up and said, "Wilkes."

"Carlton, Bob here. Sorry I was so terse with you a few moments ago but something's happened and it's thrown us all."

"Go on …"

"Another of Darke's people has been found murdered."

"Good grief," said Carlton, "another?"

"Yes, only this time it's someone much closer to him than that Gillorton woman. Do you remember Christiana his wife?"

"Good God! It's not her is it?"

"No, it was the CEO of her Christadar Holdings, Dominic Sheldon."

"But he worked for Christiana, why kill him? And are you sure that his death wasn't an accident?"

"He worked for Darke," confirmed Crowthorne, "and we believe that the only reason he ever worked for Christiana was to keep an eye on her, for him. And, we'd long suspected him of being one of Darke's top brass. As for your question about his death being accidental? He'd been tied to a chair and pushed out of a sixteenth floor window of the City Tower in Manchester."

Carlton wasn't accustomed to swearing under any circumstance, but he was so taken aback, he said, "Bloody hell!"

"Security staff found him and called us; when our lads got there they saw a note pinned to his jacket with the word 'Venio' written upon it."

"Venio?" repeated Carlton.

"It's Latin and means 'I come' or 'I am coming'."

"Blimey, ominous or what?"

"Yes, and as much as I don't like it, it would seem that we have a secret ally in our battle against Darke and his allies."

"What about Naomi and Helen, shall we still let them proceed in Skelmersdale?"

"Yes, and with a bit of luck this new turn up will take Darke's mind off them for while at least."

Chapter 16

Klossner removed a pocket watch from his waistcoat and looked at it. He'd been given his instructions, and for them to work, he had to get the timing right. He double-checked the watch, replaced it in his waistcoat pocket, and walked into the red telephone box that he'd chosen. He then extracted a business card from his jacket pocket and saw:

'B A Ware Esq
Section 5
Tel; VAU 2222'

He picked up the telephone, dialled 100 and waited.

"Operator – how may I help you?"

"I need to ring VAU 2222 but I don't know how much money to put in the box and I don't want to be cut off."

"One moment please, sir." Seconds later the operator said, "I'm putting you through now, sir."

"Wait," said Klossner, "how much money do I need to put in?"

"It isn't necessary with that number, sir, just hang on and they'll answer you in a second."

Klossner thanked the operator and waited again.

"Vauxhall 2222."

"Mr Ware in Section five please."

"And whom shall I say is calling?"

"Klossner – Axel Klossner from …"

"Thank you, sir, one moment please."

"Ware."

Klossner looked out of the windows of the telephone box and saw that nobody was looking. He put the phone back up to his ear and said, "Is that Mr Ware?"

"It is Doctor Klossner. Is everything progressing as it should?"

"It is."

There was a brief pause and then Ware said, "It is 14:40 precisely, do you agree?"

Klossner removed his watch from his pocket once again, looked at it, and said, "I agree."

"Then we have five minutes, Doctor; do you have anything to tell me?"

"I do. We may have some trouble at …"

"I know where, please carry on."

"Some of the personnel are against developing the, er…"

"The project," interrupted Ware.

"Yes, the project. They …"

"Do you have any names?"

"Yes, four right now, but there may be more."

"Understood: the names please."

"Doctor …"

"No," said Ware, "I don't need titles, just names."

"Ah, of course: Eleanor Drake, Zeena Bishop, Sandi Schmidt and David Allum."

"Eleanor Drake, Zeena Bishop, Sandi Schmidt, and did you say David Allum? Spelt A-L-L-U-M?"

"Correct," said Klossner.

"Thank you Doctor; what is the nature of their dissent?"

"They object to the, er, way, that the project achieves its aims."

"Do you envisage any immediate disruption?"

"No, the protests are vocal right now, but I was asked to inform you if I heard any hint of trouble."

"And you did the right thing. Are all of the dissenters currently on site?"

"Three are, one isn't."

"Which one isn't?"

"David Allum. He has gone to visit his sick mother."

"What form of transport did he take to visit his sick mother, and when is he expected back?"

"He took the train from Settle to ..."

"We are aware of his mother's whereabouts."

"Oh, right, he is due back on the fourth, before the ..."

"Does the Professor know about the dissention?"

"He does."

"And is he aware of our special arrangement?"

"No."

"Good. Your time is up, Doctor, thank you for calling. Goodbye."

Klossner heard the line go dead and then replaced the receiver. He turned to open the kiosk door and saw Ronnie Bowers staring in at him with a puzzled expression on his face. He opened the door and stepped outside.

"I told you to wait in the truck," he said.

Bowers ignored the comment and said, "Who were you talking to like that, and why were you giving away those names?"

Klossner glanced up the road and then back at Bowers. He said, "It's none of your business, and you shouldn't have been listening to me like that. Now please, go back to the truck and wait for me there."

Bowers was having none of it. He said, "What do you mean it's none of my business? We're all working in a top secret government establishment and I hear you on a public telephone passing the names of some of our oppo's to somebody else?"

Klossner realised how serious that sounded, but was aware that he couldn't reveal any of it. He said, "Ronnie, do you trust me?"

"Yes, course I do, but, do you trust *me*?"

"Of course."

"Then tell me who you were talking to."

Klossner said, "I can't."

"Then you don't trust me."

"It's not as simple as that."

"It is. It's just as simple as that. You either trust me or you don't."

Klossner looked up the road and saw that it was still empty. He looked Bowers straight in the eyes and decided to exert some authority. He said, "If I say that I can't tell you who I was speaking to, then you must accept that. There are things about our research that I cannot divulge to anybody but the colleagues in my own department so don't push me now."

Bowers frowned and said, "But you weren't talking to anybody in your department, you were passing names to somebody on the phone." He paused and then added, "You were talking to an English person weren't you?"

Klossner said, "What?"

"I said; you were talking to an *English* person in England weren't you?"

Klossner glowered and said, "And what do you mean by that?"

Bowers stared but didn't respond.

Klossner stepped closer and said, "I said – what do you mean by that?"

Bowers dug his heels in and said, "You're the one who started this by passing on information about some of our members to an unknown!"

"He is not an unknown to me! And that still doesn't answer my question about why you asked if I was talking to somebody in England." Klossner stepped closer.

Bowers pushed Klossner hard in the chest and sent him reeling back. He said, "Back off, Axel, I might be your cock boy but I'm still an English soldier so don't try to intimidate me."

Klossner saw red, lunged forwards and grabbed Bowers by the jacket. He said, "Are you insinuating that I'm passing information to German Intelligence?"

Bowers grabbed hold of Klossner's wrists and said, "Maybe – you are a fucking kraut!"

Klossner let go of Bower's jacket with his right hand and then he slapped him hard across the face. He hissed, *"Fucking kraut?"* He re-grabbed the jacket, yanked Bowers closer, and said, "Fucking kraut?" He pushed his face into Bowers' and said, "At least we krauts have respect for authority and seniority! Who do you think you're talking to you fucking Scheisse?"

At that precise moment, Archie Rowbottom the driver of a lorry laden with sacks of potatoes saw the unexpected altercation on the pavement ahead of him. He hit the horn to warn the grappling men of his approach.

Klossner turned, saw the truck, and pushed Bowers away from him. As he did so, he stepped back, stumbled on a raised flagstone, and fell backwards into the road.

Rowbottom had no chance. He stamped on the brakes and attempted to swerve, but the truck's radiator grille slammed into Klossner's chest and knocked him below the vehicle.

On the roadside Bowers watched in horror. He saw Klossner's body roll over twice, and then come to a stop. He looked around, saw that nobody had seen their squabble, and then he heard the truck screech to halt.

Rowbottom ran to where Klossner was lying and said, "Bloody hell! What happened? I had no chance to stop."

Within seconds a car had pulled up and the driver announced that he was a doctor. He kneeled down, examined Klossner, and then turned to Rowbottom and Bowers. He shook his head and said, "I'm sorry gents, he's gone."

Bowers heard Rowbottom say, "The police station's just around the corner, I'll run round there and get someone."

The doctor nodded and then looked at Bowers. He said, "Are you alright? You look a bit shaken."

Bowers couldn't take his eyes off Klossner. He said, "I'm okay, but what about him? What am I supposed to do now?"

The doctor said, "You need to wait here until the police arrive, and then you can tell them what happened. I'll contact the ambulance station and arrange for this man to be taken to the local mortuary. Do you know his name?"

Bowers said, "No, I've never seen him before."

He waited until the doctor looked down at Klossner's body, and then leapt back into the cab of his truck. He started the engine, and heard the doctor shout, *"Hey! What are you doing? Stop!"*

He jammed the truck into gear, and then drove away as quickly as he could.

Minutes later Rowbottom and the local Constable ran to the scene of the accident.

Rowbottom said, "Where's the squaddie?"

"I've no idea," said the doctor, "he drove off after you ran to the police station."

The policeman looked up the empty road and said, "What's his game then, and why would he do that?"

"I have the registration number of the truck if that helps," said the doctor.

"It's a start," said the policeman reaching for his pocket book.

Chapter 17

Garrison held the red telephone against his left ear, and repeated, "Hello?"

One-hundred-and-sixty miles north, near Selby in North Yorkshire, the engineers at the massive Drax Power Station watched as the final tests were completed for bringing the station back on line to all of its users. The engineers scrutinized the readouts and watched the monitors for any sign of a problem. It had been twenty days since the original blackout, and they'd been under intense pressure to restore the electricity ever since.

At the Slaidburn coal-fired power station Chief Engineer Harry Appleton and engineer Malcolm Ridyard stood by waiting for the call informing them that Drax was back on line, and to switch off the power there.

The phone rang and Appleton picked it up. He said, "Slaidburn, Appleton."

"Harry," said Ben Bromley the Chief Engineer from Drax, "sorry to keep you waiting. We should be getting the readout any second, and then you can shut down Slaidburn."

"About time," said Appleton, "we haven't been using Ferrybridge for the last three days, so I don't know why this has taken so long."

"The usual story I'm afraid, consumer demand. Slaidburn was only supplying the fringes of the power we needed, and even then it was to the outlying areas of our remit, so, as per, it got shoved to the back of the queue."

"Typical," said Appleton, "and as usual, I'm the sap stuck out here in the back of beyond."

"Hang on Harry, we're getting something now …"

Appleton heard muffled exchanges and then Bromley say, "You still there?"

"Yes."

"We're all go here, you can shut it down."

"Excellent – Mal and I will …"

"Harry, hang on, sorry to interrupt, George wants a quick word. I'll call you back."

"Can we proceed with the shutdown?"

"No, give me a minute and I'll call you back."

Ridyard looked at Appleton and said, "Is it a go?"

"No, Ben's calling us back in a couple of minutes. He says to hang on 'til then."

Ridyard leaned back in his chair at the old console and then glanced at his watch. He said, "A couple of minutes you say? We'll see about that," he shot a resigned look at Appleton, and then turned his attention back to the Daily Express crossword on the desk in front of him.

Within seconds the phone rang again, and Appleton answered.

"Harry, Ben, you can shut her down, but please stay there for the next hour or so. George isn't happy about the EP readings from boiler three and won't authorise full power until the readings settle."

"It'll be because she's been shut down for so long," said Appleton, "the readings are always a bit cranky at first."

"I agree," said Bromley, "so shut down at your end, but stay put. You know what George is like when he gets a bee in his bonnet. I'll call you again when you can leave."

"Okay, bye for now."

Ridyard put down his pen and looked at Appleton. He said, "Problem?"

"The electrostatic precipitators of boiler three are giving off some erratic readings, so Ben's authorised shutdown here, but he wants us to stay on site until we hear from him."

Ridyard said, "I don't blame him. If any of the tree-huggers found out that we'd been depositing oxides into the atmosphere, especially carbon and sulphur, there'd be hell to pay. And thinking about it – I suppose that if I was somewhere else I'd be busier than I would be sitting here doing a crossword puzzle." He pointed to the shutdown switches and said, "First things first though. Shall we?"

At McCready House Bully turned as he saw Dan and Bookie enter the previously concealed area.

"Bloody hell," said Dan, "I…"

"Shh!" Bully glared and then nodded in the direction of Garrison.

Garrison listened into the earpiece of the phone but only heard a static hiss. He said, "Hello, can anybody hear me?" He held the phone in place for few seconds longer and then removed it from his ear. He said, "Nobody's there."

"No," said Bookie, "that can't be right. Somebody's initiated that call otherwise the phone wouldn't have been ringing." He paused and then added, "Maybe somebody is there, but they're not answering you."

Garrison raised his eyebrows and nodded. He put the phone back to his ear and said, "Hello – we know that you're listening so …"

The phone went dead.

Garrison removed it from his ear and stared at it for a second. He then lifted it back and said, "Hello?" There was no static hiss. He looked at the others and said, "They've hung up."

"Blimey! So somebody was there!" said Dan.

Garrison tapped the silver buttons on the receiver cradle, put the phone back to his ear and said, "Hello? Hello?"

The phone remained dead.

The four men looked at one-another until Bully said, "Well?"

"Nothing, it's dead," said Garrison.

"Weird," said Dan.

"No, more than weird," said Bookie. "Perhaps I was wrong in my earlier assumption."

All eyes turned to him.

"I first heard that phone bleeping twelve days ago, so it would be ridiculous to think that somebody had hung onto the other end for that long."

"Bookie's right," said Dan, "it was twelve days ago. I remember because I should have been having my vasectomy on that day but they cancelled." He saw the look of surprise on everybody's face and regretted sharing that bit of info.

"So what now Mr Garrison?" said Bully.

"I don't know! What are the procedures for finding a sealed-up void with a ringing red phone that hangs up when you answer?"

"Call the police maybe?" proffered Bookie.

Garrison put the phone back on the receiver and said, "That could really hold up proceedings if we involve them."

"But what other choice do we have?"

Garrison pondered for a few seconds and then looked at his watch. He said, "Why don't I take you all to the local coffee shop for a latte while I think about this?"

"You don't have to do that," said Bully, "we can knock a coffee up here."

Garrison recalled the only other occasion that he'd agreed to have a coffee at McCready House, and winced at the memory of it. He said, "No, we'll go; besides, I think that we should keep these proceedings between ourselves until we come up with a plan." He looked at Dan and said, "Lock this room up while we're away, and then we'll decide what to do out of everybody else's earshot."

Back at Slaidburn, Ridyard looked at his watch. Forty-five minutes had ensued since they'd shut down Slaidburn, and he'd started to become fidgety. He said, "They're taking their time."

Appleton looked up from his newspaper and said, "We'll be out of here soon enough."

Following an in-depth discussion over coffees, Garrison, Bully, Dan, and Bookie, had decided that the only realistic course of action had been to contact the local police. The intrigued police operator at Hampstead Heath had put them through to the CID and it had been arranged that an officer meet them at McCready House.

As they arrived back on site, they saw an unmarked car pull up, and two men step out.

One of the men, in his mid-thirties and dressed in a smart grey suit, walked towards Garrison and said, "Mr Garrison?"

"Yes."

"I'm Detective Inspector Stuart Wood and this is Detective Sergeant Alan Fowler."

The men shook hands and Garrison indicated towards McCready House.

"You have us intrigued, Mr Garrison," said Wood.

"Just wait until you see," said Garrison, "you'll be even more intrigued."

The men made their way into McCready House, and then into the room at the end of the corridor.

Garrison pointed to the hole in the wall and said, "See for yourselves."

Wood looked at Fowler, raised his eyebrows and stepped through the wall. Fowler then stepped through, followed by Garrison and Bully.

Wood took in the whole scene and said, "Good grief gents, I see what you mean. This is truly fascinating." He turned around, looked at the red phone, and said, "And this is the phone?"

"It is."

"And it was ringing for …" he removed his pocket book from his jacket and flicked through a couple of pages. "… twelve days you say?"

"That's correct."

"And you answered it, and whoever was on the other end hung up?"

"Yes."

Wood looked at Fowler and then back at Garrison. He said, "That doesn't make sense. Why would anybody keep a phone ringing for twelve days and then hang up when somebody answered?"

"My sentiments too," said Bookie peering through the gap.

"And you are?" said Wood.

"Michael Werm."

Wood looked at his notebook and said, "And you were the gentleman who first heard the phone?"

"I was."

"And do you have any other theories Mr Werm?"

Bookie hesitated and then said, "It's not really my place to speculate, but if I was pushed, I'd say that nobody had been on the other end of the line."

Wood frowned and said, "Then who do you think was calling?"

Bookie put both hands up and said, "Sorry, no idea!" He looked at the phone and then back at the Detective Inspector. He said, "But who uses red phones?" He paused and then added, "And what was one doing here? And why was it ringing until an hour ago?"

Wood turned and looked at the phone and then turned back to Bookie. He said, "An interesting set of questions, Mr Werm." He looked at Fowler and said, "Any thoughts Al?"

Fowler looked at the phone and then said, "I've no idea how, or why, that phone would be ringing, but we do know that they're not used by just anybody."

"So what was McCready House in its past?" said Garrison.

"I don't know, sir," said Wood, "but I will find out."

"And could we trace where that call came from?" said Bully.

"Not without a connection," said Wood. He turned around picked up the phone and listened to the earpiece. He said, "And this phone appears to be well and truly dead."

"So what do we do now?" said Garrison.

"You need to seal off this entire area until we can get some forensic guys and a couple of telephone engineers down here. Maybe they can shed some light on things."

The telephone rang in the control room of Slaidburn power station.

"Home time," said Appleton reaching for it.

"Let's hope so," said Ridyard.

"Slaidburn, Appleton."

"Harry, Ben. Bad news I'm afraid. The EP readings for boiler three have got worse and George is shutting it down. You'll need to fire up Slaidburn again."

"Oh come on!" said Appleton, "How much longer?"

"Piece of string, mate, piece of string."

"It's a bloody good job that the furnaces weren't shut down."

"I know. And I'm sorry for the inconvenience but George reckons it'll only be for a couple of days, but that does mean that you and Mal will have to troll up there again to shut it down when he is happy."

Appleton made a 'tutting' sound and said, "Okay, worse things happen at sea."

"True; my apologies again, Harry."

"No problem," said Appleton, "we'll do it now, and then get back to Ferrybridge."

Back at McCready House, the two policemen stepped through the hole in the wall and waited until the others were back in the main room.

"Okay, gents," said Wood, "that wraps it up for now. Please seal this room up after we've left and we'll be in touch as soon as we have any further information."

Bully looked at Garrison and said, "Sorry to be a pain, sir, but this could bugger up the programme."

Garrison shrugged and said, "Don't worry about Peter." He looked at the policemen and said, "It's not every day that you come across a situation like this, and I don't mind admitting that I'm excited about seeing where it could lead."

"If you say so, sir," said Bully. He looked at Dan and said, "Can I leave this up to you?"

"No problem," said Dan. "Bookie and I can sort it."

"Bookie?" said Wood.

"Bookie Werm?" said Dan.

For the first time, the men saw Wood smile. He looked at Bookie and said, "We all have our crosses to bear, Mr Werm, and with a name like Wood, you can imagine that I've had more than my fair share!"

Bookie smiled back and headed for the door.

Once in the hall, Wood shook hands with everybody and said, "We'll be in touch." He turned towards the main door, and then stopped dead in his tracks. He spun around and saw everybody staring into the room. For several seconds he remained motionless, and then heard, *"bleep"*.

Everyone surged back into the room and headed for the hole in the wall.

"Guys," said Wood, "please, let me." He stepped into the void, heard the bleep and saw the light flash on the phone. He picked up the receiver, listened for a second, and then said, "Hello?" He heard nothing but static. He repeated, "Hello?" drew no response and lowered the phone. He called, "Alan!"

Fowler looked through the hole and said, "Guv?"

"Get a telephone engineer down here as quick as."

Fowler nodded and disappeared.

Wood stared at the phone for a few seconds and didn't know whether to put the receiver back on the cradle or not. He didn't want to terminate the link from the sender, but seemed to recall that if somebody else initiated a call and then held the line open at their end, the recipient could replace the receiver, but the line would remain open.

134

Garrison walked through the gap and said, "Any luck Inspector?"

"No, sir, just static."

"Can you trace it?"

"It can be traced, but we'd need trained personnel to do it."

"Police?"

Wood didn't want to get embroiled in a technical to-and-fro, and said, "It depends on the situation sir, but for now I've instructed my sergeant to get a BT engineer down here post-haste."

Garrison nodded and said, "Anything we can do?"

"Perhaps you can clear the area, sir, and seal off this room until we've completed our investigation?"

"Yes of course," said Garrison. He turned to walk back through the hole and then faltered. He turned back to Wood and said, "I don't suppose you have any idea how long this might take?"

Wood raised his eyebrows and shrugged.

"Yes," said Garrison. "Right, we'll, er, clear the area and leave you chaps to it."

As soon as he was sure that he was alone, Wood placed the red receiver on the old desk top and removed his mobile phone from his pocket. He dialled his office and spoke to one of the duty detectives.

"I want you to get me the full occupancy history of McCready House at Hampstead Heath from building completion until now. Contact somebody at Scotland Yard and try to get a directory of all the red phones in use in London from…" he looked up at the picture of King George the sixth, and said, "…nineteen-thirty-six until nineteen-fifty-two, and get a full crime-scene team down here to record everything."

The detective taking the call said, "Do you need forensics too, Guv?"

"No, that won't be necessary, but contact Maggie Bird in Archives and see if she can come up with anything."

"Right-ho, Guv. I'll be in touch."

Wood switched off his mobile phone and looked back at the red one. He put the receiver back to his ear and listened. He hoped that he would hear an interruption in the static but following nearly a minute of listening he heard no such thing. He replaced the receiver on the desk, went back out of the void, and waited for the BT engineers and crime-scene team to arrive.

Chapter 18

Garrett Hinchcliffe looked at Adrian Darke at the opposite end of the boardroom table, and even though they were sitting in a diminished light, he could see that his boss seemed to have aged. His normal Mediterranean-style good looks and dress-sense couldn't detract from his drawn face and nervous darting eyes. It was a sight that he'd never seen before.

Darke looked around the table, at Hinchcliffe, Constantin, Pike, Ajax, and then to a man that none of the others had met.

"Before we start," he said, "I want to introduce you all to an associate of mine, Detective Sergeant Mick Bryce. He and I have had a special working relationship for the past four years and he has been invaluable in being able to give us inside info, heads-up warnings, and whole lot more."

Hinchcliffe looked at Bryce and took an instant dislike to him.

Bryce was over six feet tall, slim, clean-shaven, and had close-cropped brown hair. His dark grey suit was sharp and stylish, his gleaming white shirt and tie were in excellent taste, and his black moccasin-style shoes were shiny. His looks were angular and clinically handsome but his whole countenance exuded cockiness, self-confidence, and an in-

137

built contempt for anybody he considered inferior to him. He looked at everybody in the room, but didn't acknowledge any nod towards him.

"He is here because of the unacceptable turn of events with Dominic," continued Darke, "and because I want to know …" he drew in a deep breath and then yelled, "… *what the fuck is going on!*" He slammed his right fist onto the boardroom table and then glared at everybody in the room. He waited a couple of seconds and then said, *"What's the matter with you all? Doesn't anybody have a single, goddamned, fucking clue?"*

"I'm sorry, AD," said Constantin, "I can't help because I was in Rome until yesterday."

"Garrett?"

Hinchcliffe looked at Darke and said, "I'm no wiser AD – in fact I don't even know the details of Dominic's demise."

Darke turned to Bryce and said, "Tell him Mick."

Bryce looked at Hinchcliffe and said, "He was strapped to an office chair with cable ties and launched out of the sixteenth floor of an office block in central Manchester."

Hinchcliffe's eyes opened wide and he said, "Jesus Christ! Any clues?"

"None; there was a piece of paper attached to his jacket with the word 'Venio' written upon it, but to date, that's all we have. There's no CCTV coverage, and there were no witnesses."

"What does Venio mean?" said Pike.

"It's Latin and it means 'I am coming'," said Bryce.

"Then it's a threat," said Hinchcliffe.

"Yes."

"And this has to be linked to Hayley Gillorton's death too then?"

"In my opinion," said Bryce.

138

"And I want to know who the fuck's doing it," said Darke. He tuned to Ajax and said, "Does this look like a method you would use?"

Ajax looked at Bryce and saw him scrutinising him. He didn't like the policeman either. He looked back at Darke and said, "If I was sending a message to somebody."

Silence reigned in the room for a few seconds until Darke said, "Right – it's obvious that I'm getting nothing from any of you, so this is what you'll do. You will stop everything, and I mean *absolutely everything* that you are doing now, and you will find me the fucking animal that's killing my people. 'Cos guess what? – One of you jokers could be next!" He looked from face to face and saw deep concern manifest itself in the eyes of everybody but Ajax. He looked at his impassive face, and said, "Do you have any questions?"

Ajax said, "Do you want me to postpone my instructions?"

Bryce turned to Darke with an inquisitive look upon his face.

Darke saw the look but ignored it. He looked back at Ajax, and said, "No, they stand."

Bryce said, "Anything I should know about?"

Darke looked at Bryce and said, "No."

Out of the blue, something struck Hinchcliffe, he said, "AD, can I ask you a personal question?"

Darke said, "It depends on the question."

"It isn't one that you can't answer in your inner circle."

Darke looked around the room and then said, "Go on."

"In all the time that you've been in business, have you ever ordered the individual death of anybody?"

Darke raised his eyebrows, looked at Bryce, and saw him shrug. He turned back to Hinchcliffe and said, "That's one hell of a question."

"Nevertheless," said Hinchcliffe.

Darke pondered for a few seconds and then said, "My companies and dealings may have been responsible for many deaths, in particular that consignment of non-bullet-proof vests in Africa."

Bryce dropped his head and emitted a small gasping sound.

"Not like that, AD," said Hinchcliffe, "I mean *individual* instructions to terminate somebody."

Darke felt awkward and said, "Why do you need to know such a thing? What are you getting at?"

Hinchcliffe stood up, walked across to the sideboard, and poured himself a cup of coffee. He looked at Darke and said, "If Ajax is right and somebody is sending you a message of deadly intent, then it would have to be a personal vendetta." He paused, saw that he had everybody's attention and continued, "And they result from somebody seeking revenge for the loss of a loved one, a loss that they would consider attributable to you alone."

"Oh do me a favour," said Darke, "if some murderous tribal blacky or despotic raghead lost one of his minions in a conflict with an opposing side, would the family of that individual blame me for supplying the weapons, or the prick who ordered the conflict?"

"That's why I asked you if you'd ordered an individual death."

Darke stared at Hinchcliffe for a few seconds and then said, "If I did I can't think of who it…"

"Sorry, not good enough," cut in Hinchcliffe.

Darke glared at Hinchcliffe and said, "Watch it, mister; I don't care how close we are, you don't fucking talk to me like that!"

"He's got a point though."

Darke spun around and looked at the normally taciturn Pike.

Pike shrugged and said, "We're trying to get to the bottom of this, boss, and if awkward questions have to be asked to find out who's threatening you, then we should answer them."

Darke was shocked. In his entire association with his personal bodyguard Pike, he had never heard him string so many words together in one sentence. He recovered and said, "And who says that it's me who's being threatened? Couldn't this be an attack on the organisation?"

"Maybe," said Hinchcliffe, "but what better way to destroy anything than to cut off its head?"

Darke looked around the room and then sat back down in his chair. He believed that he could trust the people around him but it still felt wrong stating that there might have been an occasion when he'd ordered the death of somebody.

He turned back to Hinchcliffe and said, "I can think of three, but even then, only one died."

"Go on," said Bryce.

Darke looked at the policeman and then back at the others. He said, "If any word of this ever leaves this room, then none of your lives will be safe. Is that understood?"

He saw nods all round except for Pike, whom he knew, wouldn't have included himself on that list.

"Okay," he said, "the first was a guy who'd tried to muscle in on my operation when I started it over fifteen years ago, but he had no family that I knew of. The next two were when I ordered the auto-destruct system to be switched on in one of the escape tunnels from Cragg Vale last year. But the ones I wanted didn't die, it was some dumb copper who'd walked into the tunnel at other end, and his family couldn't have envisaged that I'd ordered the system to be switched on just to get him."

"But did he have a family?" said Hinchcliffe.

"I don't know," said Darke.

"Who were the two you were after?" said Bryce.

Darke cast a furtive glance at Ajax and then turned to Bryce. He said, "One was an interfering cow who's screwed stuff up for me, and the other was a guard who was supposed to be escorting her."

Bryce looked down, pondered, and then back up. He said, "Given what I already know, the woman survived – what about the guard?"

Ajax looked at Darke with an inquisitive look upon his face.

Darke ignored the look and said, "I believe that he survived too."

"Then she was freed, but what happened to him?"

"I expect that he was arrested with all the other staff who were employed there."

"By whom?"

"Members of either Lancashire, or Greater Manchester Police."

Bryce looked at Hinchcliffe and said, "Do we know the guard's name?"

Hinchcliffe said, "I can find out, why?"

"Maybe he found out that you'd ordered his, and the woman's death, and he wants revenge?"

Darke looked at Pike, and then Ajax.

Ajax raised his eyebrows and said, "Could be."

Darke looked back at Hinchcliffe and said, "Okay, find out who it was and give the name to Mick. Let's see if there's anything in this."

"So, now that we're bearing our souls," said Hinchcliffe, "can anybody else think of any other situation that may have

142

engendered a revenge campaign against AD or any of us, by an aggrieved family member?"

Everybody fell silent as they tried to trawl through the various events that they'd had to order, sort out, cover up, and endure since starting work for Darke, but nobody could think of anything.

Bryce was the first to break the silence. He said, "Was anybody else killed at Cragg Vale?"

Darke heard Pike give a small cough. He looked at him and said, "What?"

Pike nodded towards the kitchen door.

Darke hesitated and then turned to the others. He said, "I'll be back in a minute." He followed Pike into the kitchen, shut the door and said, "What's on your mind?"

Pike said, "What about the guy who tried to help the Wilkes woman escape from Cragg Vale who got killed by one of the Spooners; and those people at that reservoir last year?"

"Shit!" said Darke, "I hadn't thought about them." He cast his mind back to his two previous attempts to kill Naomi Wilkes.

The first was in April 2006 when he'd instructed one of his security guards at Cragg Vale to exterminate her, but instead, the guard had tried to help her escape. Fortunately the rogue guard had been seen by one of six patrolling gamekeepers, all named Spooner, and all dressed the same to fool trespassers and prying eyes, and he'd shot and killed the rogue guard before re-capturing Naomi.

The next occasion had been in July of the same year when he'd thought that she'd been held captive in the upper floors of the old Malaterre Estate that had resurfaced from the Dunsteth Reservoir. He'd ordered Pike to fire a rocket-propelled grenade into the building, and the subsequent blast had killed three marine police officers and an innocent woman bystander on the bank. He could still recall how frustrated he'd felt when he'd found out that Naomi hadn't been there all along.

He looked up at Pike and said, "This is a waste of time, with all the other stuff that we've been up to over the years it could be anybody killing my people."

"My thoughts too, boss, but I didn't want to say it out there." He nodded towards the living room.

"You're a good man, FA Cup, and I hope that you know I didn't include you on that list when I was threatening everybody about keeping quiet?"

"I know, boss," said Pike. He pointed to the living room door and said, "Shall we?"

Darke nodded. They re-joined the others and he said, "Following a little chat with FA Cup, we've decided that it would be a waste of time trying to single out any one person who might hold a personal grudge against me, so we need to put out feelers and a substantial reward amongst those who might be persuaded to spill the beans." He looked at Hinchcliffe, Bryce, and then Constantin and said, "So let it be known that I will pay ten thousand pounds to anybody who fingers the bastards who killed Gillorton and Sheldon. Okay?"

The three men nodded.

Darke turned to Ajax and said, "And you carry on with that special task I've set you. Understood?"

Ajax paused for the briefest of seconds, and then said, "Yes boss."

Chapter 19

C sat behind his large, polished desk, in an office that looked more like an opulent, private apartment than a place of work. The decor and furniture was impeccable, and the smell of roasted coffee and expensive cigars hung in the air, and on most days the office was a place of ordered calm and luxury, but on that day it wasn't.

C was blazing; he stared at Brigadier General Sir Michael Buckley, the head of MI5's field operations, and Captain Alistair Tryon his top field operative, and said, "This is bloody outrageous, Michael! If the PM ever got to hear of this there'd be hell to pay!" He paused and then added, "And my God in Heaven, I don't even want to think about the press!"

"That's why we're here, sir," said Buckley. "And with your permission, we can sort out this mess."

C glared at Buckley and said, "What? What are you talking about?"

"The mess, sir, we can sort it out." Buckley nodded in the direction of Tryon and said, "Captain Tryon has come up with one or two scenarios that could be put into place with immediate effect, depending on the level of response you require."

C shot a glance at the handsome, but hard and dangerous looking Tryon. He knew who he was, and what he was capable of. He turned back to Buckley and said, "Go on."

"First, we have a level one response."

"Don't be preposterous!" said C, "After everything that has gone into the project we can't shut it all down now just because of that blithering idiot of a driver!" He paused and then added, "And besides, the second test is on the fifth for crying out loud."

Buckley said, "Okay, then we could implement a level two response, or indeed a level three."

"Level two may still be on the harsh side," said C, "what's your proposal for level three?"

Buckley turned to Tryon and said, "Captain?"

Tryon looked at C and said, "I will drive up to Settle with another chap from our office, we'll inform Yorkshire Police that the matter is now a military one, and that it will be dealt with by us. We'll collect all the evidence, witness statements, and records, and then we'll bring Bowers back to London."

"No," said C, "lose him."

"Publicly or privately?"

"Publicly."

Tryon nodded and said, "As you wish sir."

"And get Department Zero to carry out a full clean afterwards," C looked at Tryon and then said, "every trace, understood?"

"Yes sir."

C looked down at his blotting pad, mulled things over for a few seconds, and then looked back at Tryon. He said, "Approved; now, what about the dissenters?"

Tryon glanced at Buckley and saw him nod.

The simple action touched the already raw nerves of C. His eyes narrowed and he said, "When I ask you a question Captain Tryon, you do not need to look at Brigadier Buckley for approval."

Tryon said, "I apologise, sir; force of habit, and it will not happen again."

"Good – now get on with your report."

Tryon disliked any form of rebuke but he absorbed it, and learned from it. He looked straight into the eyes of C and said, "Sir, Eleanor Drake, Zeena Bishop and Sandi Schmidt will be dealt with in the next seven days, action is underway with David Allum."

"*Schmidt* you say?" said C. "Not another bloody German is she?"

"No, sir, she is English. She married an American GI named Schmidt and moved to the States in '35, but the marriage failed and she returned to the UK last year."

C made a grunting sound and then said, "Alright, Captain, you can go and wait in the outside office, Brigadier Buckley will join you in a few minutes."

Tryon nodded, said, "Thank you, sir," and departed.

C waited until he and Buckley were alone and then said, "By God Michael, this bloody Bowers business is too close to the bone. We've got the touchy-as-hell IRA representatives arriving in Fleetwood on the fifth, the second test of *The Halo* that same night and all on the day of the national bonfire celebrations. It reeks of potential disaster."

Buckley said, "But that's why Hallenbeck chose the fifth. He thought that any bright flashes seen by innocent bystanders could be mistaken for distant firework displays."

"Yes, yes, and I understand that, but the secrecy, the cost, the infrastructure, and the personnel are so damnably unpredictable I don't mind admitting that I've harboured serious doubts about them all since inception. It's only by good fortune and the contemptible way in which the Military's budgets are monitored that we've been able to finance the project, but if the PM and his pacifistic, arse-licking toadies ever found out we'd all be for the high jump."

"Couldn't we turn to Mr Churchill, sir? He's been spouting about the German military build-up for so long, that surely he would have a sympathetic ear?"

C frowned and said, "No, out of the question! And even if he did sympathise, he couldn't condone what we'd done. It would be tantamount to him admitting criminal deception!" He paused and then added, "It might have been different if he was PM, but he isn't, and now, I hope that we were right in believing his rhetoric and convictions that one day we'll find ourselves in conflict with Germany."

"And then we would all be complemented on our perspicacity."

C looked sideways at Buckley and said, "And that is called 'painting a positive picture on things'." He paused and then continued, "Right now we need to be ultra-careful, monitor everything that's going on up north, and above all, keep the whole operation under wraps."

"And if we suffer any more embarrassing mishaps?"

"*Mishaps?*" C almost barked; "You call that, that reprehensible episode in Settle a mishap? Good God, Buckley!"

Buckley looked down and then said, "Bad choice of words maybe, but I repeat, what if we suffer any more mishaps?"

"Then it depends on how bad the mishap is," C put both arms on his desk and leaned forwards; he said, "but I'm telling you now Michael, given all that's going on, and how close we are to the edge, I wouldn't rule out a level one response."

Buckley pondered for a few seconds and then said, "In that case, it would be prudent to put together a contingency plan."

C stared at Buckley and realised that they were of similar minds. He nodded, said, "Yes, you do that, one that can be actioned within six hours."

At K1 in Yorkshire, Hallenbeck was beside himself. Sitting in his office was Bowers, three department heads and the Sergeant-in-charge of the small unit of soldiers especially chosen for their ability to remain inconspicuous.

Bowers sat in silence with his head in his hands.

The Army Sergeant, a naturalised, Belgian and ex-French Foreign Legionnaire, named Dirk Manhaeve, looked at Hallenbeck and said, "Can I sir?"

Hallenbeck nodded.

Manhaeve turned to Bowers and said, "Look at me soldier."

Bowers sat up straight and looked at his Sergeant.

"Forget everybody else in this room, and forget how many times you've told the others what happened to Doctor Klossner, tell me."

Bowers said, "I've already told Professor Hallenbeck."

"I know," said Manhaeve, "now tell me."

Bowers let out a low groan and said, "We were driving through Settle when Doctor Klossner caught sight of the telephone box in Market Place. He asked me to pull up; he got out, and then phoned somebody."

He saw the inquisitive faces looking at him, and then his mind went into overdrive. He said, "Then I heard him begin to shout ..."

"Wait, wait!" said Hallenbeck. "You didn't tell me that Axel was shouting."

Bowers turned to Hallenbeck and said, "I'm sorry Professor, I just remembered that."

Hallenbeck said, "How could you forget anything that significant?"

"I don't know! It's not every day that you see one of your mates – sorry, colleagues – get ploughed over by a bloody great truck."

"Language!" barked Manhaeve, "and show some respect in front of the Professor and ladies!"

One of the ladies was Eleanor Drake and she couldn't believe her luck. Naturally she didn't wish anybody any physical harm, but in truth, she hadn't liked Klossner, and she hoped that his death might draw somebody's attention to their unit, and line of work.

Bowers looked at everybody and said, "Sorry."

Manhaeve continued glaring at Bowers for a second longer and then said, "Go on, what happened next?"

"I was parked with the driver's side of the cab against the pavement. Doctor Klossner came out of the box, walked to the back of the truck to come round to his side and then stumbled on the edge of the kerb. I remember seeing this lorry coming towards us and hoped that the Doctor was paying attention, but then suddenly, I heard the lorry's wheels screeching on the road as it skidded to a stop. I looked out of the passenger door mirror and saw that the lorry had hit him. I jumped out, ran across to where he was lying and saw that he looked in a bad way. A few seconds later a car pulled up and a man got out who said he was a doctor. He ran over to Axel, examined him, and then told us that he was dead."

"Us?" said Manhaeve. "Who's us?"

"The lorry driver and me."

"Okay – and then?"

"The lorry driver ran to get the local bobby, and I panicked. I jumped in the cab and drove off."

Silence fell on the room until Hallenbeck said, "This is intolerable. Not only have we lost one of our best scientists two days before the next test, but now, we're likely to have the local police and London sniffing around."

Eleanor said, "Surely you're not going to go ahead with the test now?"

Hallenbeck said, "Of course we are. Half of the equipment has already been taken to Sandscale Haws in preparation for it. It is the English bonfire night, there will be numerous pyrotechnic occurrences, and it will be two days after a New Moon giving our men complete cover from the prying eyes of local poachers and dog-walkers."

"And have we heard anything from the police or London, sir?" said Manhaeve.

"No, not yet – but I guess that it's just a matter of time."

"Then what would you like Private Bowers to do?"

Hallenbeck knew that the crestfallen Bowers and Klossner had been close. He turned to Manhaeve and said, "Even if a member of the public took the registration number of the truck it is untraceable, so I don't think that we have anything to worry about on that score. Additionally Doctor Klossner never carried any identification with him, as per all of our instructions, so that shouldn't be an issue either. My only concern is what London might do." He turned to Bowers and said, "You may return to your quarters, but do not leave this unit until I say so. Is that understood?"

Bowers said, "Yes, Professor." He looked at Manhaeve, saw him nod towards the door, and then departed.

Hallenbeck sat back in his chair and said, "Does anybody have any observations to make?"

"I think that we should cancel the test and stop development of *The Halo*."

Everybody turned and looked at Eleanor. She glared back and said, "I will not apologise for my stance on this! *The Halo* is a barbaric weapon and now we have a death on our hands. How many more will we cause if we allow this monstrosity to continue?"

Hallenbeck's pent-up frustration boiled over. He said, "I am getting very weary of your constant negativity, Doctor Drake! The test will proceed as planned, and if it's successful, it will be a testament to Doctor Klossner's hard work and dedication!"

"So, despite everything, we're still going ahead?"

"Yes we are," said Hallenbeck, "and nothing is going to go wrong!"

At Settle Police Station the local Coroner walked into the Information Room and spoke to the Constable at the front desk. He said, "Is the Inspector about?"

The Constable recognised the Coroner and said, "He is, sir, would you care to come through?" He lifted the flap of the front desk, and waited until the Coroner entered.

The Duty Inspector, Eric Long, lifted his head when he heard a tap on the door. "Come in," he called.

The Constable opened the door and said, "The Coroner's here to see you, sir."

"Ah, thank you, Tom, show him in." Long waited until the Coroner had entered. He pointed to a chair and said, "Doctor, what can I do for you?"

"It's more of what I can do for you," said the Coroner. He reached into his pocket, extracted a card, and handed it to Long. "It's strange," he said, "because in all of my years dealing with sudden deaths I've come across a lot of odd occurrences, but this one beats the lot."

Long glanced at the card and said, "How so?"

The Coroner settled back and said, "Well – when someone meets their maker in an unexpected fashion, their belongings tend to give us an insight into who they are. They usually have wallets or handbags with some kind of I.D. in, maybe a letter, or a utility bill, and sometimes their names are written on their clothes. They have money, notes, bits of jewellery, and shopping lists, etcetera, but this chappie had none, only a few coins, and that." He pointed to the card.

"So you haven't been able to identify him then?" said Long.

"No I haven't, but maybe that person can."

Long looked down at the card and saw the name 'B A Ware'.

Chapter 20

10:15am Friday 26th January 2007.
Skelmersdale, Lancashire

"By the pricking of my thumbs,
Something wicked this way comes.
Open, locks,
Whoever knocks."
'Macbeth' - William Shakespeare

Naomi looked out of her car windscreen and was amazed.

She'd found an old postcode of the Ascensis facility and had followed the route indicated by her car satnav. She'd imagined that she'd be driving into an industrial park, or an old factory site, but it was nothing like that. She glanced at the satnav screen and saw that she still had half a mile to go before arriving.

The road was narrow and she guessed that two larger vehicles would have had difficulty passing one-another. On either side, the woodland was so dense that she couldn't see much further than fifty yards in at the most.

A couple of minutes later the voice from her satnav announced that she'd arrived. She stopped her vehicle, got out, and looked around. Nothing was there. The road ahead carried on for another quarter of a mile or so and then curved around to the right. She turned, looked back, and wondered if she'd missed something, but she hadn't.

She got back in her car drove up the road, and as she rounded the bend she saw an imposing entrance on her right-hand side. She hit the brakes, reversed, and turned into a short driveway. There, she stopped in front of a pair of huge, stainless steel gates. She got out and saw two signboards warning her that the site was patrolled by a company named 'Doberman Securities' four times a day. There was an over-exaggerated depiction of a snarling Doberman dog below the text, and a contact phone number.

The double gates were at least fifteen feet high and were secured by a large padlock. One hundred feet further in, she saw a duplicate set which were also padlocked. Running either side of both sets of gates was an equally high, steel-mesh fence, topped with razor wire. The entrance was designed to intimidate, and it looked impossible to breach.

She retrieved her mobile phone and dialled the number shown on the signboards. She introduced herself, told the contact at Doberman that she was there at the request of Lancashire Police, and was told that somebody would meet her within twenty minutes.

In less time than that, a white van emblazoned 'Doberman Securities' pulled up behind her. A pleasant looking man got out, walked across to Naomi and said, "Good morning, Madam, are you Mrs Wilkes?"

"I am." Naomi shook the offered hand and said, "Thank you for coming so promptly, I hope that I haven't disrupted your routine."

"It's no problem – I wasn't far from here when I got the call." He pointed towards the gates and said, "When I let you in, please drive up to the second set of gates, and wait for me there."

Naomi nodded and waited until the guard had undone the gates. She then drove to where he requested and stopped. She saw him close the first gates, re-padlock them, and then walk up to the second set. There he removed a second padlock. She half-expected him to push those open too, but instead he walked across to a white-painted box-structure on her left, unlocked it, and pulled back a large black handle. She turned and watched in surprise as a massive locking mechanism slid a stainless steel bar from across the gates. Once completed, the guard opened them and signalled her through. She got out of the car on the other side and watched him close the box with the handle, walk through the gates, shut them, and then walk across to another box-structure on the inside. There he unlocked the door, opened it, and pulled on a similar looking handle. She turned and watched the locking mechanism slide the huge steel bar back in place.

"Good grief," she said as the guard approached, "somebody didn't want anybody getting in here, did they?"

"No that's right," said the guard, "but it's not surprising given what went on here."

Naomi recalled her suspicion and took a gamble. She said, "You mean the animal testing?"

"Yes …" the guard looked around as though he was nervous that somebody might be listening, and then added, "… not something I agree with."

"Me neither," said Naomi.

The guard pointed down the drive and said, "We can walk from here unless you'd rather drive?"

"No, it's a nice day, and after the drive from Walmsfield it'll be good to stretch my legs. I'll just get my notebook and camera."

"No, Madam, sorry," said the guard, "I'm afraid that you can't take photos in here. Not unless you have written permission."

Naomi frowned and said, "Why?"

"It's still a restricted area – hence the gates."

"It's not still in use though is it?"

"No, it shut down a few years ago following attacks by animal rights protestors on the facility and its workers, but it's still owned by Ascensis and they've just mothballed it."

"Nobody told me that," said Naomi, "I was under the impression that Ascensis had ceased trading too."

"No, they moved to some eastern European country, Romania I think, but they still own this place."

"And I can't take any photos – even though I'm carrying out an investigation on behalf of Lancashire Police?"

"No, you *can* take photos madam …"

"Please call me Naomi."

The guard smiled and said, "Thank you Naomi, I'm Rod, but as I was saying, you can take photos, but only if you have written permission."

Naomi looked sideways at Rod and said, "I won't tell if you don't."

Rod hesitated and said, "How long do you think you'll be here?"

"Not that long, why?"

Rod remained silent for a few seconds and then said, "I have to check out a couple of small places not far from here; why don't I show you where the main building is and then leave you while I check out my other venues?" He let his words sink in and then added, "That way I won't have any idea what you get up to once I'm gone."

Naomi smiled and said, "That sounds like a great idea, thank you!"

They continued down the narrow drive until it curved to the left and the building came into view.

Once again, Naomi was taken by surprise. The building was long and narrow and had two recessed doorways one third and two thirds of the way down its considerable length. It was single-storey, painted pale cream, and sat like a small island in a sea of overgrown grass. A narrow path ran along the front and disappeared out of sight around the opposite end. Two smaller paths led off to the doors on the left-hand side.

"Okay," said Naomi, "this isn't what I was expecting. Where do we go in?"

"Go in? Nobody said anything about going in. I don't have any keys to the building."

Naomi turned to Rod and said, "What? I travel all the way from Walmsfield to carry out a police investigation and I can't get into the building?"

Rod looked flustered and said, "I'm sorry – if I'd have known …"

"Brilliant," said Naomi, "flipping brilliant."

Rod pondered for a few seconds and then said, "Look, if I leave you here now, I'll try to get someone from my office to meet me at one of my other venues and bring the keys. How does that sound?"

Naomi realised that Rod was trying to be as helpful as he could and said, "Okay, thank you, but without being able to get in, I doubt that I'll need more than half an hour here at the most."

"Okay, I'll leave now and be as quick as I can. Will you be okay locked in here?"

Naomi looked around and said, "I think that I'd be safer in here than anywhere else in the north of England."

Following Rod's departure, she walked back to her car and retrieved her small compact digital camera. She took a couple of long-distance shots and then commenced walking along the narrow path in front of the building. She took several more shots and then wandered up the narrower path to the first recessed door. Out of curiosity she tried the handle, but as expected, it was locked. Because the door wasn't fenestrated, she stepped off the path, walked to the first window and attempted to look through, but it appeared to be constructed from mirrored glass, and she couldn't see in.

She continued through the overgrown grass until she reached the second door, noting on the way, that all the lab windows were the same. She tried that handle too, but found it locked. She then walked to the end of the building, where she got her next surprise.

Unlike the uniform top end, the bottom end was almost industrial in appearance. There was a wide ramp leading to a loading bay that was sealed by a large, steel, roller-shutter door. Further to the right was a grey, cylindrical container standing approximately fifteen feet in height, and at least ten feet wide. It was obvious from the funnelling at the base that it had stored some sort of liquid whilst the facility had been in use, and she surmised that it had been fuel oil. She took two photos from where she was standing, and then continued her inspection.

Past the grey container she saw two banks of extractor fans attached to the upper wall, above which was a pigeon sitting atop a CCTV security camera. This made her look twice, because she hadn't noticed any cameras as she'd walked along the front. At the far end was a single, red-painted door at platform level, in front of which, was a set of steps that led down to the perimeter path.

She continued on, and passed the doors without trying either of them, presuming that they'd be locked, too. She was about to turn and head back up the rear of the building when she heard a disturbance in the foliage off to her right. She looked, and saw that the perimeter fence disappeared into the trees in that corner. She looked at the opposite corner, saw the fence emerging from the trees, and guessed that it couldn't have been more than one hundred feet that was obscured from view.

Whilst looking at the visible corner she heard another sound come from the obscure one. Her heart rate increased, and then, two rabbits hopped into view. She smiled, shook her head, and took two more photos of the end elevation; one of the extractor fans and one of the lonely pigeon sitting on the security camera.

In the trees, a man remained stock still until he was sure that Naomi hadn't seen him. He then raised a pair of small binoculars and watched her as she made her way along the back of the building.

As she progressed, Naomi saw that the fenestration and doors were the same as the front. The doors were locked, and the windows obscured too. She glanced at her watch and saw that Rod had been gone twenty minutes. The closer she got to the top of the building, the deeper the grass got. She decided that she didn't want to step into anything that the rabbits may have left, and turned to head back to the path. At that point, she determined to check in with Helen using her mobile phone.

She heard Helen answer, and then, out of the blue, a horrific and tortured squeal erupted from the building behind her. Every last drop of blood drained out of her face. She snatched her mobile from her ear, wheeled around, and stared wild-eyed at the locked doors and mirrored windows.

A second screech followed by an agonised wail launched her heart rate to stratospheric levels, and she started to back away. And then something big and heavy slammed into the inside wall, opposite her.

Not daring to take her eyes off the building, she lifted the mobile phone back to her ear and said, "Holy Christ Helen, did you hear that? They told me that this place was deserted." She waited for a response but heard nothing. She looked at the phone and saw that she'd lost the signal. She gasped and said, "Right – just what I need."

Deep in the trees the watching man was just as shocked; he too couldn't take his eyes off the rear elevation in case something smashed its way out.

Naomi heard the sound of an approaching vehicle and began to run towards the gates. She heard the engine slow, and realised that Rod had returned. As he appeared at the top of the drive, she charged up to him and half-yelled, "I thought you said this place was deserted!"

Rod looked up and said, "It is."

"It bloody well isn't!"

Rod was shocked; he said, "It is, I assure you. Nobody's occupied this place for at least five years."

"Then how the hell do you explain a God-awful, tortured, screech coming from inside the building?"

"What?"

"A screech, a gut-wrenching wail, and then something big slamming into the inside wall?"

Rod frowned, looked at the building and said, "*What*, in there?"

"Yes in there!"

Rod looked back and said, "That can't be; show me where."

Naomi led Rod along the back of the building.

The man in the trees watched their approach, lowered his binoculars, and removed a silenced pistol from his jacket pocket.

Naomi led Rod past the first door, and then pointed to a window, she said, "In there."

The man in the trees took aim.

Rod looked at Naomi and said, "That's impossible, inside there's just old labs filled with junk. They're completely empty."

Naomi said, "I am not lying, and I'm not hallucinating! Something in there let out a horrible and tortured shriek!"

Rod looked back at the building and was dumbstruck; he stood in silence not knowing what to say.

"So come on then," said a determined Naomi, "you've got the keys, let's have a look inside."

A distraught Rod turned to Naomi and said, "I'm sorry, I don't have the keys – my controller instructed me to tell you that they were going to post a set to your office."

"Bloody typical!" said a frustrated Naomi.

Rod grimaced and said, "I'm sorry…"

Naomi drew in a deep exasperated breath and said, "Damn! But it's not your fault I suppose," she then added, "at least when I get my set I'll be able to come and go as I please."

"Well – yes and no. You'll have the keys to the building, but we'll have to let you through the perimeter gates."

Naomi let out a second exasperated breath and said, "Could you possibly make it any more difficult for me?"

Rod pursed his lips and shrugged.

Naomi stared at him and then said, "Okay, so we can't go in today?"

"Not unless you arrange to come back later."

Naomi said, "No I can't, I'm busy."

Rod shot a glance at the building and then turned to Naomi. He said, "But rest assured, before you return, I'll be back with my keys, and I'll search the building from end to end,"

"And you'll ring me?"

"I will."

Naomi stared along the back elevation one last time and then said, "Alright, then there's no point in hanging around now. I'll come back when I have my set."

Minutes later, as Naomi and Rod walked back to the entrance, the man in the trees pocketed his pistol and took out a mobile phone. He dialled a number and said, "Something's seriously wrong here boss, the weirdest damn thing just happened ..."

Chapter 21

Harry Appleton looked across to Malcolm Ridyard and said, "I don't know about you, Mal, but I'll be glad to see the back of this place."

Ridyard shrugged and said, "I don't mind here so much because it reminds me of the days when we weren't under so much pressure, it's the bloody awful drive that sends me batty."

Appleton glanced at the clock and said, "Ben said that he'd ring half an hour ago, let's hope …"

The phone rang.

Appleton picked it up and said, "Slaidburn, Appleton."

"Harry, the EP readings from all the boilers have remained static for the past twelve hours so George is happy. You can shut the power off."

"Halle-bloody-lujah," said Appleton, "I was beginning to feel as though I'd taken root!"

"Sorry Harry, and tell Mal that I'm sorry too, will you?"

"Will do – and just to confirm that I wasn't hearing things, you did say that it was okay to shut the power off didn't you?"

Bromley, calling from the huge Drax Power Station, said, "Yes I did …"

Appleton said, "Excellent," he cast a glance across to Ridyard and gave him the thumbs up.

Ridyard said, "Yes!"

"… and because of the inconvenience we've caused you, you and Mal can give yourselves a long weekend, too. We'll see you both back here next Wednesday."

"Oh, thanks, Ben, that's nice, we'd both appreciate that." Appleton saw Ridyard frown. He covered the mouthpiece and said, "Ben's given us a couple of extra days off and says that we don't have to report to Drax until Wednesday."

"Hey, fantastic," said Ridyard, "thank him for me will you?"

Appleton nodded and then removed his hand from the mouthpiece. He said, "Mal says to thank you, too."

"It's the least we could do," said Bromley, "so throw the switches and get the hell out of there, I'll drive over Monday and supervise extinguishing the boilers, etcetera."

"Thanks Ben," said Appleton, "and thanks again for the extra days off."

At McCready House in Hampstead Heath, British Telecom's Australian-born engineer Dave Gibson saw the red phone go dead. He frowned, picked up the handset and listened in. Seconds later he telephoned his contact, another engineer who'd been working with him on the project, named Art Marshall, but whose name had been switched around by his colleagues to Marshall Arts, then nicknamed Karate Kid, and reduced to KK. He said, "Did you see that KK?"

"The red phone die?"

"Yes."

"And did it screw up the connection?"

"I don't know," said KK, "I'm waiting for a call from Burnley."

"What do you want me to do now?"

KK thought for a minute and then said, "Wait there for another half hour and see if the line goes live again, if not ring me and I'll see if I have any updates."

"It'd be a bugger if we missed the last connection," said Gibson.

"We could always resort to the cluckers."

"The what?"

KK repeated, "The cluckers."

"What the bloody hell are cluckers – chucks?"

"No, it's what our counterparts in Yorkshire call the underground signal testers."

"The OSS3s?"

"Yes."

"And why do they call them cluckers?"

"Because of the sound they make when they're switched on and testing."

"Bugger me," said Gibson, "I thought we Aussie's had some weird names for things but those guys take the biscuit."

"Aye," said KK, "and there's nowt for owt up there an' all."

Gibson frowned and said, "What?"

"Nothing," said KK, "ignore me. We've made the link from Liverpool to Burnley, now the guys in Burnley are waiting to hear from our Yorkshire brethren, and whether or not we'll have to resort to yon cluckers."

"Right," said Gibson still frowning, "I'll hang on here 'til I get your call."

Back at Slaidburn Appleton and Ridyard walked to the door of the main operations room and were about to leave when Ridyard said, "Whoa, wait a minute, Harry, where's the wife's card?"

"Card? What card?

"Our anniversary card; it's our twenty-seventh wedding anniversary tomorrow and ever since I got her a vegetable rack two years ago, she's been a bit touchy about me doing the right thing."

"You got your missus a vegetable rack for your anniversary?"

"Yes, it was a beauty, yellow, washable, removable shelves – it was either that, or a new mop and bucket, but in the end the rack won. I got it from the 'Kleeneze' man."

"The Kleeneze man? The guys who do the door-to-door selling?"

"Yes."

"Have you got a death wish or something?" said Appleton, "if I'd bought a present like that for my wife, she'd have smeared Vaseline on one end and rammed it where it didn't see daylight."

"Yeah, I gathered that the wife felt like that after I'd given it to her. I thought because I'd given her some new oven gloves and an ironing board cover the year before that she'd be okay with that sort of thing ..."

"Oven gloves and an ironing board cover? Are you pulling my leg?"

"No, she was okay about them, but I didn't realise until the vegetable rack, that the previous year she'd thought it had been a joke. That's why I'd arranged with the Kleeneze guy to come one week before our anniversary, so that I wouldn't forget it."

Appleton turned and stared at Ridyard. He said, "What's your wife's name?"

"Rita, why?"

"Because I think that it should be changed to Saint Rita after putting up with you!" Appleton stared in amazement at

Ridyard for a second or two longer, and then said, "So go on, where's your card?"

Ridyard said, "It must have fallen out of my bag. Hang on." He walked back to the console, above which was the bank of switches they'd thrown. He looked on the desk, and then under the chair and saw nothing. He looked up at Appleton and said, "My bag was next to the chair, it must have slipped out under the unit."

"Well good luck with that," said Appleton.

Ridyard looked around and then noticed a long ruler on a nearby table. He grabbed it and then swept it from side-to-side under the desk until he felt something. "Ah, here we are," he said. He teased the card from under the desk and then noticed that he'd also exposed something else. With gentle sweeping movements he edged a dusty metal plate into view. The exposed side was blank, but there were small holes in each corner indicating that it must have been screwed onto something in its past.

"What have you got there?" said Appleton.

"Dunno, it was under the desk." Ridyard wiped the dust off the back and turned it over. Written on the plate was,

'Keasden Beck E1RPL'

Appleton strolled over and said, "Let me see."

Ridyard handed the plate over and said, "Keasden Beck E1RPL? What's that when it's at home?"

Appleton frowned, turned the plate over and saw that it was blank. He looked at the holes in the corners and then looked up at the bank of recessed switches. Starting on the left he looked at each one until he reached switch seven, the switch that they'd puzzled over when they'd first arrived on the 11th of January. Around that, he saw four small holes. He held the plate up to the switch and saw that the holes matched perfectly.

"Blimey," said Ridyard, "so our mystery switch is Keasden Beck E1RPL?"

"Looks that way."

"So what is it?"

Appleton pondered for a few seconds and then said, "Pass me the phone will you?" He dialled Ben Bromley's number at Drax and then said, "Ben, it's Harry, Mal and I were about to leave Slaidburn when we discovered an old metal plate that had at sometime been used to mask a switch…"

"What type of switch?"

"One of the main power switches …"

"Go on …"

"… it has 'Keasden Beck E1RPL' written on it, any idea what that is?"

Bromley paused and then said, "You're sure that it says 'E-one-RPL' and not E-I-RPL?"

Appleton glanced at the plate again and said, "No, it's E-one-RPL for sure." For a second or two he heard nothing, and then an exchange of voices at the other end.

"And are you positive that it was used to mask one of the Slaidburn switches?" said Bromley.

"As positive as I can be. The holes around the plate match with the recess around switch seven."

"*Switch seven?*" said Bromley, "We've got the schematic out here and there are only six switches shown."

"That's what we saw when we arrived."

"And did you throw it?"

"Yes."

"Did it go live?"

"It did."

"And you didn't question what it fed a charge to?"

Appleton began to regret calling Bromley but realised that the lid was off the can. He said, "It was late, Ben, it was peeing down in Biblical proportions, we were miles from home, it was the back of beyond, need I say more?"

"Nevertheless ..."

"No, nevertheless nothing," said Appleton. "We were the jokers stuck out here and we didn't just throw the switch and then walk. We waited here for an hour, and when we received no warning lights or calls, we presumed that the line was live and safe."

Bromley empathised with his colleagues and guessed that he'd probably have done the same. He said, "Questionable call, Harry, but I can understand your logic."

"So what's it all about, any idea?"

"Some, maybe, some not – I don't know where Keasden Beck is, but I do know that historically, an E1RPL was an Emergency One, Red Power Line."

"Sounds serious."

"They were; the 'red' gives it away. They were 'stand-alone' power sources to government facilities."

"That did what exactly?"

"They guaranteed a power source in the event of a national emergency."

"Bloody hell," said Appleton, "what did they power?"

"All sorts of things; early warning nuclear attack systems to local police stations, emergency distress beacons, divisional power to local telephone exchanges to power the red telephones, etcetera."

"Crikey," said Appleton, "and we switched one on?"

"No, you switched the power on to something, but that didn't mean that whatever it was got turned on."

"And you have no idea what it was?"

"No," said Bromley, "but whatever it was, it was serious."

"How so?" said Appleton.

"Because of the 'E1' part; Emergency One was the code for MI5."

"Bloody hell," repeated Appleton, "I wonder if any alarm bells have been ringing in London?"

"No idea, Harry, we'll have to see if somebody comes knocking." He paused and then added, "Leave that Keasden Beck plate on the console desk. I'll make some enquiries at this end and then check it out at Slaidburn when I get there."

"Okay, will do," said Appleton, "TTFN."

At McCready House, Dave Gibson's phone rang. He said, "Gibbo."

"It's me," said KK, "The guys from Leeds have traced the line to Keighley."

"Keighley?" said Gibson, "Where's that?"

"North west of Leeds."

"And then where?"

"Nowhere, the signal died."

"So we still don't know where it originated?"

"Not yet, but we are progressing. We know that it went from Keighley, to Burnley, to Liverpool, swept across to Lincoln, then Cardiff, and finally to you."

"Stone the crows," said Gibson, "that's a protracted route."

"Yes, and only one type of system follows a diverse route like that, the red phones."

"Well that was bloody obvious mate," said Gibson, "seeing that's what brought us here."

"True enough," said KK, "but what was so important in Keighley that required a red phone connection?"

"That's bunkum mate," said Gibson, "we lost the power in Keighley, that doesn't mean that the call originated from there."

"No, of course," said KK, "so let's hope that whoever switched it on, does so again, 'cos this time, we'll be ready."

Chapter 22

Inspector Long picked up the business card and stared at it. He saw the name 'B A Ware Esq' and the reference to 'Section 5'. He knew that the telephone number 'VAU 2222' was in London and he was convinced that it was some sort of military establishment. He'd even considered that 'Section 5' might be MI5 – but therein lay the rub. When it came to close co-operation, military and civilian forces rarely mixed. He knew that the minute he called the number, he and his force would be considered some sort of 'in-the-sticks' backwater manned by wooden-top coppers from 'oop north'.

He sat back in his chair and tapped the edge of the card on his desk as he pondered what to do.

Somebody knocked on his door. He looked up and called, "Come in."

The door opened and Desk Sergeant Michael Palmer walked in.

"Yes Mike?" said Long.

"Sorry to disturb you, sir, but we might have a lead on that mysterious army truck."

"The one that drove away from the hit-and-run?"

"Yes, sir."

Long put the business card in the top section of his filing tray and said, "Go on."

"It was a couple of visitors who reported it, sir."

"When?"

"Two days ago."

"Two days ago? Why am I only just hearing about it now?"

Palmer looked down and said, "That's a bit embarrassing, sir." He saw the look on his Inspector's face and said, "When the complainants reported it in to the station, my desk pad had run out. I'd made a note of what they'd said on some scrap paper, and put it into my pocket before going up for lunch ..." He looked at Long's face and saw how exasperated he looked. He stuttered, "... and then with other things going on, I, er, forgot about it."

"Oh for Heaven's sake!" said Long.

"The wife found it in my trouser pocket before putting them in the wash, and walked it round here a few minutes ago."

Long drew in a deep breath and said, "And what had the visitors said?"

Palmer unravelled the scrap of paper and said, "They'd been rambling on the edge of the Forest of Bowland, and had nearly been hit by an army truck."

"The Forest of Bowland? That covers two counties, whereabouts were they?"

"At Keasden, sir."

Long sat back in his seat and said, "Keasden? There's nothing there but farms and moorland."

"Yes, sir."

"So what was our truck doing up there?"

"I don't know, sir."

"Did the visitors say anything else?"

"Yes, sir. They said that after the truck had nearly ploughed into them. They'd jumped to one side and yelled at the driver, but he didn't stop. That's when they'd taken his registration number."

"And it was the same one that the doctor gave to us?"

"Yes, sir."

Long pondered for a few seconds and then said, "How well do you know Keasden, Mike?"

"I know of it, but I can't say that I know it close up like."

"And do you have any idea *why* an army truck would be up there?"

"Not unless it was on manoeuvres or something."

"Did the ramblers say which way the truck had been heading?"

"Up the beck, they said."

"Did they see it come back?"

"No, sir, they said that they'd returned to their B & B after the incident because the lady had fallen into a puddle when she'd jumped out of the way, and she'd dirtied her clothes."

Long glanced at his in-tray and saw the diminutive card sitting on top of his paperwork. He said, "All right, leave it with me, and ask one of the lads to fetch me a mug of strong tea please."

Palmer put the scrap of paper on Long's desk and said, "Will do, sir, and I'm sorry about the, er …"

Long made a sweeping motion with his right hand and said, "Yes, yes, all right, forget it – but don't forget my tea!"

Palmer touched the tip of his right forefinger to his head and said, "No, sir, I'll get one of the lads to do it right away."

Long waited until Palmer had departed, and then picked up the card. He dialled VAU 2222.

A female voice said, "Vauxhall 2222."

"Mister Ware, please."

175

"Could you please be more specific? We have more than one Mister Ware."

Long apologised and said, "Mister Ware in Section Five."

"And whom shall I say is calling?"

"Inspector Eric Long of Yorkshire Police in Settle."

"Thank you Inspector, one moment please."

At first Long thought that the line had gone dead, but then he heard the female voice say, "I'm sorry Inspector, Mr Ware is unavailable right now."

"Oh, I see, can you tell me when he will be available?"

"My apologies, but I don't have his diary."

Long looked down at the card and said, "This is the first time that I've called Mister Ware, and I see that he's in Section Five, what is that exactly?"

There was a pause on the line and then the female voice said, "When you say that you can *see* that Mister Ware works in Section Five, to what were you referring?"

"His business card."

"How did you come by the card?"

Long frowned and said, "Forgive me if I come across as being rude, but shouldn't I be talking to Mister Ware, rather than the telephonist?"

Once again there was a pause on the line, and then the female said, "One moment, Inspector, I'm putting you through to Mister Smith."

Long said, "Thank you," and then heard a voice say, "Smith." He said, "Yes, good morning to you …" the use of the name Smith had him suspicious right away, "… I'm trying to contact Mister Ware in Section Five."

"Mister Ware is unavailable right now, you can talk to me."

"Good, then first please tell me what Section Five is, and who you are working for?"

"Section Five is a division of Military Intelligence. Now, how did you get hold of Mister Ware's business card?"

"It was removed from the body of an unknown man following a traffic accident in Settle last Monday."

'Mister Smith', who was Brigadier General Sir Michael Buckley, said, "One moment please." He placed his hand over the mouthpiece of the receiver, looked at Tryon, and said, "When Doctor Klossner spoke to you on Monday, where was he calling from?"

"A public telephone box in Settle, Yorkshire."

Buckley said, "In that case we might have a situation on our hands."

Tryon said, "C isn't going to like this."

Buckley raised an eyebrow and then uncovered the mouthpiece of the phone. He said, "I'm sorry to keep you waiting, Inspector, now, how can we help you?"

"You could start by telling me who we have in our mortuary."

"Can't do, because I don't know."

"Can you tell me how he came to be in possession of Mister Ware's card?"

"No sorry, can't help there either."

Long let out an exasperated snort and said, "Then perhaps you can tell me who Mister Ware is and what connection he might have to our deceased man?"

Buckley said, "Because you are a policeman I informed you that you were speaking to Military Intelligence. Now please credit me with more sense than to be divulging information about any of our activities."

Long was taken aback by the rebuke but snapped back and said, "I wasn't prying into what Mister Ware was working on, I was trying to establish who we have in our mortuary, and what he is doing with Mister Ware's card!"

"And I apologise if this comes across as unhelpful or dismissive, Inspector, but I cannot help you on either score." Buckley heard another long, frustrated exhalation and relented to a degree. He said, "Look, I'll speak to Mister Ware upon his return, and if he has anything to offer, I'll ask him to telephone you during office hours, tomorrow. If you haven't heard from him by then, he, too, cannot help you with your enquiry."

Long said, "All right; thank you for taking the time to talk to me, *Mister Smith*, and I look forward to hearing from *Mister Ware* tomorrow."

"Yes – goodbye, Inspector."

Long replaced the receiver on the cradle, sat back in his chair, and said, "Unhelpful bastard." He knew when he was being fobbed-off, and he knew that he was no closer to finding out whose body he had. He also knew that he wouldn't hear from *Mister Ware* tomorrow either. He threw the card back in to his in-tray, and yelled, "Michael! Where's my bloody tea?!"

At MI5 Buckley looked at Tryon and said, "The longer this K1 project goes on, the more uncomfortable I'm beginning to feel. We're developing secret weapons, spending Government cash; we've got trouble with dissenters, we're getting tangled with the IRA of all people, and most our top-brass don't know a bloody thing about it."

Tryon nodded and said, "Tricky sir."

"And now this Klossner business has aroused the Yorkshire police."

Tryon nodded, but remained silent.

Buckley tapped his fingers on his desk, then looked up and said, "So what's the state of play with the dissenters?"

Tryon removed a pocket book from his jacket and opened it up to the relevant page. He said, "David Allum met with an unfortunate traffic accident in the early hours of this morning."

Buckley raised his eyebrows and said, "How?"

"He'd been, er – drinking."

"Ah," said Buckley, "do the staff at K1 know about it?"

"Not yet, sir."

"And the others?"

"We're leaving Eleanor Drake until the end, because she is the high profile figure. Sandi Schmidt will be dealt with week commencing the fifteenth, and I'm dealing with Zeena Bishop next week."

"And Bowers?"

"Already eliminated."

Buckley said, "All right," he looked down, shook his head, and then looked back up. He said, "Now I've got the odious task of reporting this lot to C."

Tryon said, "Ouch! Good luck with that one, sir."

Chapter 23

Helen sat in front of her laptop scrolling through the photos that Naomi had taken at the Ascensis facility. Something had taken her eye, but as she scanned through them for the second time, she couldn't recall what it was.

She'd listened to Naomi's account of the weird screech coming from the within the building, and she too had been convinced that something must have been in there, but Naomi's graphic account of what had happened, had so enthralled, and horrified her, that she'd forgotten what had caught her eye on the photos.

"What's really annoying," said Naomi, deepening Helen's temporary amnesia, "is that the security guard, a guy named Rod, said that he'd call me after inspecting the interior."

Helen looked up and said, "He'd call you? Why?"

"He said that he'd go back to site with a set of keys, check out the interior, and then give me a call."

"And he never called?"

"No."

"Did you try ringing him?"

"At Doberman Securities?"

"Yes – unless he gave you a mobile number."

Naomi pondered for a second or two and then picked up the telephone.

"Doberman Securities, good morning," said a friendly-sounding male voice.

"Good morning – could I speak to Rod please?"

"Do you mean Rod Carroll?"

"I don't know, I didn't ask his surname. Do you have more than one Rod working for you?"

"Who's calling please?"

"My name's Naomi Wilkes, I'm a historic researcher working with Lancashire Police. I met Rod when he gave me access to the old Ascensis site in Skelmersdale."

There was a pause on the line and then the man said, "Hang on a sec, Naomi, I'm putting you through to Dave Nicholls, he's our Head of Security."

Naomi said, "Okay," and then heard another man's voice say, "Is that Ms Wilkes?"

"Yes it is, but Naomi's fine."

"Thank you. Do you mind if I ask you a couple of questions?"

"No, fire away."

"When did you last see Rod?"

"Last Friday."

"At the Ascensis facility?"

"Yes."

Something about the conversation alerted Helen and she began to listen.

"And how did he seem to you?" said Nicholls.

"Absolutely fine, why?"

"Did you see him again, after your first meeting?"

"Yes, he had to let me out."

"So he didn't stay with you whilst you were there?"

"No – look, what …?"

"And was everything all right whilst you were there?"

Naomi hesitated and said, "Before I answer you, why are you asking me all of these questions?"

Helen tapped Naomi on the elbow and indicated for her to switch the phone to loudspeaker.

Naomi pressed the button and put the phone between them.

Nicholls said, "Because nobody's seen Rod since then."

"What?" said Naomi.

"We heard from him on Saturday, but since then he seems to have disappeared off the face of the earth."

"Have you reported this to the police?"

"No, because we weren't sure what to do; Rod was due to have the weekend off so we thought that he might have gone away and switched his mobile off, but when he didn't report for duty this morning we phoned his digs, and his next-door neighbour said that he hadn't seen or heard Rod since last Friday."

Naomi's heart started to beat faster and she felt a pressure on her left shoulder, a pressure that she took to be a psychic alarm bell. She looked at Helen and then said, "The first thing that you should do is to ring the police; ask for Superintendent Bob Crowthorne at Greater Manchester Police, not Lancashire Police, and tell him that I advised you to call."

"Before I do, do you know something that we don't?"

Naomi explained that Rod had promised to re-visit the site, inspect the interior of the building, and then call her.

Nicholls listened with growing concern and said, "And why did he need to ring you after he'd inspected the interior?"

Naomi glanced at Helen and saw her mouth, "Tell him," she said, "because I heard a weird screech come from within the building." The feeling of the thumb pressing down on

Naomi's shoulder increased and she heard a quiet female voice say, *"Careful poppet..."*

Nicholls said, "You heard what?"

"A screech come from within the building."

Nicholls was stunned; he said, "Bloody hell, what kind of screech? Animal, human?"

"I don't know; that was what Rod was going to investigate." Naomi heard the voice in her head repeat, *"Careful ..."* she became confused and wanted to say "Why?" but knew that she couldn't. She said, "But wait a minute – you said that you'd heard from him on Saturday. If he was supposed to be off duty, why did he call you?"

"He didn't speak to us in person – the switch controller that night left his desk and went for a pee, but when he got back he saw that a message had been left on our voicemail. He pressed 'play' and heard Rod say, 'It's me.'"

Naomi waited for a second expecting Nicholls to say more, but he didn't. She said, "And what else?"

"Nothing else, he said, 'It's me' and then the line went dead."

"And you're sure that it was Rod?"

"Positive, we all know his voice, it's so distinctive."

Naomi recalled the soft timbre of Rod's voice and his mild Dorset accent. She opened her mouth to respond, and then heard the voice in her head command, *"Stop!"* She put her hand up to her left shoulder and rubbed it as the pressure intensified.

Helen saw the movement and the look of confusion on Naomi's face, and knew that she was experiencing some inner turmoil. She turned the phone towards her and said, "Dave, I'm Helen Milner, I work with Naomi, and I've been listening in to the conversation. Do you mind if I ask you a couple of questions?"

"No, not at all, shoot."

"When Rod left the message on your voicemail did it sound as though it had been cut off?"

"Not really, it was just a simple 'It's me'."

"And didn't you find it odd, that he'd just phone and say that?"

"Well, yes," Nicholls paused and then added, "especially at that time."

Helen frowned and said, "What time?"

"It was 3:10 a.m. on Saturday morning when we got the call."

"3:10 a.m.?" said Helen, "Are you kidding? And you didn't do anything about it?"

"What was to do? He didn't indicate that he was in trouble; his voice sounded calm, and Martin, the controller, thought that Rod had phoned him by mistake and just terminated the call."

Naomi leaned forward to speak but heard the voice in her head say, *"No, don't ... "* She leaned back with an even-more puzzled expression on her face.

Helen said, "And you haven't seen or heard from him since?"

"No."

"Did he collect the keys to the Ascensis site?"

"On Friday afternoon, yes."

"Did he return them?"

"No."

"Did you hear from him after he visited there?"

"No."

"And you did nothing?"

Nicholls started to feel under pressure and said, "Look, Ms Milner, give us a break will you? We're permanently short-staffed here and the people who work for us aren't exactly Oxford Undergrads. Martin had been working from 5 p.m. the previous evening and when he got a half-assed message from Rod at three in the morning he wondered if he'd been out on a stag-do or something and had rung the wrong number. He just dismissed it and went back to work."

Helen empathised with Nicholls and said, "Yes okay, sorry. But I concur with Naomi that you should now ring Superintendent Crowthorne at Greater Manchester Police and tell him what you've told us."

"Okay, I'll do that now."

"Good," said Helen, "but before you go, do you have another set of keys for the Ascensis building?"

"Hang on," said Nicholls, "I'll just check."

Helen looked at Naomi's troubled face and said, "Are you okay, hun?"

Naomi removed her hand from her shoulder and said, "I heard one of my voices warning me to stop talking."

Helen said, "That's weird; why should you stop talking?"

"I've no idea; it doesn't make sense to me."

"Nor me."

"The voice was a woman's and she called me poppet."

"Blimey," said Helen, "sounds like she knows you."

Naomi thought about the remark and tried to conjure up the sound of the voice again. She said, "If she does, I can't say that I recall her."

Helen heard the phone being picked up, and listened.

Nicholls said, "Are you still there?"

"Yes I am."

"Sorry to be a bother, but can I ring you back in a few minute's time?"

"Yes, no bother," said Helen. She looked at Naomi and said. "Did you hear that?"

Naomi nodded and then heard the female voice say, *"It's K2."* She frowned and said out loud, "What?"

Helen said, "I said, did you hear that?"

Naomi stuck her right hand up in the air, looked at Helen and said, "Shh, not you …" She then said, "What?" again.

"K2 poppet, it's K2, and you need to keep it to yourself."

Out loud, Naomi said, "Why?"

"Because it will get you killed like the rest of us."

Naomi's heart leapt into her mouth, she said, "The rest of you? Who are you, and who's the rest of you, and what's K2?"

Helen was mesmerised by the one-sided conversation. She'd known that Naomi had this side to her, but she'd never been party to anything like this.

The phone rang on the desk and made both girls jump.

Helen snatched it up and pressed the button. She said, "Walmsfield Historic Research, Helen Milner."

Naomi listened and realised that she'd lost the psychic link. She tried to reconnect, but nothing happened.

"Erm, we seem to have a bit of a problem," said Nicholls, "we don't have another set of keys, and we can't find a contact number to get some more."

Helen frowned and said, "So who pays you?"

"A management company in Hertford."

"Then ring them and ask for another set."

"We already did that, and the contact number's gone dead."

"And you have no other contact numbers?"

"No."

"Then what will you do?"

"We'll suspend the service until we make contact with somebody in Romania."

"Romania?" said Helen. "Why Romania?"

"That's where the site owners are situated now."

Helen expelled an exasperated gasp and said, "But …"

Naomi snatched the phone up and said, "Dave, listen to me! Phone Superintendent Crowthorne at Greater Manchester Police now, and get down to that site as soon as you can! Do you hear me?"

The voice in Naomi's head suddenly reconnected and the female voice said, *"No, no …"*

Naomi ignored it and said, "Whatever it takes, get into that building. Rod's life may depend on it!"

"Bloody hell," said Nicholls, "that sounds a bit ominous; are you sure that you don't know something we don't?"

"No I don't, now please get off the damned phone, call the police, and get down to the site. I'll see you there in an hour's time."

Something about Naomi's urgency triggered in Helen's brain, she turned back to the photos and scrolled through them again. One-by-one she inspected each image until at last she said, "N, you need to see this."

Naomi watched as Helen turned her laptop, and then pointed to the photo of the pigeon sitting on top of the security camera; the only photo that she'd taken for fun. She said, "What am I supposed to be looking at?"

"The extractor fans."

Naomi looked below the security camera and recalled the banks of grilled vents on the rear elevation. She looked at each one in turn and then stopped at one. She pointed to it, frowned, and said, "This one looks different."

"Exactly," said Helen, "if you look at all the others you can see the blades of the fans behind the grilles, on that one you can't."

Naomi pulled the laptop closer, positioned the mouse's cursor over the zoom facility, and zoomed in. The image behind the grille appeared to be blurred. She then zoomed in to all of the other grilles and saw that the fan blades were clear and well-defined. She turned to Helen and said, "That one's switched on ..."

Chapter 24

Ben Bromley walked into the control room of Slaidburn Power Station and ambled over to the bank of switches on the centre console. Under his arm he had a printout of the schematics. He laid them on the desk and turned to the page indicating how many operational power switches there should have been. It showed six. He looked at the switches, counted seven, and then picked up the metal plate that Mal Ridyard had found on the floor below the desk. On it, in red letters and numerals he saw the 'E1RPL'. He looked at the screw holes in the corners, and then offered it up to the front of switch seven. Once in place he removed a propelling pencil from his jacket pocket and found that the holes in the plate matched the holes around the switch; just as Appleton had said.

He expelled an "hmm" sound, put the plate down, and then telephoned the oldest employed engineer at Drax, Edwin Dawe.

"Dawe."

"Ted, it's Ben, I'm at Slaidburn – there is a switch seven, and Harry was right about that plate."

"Okay, what do you propose?"

"Check the monitors there and I'll switch it on. Tell me if there are any spikes."

Dawe said, "Okay, ready when you are."

Peter Tyrrell, the British Telecom senior engineer at Leeds, saw the mystery line come live. He immediately activated the tracing equipment.

At McCready House in Hampstead Heath, Dave Gibson was sitting with a flask of coffee in the room adjacent to the concealed compartment. He heard the red telephone begin to bleep again. He leapt to his feet and raced into the void. He snatched up the red phone and listened, but only heard the familiar hissing of static.

He rang KK and almost yelled down the phone, "It's live again!"

At Drax in North Yorkshire Dawe studied the readouts and saw nothing. He put the phone up to his ear and said, "Nothing's showing up here Ben, are you sure it's gone live?"

Bromley glanced up to the red light above switch seven and then looked at the old-fashioned needle flickering from left to right as it monitored the small fluctuations in power output. He said, "Yes, positive."

"Then obviously there are no back-up systems diverting power to Drax in the event of failure at Slaidburn," said Dawe.

"Right, which in turn says that whatever this was powering, was no longer needed when Drax took over."

"Yes."

Bromley pondered for a few seconds and then said, "Any suggestions?"

"Not without physically tracking the lines. That switch has turned on the power, but we don't know who, or where, the recipients were."

"They can't have been far; otherwise the switch wouldn't have been here."

"And there's something else," said Dawe, "if the power output dial is showing a fluctuation, that means that whatever is being powered is still intact, and that power is being used."

"Christ," said Bromley, almost as though he'd just had a revelation, "of course, somebody somewhere is using the power."

"Right."

"Shit, so someone may be trying to track where it's coming from, or going to, right now?"

"Precisely."

"Then we need to leave it switched on."

"Yes."

Bromley's mind was in turmoil. He said, "Right, send some more guys to help the boys here to keep the boilers fired up, and despatch an outside unit to track the live lines from the main power grid."

"Will do. What will you do?"

"I'll stay until they get here and see if I can figure anything else out."

"Okay," said Dawe, "I'll be in touch."

At Hampstead Heath police station, the telephone rang on Detective Inspector Wood's desk. He picked it up and said, "Wood."

"Hello, Stuart."

Wood instantly recognised the soft voice with the last traces of a Welsh accent and knew that it was Maggie Bird the Curator of the Metropolitan Police Museum, and Head of the Archives Department.

He said, "Hello, Maggie, this is a pleasure. I thought that you'd be too busy with your black museum project to ring me yourself."

"I'm never too busy to ring one of my oldest friends," said Maggie.

"Hey! Stop right there," said Wood, "I'm not that old!"

There was a brief pause on the phone and then Maggie said, "Well let's see. We joined the force together as cadets. I was the baby of the group, then there was Sam Chance, and Tiny Gent, Terry Hulley, and…"

"Okay, okay, I get it – I was way before that lot."

"And I should know; I'm the archivist don't forget."

"Yes," said Wood, "how can I?" He thought about his past colleagues, and then said, "Do you ever hear from any of the old gang?"

"Only Sam Chance every now and then."

"Sam Chance, *'Rasputin the mad monk'*? Blimey, he was a case! What's he up to nowadays?"

"He's a professional yacht master living with his wife on the South coast."

"Oh nice: now, what can I do for you?"

"It's what I can do for you, Stu, Al Fowler rang me, and then not long afterwards The Yard rang me, too. Both were trying to establish who red phones belonged to in the Met area."

"Yes, I asked Al to contact The Yard, and you. I didn't think that *they'd* come straight to you as well."

"Right – well I've managed to get hold of a 1930s directory of who had the phones, but there is a sting in the tail."

"Go on …"

"McCready House is listed, but it doesn't give a geographical location to where the phone was linked."

"Does it list *who* the phone was linked to?"

"No, sorry."

Wood said, "Bugger," he thought for a second and then said, "Does the directory state what the red phone at McCready House belonged to, a government department, an Embassy, a minister or someone?"

"Oh, it did that okay," said Maggie savouring the moment, "it belonged to 'SE1'."

"SE1?" said Wood, "What the hell is SE1?"

"Now that's the big question Stu; there is no SE1."

"Then how did you get a directory entry listing SE1?"

"No idea, and nobody I spoke to can help."

"Could it be the military?"

"If it is nobody's admitting to it."

"What about the intelligence services?"

"I tried MI5 and MI6 with the same result."

"Brilliant," said Wood, "so now we have a red phone ringing in a building in Hampstead Heath. Nobody knows where the call's come from; nobody knows who activated it; nobody knows who would have answered it, and nobody even knows who SE1 were?"

"In a nutshell," said Maggie.

"Bollocks," said Wood.

"In a nut sack," said Maggie.

Wood hesitated, and then couldn't help laughing. He said, "Maggie Bird! What would your old Welsh mum and dad say if they heard you talking like that?!"

Maggie laughed too and said, "Don't ask!" She paused and then added, "I will keep on trying to find out who SE1 were, and if I come up with anything I'll let you know."

Wood said goodbye to Maggie and put the phone down. He leaned back in his chair and repeated, "Bollocks."

The phone rang; he picked it up and said, "Wood."

"Inspector Wood, this is Dave Gibson the BT engineer at McCready House."

"Yes Dave?"

"We've got it."

"Got what?"

"The last exchange on the red phone trace."

Wood sat bolt upright in his chair and said, "Whoa! Well done! Where did it terminate?"

"In Settle, Yorkshire, but it didn't terminate there, that was the last exchange on the trace."

"I'm sorry," said Wood, "I don't understand."

"We've been able to trace the red phone from exchange to exchange as it weaved its way up country, but there has to come a point where the line leaves the final exchange and terminates at the subscriber's office or place-of-work."

"And Settle was the last exchange?"

"Yes mate, er, sorry, sir."

"So what now? Can you trace the line from the exchange to the subscriber?"

"We can, especially if it remains live."

Wood was astounded. He said, "What? It's gone live again?"

"Yes it has."

"Okay, thank you for letting me know, and ring me as soon as you know where the line terminates will you?"

"We will."

Wood sat back in his chair and put his hands up to his face. His mind was racing ten-to-the-dozen. He thought about his conversation with Dave Gibson and Maggie Bird, and he tried to speculate what the acronym 'SE1' might be, but following one or two possibilities, he realised that it was a pointless exercise.

Somebody knocked on his office door. He looked up and said, "Come in." The door opened and one of his detective constables walked in with a handful of paperwork. He said, "More bum-fodder?"

"More-or-less, guv," said the DC in an almost disinterested tone.

Wood nodded and said, "Okay, put it in my pending tray."

The DC turned to walk away, and then hesitated. He turned back and then said, "You know that McCready House gaff we're working on, Guv?"

Wood looked up and said, "Yes."

"Some old gooseberry rang ..."

"Woman," said Wood.

"... sorry, Guv, some old woman rang from the house next door ..."

"Not Esme Pilchard?"

"... no, not that sour old Chairman – it's a pal of hers by all accounts. She rang to say that she's seen that we're all searching for something at McCready House – and she knows what it is."

Wood frowned and said, "What? When did we get the call?"

"Yesterday."

"And why the fuck are you just telling me about it now?"

The shocked DC said, "Because we thought that she was referring to the red phone, and we've already found it."

"And did anybody *ask* if that was what she was referring to?"

"No, Guv, we just thanked her, and said we'd be in touch."

"Pass me the paper."

The luckless DC handed the message to Wood and stood in silence.

Wood saw that there was no telephone number, just the name 'Mrs Ware' and an address. He looked up at the DC and said, "Get my car round here now."

Chapter 25

10pm Friday 5th November 1937. H.M. M34
'Spartan', 54.15degN x 3.51degW Twenty
nautical miles west of Gutterby Banks,
Whitbeck, Lancashire

Patrick Boyle stepped out onto the lower aft, port side deck of
the old Coastal Monitor HMS *Spartan* and looked into the
night sky.

The weather was crisp and cold, and it had been a new
moon forty-eight hours' earlier, rendering the night as black as
a serial-killer's heart. The only bonus was the incredible
starscape. The Milky Way appeared to have been painted
across the sky in a vast white stripe and the millions of
twinkling stars stretched from one horizon to the other.

He pulled his overcoat tighter around his chest and
allowed the enormity of the universe to wash over him. He
could hardly believe that he was on his way to Westminster to
negotiate the possibility of returning the Republic to Ireland.

Since Robert Somersby's visit to Cork on the 27th
October, he and other top members of the IRA had been in a
constant state of flux. Some had wanted the status quo to
remain the same, not ever trusting anything the English had to
say, whilst some of the old-corps not only welcomed the
possibility of a return of the Republic to Irish hands, but also a
long-awaited cessation of the dreadful hostilities.

The most vociferous anti-English voice had come from one of his closest colleagues, Michael Duffy, who had gone to extraordinary lengths to try to persuade the IRA Army Executive to oppose the meeting, and to forge bonds between themselves and Germany against Great Britain. But, the lure of reclaiming the Republic had overcome everything, and now he and three other top members of the IRA leadership were on the first leg of their journey to London.

He looked at his watch and saw that it was 10 p.m. Before leaving Belfast he'd been told that the *Spartan*, a veteran of the First World War, was capable of ten knots, but the reality had been much worse. She'd struggled to maintain seven to eight knots at best. He'd set off on the one-hundred-and-thirty mile journey from Belfast at 10 a.m. expecting to arrive in Fleetwood at 11 p.m., but he'd been informed by the down-to-earth crew, that they expected to arrive at approximately 3:30 a.m.

He drew in a deep breath and looked east hoping to see some fireworks on the English coast twenty miles distant, but upon seeing nothing, he decided to head back to his sparse, but functional quarters.

The M34 *Spartan* had been built at the Workman Clark yard in Belfast in 1915, and whilst she had been tied up near her original construction site awaiting the arrival of the IRA contingent, two of Duffy's men, and two shipbuilding, IRA sympathisers, ones who'd been involved in *Spartan's* original construction as young apprentices, had concealed a small but powerful explosive device in the engine room. They'd followed Duffy's instructions to position it in a place that would cause the maximum damage without blowing the whole vessel to smithereens.

He'd also instructed his men to set the device to detonate twelve hours after her departure, expecting that she'd be just one hour away from Fleetwood. That way he'd hoped to disrupt the meeting, and engender a deep mistrust of the English, whilst knowing that the vessel would be close enough to shore, for his colleagues to be able to survive the experience. Thereafter he planned to propose that the English may have faked the onboard explosion as a ruse to give them the opportunity to eliminate the top echelon of the IRA.

And in secret, it didn't matter to him whether his colleagues died in the explosion or not, he could still blame the English, whatever the outcome.

At 10:05 p.m. the minute hand on the timer reached its appointed place and the bomb detonated. The ear-splitting blast ripped two nearby stokers to shreds, and tore through the old half-inch deck plates below the waterline. In an instant, *Spartan* started taking on a deluge of water.

Up in the tiny wheelhouse everybody heard, and felt the blast. 'General quarters' was sounded and the remaining sixty-five crew began running to their posts.

Captain Thomas Middleton snatched up the bulkhead phone and called the engine room. Nobody responded. He turned to his First Officer and said, "Number One, get down to the engine room, and report."

The First Officer nodded, and disappeared from view.

Middleton shouted to his panic-stricken Radio Officer in the tiny radio shack behind the wheelhouse, *"Coms, put out a mayday."* He then called the Ammunition Room amidships.

"Yes, sir?"

"Report," said Middleton.

"The blast appeared to have come from astern, the engine room I think."

"And is everything okay in there?"

"Yes, sir."

"Is anybody with you?"

"Yes sir, Able Seaman Car …"

"Send him to the engine room and tell him to ask Lieutenant Smyth to return to the wheelhouse."

"Yes, sir."

Middleton hung the phone back on the bulkhead hook and poked his head into the adjacent radio shack. He said, "Any response?"

"No, sir."

Middleton frowned and said, "Nobody at all?"

"No, sir, not yet," the Radio Officer paused and then added, "I would have expected a few fishing boats out tonight, but maybe it has something to do with the bonfire night celebrations."

Middleton nodded and said, "Maybe – keep on trying."

"Yes, sir."

Boyle raced out onto the lower deck and saw his three colleagues staring in wild-eyed confusion.

"What happened?" said Brendan Jackson his closest friend.

"I've no idea," said Boyle.

"Was it one of the boilers?" said another of his other colleagues.

Boyle said, "How the hell should I know?"

"What should we do now?" said Jackson.

Boyle's mind was in turmoil and he couldn't take the inane questions. He said, "What am I – the fucking Oracle?"

"I just thought…"

"No you didn't!" snapped Boyle. "Now shut your damned mouth until we find out what's happened!"

"Sir!"

Middleton turned and saw the Radio Officer looking at him. He said, "Yes?"

"We've had a response …"

The phone rang on the bulkhead. Middleton said, "One minute," and snatched it up. He said, "Captain."

"It's Carter, sir, down in the engine room. There's been an internal explosion by coal bunker four and we're taking on a lot of water."

"Good God. Any casualties?"

"Yes, sir, two dead and more injured."

Middleton closed his eyes and then said, "An *internal* explosion you say?"

"Yes, sir."

"Can it be shored?"

"The lads are trying, sir, but because of the buckling of the plates, and its awkward position, there's nothing much we can do. It couldn't have been in a worse spot."

"What about the boilers?"

Carter glanced at the pressure gauges and said, "All okay at the moment, but at the speed we're taking on water, I'd say that we'll have about an hour – two at the most."

"Can you see what caused the explosion?"

"No, sir, but it doesn't look as though it was anything to do with an engine room fault."

Middleton said, "Right, do what you can, and keep me informed."

"Yes, sir, understood."

Middleton turned to the Radio Operator and said, "Okay, report."

"We've had a response from *HMS Express*, an E-class destroyer. She's twelve miles northwest of Portpatrick on the Mull of Galloway."

"How soon can she get to us?"

"At full speed, to this position – three hours."

Middleton pursed his lips and said, "Okay, ask her to respond but tell her that whilst we have propulsion we'll head due east from this position and make for the coast. Acquaint her with our exact lat / long and inform them that we'll update them as they draw closer." He saw the Radio Operator nod, and then turned to his Navigation Officer. "Where are we?" he said.

The Nav Officer placed his finger on the chart of the Irish Sea and said, "There, sir, Forty-two miles northwest from Fleetwood, and twenty-eight miles from Barrow-in-Furness by the time we've rounded the Isle of Walney."

Middleton studied the chart and said, "What about there?" He pointed to the Duddon Channel north of Sandscale Haws and said, "How far's that?"

The Navigation Officer placed his dividers on the chart, opened them up from their position to the mouth of the Duddon Channel and then checked the distance with the latitude scale on the right-hand side. He said, "Twenty-four nautical miles to the navigable entrance, sir."

"Then if the boys in the engine room are right about the speed of water intake our best option would be to steer towards the Gutterby Banks, then hug the shore down to the Duddon Channel."

The Nav Officer looked at the chart and said, "We'll have the depth, but it's tidal, and we'll need to stick to the middle when we get there."

"If we get there," said Middleton. "What's the bottom like?"

"Sand and shell further out – sand, mud, and shale closer to shore."

All the better," said Middleton, "then if we're lucky enough to make it to shore, and it looks as though we aren't going to make it to the channel, we could launch the lifeboats and then ground her."

He saw the Nav Officer nod in agreement and then shot a last glance at their position. He said, "Right, Coms, make sure that the *Express* is clear about our intention, keep on trying to raise somebody else, and get a message off to the Admiralty about our current situation. Helm, steer 090."

At exactly the same time, at the Ministry of Defence rifle range at the eastern edge of Sandscale Haws, Hallenbeck stared at *The Halo* strapped to the bottom of the gondola below the dirigible.

As it floated thirty feet above the ground, he marvelled at how innocuous and innocent it looked. He shook his head and then turned to his new second-in-command, an English physicist named Doctor Reginald Fisher. He said, "I wish that Axel was here right now."

"Me, too," said Fisher, "but everything is well under control."

Hallenbeck looked at his watch and said, "Okay, run it past me one last time."

Fisher said, "We've been over this a dozen times, Karl, do we need to do it again?"

"Yes please; humour me."

Fisher drew in a deep breath and said, "We launch at midnight. The dirigible pilot does a steep ascent to three-hundred-and-fifty feet on a heading of 270 degrees. At that height, he will level out and set the autopilot to take her out of the Duddon Channel at a constant speed of ten knots. He will then activate the timer, which is set for twenty-four minutes, and parachute out. The pilot will be picked up by our launch and returned here. Twenty-four minutes after switching on the timer, *The Halo* will detonate. She will be at least four miles due west of the launch site, and with the wind behind her."

Hallenbeck nodded and said, "Okay – and you personally set the timer?"

"I did."

"Is the boat standing by?"

"It is."

"Then it would seem that we are set to go. Have we had the latest weather report?"

Fisher turned to his immediate assistant who'd been listening to the exchange. He raised his eyebrows in question.

The assistant looked at Hallenbeck and said, "Yes we have Professor, and it is the same. Clear skies, good visibility, and a westerly wind of five miles per hour."

Hallenbeck thought about the fallout and dispersion, and said, "That's perfect." He paused for a second trying to think if he'd missed anything, but then saw the expectant looks on the faces of his team.

He drew in a deep breath and said, "Alright, ask the pilot to board, and raise the dirigible to the top of the mast. We launch at midnight as planned."

Chapter 26

Inspector Wood stepped out of the police car, strode up to the house number given by Mrs Ware, and rang the doorbell. He waited for a few seconds, saw the door open, and then half-opened his mouth in surprise.

Knowing that the old lady was a friend of the acerbic and foul-mouthed Esme Pilchard, he had been expecting to see another person of the same ilk. Instead, the woman who stood before him looked amazing. She was approximately five feet two inches tall, she was slim; she wore a figure hugging black jacket and skirt and white silk blouse. Her hair and make-up were perfect, she had near-flawless, lightly-tanned skin, and she looked to be in her early sixties rather than the eighties of her card-playing contemporaries.

He gathered his shaken equilibrium and said, "Good morning, Madam, I am Detective Inspector Stuart Wood, are you Mrs Ware?"

"I am, please do come in."

Wood was offered a seat in a tastefully decorated lounge and accepted the cup of coffee that he was offered.

As he waited for Mrs Ware to re-appear he looked around and noted one or two photos. In each of them he saw only what he took to be the younger Mrs Ware with a man, but none showing any children. Nothing else about the room gave away anything of interest. Seconds later he heard her returning, and resumed his position.

"Do you take sugar Inspector?"

"No, thank you, just milk."

The lady smiled, placed the coffee in front of Wood and then sat down opposite. She said, "Now, do I take it that you've come in response to my message?"

"You do."

"Good, then let's clear one thing up first. My name is not Ware: I am Ulyana Vetochkin an ex-Russian-born Intelligence Officer who'd been working with my colleague Mademoiselle Evelyn Picard at McCready House before the outbreak of World War Two."

Wood raised his eyebrows and said, "Whoa, that's some statement Ms Ve …"

"Vetochkin."

"… Ms Vetochkin," said Wood.

"Please call me Ulyana."

"Thank you Ulyana: perhaps you could elucidate?"

"Before I do, was the print of King George the Sixth still hanging in the void at McCready House?"

Wood sat back in his chair and placed his coffee on a side table. He said, "You know about the void?"

"I do, and a lot more besides, but first, is the print there?"

Wood recalled seeing it and said, "Yes it is."

Ulyana nodded and said, "Good."

Wood frowned and said, "What …?"

Ulyana stuck her right hand up and said, "Please wait, Inspector. I will explain all in due course. It is now sixty-eight years since the operation at McCready House closed down, and though I was informed that I was bound by The Official

Secrets Acts of 1911 and 1920, the unit at McCready was never de-classified, because apparently, it never existed."

Wood's frown deepened. He said, "Go on."

"The unit consisted of six personnel, all employed by …" Ulyana hesitated and then said, "… if I proceed, can I have your assurance that no action will be taken against me by any government department, either now, or at any time in the future?"

Wood hesitated, unsure of the ramifications of discovering something that may have been required to be bound by The Official Secrets Act.

Ulyana took the initiative and said, "Perhaps you need to go away and consider your options before I go any further."

Wood remained silent for a few seconds longer and then said, "Maybe I will do that; but, if it doesn't stretch your admirable loyalty to the Crown too far, can I ask if there are any other members of your team still alive?"

Ulyana looked down, and then back up again. She said, "Maybe."

"Can you say who they are?"

It was Ulyana's turn to ponder. Following several seconds she said, "For now I can tell you one – Mademoiselle Picard."

"Obviously she is of French origin," said Wood, "did she return home?"

"No, she still lives in London."

"And do you think that she would be willing to speak to us if I can give you both assurances that no action will be taken against you?"

I don't know. We are still good friends, but we never speak about the McCready House operation."

Wood's curiosity intensified. He said, "You weren't a military installation were you?"

Ulyana raised her eyebrows and said, "Inspector, please …"

Wood pursed his lips and said, "Sorry, my copper's desire to investigate took too big a hold, I apologise."

Ulyana nodded and said, "It's understandable," she looked into Wood's eyes and believed him to be 'a good cop'. She added, "And I promise you, that if you are able to offer us those assurances, you will not be disappointed."

Wood nodded and got to his feet. He extended his hand and said, "It has been a most stimulating encounter Ulyana Vetochkin, and I look forward to our next meeting, which I promise, will be very soon."

Ulyana shook the offered hand, led Wood to the door, and bid him goodbye.

She then went upstairs to her bedroom and walked across to an ornate, wooden make-up box on her sideboard. She picked it up, and turned it end on.

The veneer of the marquetry was made up of different coloured woods, inlaid in the form of small diamonds. She pressed one; turned the box around, and pressed another on the opposite end. She then turned the box back, and pressed the first one again. A shallow drawer popped out at the opposite side of the box, close to the base. She extracted it, removed a false bottom, and saw her business card, and a key.

She took out the card and saw the inscription;

'B A Ware Esq
Section 5
Tel; VAU 2222'

She put the card down and retrieved the key. It was small, made of brass, and was in pristine condition. She then put the key back in the drawer and picked up the card. She walked downstairs and looked at the handset of her landline phone. She saw the letters adjacent to the numbers and wondered whether or not dialling VAU 2222 would draw a response. She pondered for a few seconds then walked across to her back window.

She stared for a long time at the thick, grey, cumulonimbus clouds, and then said, "Soon my loves – soon …"

Half an hour later Wood walked into McCready House and sought out Dan Lowe. "Sorry to trouble you," he said, "but do you mind if I take another quick look in the void?"

Dan raised his eyebrows and said, "No, help yourself: we've put a screen over the entrance to keep out the employees."

Wood said, "A screen? Don't tell me that your guys have been wandering in and out of there?"

"No! Of course not," said a flustered Dan. "They're all aware that they could be sacked if they do."

"And that the room is part of an ongoing police investigation?" said a stern Wood.

"Yes, yes, right."

Wood glared for a few seconds and then said, "Good – okay, I won't be long."

Dan stayed rooted to the spot until he realised that that was his cue to leave. He cleared his throat, pointed towards the old scullery and said, "I'll be in there if you need me."

Wood nodded and then made his way into the void.

He couldn't get Ulyana's question about the print of King George the Sixth still being there, out of his head. He walked across to it and stared at it.

It had a plain, dark wood frame, mahogany he thought, approximately eighteen inches wide by two feet in height. The print was in colour, but the individual colours had faded, giving it the appearance of having once been black and white, and then coloured in. In front of it, was plain glass. He studied every inch and saw nothing to attract his attention. He stared at the frame, but again saw nothing. He then removed a propelling pencil from his pocket and carefully slipped it behind the side of the print and eased it forward an inch.

With his head flat against the wall, and with the aid of his small pocket torch, he saw that it was hung by a sturdy length of twine attached to two eyehooks screwed into the back of the frame and then hooked over a standard picture-hook.

He put the torch and pencil back in his pocket and then lifted the print off the wall. He turned it over and examined the back. Once again, he saw nothing to catch his eye. The backing board was a thin piece of wood, secured in place by numerous half-inch panel pins.

He laid the print face-down on the desk and stared at it for a few seconds. He then gathered resolve, and with the aid of his Swiss Army knife, removed enough pins to be able to lift off the backboard. Underneath was just the plain, age-tempered, white back of the print.

He studied it for marks, writing, or clues of any sort, but saw nothing. He then inspected the inner side of the backboard, but that too was blank. He removed the paper print, laid it on the desk and then examined the inside edge of the frame. Nothing was there.

In a state of high frustration, he put it all back together again, re-hung the print, and walked back to Dan.

"All done," he said.

"Did you find what you were looking for?"

Wood realised that Dan's question was more a courtesy one than a direct one. He said, "So, so; it was more curiosity than anything specific."

"So you're all done?"

"Yes, thank you."

Dan nodded and said, "I'll walk with you to the front door, it's bloody dusty in that old scullery. I swear that most of it hasn't been touched for years."

"Anything valuable?"

"Nah, if there had been, it would have been nicked long before we'd moved in. It's just the usual – old pots and pans, baking trays, utensils, boxes, shit, shit, and more shit, you know."

"Sounds like my dad's garage," said Wood, "there so much crap in there that he hasn't been able to park his car in it since the 1980s."

"Bloody hell," said Dan stepping outside into the grey, cold, day and pointing towards the double green doors at the end of McCready House. "Don't even get me started about the garage! I think that everybody's been avoiding that, and it's going to be up to muggins here to clear it."

Out of the corner of his eye he saw Esme Pilchard pull back a curtain and stick her middle finger up at him. He turned to face her, stuck two fingers up, pointed at her, and mouthed, *"You, fuck – right – off."*

Wood saw the gesture and said, "Whoa – something I should know about?"

Dan shook his head and said, "No, don't ask."

Chapter 27

Naomi sped along the narrow road, turned into the drive leading to the old Ascensis facility and expected to meet somebody from Doberman Securities there. Instead, there was a police car blocking the open gates. She pulled up and said to the approaching police constable, "I'm Naomi Wilkes, I'm…"

"That's all right Ms Wilkes; we were expecting you, you can go through."

Naomi watched as the policeman gestured to the driver of the police car to move, and then turned to wave her on. She waved a 'thank you' at him and then drove down the narrow road to the building. As she approached, she was shocked to see so many vehicles. There were two police patrol cars, one white van marked 'Police Dogs', an unmarked car with Bob Crowthorne standing by it talking to a thick-set man, and three Doberman Securities vans.

She pulled up, got out, and walked across to Crowthorne. She opened her mouth to say something, but was cut off.

"With your permission, sir?"

Everybody turned and saw two burly policemen standing with a battering ram by the central door.

"One minute," called Crowthorne. He turned to the man opposite him who was on a mobile phone, and said, "Well?"

212

He then turned to Naomi, smiled, and said, "One sec, and I'll be with you."

Naomi nodded and smiled back.

"Oh yeah, that'd be right, you plank!" said the man on the mobile phone, "What? Do me a favour and credit me with some sense …"

Naomi shot Crowthorne a glance.

"It's the Area Manager of Doberman," said Crowthorne, "he's trying to see if he can locate another set of keys before we batter the door open."

"And not having much luck by the sound of it."

"You could say that."

"Yeah," said the Area Manager, *"Yeah?! What?* Hey, hey! I'll tell you what – go fuck yourself!" He almost punched the off switch on the mobile, and then saw Naomi. He said, "Romanian fucking twats!"

"All right, all right," said Crowthorne, "we can do without the language."

The Area Manager ignored the comment and said, "They said that we had all the keys for here, and that if we damage anything trying to get in, we'd be responsible for it!"

Crowthorne raised his eyebrows and said, "Sounds reasonable."

"But we didn't have *all* the keys as they were suggesting! We just have the one set."

"How many did they think you had?"

"Three!"

"And did you? Ever?"

"No way! We only ever had one set."

Naomi frowned, but said nothing.

"So why did they think that you had?" said Crowthorne.

"Are you asking me?"

Crowthorne looked around and said, "I believe so, yes!"

Naomi looked down and smiled to herself. She knew Crowthorne of old, and could tell when he was starting to get irritated.

"Well I don't bloody know!" said the Area Manager.

Crowthorne drew in a deep breath and said, "Okay, then we have no option but to use the ram."

"We aren't paying for any damage!" said the Area Manager.

"And neither are we," said Crowthorne. He looked at the frustrated manager and said, "Now, unless you have any other suggestions?"

"I do," said Naomi.

Both men turned and looked.

"The roller shutter door at the end of the building is secured by a padlock. If you get some bolt-cutters, it would be a lot less expensive to replace that, than a new door."

The two men looked at each other, and then back at Naomi.

"We carry them in all our vans," said the Area Manager.

Seconds later, Naomi, Crowthorne, two police officers, and a police dog handler with an eager German Shepherd, watched as the Area Manager snipped through the padlock. It sheared and dropped to the floor. He attempted to lift the shutter door, but following one or two heaves and loud grunts, he said, "Bloody hell, this doesn't want to shift."

Crowthorne nodded to the two police officers and watched as they positioned themselves at equal distances apart.

One said, "Okay – one, two, three…"

All three men heaved upwards and the heavy door opened.

In an instant the police dog was straining at the leash. "Steady boy," said the handler.

"Right," said Crowthorne, "keep the dog on the leash, but give him free reign. And don't anybody go in front of him. Understood?"

The police officers said, "Yes, sir," and then followed the straining dog inside.

"Can we go in, too?" said the Area Manager.

"Yes, but after the dog's moved onto the next room; we don't want to contaminate anything."

"Do you want me to wait here?" said Naomi.

"No, I want you to walk over there, into the trees."

Naomi looked at where Crowthorne was pointing, and saw that it was the corner that she'd seen the rabbit come from." She said, "Why?"

"You'll see. And when you've finished over there, we'll be ready for you here."

With a puzzled expression on her face, Naomi turned and looked into the corner again. She said, "Okay," cast another look at Crowthorne, and saw him nod in confirmation. She then walked to the end of the loading bay platform, descended the steps, and with a mind brimming with curiosity, walked into the trees.

For several seconds, she saw nothing.

"Hello," said a voice behind her.

She whipped around and saw Leo Chance standing beside the trunk of a broad Elm.

"Oh my God!" she said. "Leo! What are you doing here?"

"Watching your back – as usual!"

Naomi rushed forwards and threw her arms around him. "It's so lovely to see you," she said, "but what do you mean, watching my back?"

"Our esteemed Superintendent has asked me to be your guardian angel until your old adversary Adrian Darke is back behind bars."

Naomi was shocked. She said, "Are you serious?"

"I'm afraid so," said Leo.

"But why, surely Bob doesn't think that I'm in that much danger from him?"

"He isn't taking any chances with you, and I must say, that I concur."

Naomi looked at Leo and saw that he was wearing dark brown corduroy jeans, walking boots, a thick, round-necked sweater below a green waxed overcoat, a Harris Tweed hat, leather gloves, and a scarf. Around his neck was a small pair of binoculars and a camera. She said, "How long have you been out here?"

"Today, or since you starting coming here?"

Naomi was shocked again, she said, "Was it you I heard the last time I was here?"

"No, it was the rabbit."

"So you were here?"

"Guilty as charged."

"Did you hear that weird scream?"

"I did," Leo leaned down towards Naomi's left ear and said, "and I'll be forced to kill you if you ever tell anybody this, but, it nearly sent a shiver down my spine."

Naomi playfully jabbed Leo with her right forefinger and said, "You're impossible, Leo Chance!" She saw him smile and wink, and then said, "So, how long have you been my guardian angel?

"Since you came back from America."

Naomi was shocked for a third time and said, "My God! You've really been keeping tabs on me since then?"

Leo nodded and said, "I have."

"Day and night?"

"Yes."

"Just you?"

"No, I have had help."

"Even at my house?"

"Everywhere."

Naomi repeated, "My God." She lapsed into silence as she tried to recall seeing anything that could have been construed as 'a tail', but nothing came to mind until she realised where she was standing. She looked into Leo's striking blue eyes and said, "So if you were in these trees the last time I was here, how did you get in?

Leo put his hand into his pocket and pulled out two sets of keys. He threw one set to Naomi and said, "For you."

Naomi looked down and her mouth fell open. She said, "Are these the missing Doberman keys?"

Leo raised his eyebrows and nodded.

"How on earth…"

"Don't ask."

Naomi looked at the keys again and said, "I just heard their Area Manager telling Bob that they only ever had one set."

"He was lying."

"So, we've got two. What about their third set?"

"That's why we're here. We believe that your guard was still in possession of them when he went missing."

"And you think he's inside do you?"

"We don't know, but last Friday, something did screech or wail, whatever, inside that building."

"And it did send a shiver down my spine!" said Naomi poking another dig at Leo.

Leo smiled back and said, "Yes, it was, er, memorable."

Naomi drew in a deep breath, shook her head, and said, "You really are impossible; do you know that?"

"If you say so."

Naomi shook her head again and then said, "Okay, back to business – if you've been watching over me in secret for the last few months, why did Bob want me to know now?"

"Because you appear to have stumbled on something here, that's bigger than the Darke problem."

Naomi recalled the psychic warning about keeping things to herself, *'because it will get you killed like the rest of us'* – but she hadn't heard anything since, and she was unsure about mentioning it. She knew that Crowthorne had become accustomed to her 'strange interludes' but she wasn't sure how Leo would respond. She dismissed the idea for the present, and said, "Something *bigger* than the Darke problem? Like what?"

For the first time, she saw Leo falter. She said, "Come on, you know that you can tell me."

Leo looked at Naomi and said, "In keeping with being impossible, let's just say, that all's not what it seems here."

"Well that's flipping obvious!" said Naomi making a sweeping gesture towards the police activity.

Leo faltered again and then said, "Without going into detail, you need to know that things could soon become, let's say, 'lively', but we will be watching your back at all times. We've given you the keys to this place, including those to the entrance gates so that you can investigate the missing women, and …"

An astounded Naomi said, "You know about them?"

"Of course, Violet Burgess and Denise Lockyer."

Naomi frowned and said, "Whoa, whoa; wait a minute, has all of this been a set-up?"

"In a way yes: we wanted you to leave Walmsfield until Darke was caught, but when you refused, we…"

"Came up with a reason for me to work in Skelmersdale!"

"Not ex …"

"So Percy was in on it too?"

"Er …"

"And Carlton, was he a part of this?"

Leo looked down at Naomi and said, "Look, I'm sorry, we only had your best interests at heart."

"Best interests? – What do you think I am – some sort of wayward schoolgirl who can't look after herself?"

Leo raised his eyebrows and said, "You can't deny that you've been in more than your fair share of sticky situations."

Naomi opened her mouth to object, but then images of Darke's drugs facility, her cell, her near-death experience with the security guard, and of being held captive at the top of Bellthorpe Grain Mill popped into her mind. She faltered and said, "Okay, I admit, but …"

"But nothing, we, I, lost you once, and it's not going to happen again. We're going to make sure that you're safe, at all times, regardless of how much you may rail against it."

Naomi realised that it was pointless to object, and in the seconds that followed, took comfort from the thought. She resigned herself to her new circumstance and then returned to Leo's remark about Ascensis. She said, "Okay, moving on, do you have any clues about what I may have stumbled on that could be bigger than the Darke problem?"

"It's nothing specific, but it is intriguing. When we heard that sound last week, I reported it in and asked the boys at CID to get details on Ascensis, their activities, the building, plans, access, security systems – the usual, and at first all seemed routine. But then we unearthed a conundrum." Leo paused and then said, "Nobody was able to find anything about the place prior to the late 1960s."

Naomi frowned and said, "Such as what?"

"We couldn't find any reference to who built the unit, who the architects were, when it was constructed…"

The thumb pressed down on Naomi's shoulder and she heard the female voice say, *"Poppet...be careful..."* She looked at Leo and said, "And is this just a temporary state of affairs?"

"No, I don't think so; our guys were exhaustive in their search and they weren't able to locate a thing."

Naomi opened her mouth to reply, but then heard the voice say, *"And they won't. Everything about the construction of K2 was destroyed except for the building itself."* She'd heard it again; the name 'K2'. She looked at Leo and said, "I'm going to tell you something that I wouldn't even confide in Bob."

Leo's whole persona changed; he turned to face Naomi head-on and said, "Okay."

"I believe that you are aware, that I have help from my psychic ..."

"I do know about that, yes," said Leo, "go on."

Naomi remained silent for a few seconds and then said, "Have you ever heard of anything, or anywhere, named ..."

"No! No! Don't ..." the voice in Naomi's head almost yelled.

She couldn't help herself; she turned away from Leo and said out loud, "I have to trust in someone!"

Leo was shocked, but remained silent.

Naomi turned back and said, "I want you to find out about something, or somewhere, named, K2."

Leo looked physically shocked and Naomi saw it. She said, "You already know don't you?"

Leo didn't know how to respond.

"You do don't you?"

Leo faltered and then said, "How the hell did you ..."

"Never mind that," pressed Naomi, "what do you know?"

Leo swallowed and then said, "I only know that I can't tell you anything about it, and that if anybody apart from me ever learns that you know about K2, your life could be in the utmost danger."

"Naomi!"

Naomi turned and saw Crowthorne beckoning her. She called back, *"Coming,"* and then turned to face Leo. She said, "Okay, so what now?"

Leo's concern for Naomi's safety had leapt to stratospheric heights; he pondered for a few seconds and then said, "Dig, but not too deep. You can try to find the missing women, but only ever talk about Ascensis, or the St. Mary Cross Animal Research Unit who occupied the building before them, not K2. There's a lot more to the disappearance of those women than meets the eye, so please do as I say. Dig, but not too deep. I will keep an extra-special eye on you from now on, but by God, if you don't heed my warning, or if you slip off my radar, you could be in extreme danger."

Naomi repeated, *"The St. Mary Cross Animal Research Unit?* – Damn! I knew it. Did you know that Violet Burgess's husband worked at Ormskirk Zoo?"

"Ormskirk Zoo?" said Leo, "That's a new one on me."

"And if he worked there, could there have been a bit of collusion?"

"Hey, don't go jumping to conclusions, stick to the facts."

Naomi felt silly, she looked down, and said, "Of course, sorry." She looked back up again and said, "When you told me not to dig too deep, were you hinting that the women disappeared through some sort of …"

"Stop!" said Leo, "I'm not hinting at anything." He stepped forwards and took Naomi's hands in his. He said, "I will continue to make discreet enquiries at my end and if I find anything out I'll let you know, but whatever you do, don't mention the name K2 to anybody. Not your friend Bob over there, not Helen, and not even to Carlton. Do you understand?"

Naomi frowned and said, "What? *Not even Bob?* I thought that you guys shared info?"

"Yes we do – mostly, but on this occasion, not even Bob; do you understand?"

"Yes."

"Good," said Leo, "then I think that you should go and see him, he's waiting for you."

Chapter 28

Hallenbeck stared through the powerful, Zeiss, self-adjusting binoculars into the near pitch-black sky, as the dirigible levelled out and flew at five knots towards the Irish Sea.

Being only two nights after a New Moon, made him realise what a good idea it had been to put the dirigible's navigation lights on, otherwise he would have lost sight of it within minutes. He looked down and also saw the single white nav light of the launch matching its progress in the sea below.

From in the sky, he heard the sudden increase in sound as the dirigible's engines accelerated to ten knots. He then saw the pilot ignite a small flare, jump from the gondola, and deploy his parachute. He lowered the binoculars to make sure that the boat was still there, and then raised them again.

For a split-second, everything appeared to have vanished. He swept the binoculars to the left, but saw nothing. He swept them to the right, and saw nothing. He frowned, lowered the binoculars, and relocated the launch. He saw that it had veered hard to starboard and was racing on a north-westerly heading towards the descending pilot. He muttered, "What?" and then looked back at the pilot. Through the light of the flare, he saw that the parachute was angled at least thirty degrees off centre, and was being blown towards the opposite shore of the

Duddon Channel. He felt his heart rate increase as he muttered his first, "No ..."

He then turned to look at Fisher who was also tracking the activity. He saw Fisher drop his binoculars and look at him in a searching way. He lifted his binoculars and saw that the pilot had landed, but that he was far off the expected mark. He then raised them, looked at the dirigible, and saw that he could no longer see the port side red nav light, only the white stern light. His heart rate stepped up another few notches and he said, "No, no ..." He snatched the binoculars down, turned to Fisher and said, "Are you seeing this?"

Fisher felt a huge lump in his throat; he swallowed hard, and nodded.

Hallenbeck raised the binoculars again and saw that the dirigible had not returned to its planned course. He said, "This cannot be. Why hasn't the auto-pilot corrected the heading?"

In the small wheelhouse of HMS Spartan Captain Middleton snatched up the bulkhead phone and dialled the engine room. He heard Able Seaman Carter answer. He said, "Captain – what's the situation?"

"It's hopeless, sir, we can't stop the flooding, and the explosion's ruptured the water circulation pipes to the boilers."

"Are they're beginning to overheat?"

"Yes, sir."

"How long to critical?"

"Thirty, maybe forty minutes – if we're lucky..."

"Right, get out of there now, and seal that door."

"Yes, sir."

Middleton looked out of the wheelhouse window and saw that miraculously, and with the help of the spring tide, they'd made it to half a mile off-shore, halfway between Kirkstanton, and Haverigg Haws. He looked at the chart and called, "*Helm, alter course to one-three-zero*. Number One, give the order to lower the lifeboats."

The Nav Officer looked at the chart and frowned. He said, "One-three-zero sir? That'll run us straight into the sandbanks off Haverigg Point."

"I know where it will take us, Mister!"

The Nav Officer faltered and then said, "What's your thinking, sir?"

"We're already listing ten degrees to port and the boilers are beginning to overheat. The degree of list will hamper the boat being lowered on the starboard side, so we need to get the portside boat swung out and down, before the boilers blow."

The Nav Officer said, "Thank you, sir. Now I understand."

Middleton nodded and shouted, "Coms contact the *Express* and …"

"*Sir, you need to see this!*"

Everybody turned and saw the lookout on the port side of the wheelhouse pointing into the night sky.

At Sandscale Haws Hallenbeck continued to watch the track of the dirigible as it veered slowly to starboard. He said, "I don't understand it, if the wind's veering her off course, why can't *we* feel anything?"

One of the observers said, "Because we're sheltered here, whereas, at the mouth of …"

"*No! No!*" Fisher's two simple words stopped everybody dead.

Hallenbeck lowered his binoculars and said, "What?"

Fisher looked at Hallenbeck and then pointed across the channel.

Hallenbeck looked and saw nothing. He repeated, *"What?"*

"Look through your binoculars."

Hallenbeck raised his binoculars and looked at where Fisher was pointing. At first he saw nothing, and then he gasped in shock and disbelief. He said, *"Mein Gott im Himmel!"*

Shining like two bright stars in the night, he saw a ship's white masthead light and a red, port, navigation light on a converging course with the dirigible.

"Nein, nein, nein!" he said. He let go of the binoculars and looked at the pocket-watch in his left hand. The time showed 12:23 a.m. – the stopwatch showed eleven minutes to detonation. He dropped the watch, snatched up the binoculars, and looked at the oncoming vessel. This time he saw the white masthead light, and the red and green nav lights, indicating that the vessel had turned more to port. It was now coming straight at them. He gasped and said, "Heilige Mutter Gottes …"

Aboard the *Spartan*, Boyle and his associates crowded against the port rail of the lower deck and looked at the oncoming dirigible.

All around them the non-essential crewmembers jostled in their lifejackets as they watched the deck crew preparing to swing out the port side lifeboat.

The Petty Officer in charge yelled, *"Stand by to board!"*

Brendan Jackson pointed at the dirigible and said, "What's that?"

Boyle looked at Jackson and said, "Are you serious?"

"Yes, what is it?"

An incredulous Boyle said, "Where the fuck have you been most of your life, in a potato field? It's an airship!"

Jackson looked at the approaching craft and said, "What's that below it?

Boyle looked up and saw a cylindrical metal object slung below the gondola and frowned. He said, "If I didn't know better, I'd think that was a bomb."

The word 'bomb' made everybody nearby turn and look at the approaching dirigible.

Boyle heard one or two shocked remarks and then became filled with suspicion. He said, "Surely they wouldn't?"

Up in the crowded wheelhouse, everybody else had seen the strange looking object below the dirigible, but it was the First Officer who made the connection. He yelled, *"Hard-a-starboard!"*

Middleton looked at his First Officer and said, "What?"

"It's a bomb, sir!"

"What?"

"A bomb, sir, strapped to the underside of the gondola!"

Middleton frowned and yelled, *"Helmsman, belay that order!"* He glared at his First Officer and said, "Even if it is, why would you give such an order? They're not going to drop the bloody thing on us!"

The helmsman swung the wheel back to port and resumed the course to shore.

At Sandscale Haws, Hallenbeck watched the hands on the stopwatch. It was as though life around him had ceased. He was numb. He felt nothing, he heard nothing, and he only had one thing to do – to watch the second-hand tick its way around to the final zero. As it did, he lifted his head and looked across the Duddon Channel.

The detonation was awesome. The napalm derivative and hydrogen lit up the night sky in a spectacular, sun-bright, halo.

Seconds later the hydrogen in the dirigible's ballonets ignited too, adding to the already breath-taking spectacle.

Fisher couldn't help himself, he said, "Fucking hell!"

Hallenbeck saw that the vessel, now bathed in light, appeared to be some sort of warship; he dropped to his knees, grabbed his face in both hands, and began to weep uncontrollably.

Aboard the *Spartan* was a scene from the deepest recesses of hell.

As *The Halo* had detonated it had consumed every last ounce of oxygen within its range. It had sucked it out of the atmosphere, and out of everybody's lungs. And then, as the oxygen had sped back into the vacuum, everybody had inhaled and sucked in the searing, choking, chemical. They began gagging and clawing at their throats as the inextinguishable napalm burned their tongues, windpipes, and lungs. Within seconds more of the horrific chemical fell onto their heads, faces and hands. Everywhere men were screaming and clawing at their skin as the napalm seared its way through everything it landed upon. Those men able to do so began batting at the burning specs, but as more and more rained down upon them, the multiple spots turned into a raging conflagration, and their clothing and lifejackets erupted into flames.

Everywhere, men threw themselves into the sea, but even as they sank to their tortured, watery graves the chemical continued to burn and sear its way into their agonised bodies.

Within minutes the ordered world of a British warship had gone to hell; and along with it, the bodies and souls of the screaming, writhing, agonised men.

And then, way earlier than Carter's estimate, the number one, oil-fired, watertube boiler exploded, followed immediately by boiler number two. The ensuing explosion ruptured the bulkhead to the adjoining Ammunition Room and everything in there detonated, too.

The effect was utterly devastating and catastrophic.

The one-hundred-and-seventy-seven foot, M34, blew apart from stem to stern, reared up, and then plunged below the blazing surface of the Irish Sea.

Above her final resting place, the eerie glow of the fiery chemical continued to drift onto the tortured souls still writhing in their burning lifejackets.

On land at Sandscale Haws, everybody except Hallenbeck watched in abject horror.

Twenty-three miles away, close to the position that *Spartan* had first put out her mayday, the Captain and bridge crew aboard *HMS Express* first saw, and then heard the series of explosions.

All those who could, rushed out onto the bridge wings, and stared into the distant, glowing night sky.

"What the hell was that?" said the First Lieutenant.

The Captain turned to his Radio Officer and said, "What was the last position of the *Spartan*?"

"Fifty-four degrees, twelve minutes and eight seconds north, by three degrees, twenty-one minutes, and twelve seconds west, sir," he glanced up and added, "where that explosion came from."

The Captain turned and looked at the diminishing glow in the distance and shook his head. He said, "God rest their souls. That must have been the boilers and ammo." He strode back into the bridge, snatched up the phone to the engine room, and spoke to his Chief Engineer. "Chief," he ordered, "I want every last drop of speed you can get out of this old rust-bucket, do you hear?"

Chapter 29

As Naomi walked across to the main building she couldn't get Leo's warning not to say anything to anybody about 'K2' out of her mind. She also found it more than odd that Leo had warned her not to say anything to Bob Crowthorne, and wondered why members of the same force would keep things from one another. She looked up and saw Crowthorne gesturing for her to join him. She nodded and then extracted her pocket book and scribbled down the name 'St. Mary Cross Animal Research Unit'.

Next were the extractor fans. As she approached them she glanced up to the one that Helen had pointed out and saw that the blades weren't moving. She frowned, and walked across to Crowthorne.

"Pleasant surprise?"

Naomi said, "Not sure about pleasant. Of course it was nice seeing Leo again, but you could have told me that I was being watched."

"I could, but would you have acted so naturally?"

Naomi shrugged and said, "Don't know." She nodded towards the Ascensis building and said, "So, are you going to enlighten me about this place?"

Crowthorne raised his eyebrows and said, "I'm not sure that I can. As far as we were concerned this was an empty, but at one-time mega-contentious, ex-research unit, until both you and Leo heard the unusual sound. Then we received the missing persons call from Doberman, and here we are."

"Okay."

Crowthorne looked at Naomi and saw that she wasn't comfortable. He said, "Are you happy to go inside?"

Naomi paused and then said, "To be honest, I'm not sure."

"Would you rather wait here?"

"No."

Crowthorne looked at Naomi's troubled face and said, "Is it one of your unusual feelings again?"

Naomi remained silent just long enough, and was then cut off before she could answer.

"You know that I haven't always been comfortable with your odd episodes, but you do know that you can tell me don't you?" added Crowthorne.

Naomi wanted to be open and honest, but she was racked by Leo's warnings. She said, "I'm sorry, Bob, I can't put my finger on it."

"And no direct messages?"

"No."

Crowthorne knew that something wasn't right. He waited for a few seconds and then said, "Okay, if you say so," he pointed towards the door and said, "Shall we?"

Naomi looked into the opening and said, "Yes."

The inside of the modest-sized loading bay was like any other that she'd seen in the course of her work. The platform was raised three or four feet above ground level and there was room for one vehicle to be loaded or unloaded at a time. Looking in, she noted that the left-hand side was dedicated to the raised platform alone, allowing access to any vehicle side doors. At the back, on the right, was a single door, which she guessed would have been to the dispatcher's small office. To the left of it was a set of double-doors which appeared to be the soft plastic sort that could be pushed open by a forklift truck. On the right-hand side, the bay was much wider. She presumed that that was where the goods would have been stacked before being loaded or unloaded.

As she approached the halfway-in mark, she stopped, turned, and looked back out. Up on the left she expected to see the back of the extractor fans, but nothing was there. She looked down and saw another office in the corner of the bay, from which, she presumed, anybody could exit the building through the external red door that she'd seen on the outside.

She turned to Crowthorne and said, "Can we look in there?"

Crowthorne looked at where Naomi was pointing and said, "Yes, sure, but let me check if the dog's been in first." He looked at Naomi's face, and his suspicion that all wasn't right intensified. He said, "Do you want to do it now, or shall we do it on the way back?"

Naomi tried to connect to something psychically, but nothing happened. She said, "On the way back'll be fine."

Crowthorne held up his arm and indicated for Naomi to go first. They walked through the double doors, and entered a large storeroom filled with empty racks. At the far end was a single green door with a sign stating 'Authorised Personnel Only' that had been overwritten with the words *'murderous bastards - rot in hell'* in red graffiti.

They walked through it and entered a long corridor with more doors to the right and left, along its full length. Ahead they could hear the eager police dog as it snuffled its way around each room.

"Best not to get too close," said Crowthorne, "let's take our time."

Naomi nodded and then felt a pressure begin to assert itself on her left shoulder. For some odd reason she knew that it wasn't anything to do with 'K2' or the lady who'd called her Poppet, it was to do with a feeling of deep depression about where she was; in a place of unspeakable suffering.

She looked around and saw that the old magnolia doors, walls, and skirting boards had become flaky and musty-smelling. Below the ceiling white polystyrene tiles had been suspended, of which, some were missing and others had been punched through to access the void above. The floor was strewn about with chunks of paint, plaster, polystyrene, torn backing paper, and other detritus, making it squishy and crunchy to walk across.

Crowthorne said, "This isn't what I expected."

"No, me neither. The outside looks in much better condition."

"Yes..."

They walked in silence from room to room, keeping well behind the dog. Some were devoid of anything, some contained empty cupboards and worktops, and the larger rooms appeared to have been the labs. Old and rusting cages had been strewn about, drawers had been pulled off their runners, doors were hanging off wall cupboards, and copious sheets of printed paper were scattered about in wild disarray. And like the door to the corridor, everywhere was covered in foul-language graffiti decrying the activities of the occupants.

Crowthorne glanced at Naomi and said, "Animal rights protestors – not the calmest of people."

Naomi nodded and said, "It must have been terrifying for the workers here." She surprised herself by feeling like a hypocrite, but she couldn't help empathising with the fearful researchers, even though she despised their activities.

She saw that some of the scattered paper contained letter-heads. She bent down to retrieve one from below a bench, and then noticed something unusual. Directly below the worktop, a black metal pipe had been let into a groove. She dropped down to her haunches and looked closer. The pipe extended from bench to bench through a series of grooves until it disappeared into the wall at the far end of the lab. She then turned in the opposite direction and saw that it came from the room she'd just left.

Thinking that it was a gas pipe, she stood up and expected to see a series of Bunsen burner extensions on the bench tops, but nothing was there. With a puzzled expression on her face she tapped Crowthorne on the shoulder and said, "Two secs Bob, I'm just going back next door."

"Have you seen something?"

Before she could respond, the pressure on her shoulder intensified and the female voice almost yelled, *"No!"* She held steady, looked at Crowthorne, and said, "Not really, I'm curious about the general layout and I forgot to make a note of it as I went along."

Crowthorne nodded and turned back to what he was doing.

Naomi walked back into the previous room and estimated where the pipe should have come through the wall, but there was no sign of it.

She remembered an old trick her father Sam had shown her about detecting hollow spaces behind walls – and, keeping as quiet as she could, she ripped off the old and peeling paper, and laid it on the floor. She then removed her pen from her notebook, placed it between her forefinger and thumb, and ran it lightly across the surface of the exposed plaster. At first she heard nothing but as she got to the point where she estimated the pipe to have entered the wall, it sounded hollow.

"What are you doing?"

Naomi whipped around and saw Crowthorne standing in the doorway. She kept her cool and said, "I'm just checking the integrity of the plasterwork."

"Why?"

"Habit I suppose. Whenever I enter anywhere with peeling paint and paper I check to see if it was an internal or external thing."

"I don't follow," said Crowthorne.

"If the walls are peeling because of an internal problem such as being over-papered or painted, then the plasterwork won't usually be affected, but if it was because of external damp, then the plaster would often become hollow and detached."

Crowthorne frowned and said, "But this is an internal wall."

"I know," said Naomi, "but I wanted to do this before trying anywhere else."

Crowthorne wasn't convinced. He said, "Is there something you're not telling me?"

The voice in Naomi's head said, *"No poppet!"* She looked at Crowthorne and said, "Do you trust me?"

"Of course."

"Then please don't ask me any more questions until after we leave."

Crowthorne stared at Naomi for a few seconds and then nodded. He said, "Okay, have it your way – but only for now."

Naomi smiled, thanked him, and said, "Now buzz off and leave me alone for a few minutes." She waited until Crowthorne had departed and then swept the pen across the other walls. Only the place where she suspected the pipe entering sounded hollow.

She walked back into the lab, and feigning picking up more pieces of paper, she followed the pipe to where it disappeared into the wall at the opposite side, and noted on the way, that it didn't have any junctions off it.

She stepped back into the hall, walked up to the next door and opened it. It was a utility cupboard and the ceiling wasn't covered by suspended polystyrene, it was exposed, and numerous pipes ran across the top of it.

She said, "Typical," and tried to estimate which of them, was the one leading from the lab, but, with the exception of one obvious over-sized pipe, they all looked the same. She let out an exasperated breath, and knew that it would be pointless trying to trace it whilst anybody else was there. She stood in the corridor considering her options, and then remembered her set of keys. An idea started to form.

Seconds later she heard a sound to her left, and saw the dog-handler heading towards her from the opposite end of the building. She smiled as he drew near and then saw him look over her shoulder.

"All clear that end, sir," said the dog-handler.

"Nothing at all?" said Crowthorne.

"I thought that we had something in Lab 4," said the handler, "but it was nothing in the end."

"Lab 4?"

"Yes, sir, it's the only room with a name on it, second door on the right up from here."

Crowthorne looked up the hall and said, "Okay, are you finished now?"

"No, sir, there's still the small room off the loading bay."

Naomi felt the pressure on her shoulder again, but held her tongue.

"Okay, I expect that you'll be done by the time we get there."

"Yes, sir – unless we find something."

Crowthorne nodded and then waited until the dog-handler had moved on. He turned to Naomi and said, "Well, off you go, but you know the score."

Naomi smiled and said, "Thanks, Bob, I can see why Helen has a soft spot for you." For the first time since she'd known him, she saw Crowthorne blush. She stared at him for a second or two, stepped closer, and then said, "Why Bob Crowthorne, did you just blush?"

Crowthorne checked that nobody was nearby and said, "I, er ..."

"You did, didn't you?"

Crowthorne gathered his composure and said, "I did no such thing, it was a ..."

"Blush?"

"No, nothing of the sort," he made one of his 'harrumphing' sounds, and then said, "now, let's get on shall we? We have work to do."

Naomi watched in amused fascination as Crowthorne turned on his heel and almost scurried off.

Room-by-room they moved along, but saw nothing out of the ordinary. Naomi didn't attempt to search for any more concealed pipes, because she'd decided that she was going to return to the site alone. She wasn't sure how she'd evade Leo's watchful eyes, but she was determined to do whatever it took to get to the bottom of whatever was going on.

Suddenly, the dog barked.

Everybody headed for the loading bay and then waited outside the door until the handler came out.

"I don't know what to make of this, sir," said the handler, "The dog appears to have picked up something, but it doesn't make sense."

Crowthorne nodded to Naomi and said, "Come with me."

The Doberman Area Manager, who'd remained quiet for most of the time said, "Can I come too?"

Crowthorne said, "Not right now if you don't mind, if the dog's found anything we don't want too many feet going in there." He turned to the two PC's and said, "You two wait here and don't let anybody in."

The PCs said, "Yes, sir," and took up a position either side of the door.

Crowthorne turned to the dog-handler and said, "Right, now what's going on?"

"Stay behind me and watch this," said the dog-handler. He let the dog sniff the item of clothing that belonged to Rod Carroll, and set it free.

The dog sniffed around for a few seconds and then started wagging its tail. He followed a distinct trail until he neared the opposite wall, and then turned left. He continued along its full length, got to the red door that led to the exterior, and turned left again; he followed that wall to the end, and then turned left once more. Seconds later he was back where he started.

Crowthorne frowned but didn't comment.

The dog-handler said, "See what I mean, sir? Apache has picked up a scent, but all it appears to do is go around in a square, and he doesn't show any interest in, or around, the exit door."

"What about outside?" said Crowthorne.

"We've tried there but he hasn't found any trace."

Crowthorne looked at Naomi and said, "Any ideas?"

Naomi shrugged her shoulders, walked out of the office, and back into the loading bay. She saw empty boxes strewn about, one or two thick cardboard cores which she surmised had come from rolls of packing material; general dust, dirt, the odd discarded beer can, a pair of old wooden ladders lying on the floor near the back wall, and nothing much else. Next she turned her attention to the concrete floor itself. She wondered whether somebody might have thrown disinfectant or bleach over it, to mask any smells that the dog may have been able to pick up, but if they had, she couldn't tell. Everywhere looked uniform in colour. The only odd-looking thing was the cut-off appearance of the boxy office that didn't stretch all the way up to the sloping roof.

She walked back into the office, glanced up, and shook her head. Something looked wrong. She looked at Crowthorne when she heard him ask, "Anything?" and replied, "Not that I can see."

"Nor me," said the dog-handler, "and Apache didn't detect anything either."

"Just this trail going around in a square?" said Naomi.

"Yes: I said that it didn't make sense."

"All right," said Crowthorne, "then let's leave before we contaminate any more bits of potential evidence. We'll get forensics down here." He looked at Naomi and then thought about her special gift; he said, "Before we leave, would you like a few minutes alone?"

Naomi was shocked by the down-to-earth policeman whose ideas had changed so much since meeting her. She said, "Yes, if you don't mind, I won't touch anything."

Crowthorne nodded, and left with the dog-handler.

Naomi wasn't interested in anything psychic; she was interested in the open space above the office, and how the back wall of it formed a part of the main gable wall of the bay. On the underside of the sloping roof, she could see the silver box-work of the overhead air-conditioning unit, and how it led

240

to the extractor fans, but there was something else. Coming in through the gable wall, above and to the right-hand side of the external red door, were three pipes of a similar diameter to the one she'd seen under the laboratory bench. Two of them turned upwards and then ran back towards the labs at ceiling level, but one didn't. It came in for approximately six inches, turned down for two feet, and then turned back out through the same wall. It didn't make sense.

She knew that the floor height of the office would be the same as the exterior loading platform, and recalling that the outside of the wall was cladded in moulded aluminium, she counted the courses of bricks up to where the pipe came in through the wall, and to where it went out. Knowing that thirteen courses amounted to one metre in height, she made a note of each measurement in her notebook, and then rejoined the others in the loading bay.

"Anything?" said Crowthorne.

Naomi shook her head and said, "No, sorry."

"Right, let's leave until forensics has done their stuff."

Naomi was deep in thought when she heard the Doberman Area Manager say, "Bloody weird eh?" She shook herself out of her out of her cogitation and said, "I beg your pardon, what did you say?"

"I said that it's bloody weird that we didn't find anything to account for that sound you heard."

Naomi frowned and realised that she hadn't given that any thought. She said, "Yes, strange indeed."

They went outside, watched the police personnel close the shutter doors, and then turned to head back towards the vehicles.

On their way, Naomi stopped and turned to the Area Manager. She said, "Excuse me for just one minute will you?"

The Area Manager nodded and ambled across to the other men.

Naomi waited until everybody had become engrossed in their conversation, and then walked around to the opposite side of the cylindrical fuel container. She took her tape measure out of her bag, clambered onto an industrial bin, and then measured upwards, the two distances that she'd noted in her book.

The pipes appeared to have gone into the building from behind the extractor fan that both she and Helen had seen switched on, and the pipe that went in and then led down, appeared to have come out again, into the back of the steel fuel container.

She hopped off the bin, wound in her tape, and then took another photo of the extractor fans and surrounding elevation. None of it made sense. She pressed the side of her head against the cladding and tried to see if she could see the pipes going into the rear of the container, but it was so closely abutted that she couldn't tell.

She frowned, made an exasperated grunting sound, and headed back to Crowthorne and the others.

Out of nowhere the voice in her head said, *"There we are then poppet, now do you understand?"*

Naomi looked down and almost hissed, "No, I don't; I really, really, don't!"

Chapter 30

The CID office was unusually quiet. Detective Inspector Wood leaned his office chair back to its maximum tilt, and looked around. Mounds of paperwork lay in numerous trays atop half-a-dozen or so desks. It was in 'in-trays', 'out-trays', and the 'I don't-know-what-the-hell-to-do-with-this' trays, and he knew that most of it represented unsolved cases. He also knew that if he had more personnel, their crime-solving rate would improve, but as usual, it always came down to the same thing; money, or more realistically, the lack of it. The desks were functional, but old, the chairs were well past their use-by dates, and the office walls appeared to have been decorated following the queen's coronation. He drew in a deep breath and was about to pick up a case file, when the telephone rang on his desk. He picked it up and said, "DI Wood."

"Inspector, this is Dave Gibson from BT Engineers."

"Yes Dave, what can I do for you?"

"We've had a call from Leeds and our guys have traced that line you were after."

Wood sat bolt upright and said, "Excellent! Where did it terminate?"

"Nowhere."

Wood frowned and said, "Nowhere? What do you mean nowhere?"

"I mean nowhere Inspector. They followed the telephone line from Settle onto the Yorkshire moors and out towards a place named Mewith Head, and then it disappeared."

"Mewith Head," repeated Wood, "I've never heard of that before; where is it?"

"You can find it on any online map, but it's on the Yorkshire edge of the Forest of Bowland."

"And when you say that the line disappeared, what do you mean exactly?"

"It was a line-of-sight trail. The guys followed the telephone line as it passed from pole to pole. They went northwest from Settle to a place named Giggleswick, and then followed it onto a railway line until it cut off at …"

"Hang on," said Wood, "I don't mean to be rude, but can we skip the detail?"

Gibson blushed and said, "Oh, sure, sorry Inspector, right, now, the line led to a deserted temperance hall, and then ran into the ground."

"A deserted temperance hall? I thought you said it was on the Yorkshire moors?"

"It was."

"What the hell's a temperance hall doing in the middle of the Yorkshire moors?"

"Don't ask me Inspector, I'm just telling you, what they told me."

Wood frowned and said, "And then what?"

"The line ran down an interior wall and then disappeared into the ground."

"Is that normal?"

"No it isn't, they normally terminate at a junction box or wall-socket."

"Okay, so what happened next?"

"The guys were able to track the signal underground until it got close to a small river named Keasden Beck, and then they lost it."

Wood sat in silence for a second and then said, "How could they lose it?"

"There could be any number of reasons but the most logical would be if the line went so deep that the trackers couldn't pick up the signal."

"So couldn't the engineers dig down and pick it up again?"

"Sure – but if you were out on the moors, next to a river, how deep and how far would you keep on digging to follow a line? It could go on for miles."

"And the line was still live?"

"Yes: we just couldn't find where it went to."

Wood shut his eyes and then said, "Not *'couldn't'* Dave, *'didn't'*."

Gibson didn't bite, he answered, "Not me personally Inspector."

"No, of course not," Wood paused and hoped that Gibson hadn't heard the sarcasm in his voice. He said, "So the bottom line is, a red phone goes off in London, and all we can do is to track it to some obscure river bed on the Yorkshire Moors?"

"And we weren't the only ones either. When the boys got back to their vehicle, a van from Drax Power was parked next to them. It turns out that they'd been instructed to follow the power lines from Slaidburn Power Station to see who'd been consuming the electricity."

"Slaidburn, where's that?"

"About ten miles south of Keasden, just over the Lancashire border."

"This Keasden, is it a village or something?"

"It may have been at one time, which might account for the Temperance Hall, but apart from the odd farm here and there, there's nothing. Keasden must just be the name of the area."

"So it was Slaidburn Power Station that powered your telephone line?"

"Yes: the Drax boys knew that somebody was consuming power, but they didn't know who, so they followed their lines and eventually found out that it was us."

"But none of you could find where the telephone line went to?"

"No."

"So nobody's any the wiser?"

"Not in so many words, but we do know that the power's coming from Slaidburn, we know that the line terminated at the red phone in McCready House, and we know that it originated from somewhere near Keasden, that's more than we knew before."

"And all of that amounts to nothing if we don't know where the signal's coming from."

Gibson paused and said, "I'm sorry Inspector, but nobody was on the other end of the line when the red phone was picked up, so we're not about to go digging up Christ knows how much of Yorkshire moorland to find a phone that nobody's on."

"Then how do you account for the signal? Somebody must be activating it."

"Not according to the boys from Drax. They said that the signal stops when they turn off the power."

Wood pondered for a few seconds and then said, "So at sometime in the past, somebody activated a call, or signal, to a red phone in London, and for some reason, someone else cut the power to it?"

"It looks that way."

Wood's curiosity started to run riot. He said, "Then that must mean that somebody at Slaidburn Power Station, for whatever reason, didn't want somebody else from Keasden, speaking to somebody at McCready House; is that it?"

"We don't think so. We think that it was an emergency response."

"What – like a panic button or something?"

"Kind of: back then the red phones could be activated in two ways. One was by picking it up and pressing the contact button, the other, for example, in the event of a fire, or any situation that might not have allowed the subscriber access to the phone, by activating an emergency switch that sent out a repetitive signal."

"So somebody activated an emergency switch near Keasden, from a set-up that warranted the installation of a red phone, and the response was to cut the power off?"

"Ah, now that's the question that's got us all talking. Did the power get cut off before anybody responded, or did it get cut off because somebody responded?"

Wood frowned and said, *"Because somebody responded?"*

"Yes. Nothing else accounts for the signal remaining active. If somebody had responded to it, there wouldn't have been a need to keep it live. Therefore, somebody either cut off the power to stop the emergency response being received, or alternatively, they received it, but didn't want anybody else to know about it, and cut the power off."

Wood said, "Bloody hell Dave, that's some assumption!"

"Maybe," said Gibson, "but nothing else makes sense."

"But that would be horrendous," Wood paused and then said, "and we have no idea who, or what outfit sent the signal?"

"No, except that it's connected to MI5."

If Wood had been slapped across the face he couldn't have been more shocked. He said, "*MI5?* How on earth do you know that?"

"The boys from Slaidburn told me that the power to Keasden ran from an undesignated switch that had been masked by a missing blank plate, but then last Friday one of their senior engineers dropped something below the control panel desk and they found it. It fitted perfectly: they then turned it over and saw the inscription 'E1RPL' printed on the other side. And according to the senior engineer at Drax, the 'E1' part was an old code for MI5."

Wood felt drained. The whole investigation had just taken a massive nose dive. He knew that any dealing with any of the secret services was a major pain in the backside, and that their secrets, always bound by the Official Secrets Act, could be classified for anything up to a hundred years.

His heart sank at the thought of dealing with them, let alone trying to investigate them. He drew in a deep breath and said, "Okay Dave, thanks, but that's a major bummer."

"Call me Gibbo will you Inspector? I'm an Aussie and we aren't big on proper names."

"All right Gibbo, thanks for your help."

"Right, last thing, apparently the guys from Drax, told our boys, that they would be reporting their findings to their bosses, after which, the power to Keasden would be turned off again."

"Whoa whoa!" said Wood. "They can't do that! This is still part of an ongoing investigation."

Gibson frowned and said, "But you know everything that we know, why do you still need the line connected?"

Wood knew that Gibson's statement made sense, but something about turning the power off, didn't feel right. He said, "Because I want it left on." He paused and then added, "I want it left on until we've exhausted every last avenue of search from a police point of view."

"Okay," said Gibson, "then you need to talk to the boys at Drax."

Wood said, "I will, and thanks for the call." He said goodbye, waited until the line had cleared, and then sat back in his seat. He couldn't believe that everybody had gone to so much trouble for it to end with nothing. He rested his head back on his chair, stroked his chin for a few seconds, and then reached for his A4 notepad. On it he wrote;

1. Drax Power, Yorkshire – dead end (give them a call)
2. BT: London to Keasden – dead end
3. Slaidburn Power Station, Lancashire – dead end
4. McCready House, Hampstead Heath –

It hit him like a hammer blow. He snatched up his telephone and dialled the number of his Chief Superintendent.

One hour later Wood stepped out of his car and knocked on Ulyana Vetochkin's door.

"Inspector Wood," said Ulyana, "how nice to see you so soon."

"Likewise," said Wood, "I have those assurances for both you and Mademoiselle Picard. Can I come in?"

Chapter 31

"Necessity knows no law."
Old Latin Proverb

Zeena Bishop, Sandi Schmidt, and Eleanor Drake trudged up the narrow, made-up road track that cut through the starkness of Turnerford Brow like a single, curving pencil line, and they were not happy. The incline was steep and unforgiving, and the higher they got, the more exhausting it became.

Sandi looked at the acres and acres of bleak, windswept grass, and pulled her overcoat tighter around her waist. She said, "I forgot how freezing it can get up here."

"And it's not even winter yet," said Zeena. She then turned to Eleanor and said, "You're quiet, are you okay?"

"What do you think?" snapped back Eleanor. "First we get sent on some wild-goose chase by Hallenbeck, which was only an excuse to have us not around when the second test was done, and then the bloody car breaks down!"

"I can understand why you're a bit peeved about the goose chase," said Sandi, "but the car breaking down wasn't Karl's fault."

Eleanor glared at Sandi and said, "Are you so sure?"

"Oh come on," said Zeena.

"No!" snapped Eleanor. "It wouldn't surprise me one bit if he hadn't got one of his moronic soldiers to tamper with the engine!"

Zeena shot a glance at Sandi; they knew better than to argue with Eleanor when she was in one of her angry moods.

Eleanor fumed for a few seconds longer and then said, "And now we're going to be late!" She turned to her companions and said, "And I have never been late for anything, anywhere, ever, before!"

The companions continued up the hill until they saw a near-circular hole, cut into the side of the moor several feet off the road. It was approximately four feet deep, lined with dry stones, and the number '7' was painted in black beside the narrow entrance.

"I've seen this as we've passed before," said Sandi, "any idea what it is?"

"A shooting box," said Eleanor, "they were constructed for people to hide in during grouse-hunts and …"

In that instant, the kitten heel broke off Eleanor's left shoe. She staggered over; hit the steep camber at the edge of the narrow road, and fell into a grassy ditch.

Zeena and Sandi rushed across and expected Eleanor to be fuming, but instead they saw her sitting in a shallow stream. She had an exasperated, but bemused expression upon her face. Almost in unison they said, "Are you all right?"

Eleanor looked at her friends, looked down at her wet skirt and laddered stockings, and then looked back up again. She said, "I'll give you two guesses!"

Zeena saw the funny side of it and said, "Here, give me your hand." She reached forwards, took hold of Eleanor's hand and pulled.

The moorland Gods struck again.

As Zeena pulled on Eleanor's right arm, her feet slipped from under her, and she landed on her bottom on the side of the road.

Both women started to giggle until Sandi saw something in the distance. She stared for a couple of seconds and then said, "Hey, look at this: there's a man being chased over there."

Eleanor and Zeena clambered to their feet and looked at where Sandi was pointing.

In the far distance at the top of the hill, they saw a man running from their right-to-left and intermittently turning to look at the man chasing him. They followed his progress for several seconds and then saw him stumble and fall. As the man stood up, they saw him lift his hands in the air and stand still.

"Crikey," said Zeena, "it must be a poacher."

"And the farmer's got a shotgun," said Eleanor.

The friends watched in silence as the man with the gun drew closer, and then to their horror, they saw him raise it to his shoulder, and fire.

The man with raised arms staggered backwards and fell as the sound of the shot reached them.

"Holy Christ!" said Zeena, "Did you see that?"

Eleanor snatched hold of her friends' arms and pulled them down to a level where they could just see.

They watched the man with the gun walk across to the shot man, raise his weapon again, and fire down.

"Jesus Christ," said Zeena, "he just shot him again!"

They saw the distant man lower his gun, then turn around to look. All three women ducked.

Eleanor whispered, "Keep your heads down and get into that shooting box."

Zeena and Sandi nodded, then crawled through the long grass, and squeezed through the narrow entrance into the cramped interior.

Eleanor slowly raised her head and saw the profile of the man as he appeared to be scouring the moor top. She put her hand up to her mouth, then turned to her friends, and whispered, "He's a soldier!" Without waiting for a response, she raised her head again, and saw two other uniformed men join the first and begin looking in all directions.

"There are two more of them," she said, "and they appear to be looking for someone."

"What should we do?" said Zeena.

Eleanor ignored the question, and then said, "Oh my God, they've split up, and one's coming this way!"

Sandi began to panic and repeated Zeena's question, "What shall we do?"

Eleanor looked around and saw a small, rusting, corrugated steel shed, a hundred yards to her left. She said, "You two hide in that shed, and I'll attempt to make my way down the ditch to that schoolhouse at the bottom."

"But that's three miles away," hissed Zeena, "you'll never make it without being seen."

"Why don't we just make ourselves known?" said Sandi, "We haven't done anything wrong and that man might have been a deserter."

"Soldiers don't shoot deserters!" snapped back Eleanor, "And are you willing to stake our lives on being safe from them?"

Sandi looked at Zeena's troubled face, and then said, "No; we'll go."

"All right, keep low, and keep moving. Don't look up, and don't stop until you get there." She extended her right hand, gave the hands of her friends a quick squeeze, and said, "Good luck, I'll get back to you as soon as I've got help."

She watched her friends scurry away towards the steel shed, and then raised her head to see where the soldier was. Her heart leapt into her mouth, and she ducked back down. He was much closer than she'd anticipated, and he was heading straight towards her.

In blind panic she looked around, dismissed the shooting box, and saw that her only hope was the ditch. Like a child scurrying on all fours across a living room carpet she started crawling down the side of the hill in the ditch. She didn't know how far she'd got, but she knew that within minutes, the soldier would see her. She shut her mind to the possibility of being shot in the back, and then, as if the moorland Gods had suddenly taken pity on her, she fell through some thick grass into a deeper section of the roadside stream.

The freezing water ran down the side of the road, beneath her, and soaked her clothes. She ignored it, rolled over, and looked up. She realised that she must have been two feet down in the ditch with thick, moorland grass above her. As quick as a flash, she adjusted it so that she couldn't see any sky. She looked down at her feet and saw that they were covered, too. She heard footsteps coming down the road and thought that the beating of her heart was going to give away her position. She clapped her hands over her mouth and tried to remain as still as possible.

The footsteps stopped close by. She heard some movement, and then a match being struck. She gathered that the soldier had stopped to light a cigarette. The spent match fell into the grass above her head, and then she heard a whistle blow in the distance. She heard the scuffling of boots, and then the sound of running away.

Not daring to breathe, she lay stock still, aware that her clothes were now saturated. She wasn't sure how much time had elapsed, but then she heard two shots, followed by a third. Her heart rate increased again, and she was filled with a terrible feeling of anxiety about her two friends.

Shivering like crazy, petrified, and filled with deep foreboding, she lay for hours in the stream, not daring to move. She didn't know if she'd be able to survive until dark, but she remained silent and still even as she heard a procession of trucks trundle past in convoy. Then hypothermia took over, and she slipped into unconsciousness.

"She's waking ..."

Eleanor opened her eyes and saw a kind-looking older woman peering down at her. Next, the weather-beaten face of an older man come into view, and she heard him say, "How are you, lass?" She looked around and saw that she was in a small bedroom. She said, "Where am I?"

"Stoops Farm," said the man. "I'm Gerry Butterworth the farmer, and this is my good lady wife, Mabel."

Eleanor pushed herself up onto her elbows and said, "How did I get here?"

"Patch found you after t'Ministry of Defence lads declared the all-clear." Gerry nodded towards his black and white sheepdog, sitting in the corner of the room. "And it's a miracle you survived. You were so cold when 'e found you, that I thought you were a goner; and if it weren't fort' missus 'ere, and 'er 'omemade broth, I doubt you'd still be with us."

Eleanor didn't know what to say. She wanted to ask about Zeena and Sandi, but instead said, "The all-clear?"

"Bless 'er soul," said Mabel looking at her husband, "I told you that she wouldn't remember owt." She looked back at Eleanor and said, "After the accident love, up on yon moor."

"Accident? What accident?"

"On Sat'day, after they tested that bomb thing."

Before she could stop herself, Eleanor said, "What - *The Halo*?" She saw Mabel frown, and then heard Gerry say, "Language, lass, if you don't mind. We know you've been though it an' all, but we try to keep a civil tongue in 'ere."

Eleanor frowned and realised that they must have thought she'd said, "What the hell." She looked up at Gerry and said, "Sorry, I didn't mean to cause offence," she saw Gerry nod, and then said, "but what 'bomb thing'?"

"Lord 'elp us," said Mabel, "you must be in a bad way if you've forgotten that."

Eleanor looked at Mabel and said, "I'm sorry, what happened again?"

Gerry pulled a chair next to the bed and sat down. He looked at Mabel and said, "I'll tell 'er, you put kettle on." He waited until his wife had departed and then said, "What's your name, lass?"

Eleanor nearly said her name, but then hesitated. She recalled the name of her old Sunday school teacher and said, "Violet, Violet Burgess."

"Right, Violet," Gerry paused and then said, "You don't mind me callin' you Violet do you?"

Eleanor said, "No, not all."

Gerry smiled and then said, "Good: right, it seems that old man Bagshaw 'oo owns that small croft ont' top of Tatham Fell, gave the Ministry of Defence permission to let off one of their new-fangled chemical bombs, the same as they used int' Great War like. It wasn't supposed to be a big 'un, they said, so 'e let 'em do it. Like as not, they paid him a goodly amount of brass, or 'e'd never 'ave agreed int' first place.

"Any'ow, by all accounts summat went wrong – a change int' wind direction they said – and before we knew it, we 'ad soldiers knockin' ont' doors and tellin' us to stay inside until it were safe to leave. It were a right buggers-muddle by all accounts."

"And when was that?" said Eleanor.

"They first come knockin' on Sat'day afternoon." Gerry paused, frowned, and then said, "but 'ow come you was out and about ont' moor like?"

"I wasn't aware of any restrictions, my ..." Eleanor was going to say that her car had broken down, but changed tack. She said, "... friends had told me how beautiful it was up here, and I was lucky enough to thumb a lift from the railway station. I was dropped off at the bottom of the brow and just walked up."

"And 'ow comes you ended up int' ditch?"

"The heel broke off my shoe; I lost my balance, and the next thing I knew I was here."

"Well first off, them shoes wasn't fit for 'ill climbin', but 'avin' said that, I 'ave repaired t'eel for thee ..."

Eleanor said, "Oh, thank you very much."

Gerry nodded and then continued, "... and second, you must have fallen over and banged your 'ead as you fell int' ditch." He paused and then added, "And when t'lad over there ..." he indicated towards Patch. "... found you, it didn't look like you was long for this world neither."

Eleanor looked down and saw that she was wearing a thick cotton nightdress. She said, "Who?"

"Mabel – and don't worry, she dried your clothes for when you're ready to leave."

Eleanor looked at the bedroom window and saw that it was light. She said, "What time is it please?"

Gerry pulled a pocket-watch out of his waistcoat and said, "'alf-past-nine."

Eleanor looked out of the window and repeated, "Half-past-nine?"

"Yes lass: you've been 'ere since yest'day afternoon."

"It's Wednesday?"

"Aye, all day."

Eleanor was shocked, she said, "I have to get back to my friends, they'll be wondering where I am."

"That's all right, lass," said Gerry, "as soon as you feel fit enough, we'll take you t'station int' motor."

An hour-and-a-half later, at 11 a.m., Eleanor climbed into Gerry's Morris 8 car and closed the door.

"All set lass?"

Eleanor nodded and said, "Before we go to the station, would you be kind enough to take me up to the top of the moor so that I can see it in all its glory before I go?"

"I'll do my best lass, but old Betsy here," Gerry patted the steering wheel and said, "is a Morris 8. They have the reputation for needing to drop a gear if you was to drive over a penny."

Eleanor smiled and watched as they made their way from the farm to Turnerford Brow and then up the hill. She saw nothing as she passed the number seven shooting box, nothing as they passed the corrugated steel shed, and nothing else to indicate that anybody had been there at all.

"Shame about sheep."

Eleanor turned and said, "What about them?"

"Seems MOD lads had to kill 'em in case they was infected like."

Eleanor recalled the men with guns, and then said, "Do you come up here often, Gerry?"

"I 'ave no cause; my land's back down brow, and by the time I've finished work of a day, I 'ave no mind or inclination to go wandering."

The car breasted Keasden Head and Gerry pointed through his windscreen. He said, "That's Bagshaw's land over yonder."

"Where they let the bomb off?"

"Aye, do you see all t'burned grass like?"

Eleanor said, "Yes," but she wasn't looking at where Gerry was pointing. She was looking for the private approach road to the K1 research facility.

It had gone.

Chapter 32

Ulyana Vetochkin led Detective Inspector Wood into her lounge and gestured towards a chair. She said, "Do you have the assurances that Evelyn and I won't be prosecuted, in writing?"

Wood reached into his jacket pocket and handed over a piece of paper.

Ulyana looked at the letter-headed Metropolitan Police note signed by Wood's Chief Superintendent, and saw that whilst it guaranteed that neither she nor Evelyn Picard would be subject to prosecution, it did state that there was no guarantee that the information provided would be acted upon, and that it may have to remain secret for the duration of its classification period in accordance with the Official Secrets Act 1911 - 1989.

She looked at Wood and said, "May I keep this?"

"It's your copy."

Ulyana thanked Wood, folded the document, and placed it in her handbag. She said, "Before we start, would you like a drink?"

"No thank you, I'm anxious to hear what you have to say."

Ulyana perched down on the edge of her settee, faced Wood, and clasped her hands on her lap. She said, "Okay: let's start with McCready House," she looked down for a second and then continued, "McCready House was the ultra-secret headquarters of a pre-war, weapons development unit that few people knew about. And when I say few Inspector, I mean very few. Not even Neville Chamberlain the PM at the time, his top ministers, or his civil servants knew anything about it.

"The unit, codenamed K1, was situated at a secret location in Yorkshire, and its function was to 'develop a devastating and demoralising weapon, hitherto unknown by man'. At its head was a Jewish, German Physicist named Professor Karl Hallenbeck who'd been given sanctuary in the UK in return for helping to develop the weapon. His remit, and the funding to develop it, had been given to him by the then head of the Secret Intelligence Service, Admiral Sir Iain Vincent, known to us in the field, as 'the controller' or 'C'."

She stopped and asked, "Do you want to take notes?"

Wood shook his head and said, "Given the OSA restrictions, no thanks."

"OSA?"

"Official Secrets Act."

"Ah yes, of course," Ulyana re-composed herself and continued. "The staff at McCready House consisted of three men and six women, of who three remain with us today: me, obviously, Mademoiselle Picard, and Lady Jocelyn Fitton-Kearns, who owned the property and who was the team leader of the women's section."

"Lady Jocelyn owned McCready House?"

"Yes, and she had given the SIS permission to use it, maybe in return for some remuneration?"

"Did she remain living there while it was in use by the SIS?"

"Yes."

"And do the three of you still live in London?"

"No, Jocelyn lives in Bournemouth with her long-term lady companion, and though she's getting on in years – as are all the rest of us – I understand that she's still as sharp as a pin."

Wood nodded but said nothing.

"Each member of the unit, at McCready House and K1, were given cards with the name 'B A Ware' upon, and a contact number to ring in the event of an emergency, and anybody ringing that number would activate a red phone at McCready House." She looked at Wood and added, "The one that's been bleeping."

Wood was surprised, and said, "You know about that?"

"I do."

"Then do you know who activated it?"

"Please let me finish. The red phone had a second function; it would also activate if anybody at K1 had thrown an emergency switch which was located in the central lab. It had been installed there in case the staff had become incapacitated, or if contact had been impossible in any other way.

"Our orders were to respond to the voice calls, and to transfer the callers to specific members of the service; or in the event of the emergency signal being received, to deploy a military response unit from the Special Operations Executive based at Claughton in Lancashire."

Wood nodded and said, "Was there any way to tell the difference between a voice call and the emergency signal from K1?"

"Yes; if it was a voice call the phone would ring and the centre of the dial would flash; if it was the emergency signal, the centre of the dial would flash but the phone would bleep. If this happened we were instructed to push the centre of the dial, and we would be transferred to the SOE in Claughton."

Wood raised his eyebrows at the thought of missing something as simple as pushing the centre of the dial and then said, "And are you saying that's what's happened now? That somebody has activated the emergency response?"

"No, that would be impossible after all this time, but there may be something to explain it.

"At the beginning of November 1937, we were informed that K1 had been shut down and that a new unit codenamed K2 had been set up in Skelmersdale, Lancashire. According to our senior officers, K1 had been closed because the staff there had been given new instructions to concentrate on developing chemicals for use in weapons, rather than developing a weapon itself. We were told that this measure had been a twofold one. One, to cut costs, because the new unit had been specifically built to meet the working requirements of the team, and two, that if the work at K2 had ever been uncovered by a foreign power, it could be explained away as Britain developing new vaccines to aid field-deployed, allied, armed forces."

"And you all bought that did you?"

"Nobody questioned it. Our type of work was such that we weren't always meant to know what was going on in the departments around us, and we were chosen for our positions because we were the types who didn't ask questions." Ulyana paused and then added, "Except for one person I recall, who became the subject of a nationwide search by MI5, for years."

"Why, what had he done?"

"Not a 'he' Inspector, a 'she'. She was Doctor Eleanor Drake, a dissenter from K1 who threatened to expose the work going on there."

"Why did she do that?"

"Because she disagreed with what they'd come up with."

"So a weapon had been developed?"

"Apparently."

"What was it?"

"We weren't given details."

"Was it ever deployed?"

"I don't know."

Wood began to get the feeling that Ulyana was becoming evasive. He tried one last direct question. "Was the development of the weapon the reason K1 was shut down?"

Ulyana remained calm, and considered the ramifications of a speculative answer, despite the Inspector's assurances. She played safe and said, "No, it was because of costs."

"And what happened to the weapon?"

"It, and everything to do with it, was scrapped."

"Was Doctor Drake ever found?"

"Not as far as I know."

Wood pondered for a few seconds and then said, "Okay – you said that there may have been something to explain why the red phone was bleeping now?"

"Yes: I was on duty the night K1 was shut down. It was the Saturday after bonfire night I recall, which would have been the sixth of November 1937. The red phone began bleeping just before midnight. I pushed the centre of the dial, but heard nothing. At first I thought that there was a line fault and I called my senior officer, Jocelyn. She listened in and then informed me that she would take over. She disappeared into her office, and then reappeared minutes later and told me that she'd contacted Military HQ, and that everything was in hand. Thereafter, I didn't think any more about it."

"Were you aware that K1 had already been shut down when you received the red phone signal?"

"No, we learned about it the next day."

"Did you link the two occurrences?"

"The closure and the call? No."

"Did you ever hear the red phone activate again?"

"No, I didn't, but according to Jocelyn, over the course of the next year, it did begin bleeping again three more times. She told me that on each occasion she'd contacted C's office and had been told to leave it up to them."

"Didn't Lady Jocelyn ever question *why* the phone began bleeping again?"

"Yes; she came up with a theory that somebody must have accidently thrown the emergency switch before leaving K1, and that its signal had been curtailed by cutting the power to it; and that on subsequent occasions, when for whatever reason, the power had been re-connected, it re-activated the phone."

Wood frowned and said, "So why didn't she ask somebody to go back to K1 and turn the emergency switch off?"

"Because all traces of the unit had been obliterated."

Wood's alarm bells activated; he said, "Obliterated? How, and why?"

"The 'how', I don't know, but I understand that the modern idiom for 'why', is plausible deniability, Inspector."

Wood said, "Yes, so I believe." He thought for a second or two and then said, "But that doesn't make sense; if the unit had been obliterated, how could the signal still emanate from there once the power had been switched back on?"

"I have no idea, Inspector."

"Okay, but Lady Jocelyn must have questioned the same thing?"

"You'll have to talk to her about that."

Wood felt the evasiveness begin to return; he said, "Okay," and put his left hand up to his mouth; he stared at Ulyana's impassive face for a few seconds and then said, "Couldn't Lady Jocelyn have had the red phone disconnected at Macready House?"

"Ah, now we come to it, Inspector. As the years passed by, Jocelyn became less convinced that the phone would only activate when the power was re-connected to the K1 signal. She would often say to me, 'What if somebody with a 'B A Ware' card, like the missing Doctor Drake, wants to make contact: how would they stand a chance if I disconnected the phone?' She became obsessed by it, and even when the SIS shut down ops at McCready House after the outbreak of war, she had the desk, the phone, and the picture of King George preserved and walled up, so that there would always be that capability."

"And sealed up in the void?"

"She didn't have the void sealed until she sold Macready House nine years' ago. Up until then, there was a door into it."

"And *did* anybody ever make contact?"

"If they did, she never told me."

Wood nodded, took stock, and then said, "Did you ever visit the K1 site?"

"No."

"Did you know where it was located?"

"In Keasden, North Yorkshire – hence the 'K' in K1."

Wood frowned and shook his head on hearing the name Keasden again.

Ulyana saw and said, "Inspector?

Wood said, "Circles within circles."

"I don't follow."

"Circles within circles Ulyana. Both BT and Drax Power have traced the live signal to an old temperance hall in Keasden, but there, the telephone line sinks into the ground, and moves underground towards Keasden Beck."

"Keasden Beck; now there's a name I've not heard since those times."

"Does it have a particular significance for you?"

Ulyana thought for a second or two and then said, "Perhaps not: I do recall hearing some people refer to the unit as Keasden Beck as well as K1, but I never knew the difference."

"The difference is, K1 was the name of the unit, and Keasden Beck is the name of a small river."

Ulyana nodded and said, "And when that telephone line got to Keasden Beck, where did it go to then?"

"The engineers couldn't trace it."

"Why?"

"They said that it went too deep into the ground."

"If it was that deep, how did the nineteen-thirties telephone engineers lay it in the first place?"

Wood didn't know what to say; he opened his mouth to respond but nothing he thought of sounded rational. He drew in a deep breath and then saw Ulyana stand up, walk across to her window, and look out. He said, "You okay?"

Ulyana turned and said, "You said that the line went to an old temperance hall and then sank into the ground?"

"Yes."

"Where, inside or outside?"

Wood hesitated and then said, "I didn't ask."

"Then, has anybody looked below the floor?"

Wood was shocked; he could have kicked himself.

Ulyana saw and said, "Not thought of that?"

Wood pursed his lips and said, "I'm supposed to be the Detective Inspector here, but I've become so engrossed in the multi-tangled web of everything, I didn't ask the most obvious question."

He stood up, shook Ulyana's hand and said, "I need to go, but I'll be in touch, I promise."

Ulyana watched Wood head towards the door and then said, "May I be permitted to see inside the void at Macready House?"

"Yes of course."

"And may Evelyn come with me?"

"Certainly, it'll be a pleasure to meet her." Wood turned to go, but then remembered something. He turned back and said, "The last time that we met you asked me if the picture of King George was in the void. Why?"

"Curiosity Inspector: before Jocelyn moved to Bournemouth she gave me a small key that unlocks a part of the frame."

"Unlocks the frame? I inspected every last inch of it, and I couldn't see any indication of anything that would unlock."

"You weren't meant to."

"What does it unlock?"

"A small compartment that contains the name and contact details of the person who'd been assigned to run K2, from K1."

"Professor Hallenbeck?"

"No, definitely not him; we were told that after K1 had closed, he and his wife had re-located to the USA."

Wood said, "Okay, I'll try to locate them through our American counterparts," he turned to exit again, and then heard Ulyana say, "And that's not all." He turned once more and said, "Go on."

"Over the years Jocelyn became convinced that there was more to K2 than met the eye. It operated under the name of the St Mary Cross Animal Research Unit."

"An animal testing place?"

"They didn't have the same stigma then Inspector, and vaccines, those days, always had to be tested on animals first."

"So what made Lady Jocelyn suspicious?"

"Even after it had been sold in the nineteen-eighties, Jocelyn told me that she had seen sporadic news items about people going missing near there, and she was convinced that it had something to do with whoever was still running K2."

"*Still running K2?* But you said that it had been sold in the eighties?"

"It had, to a company named Ascensis, but Jocelyn remained steadfast that something still wasn't right about the place."

"And you say that the name of the person who'd been assigned to run it by the SIS, is in that frame?"

"Yes; but please don't attempt to get to it without my help, because it has a small charge attached to it that will destroy the document inside, unless it's opened in the correct sequence."

Wood shook his head and said, "My God, Ulyana Vetochkin, you continue to amaze me, he paused and then said, "I'll clear all of this with my Chief Superintendent, and then collect you and Mam'selle Picard for a visit to McCready House as soon as I can. I'll also contact the police in Lancashire to see if they can come up with anything on that building in Skelmersdale, and then I'll ask the police in Yorkshire to do a bit of digging at that temperance hall."

Ulyana nodded and said, "Good, that's a start."

Wood shook hands with Ulyana and said, "Thank you; you may have changed everything." He smiled, turned, and went back out to the waiting police car with more questions than he'd arrived with.

Chapter 33

Crowthorne looked around the room and saw Uniformed Duty Inspector Peter Milnes, Detective Sergeants Tasha Andrew and Leo Chance, and Detective Constable Roger Walburn sitting and looking at him. He said, "Thank you all for coming: on the twenty-second of this month a decision was taken to encourage Naomi Wilkes, whom I know you are all aware of," he cast a glance across to Tasha and Walburn.

Tasha and Walburn had both been injured by Adrian Darke's thugs whilst on night protection duty watching over Naomi. Tasha had been punched in the face by a man wearing silk gloves, causing her a terrible facial injury, and Walburn had been shot in the chest with a taser.

"The decision was prompted by intelligence received that Darke was still alive and that he may have been planning some sort of personal vendetta against her; but as you know, events took a turn when some of Darke's top generals began being assassinated." He paused, looked from face to face, and then said, "And it's happened again." He saw a look of shock

271

appear on everybody's face except Leo's, whom he knew from old, never showed any emotion about anything like that.

"Good grief, sir," said Tasha, "do we have a name?"

"We do: Garrett Hinchcliffe. He was Darke's number one, his top man."

"My God, that's going to hurt the son of a bitch."

"How was he despatched, sir?" said Walburn.

"He was strapped into the driver's seat of his car, propelled onto a level crossing, and hit at ninety miles-per-hour by the London to Manchester express, near Wilmslow."

"The incident that was reported on the news yesterday?" asked Milnes.

"The same."

"It's damned lucky that the assassin didn't kill a whole raft of people with stunt like that," said Milnes.

Crowthorne looked up and said, "Apparently not: according to the driver of the train, the crossing was clear until he was almost upon it. At the last moment the car surged through, and his engine only hit the bonnet, sending it spinning off into the trackside bushes. He recorded in his statement that it looked as though the incident had been timed to cause the least effect on the speeding train."

"Nobody was killed or injured either, were they, sir?" said Walburn.

"No they weren't, in fact not many knew that an incident had taken place until the train made the unscheduled stop."

Leo said, "Another professional hit, and another huge statement to Darke. He must be going ape right now."

"Not so: we haven't released Hinchcliffe's name. My contact in the Cheshire Force was aware of my interest in Darke and his cronies, and when they identified Hinchcliffe's body, he called me. As a consequence they've released a statement stating that to date; the driver of the car remains unidentified."

Leo nodded and said, "Same assassin, sir?"

"If not, then whoever's doing it, are in cahoots. The same warning that was on Sheldon's jacket, was found pinned to Hinchcliffe's, too."

"What was it again, sir?" said Milnes.

"Venio – Latin for 'I am coming'."

"Seems a shame we can't let Darke know that Hinchcliffe was hit," said Tasha, "I'd love to see the panic on his face." She reached up and touched the three-inch scar on her cheek.

"That had been my plan, too," said Crowthorne, "but something else has come up and muddied the water." He looked around and saw the eager, attentive faces looking at him like wolves at feeding time. He said, "Part of the plan had been to get Naomi Wilkes out of the Walmsfield area by asking her to aid the Lancashire force in an investigation into the disappearance of two women. The link had been an ex-animal research laboratory owned by a Romanian Company, named Ascensis. We had thought that this would amount to nothing more than an intriguing distraction for her, but, and it is a big but, I probably should have known better.

"In Naomi's inimitable style, and with Leo here watching her from a discreet distance, she uncovered more than we'd bargained for, because whilst she was on the case, not only did she, and Leo, hear an unusual sound emanate from a supposedly deserted building, but also, another man went missing, who is to date, still unaccounted for.

"In the company of the dog section we searched the building, and the dog picked up some confusing signals which resulted in us detailing forensics there, but so far, nothing has been found to account for the unusual sound."

Tasha said, "Sorry to interrupt, sir, but what kind of sound was it?"

Crowthorne looked at Leo and said, "Leo?"

"It was difficult to identify; my first instinct was that it was animal. It was a high-pitched wail, as though something was being subjected to pain."

"Which would fit in with where you were," said Tasha.

"Yes, but as Superintendent Crowthorne said, we carried out an extensive search of the place, and found nothing to account for it."

"Have you got any construction plans for it?"

"Stop," said Crowthorne, "now we've come to the main reason for the meeting."

All eyes turned to look at him.

Crowthorne looked at Leo, and then turned to face the others. He said, "I won't go into detail now, but during his investigation, Leo had uncovered an unusual link to the Ascensis facility in Skelmersdale. He, like you, Tasha, decided that the best plan of action would be to obtain the plans for the building, but when he tried to locate them, there weren't any to be found." He stopped and then said, "Perhaps Leo should continue."

Leo nodded and then said, "I tried every avenue to locate anything to do with the construction of the building, but found nothing. No construction company records, no architectural company records, no planning permission records – it was crazy, it was as though the building had just materialised out of nowhere, and nobody knew anything about it."

"What about Council Business Rates?" said Walburn.

Leo shook his head and said, "When I contacted the Council department responsible, they hadn't even heard of the Ascensis facility."

"That's impossible," said Milnes, "what about the other services – electricity, water, sewage?"

"You think?" said Leo. "There are no accounts anywhere for any services to and from that facility."

"Good Lord," said Tasha, "how intriguing: what did you do next?"

"I went to Skelmersdale Library and started trawling through their old newspapers. There I got lucky. I found a newspaper article dating from 1973, reporting the disappearance of a woman named Violet Burgess, one of the women that Naomi had been sent to investigate, and it mentioned that she'd been employed by the St Mary Cross Animal Research Unit in Skelmersdale, which had been the name of the facility before it changed to Ascensis. No more information was forthcoming from that particular newspaper, but at the end of it, there was cross-reference to what must have been a local rag. A newspaper named the 'The Skelmersdale Bugle'. I found the article, and in it, there was reference to an interview with an elderly local who had let it slip that the building had once been named 'K2', and that it had been owned by the Ministry of Defence.

"Next I phoned the MOD in London and got put through to somebody who wouldn't reveal his name. I told him that I was investigating the disappearance of two women that had been linked to their K2 building in Skelmersdale. I was put on hold for about ten minutes, and then transferred to another man who wouldn't identify himself. He asked me where I'd picked up the name 'K2' and I, thinking that we were on the same side, told him. He then told me in no uncertain terms, that anything to do with that building was highly classified under the Official Secrets Act until the year 2087 no less, and that any investigations into the history, construction, or personnel of the facility, up to, and including the year 1953, would be dealt with, with extreme force."

Walburn couldn't help himself, he said, "Bloody hell!"

"Yes," said Leo, "tell me about it!"

"And what happened next?" said Tasha.

"I was about to challenge the statement, but the phone was put down on me."

"And that was it?" said Milnes.

"Not quite," said Leo, "following that episode, I returned to Skelmersdale Library intent on printing out the article from The Skelmersdale Bugle, but when I searched the records, it had gone."

Tasha frowned and said, "How long after the phone call to the MOD, did you go back to the library?"

"Just short of two hours."

"And it had already gone?"

"Yes."

"So in less than two hours, somebody went there, accessed the records, and deleted them?"

"Yes."

"Did the library staff see anybody do that?"

"No."

"Amazing," said Walburn, "those guys don't bugger about do they?"

"More to the point," said Crowthorne "is where that leaves us now."

"Pretty obvious isn't it, sir?" said Milnes, "We back the hell away, and drop the investigation."

"If only: I received a telephone call from Detective Inspector Wood of the Metropolitan Police at Hampstead Heath, informing me that he was on his way here to liaise with me about a building in Skelmersdale, previously owned and run by a department of MI5, named K2."

"God in Heaven," exclaimed Tasha, "does he know about Leo's warning?"

"No," said Crowthorne, the message was left on my desk by the 10 p.m.-to-6 am, duty Inspector, who received it at 5:30 a.m. this morning."

"So he's already on his way here?"

"Yes he is."

"Right," said Leo, "what are your orders?"

"We listen to what Inspector Wood has to say about K2 without divulging the warnings received from the MOD, next, Leo, Tasha and Roger will continue their investigations into St Mary Cross and Ascensis without attracting any unwanted attention."

"And me, sir?" said Milnes.

"You'll be the front, the implacable face of this investigation, who knows nothing about any MOD involvement, only about our enquiries into the missing persons." He saw everybody nod their acceptance and then said, "But first and absolute foremost, we stop Naomi Wilkes going anywhere near that building."

One hour later, in the Historic Research Department of Walmsfield Borough Council, Naomi looked across at Helen and said, "I'm going to tell you something, and you aren't going to like it."

Helen stopped writing and looked up. She said, "Go on."

"I'm going to that Ascensis facility on my own."

"Oh no you are not!" said Helen.

"Oh yes I am, and neither you, nor anybody else will stop me."

Helen let out an exasperated gasp, and said, "Have you forgotten …"

"I haven't forgotten anything," said Naomi with gritty determination, "and I am going! Now, I really could do with your help; are you with me or not?"

Helen knew that it was impossible to stop Naomi when she had the bit between her teeth. She said, "Okay, okay, when are you planning to go?"

"Tomorrow at 9:30 p.m."

"Oh bloody hell," said Helen, "night time; are you kidding?" She saw Naomi's set face and knew that it was pointless to argue. She drew in a deep breath and said, "Okay, but it doesn't give us much time to plan."

Naomi said, "It's plenty. I made Val Lockyer a promise, and in the course of trying to find her mum and daughter we lost Rod Carroll, too. Now I've had enough; we're going to find out what's going on at that poxy site come hell or high water!"

Chapter 34

"All report," C looked at his inner circle of trusted staff and his eyes lighted upon Tryon. He said, "You first, Captain."

Tryon stood up and said, "The closure of K1 is complete."

C continued looking at Tryon in silence until he realised that the report was finished. He said, "Is that it?"

"Yes, sir."

"A full, level one response?"

"Yes, sir."

C glanced across to Buckley and then to Colonel Paul Stansfield-Smith the leader of the undercover Military Unit deployed to K1. He said, "Did everything go according to plan, Colonel?"

"Mostly, sir."

C glared and said, "Mostly? What do you mean, mostly? This was supposed to be a level one response!"

Stansfield-Smith kept his ice-cold, grey eyes on 'C's flustered face and didn't respond.

"Well?" said C, "Are you going to enlighten me?"

"You know that I was against this measure, sir, do you really want all of the gory details?"

C felt his prickliness rise. He said, "No of course not damn it, just those that occasioned the word 'mostly'!"

279

Stansfield-Smith sat forwards in his seat and placed a stack of business cards on the briefing room table. He said, "These are all of the 'B A Ware' cards from K1, minus one. All but three of them were found on site, two were then located on Turnerford Brow, and the third is still missing."

C turned to Buckley and said, "I thought that you'd timed this operation to coincide with all the staff being on duty at K1?"

"I did, sir," said Buckley, "but there is no accounting for happenstance."

"Go on..."

"Three female members were meant to be on site at 0800 Zulu. Two had attempted to get there in their motor car but it had broken down. During their walk up Turnerford Brow they'd seen another member of the K1 staff being pursued by the Colonel's men, and then eliminated. They'd then been found hiding in a sheep shed."

"And the third, had she been with the other two?"

"Impossible to say, sir."

"Didn't the Colonel's men question the two in the shed?!"

Buckley looked down and then back up. He said, "No they didn't."

C couldn't believe his ears; he banged his clenched fist down on his desk and yelled, "*How many more times am I going to hear this?* It's incompetence, sheer, unadulterated, bloody, incompetence!" He glared at Buckley and then said. "We spend thousands of pounds training our men to ask questions first, not bloody shoot!" He looked around the table and saw that everybody except Stansfield-Smith was looking down. He made an exasperated sound, got up, and walked across to his office window. He watched a barge chugging down the Thames towards Tower Bridge until his jangling nerve-ends steadied. He then returned to his seat and said, "Right, who's missing?"

Buckley knew that C wasn't going to like what he was about to say. He drew in a deep breath and said, "Doctor Drake."

For a split-second nothing registered, and then the penny dropped. C said, "Wasn't she one of …?"

"The dissenters? Yes, sir."

C felt a physical tightening around his temples. He glared at Buckley with a mixture of raging anger, and unadulterated contempt. He said, "My God in bloody Heaven; isn't that just perfect?!"

Buckley looked down at the table and remained quiet.

C glared daggers at Buckley and then got up and walked back to the window. The barge disappeared under Tower Bridge. He felt his heart hammering, and right then he wanted more than anything, to be on the boat, leading the simple, uncomplicated life of a river-boat skipper.

He wasn't aware of how long he remained staring out of the window, but by the time that he'd returned to his seat, his nerves had calmed, and nobody had spoken a word.

He looked at Buckley and said, "Could Doctor Drake have been with the other women on Turnerford Brow?"

"It's impossible to say sir: the men only reported seeing two women, and they were both accounted for. Their car was found some time later, and disposed of in the usual manner."

"And?"

"And everything is being done to locate her. The police have been informed that she's wanted for questioning by the SIS. Her friends and family are being watched day and night. All of the telephone exchanges within a hundred mile radius of her family are on the alert for anybody asking to speak to any of them, and we have detailed three of our top men to search for her."

C nodded and said, "Has anybody here, or anywhere else, ever her seen her face-to-face?"

"Only *our* man from K1, sir."

"Do we have any photographs of her?"

Buckley knew that his answer would be contentious; he looked at C and said, "They've all gone."

"Gone? Gone? How the hell has that happened?"

"Doctor Drake is a very intelligent woman, sir; we believe that she must have accessed her file and removed all of her photographic records."

"What about her I.D. photo?"

"That, too, sir."

C shook his head, ruminated for a second, and then drew in a deep breath. He said, "Damn the woman!" He turned to Buckley and said, "What about the press?"

"We've given them her full description and told them that she'd been uncovered as a German spy who'd been working on a top-secret project for British Military Intelligence. We also told them that she may now be hoping to divulge what she'd been working on in exchange for a ticket to freedom. They know that if they are approached, they must agree to her terms, but to contact us immediately."

He paused and then added, "But there is a caveat: not only is Doctor Drake an intelligent woman, she is resourceful, too.

"At the outbreak of the Spanish Civil War, she'd been working in Seville with the Republican Spanish Army. She was then captured by one of Franco's Military Units and interred in the castle there. Through her guile and wits alone, she escaped, and made her way uncaught, right across Spain, crossing into France twenty miles south of Perpignan."

C raised his eyebrows and said, "Impressive, but I want her eliminated as soon as possible. No questions and no considerations, understand?"

"Yes, sir."

C turned to Royal Engineers Colonel Martin Chivers and said, "What about the terra-forming?"

"Complete, sir."

"No sign?"

"Nothing, sir."

"And the locals?"

"No problems encountered."

"Relatives?"

Chivers said, "Please don't trouble yourself, sir, everything, and I mean everything, is accounted for."

C sat back in his chair and said, "Good: now, I want K2 up and running as soon as possible, and we are to continue our research into the production of chemical weapons and antidotes. We've received intelligence that Hitler's Nazi lunatics are developing new devices, so if they're prepared to use them on us, then by God, we'll be ready with a robust response." He paused and then added, "Unlike K1, this unit has the full backing of the PM and the Joint Chiefs of Staff, but it, and all of its activities, are to be kept ultra-top secret. Any breaches by any members of staff are to be handled with immediate effect, and the offenders are to be taken to the facility in St Mary's – understood?" He saw nods of agreement all around.

"Given his unique qualities, and being the only person who can identify Doctor Drake, our man from K1 will head the new unit. I want all of you to do everything in your power to protect his identity and to assist him wherever it's needed. You will have unlimited resources at your disposal to achieve that end.

"I will convey to him that Doctor Drake is at large, and that if he ever encounters her, he is to detain her until we arrive.

"Now, does anybody have any questions?"

Tryon put his finger up and said, "Changing tack, sir, can you tell us what happened on the night of the second test?"

C pondered for a few seconds and then said, "Yes, it seems that providence was on our side for once. The vessel that went missing was M34, an old Coastal Monitor named *HMS Spartan* that had been on patrol duties in the Irish Sea. She had been ordered to carry four members of the IRA High Command from Belfast to Fleetwood."

"Ouch!" said Tryon.

"Ouch indeed, Captain: but as I said, providence had been on our side. By all accounts certain members of HM Government had been trying to broker a deal with the IRA to join forces with the UK in the event of conflict breaking out between us and Germany. In return for this accord, the Government was going to return Northern Ireland back to the Irish."

Several sharp intakes of breath could be heard around the table and C halted his narrative.

"Return a United Ireland to the Irish?" said an incredulous Stansfield-Smith.

"That was the notion, yes."

Stansfield-Smith shook his head and said, "That would never have worked. Too many unionists would have been up in arms."

"And not only the unionists," said C. "Certain factions of the IRA didn't want it either.

"The mayday that was intercepted by *HMS Express* stated that there'd been an explosion in M34's boiler room that'd been triggered by an explosive device.

"The Captain had ordered the helmsman to head to shore and to hug the coastline until they reached the Duddon Channel north of Morecambe Bay. There they'd hoped to make it to nearby Haverigg. That was when they encountered the dirigible carrying *The Halo*.

"Hallenbeck had instructed the pilot to climb to three-hundred-and-fifty feet and to set the auto-pilot on a heading of 270 degrees. That would have taken the dirigible out of the channel and into the Irish Sea. He was then to set the timer, and to exit the gondola.

"But that didn't happen; the pilot set the timer *before* setting the auto-pilot, and then found that the auto-pilot was faulty …"

"Surely Hallenbeck's ground staff had checked the equipment prior to take off?" said Chivers.

C turned and said, "One would have thought so, Colonel." He paused long enough to convey suspicion, and then continued. "According to Professor Hallenbeck, the pilot then attempted to switch off the timing mechanism to the bomb, but realised that it couldn't be undone once it had been turned on. He tried again to activate the auto-pilot, but seeing that it was a lost cause, he parachuted out."

"Did the pilot give any indication about what had caused the failure, sir?" said Tryon.

"No he didn't: he saw that the compass heading was correct, threw the switch, and nothing happened. By all accounts he tried several times before bailing out."

Tryon raised his eyebrows, looked around the room, and saw that everybody appeared to be harbouring the same doubts.

"Anyway," said C re-commencing his narrative, "as the dirigible approached the mouth of the Duddon Channel it was hit on the port beam by a force three south-westerly that turned it into the path of the oncoming M34. Minutes later *The Halo* detonated, like as not killing everybody aboard. The ship's boilers then blew, sending her straight to the bottom.

"The Captain of the *Express* reported that he'd seen and heard the explosions in the distance, and that he'd presumed, following the first explosion, that the boilers had gone up, too. The only reservation in his report had been why the Captain of the *Spartan* hadn't ordered the 'abandon ship' before it all went up."

"And the IRA?" said Tryon.

C turned and said, "Unusually quiet: we thought that there'd be an absolute uproar, but instead, we've received what can only be described as 'puzzling messages of sympathy' for what had happened."

"Messages of sympathy?" repeated Chivers.

"Yes, which leads us to suspect that the bomb had been planted by IRA extremists in order to disrupt the planned meeting; and that when they'd heard what had happened, they'd presumed that the sinking had been their fault.

"The end result is, they've closed ranks, and said nothing but eulogies."

"I see what you mean when you said that providence had been on our side, sir," said Tryon.

C said, "Yes indeed, Captain."

He looked at his watch and then around the room. "Now," he said, "you all know what you have to do; and I have another meeting to attend."

Chapter 35

Crowthorne was an industrious man of routine; every day he would check and clear his in-tray of all the most pressing items, and then he would order a cup of coffee and ponder those items that required more thought. It was his work ethic; a practice that had served him well for all his years as a senior police officer, and one that meant nothing ever got overlooked. But since arriving in the office, nothing had been done, and he hadn't given his in-tray a single thought.

In his hand he held his departed mother's favourite letter-opener; it was made of stainless steel, and the handle had multi-coloured fine wires wrought around it in a dazzling, interwoven pattern. He liked the feel and weight of it, and whenever anything played on his mind, he'd pick it up and tap the blade on the sponge-based mouse mat next to his computer keyboard.

He stopped tapping, put the letter-opener down, sat back in his chair, and said out loud, "Oh come on Crowthorne, get a grip."

He was convinced that he'd missed some vital piece of evidence at the Ascensis building, but for the life of him, he couldn't think of what. There seemed to be nothing to account for the erratic behaviour of the dog or the sounds experienced by Naomi and Leo, and it was driving him crazy, and the last thing that he wanted, was to appear clueless if he was questioned by MI5.

His troubled rumination was interrupted when he heard a knock on his office door. He called, "Come in."

Milnes walked in and said, "Sorry to disturb you, sir, but D I Wood arrived a few minutes ago."

"Ah, where is he now?"

"I sent one of the lads to show him where the canteen and toilets were, so that you would have ten minutes to prepare."

"Thoughtful, Peter, thank you; let him finish his tea and then send him down."

Fifteen minutes later Milnes showed Wood into Crowthorne's office and departed. The two officers shook hands and settled into their seats.

"Good journey, Inspector?" said Crowthorne.

"Yes, thank you, sir; I have relatives who live in this neck of the woods and I always enjoy coming back."

"Have you got somewhere to stay?"

"With the relatives sir, yes."

"Good: then what have you got to tell me?"

Wood reached into his jacket pocket and placed his notebook on the corner of Crowthorne's desk. He then told Crowthorne about the events at McCready House, about its link to K1, the temperance hall, and MI5, and about his meeting with Ulyana Vetochkin, and by the time that he'd finished he hadn't referred to his notebook once.

Crowthorne sat in silence the whole time, but the mention of the link to the mysterious K1 had shown him that he was dealing with a much bigger problem than he'd first thought. He decided that Leo should be present and said, "Excuse me,

Inspector, I'm going to send for our Detective Sergeant Chance, he, too, is involved in this case."

A few minutes later there was a knock the door and Leo entered. The introductions were made and Wood recounted once more, all that had happened.

Leo listened with growing concern until at the end; he looked at Crowthorne and said, "This is a lot more involved than we first thought, sir, do you mind if I have a private word?"

Crowthorne looked at Wood and said, "Do you mind, Inspector?" he nodded towards his office door.

Wood said, "Not at all," and stepped out.

Leo waited until Wood had closed the office door, and then said, "Given the new circumstances I think that we should include D I Wood in everything we know."

"Agreed," said Crowthorne. He called Wood back in, and over the course of the next fifteen minutes, told him everything that they knew, about the missing people, the Ascensis site and its link to the Ministry of Defence, and MI5.

Wood, like Crowthorne before him, was just as shocked by the increased complexity of events, but digested it and then mooted the question, "Have you tried contacting anybody at MI5 about the Ascensis site?"

Crowthorne nodded towards Leo and said, "D S Chance did, and he was warned to back off. He was told that the building, its history, construction, and staffing, up to and including 1953, were classified until 2087, and that any investigations involving anything within that period, would be dealt with using extreme force."

"Extreme force?" exclaimed Wood. "Christ, that's either way over-the-top, or somebody being over-dramatic."

"It is," said Crowthorne, "but it does make us wonder why they're so sensitive about a building they abandoned in 1953."

"I should think so, too! Did they comment on your missing persons?"

"No, and they didn't impose any restrictions on us searching for them either."

Wood turned to Leo and said, "Did you tell them that you thought the missing persons were connected to their old site?"

"No," said Leo, "I told them that persons had gone missing near there, and asked them if they had any old construction plans. That's when they got shirty."

"So they have got something to hide?"

"You'd have to say so."

Wood pondered for a second or two and then said, "You said that the building had been purchased by a Romanian company?"

"Yes, Ascensis."

"And who are 'Ascensis'? Have you checked?"

Leo exchanged glances with Crowthorne and said, "No, sir, we haven't."

Wood made a 'Hmming' sound and then leaned back in his chair. He looked at Crowthorne and said, "I was tempted to ask your permission to check them out, sir, but I have a gut feeling about where it may lead us." He saw Crowthorne nod, turned to Leo and said, "And you searched the place from end-to-end without result and they still threatened you with 'extreme force'?"

"Not just me," said Leo, "anybody."

Wood turned to Crowthorne and said, "This is stating the obvious I know, but something's not right. In today's age we don't get bodies like MI5 threatening 'extreme force' unless it's in the fantasy world of stuff like James Bond films."

"I concur," said Crowthorne, "but the threat was made nevertheless."

"So where do we go from here, bearing in mind the threat?"

"Before I answer that, "said Crowthorne, "who are you dealing with in the Yorkshire and Lancashire forces?"

Wood said, "DCI Kelsall in Yorkshire, and DI Maurice Finney in Lancashire."

"Ah, I know them both," said Crowthorne, "they're good men."

"I know Howard Kelsall, sir," said Wood, "we were Cadets together in the Cheshire force before I transferred to the Met."

"So you're a local lad then?"

"Stockport to be exact, it's where I was born, and lived until my transfer in 1987." Wood thought of something else and said, "Getting back to our dilemma, has anybody contacted MI5 about the K1 site?"

"No," said Crowthorne, "and we have no intention of doing so. We've already had our fill of them, and we don't want any more threats hindering further investigations."

"So no men in black sniffing about then?"

"Not as far as we know, said Leo."

"Then we should keep any digging around at that old temperance hall very low key, too," said Crowthorne.

Wood said, "You say 'we', sir, don't you mean Howard's men?"

"No, most of Keasden Beck is in Yorkshire, but that temperance hall is just inside the Lancashire border."

"Hang on a minute," said Wood, "Ulyana Vetochkin was a precise woman. She told me that K1 was in Yorkshire, not Lancashire."

"Then the site of the facility must have been closer to Keasden Head than the temperance hall," said Crowthorne, "because the hall is in Lancashire."

Leo sat in silence pondering the new information and then a troubling thought crossed his mind. He said, "When are we planning to go to the hall?"

"I've spoken to Lancaster HQ and they've given us inter-force carte blanche, so I'd panned to go tomorrow, why?" said Crowthorne.

A feeling of unease began to manifest itself in Leo's chest. He frowned and said, "Has anybody from either force done *any* poking about up there yet?"

Wood looked at Leo, and frowned.

Crowthorne said, "What are you driving at?"

"To ask about gaining access for example?

"It's possible," said Crowthorne, "I did mention it to Inspector Milnes this morning."

The penny dropped, and Wood said, "No, no, no ..."

The remark was lost on Crowthorne; he frowned and said, *"What?"*

Leo said, "Couldn't any kind of poking around up there put us on MI5's radar?"

Crowthorne gasped and said, "Bugger, I hadn't thought of that!"

Leo leapt to his feet and said, "Excuse me, sir, I need to check right now."

Crowthorne said, "Yes, and while you're at it, find out where Naomi Wilkes is."

"Will do," Leo almost ran out of the room.

Wood looked at the retreating figure of Leo, and then turned to Crowthorne. He said, "I get the feeling that this is morphing into something much darker and more serious than we first thought, sir."

"Yes," said Crowthorne. He sat back in his chair, picked up the letter-opener and began tapping it on the corner of his mouse mat.

Minutes later Leo tapped on the door, and let himself in. He said, "We're too late; a patrol car went to the temperance hall early this morning. The lads found it locked and drove to a nearby farmhouse to ask who owned it. The farmer told them that it was owned by a management company in London, and gave them a number to ring."

"No, please don't tell me ..." said Wood.

"They did, and they were put on hold. Several minutes later a woman asked who was calling. They said that they were from Greater Manchester Police investigating a case that required access to the old temperance hall at Keasden, at which point; they were put on hold again. A few minutes later they were told that they hadn't been able to contact the owner, but not to go anywhere near the place until they'd received the proper permission. The lads asked how long that could be, and were told that someone would ring Bury HQ tomorrow morning."

Wood looked at Crowthorne and raised his eyebrows.

"Great," said Crowthorne, "that's all we need."

Leo raised his eyebrows and said, "MI5, sir?"

Crowthorne nodded.

"My thoughts, too," said Wood.

Crowthorne sat back in his seat, pondered for a moment or two, and then said, "This is ridiculous: if that Russian lady was right about a secret weapons facility being shut down in 1937 for financial reasons alone, what the hell is all the fuss about? We've already had MI5 threatening us about their Skelmersdale site, and now we may have them sniffing around there, too!"

Wood looked at Leo and then at Crowthorne. He said, "What we need here gents, is a bit of lateral thinking, and a new approach."

Crowthorne looked sideways and said, "Go on."

"We need to be investigating a good old-fashioned break-in at that temperance hall."

Crowthorne guessed where the conversation was going, but knew that it would be illegal; and then in line with the lateral thinking process, a name popped into his mind. He looked at Leo and said, "Have you ever come across EMDW?"

Wood frowned and turned to face Crowthorne.

"No," said Leo, "but wasn't he or she the person you and Percy were talking about?"

"EMDW – Percy?" said Wood.

Crowthorne looked at Wood and said, "Postcard Percy is a local character who has helped us on numerous occasions. He and his unusual bunch of friends are something of amateur historians and sleuths and they've been an invaluable aid to Naomi Wilkes the historic researcher we told you about earlier. He's a prolific collector of memorabilia and old postcards; hence his nickname, and amongst his oddball chums is one known as EMDW."

"And what does EMDW stand for?" said Wood.

"Elementary, my dear Watson."

Wood and Leo frowned.

Crowthorne said, "EMDW, or EM for short, is Jewish, and was named Shylock Silverman, but whilst he was still a young boy, his parents divorced, and his mother married a gentile by the name of Philip Holmes. She and Shylock adopted the new surname which meant that poor lad became Shylock Holmes. He endured endless ribbing from school friends, workmates, and anybody else who found out his name, and in order to combat the mickey-taking, whenever anybody asked him a question, he would always precede his answer with, 'Elementary, my dear Watson'.

"Over time he became known as EMDW, which then shortened to EM."

"Okay," said Wood, "but what about him, and this Naomi Wilkes?"

Crowthorne said, "Don't worry about Naomi; she's under our wing for other reasons. But EM on the other hand, has a criminal record for breaking and entering."

The penny dropped with Leo and Wood at the same time.

"Good Lord," said Leo, "you're not suggesting that we send him to that temperance hall are you?"

"And what if he's caught by any of our men?" said Wood, "He couldn't say that we'd asked him to break in, could he?"

"Wait, wait," said Crowthorne, "think about it for one second. What do you think is going to happen if our men *have* tipped-off MI5? Do you think that they'll telephone tomorrow, refuse permission, and then ignore it? They're threatening dire consequences if we poke about at the K2 site, so what do you think they'll do when they see that we've moved our attention to their K1 site; sit back and let it happen?" He looked at Leo and said, "How quick did they move when it came to removing that reference to K2 from Skelmersdale Library – under two hours you said."

Leo nodded, then looked at Wood and said, "I'll fill you in later."

"So what do you propose," said Wood, "that we send this EM character into the temperance hall to rip the floor boards up and have a look?"

"No, we'll do that after he's broken in and vanished."

Leo looked at Wood and then back to Crowthorne. He said, "And how would we explain being on the moor at that time of night?"

"We could be showing Inspector Wood the temperance hall and 'come upon' the break-in. We would then send for 'scene-of-crimes' and have a poke about whilst we we're there."

"And all of this before we receive an answer from London?" said Wood.

"Yes."

"You do know that we could have men in black crawling all over the place and accusing us of all sorts jiggery-pokery don't you, sir?" said Leo.

"What? Accusing us of investigating a crime scene?"

Leo pursed his lips and said, "Hmm …"

Wood looked at Leo, saw him ponder and then nod in uncertain agreement. He looked back at Crowthorne, and then at his watch. He said, "Okay, it's 2:35 p.m.; if we're going to do this we've a shed load to do first."

Crowthorne said, "Leo, before we do anything, I have a strange feeling about Naomi. When she left the Ascensis site last Monday she was pensive and quiet. That, to me, means that she's scheming, and we know what kind of scrapes she gets into; so under no circumstances let your men lose sight of her, is that understood?"

"It is."

"She's bright and imaginative, don't let her fool them."

"No, sir, I won't; I've suffered enough consequences for losing sight of that girl, so I'm not about to let it happen again."

"All right," said Crowthorne, "then if we are all agreed, let's give this a go." He saw nods of approval from Leo and Wood, and then said, "Okay, I'll contact Percy and EM now, and we'll reconvene here in one hour."

296

Chapter 36

At 9:35 p.m., the police car containing Crowthorne, Wood, and Leo meandered along the narrow and twisting Mewith, Bloe Beck, and then Hollin Lanes. A nearly full moon illuminated the cold and crystal clear night, and the driver took extra care in case he hit any patches of black ice. The car drove up a curving left-hand bend, and then swept down towards the bubbling Keasden Beck as it ran below a narrow bridge.

The driver broke the silence and said, "That's the place in front, sir."

Everybody leaned forwards and looked out of the window as the car's headlights illuminated the simple, stone-built building in front of them.

Wood shook his head and said, "What? That's ridiculous: here we are in the back of beyond, with nothing but the odd farm, sheep, and miles of empty moorland, and what do we find? A temperance hall for God's sake!"

"It wasn't always that, sir," said the driver, "my grandparents grew up around here and they told me that the building used to be Clapham Wood Hall, a kind of community centre. There were more people living here then, and there

297

was even a small schoolhouse further up on Turnerford Brow."

"Turnerford Brow?" said Wood.

"Yes, sir: it's another half a mile further up the moor; it's named Keasden Road now, but at one time it was named Turnerford Brow." As the car drove down the other side of the narrow bridge the driver pointed into the trees alongside the beck and said, "And that's Turnerford Wood."

"It makes you wonder why they needed a temperance hall," said Leo.

Wood looked around and said, "After living in London for twenty years, it'd drive me to drink if I had to live here."

"And it'd drive me to drink if I had to live in London for twenty years," said Leo.

Wood smiled and said, "Touché."

The car stopped to the left-hand side of the old temperance hall and everybody got out.

"Good grief," said the driver, "talk about luck, look at this!" He pointed to the front door.

The building was a small, single-storey, stone-built structure with a slate-covered gable roof, set at the side of the road; it had a grey wooden door set in the centre of its grey pebble-dash facade, and two narrow, boarded-up windows either side.

"It looks as though somebody's broken in," said the driver, pointing to the gaping door.

"You'd better get the flashlight," said Crowthorne, "but be careful, whoever did it may still be in there."

The driver retrieved the flashlight from the car, switched it on and started to walk across to the temperance hall.

Halfway over he stopped, aimed the light at the road surface, and said, "Whoa, wait a minute…"

Crowthorne, Wood, and Leo watched the driver crouch down, touch the road surface with his left forefinger, and then aim the flashlight at it. He examined it, smelled it, and then looked back at the car. He said, "You need to see this."

Crowthorne, Wood, and Leo exited the car and walked across to where the driver was crouched down. They saw what appeared to be fresh blood.

A horrible feeling overtook Crowthorne. He saw the driver lean down to touch it again and said, "Stop! It could be human."

The driver said, "Human, sir? Surely not; it's more like a fox with a rabbit or something." He looked up at Crowthorne and said, "Don't you think?"

Crowthorne knew that the driver wasn't aware of the plans they'd concocted earlier and said, "Yes, you could be right, but until we establish that, don't touch it again." He looked at Wood and Leo, and saw troubled looks on their faces too.

Leo's discomfort level rose the more he looked at the gaping door, and instead of reaching for his torch, he undid the belt loop of his shoulder-holster and extracted his handgun.

Crowthorne saw the action and realised that they were on the same wavelength. He shouted, *"Everybody down!"*

In that instant, a boom erupted from the temperance hall and a number four shot screamed over Wood's head. The door was yanked open and a second shot boomed out.

As quick as greased lightning, Leo rolled to his right, brought his handgun up, and shot the perpetrator in the chest.

The figure fell, but nobody moved. With straining eyes and ears the colleagues remained motionless waiting to respond to the slightest movement. The seconds ticked by; the driver looked back at Crowthorne and indicated that he was going to approach the hall.

Crowthorne nodded but whispered, *"Be careful ..."*

The driver nodded, got partway up, and then the door opened some more and another shot boomed out.

The driver's head shot backwards as part of it disintegrated in a shower of blood and tissue.

Leo raised his gun and fired twice into the darkened room.

Once again, nobody moved. The echo of the shots dissipated and everywhere returned to deathly silence except for the trickle of the nearby beck.

Crowthorne wondered why nobody had come to investigate from a neighbouring farm, but then realised that the sound of the odd gunshot would not have been out-of-place in that part of the country.

The seconds ticked by until out of the corner of his eye, Wood saw Leo roll to his left and then scramble along the floor until he reached the gable wall of the hall. He looked up and saw two narrow, boarded-over windows above Leo's head, saw no sign of movement from them, and then nodded to Leo that it was safe to stand.

Leo got up, extracted his high-powered, Led Lenser torch from his belt pouch, narrowed the beam to a point, and then placed his left thumb over the switch that would activate a blinding flash of light. With the gun in his right hand and the torch in his left, he ducked down and crept along the facade of the hall, to the door. He then stood up, kicked it wide open, and sent a brilliant flash of blinding light into the dark interior. Against the back wall he saw a figure poised with a double-barrelled shotgun aimed at waist height. He leapt to one side as the shooter, temporarily blinded by the light, fired straight ahead. He ducked, swung in low, fired at the head of his target, and saw it drop to the floor, face down.

Staying low, he switched on the torch, widened the beam, and looked around. On the floor were two bodies, both dressed from head-to-toe in black and wearing black facemasks. He walked across to them, rolled them over and lifted the masks. He was shocked to see that one was a man, the other was a woman, and that they appeared to be at least seventy-plus, years old.

He listened for any other signs of movement, and then went to the door. "All clear," he said.

Wood looked at Crowthorne and said, "Holy Christ, that was fraught" He got up, checked the surrounding vicinity, and then saw Crowthorne crouching by the dead driver. He walked over and said, "Poor bugger didn't stand a chance – shall I send for back-up?"

Crowthorne was mortified at the turn of events but was determined that the driver's death wouldn't be for nothing. He said, "Not yet, get the crowbar, spade, and arc lamp from the back of the car."

Wood was shocked: he said, "What now? After this?"

"Especially after this," hissed Crowthorne. "Do as I say!"

As the men wrenched and heaved up the thick wooden floorboards adjacent to the telephone line, Leo looked at Crowthorne and said, "Are you as puzzled by all this as I am, sir?"

Crowthorne looked up and said, "We'll talk later, let's get on; we've no time to waste."

Within minutes numerous boards were up. They aimed the light from the arc lamp into the three-foot void and saw clean soil. No grass, no moss, no lichen, and no weeds. They remained silent for several seconds until Crowthorne said,

"All right, Leo, get down and expose where that telephone line goes into the ground."

Leo nodded, and dropped into the void. He expected to land on soft soil, but instead, landed on something hard and unforgiving. The shock of the abrupt landing made him say, "Whoa, I wasn't expecting that!" He picked up the spade, rammed the blade down, and heard a metallic clang as it hit something solid. He scraped away the soil; saw that it was less than six inches deep and that it was covering solid concrete. He scraped away more and more, and then looked up and said, "Crikey …"

"Be quick," said Crowthorne, "clear that area around the phone line."

Leo scraped and brushed the soil from where indicated, and saw that it too, disappeared into the solid concrete.

All three stood in silence trying to rationalise what they were seeing, until Wood spotted something. He said, "Leo, what's that?"

Leo turned to where Wood was pointing, and saw something metallic in the surface of the concrete by the left-hand wall of the building. He got down on his haunches, cleared the soil away and then switched on his torch for a closer look. He looked back up and said, "It's the knuckles of a metal hinge."

"How many knuckles?" said Crowthorne.

Leo looked again and said, "Three."

"Then it's the back plate, not the door plate. Which way is it facing?"

Leo looked again and said, "It's level with the ground; it must have belonged to a trapdoor."

"Are you sure?" said Wood, "What would a trapdoor be doing here?"

Crowthorne turned and said, "Can you think of any other reason why a hinge would be there?"

"What are you hinting at," said Wood, "a cellar?"

"If it was a cellar, it wouldn't have been situated like this; there would have been a trapdoor in the floorboards and steps down to it."

"So what are you saying that this is some sort of entrance, or secret passageway?"

Crowthorne shrugged and said, "I don't know; maybe," he turned to Leo and said, "Clear away more soil each side of it, and see if you can see a corresponding hinge."

Leo cleared away several more shovels full of soil, saw no hinge, but then faltered and said, "Hello ..."

Crowthorne and Wood looked at where Leo was tapping with his spade.

"What is it?" said Crowthorne.

"The ground here is soft."

"Then follow the contours of the concrete and see how big it is."

Leo poked the spade into the soft earth and followed it around the concrete until he saw that it covered an area of six square feet. He looked up and said, "Fascinating: what's this all about?"

Crowthorne looked at his watch and saw that more than half an hour had elapsed since they'd arrived, and he knew that they had to get the floorboards back. He said, "I think that we've seen enough for now, smooth that soil back and let's get out of here."

Fifteen minutes later the floorboards were back, dirt had been rubbed into the excavation marks, and nothing looked disturbed.

They walked back outside and Crowthorne said, "Right, I'll send for back-up," he looked at Wood and said, "You see if you can find any more blood, and if so, what it leads to." He turned to Leo and said, "You wait by the car in case we get a call."

Leo nodded and took up his post.

Wood switched on his torch and followed the trail of blood towards the opposite side of the road, and then saw two deep score marks running through the frost-covered grass. He muttered, "No," and almost not daring to look, he lifted up the torch beam and aimed it down the small incline towards the beck. He saw two feet sticking out from behind a tree, closed his eyes and said, "No, no."

Leo heard Wood and said, "You okay, sir?"

Wood shook his head and said, "It looks like we have another body."

Crowthorne had just terminated his call to control, when he heard Wood's remark. His spun around and said, "What? Where?"

"Behind that tree, sir,"

Crowthorne walked down the incline, being careful not to contaminate anywhere marked, and looked at the body. It was EM; he was mortified. And then he got angry; he said, "*Why would anybody do this?!* And what kind of *fucking* moron, or morons, would react to a break-in like this?"

Leo had never heard Crowthorne swear before, and wondered whether his reference to 'morons' was about the MI5 connection. He turned and looked into the door of the hall, recalled the age of the bodies inside, and frowned in dismay.

"*By God,*" continued the raging Crowthorne, "somebody's going to pay for this!"

Wood was about to respond but saw Leo warning him to keep quiet by putting his finger up to his mouth. He turned back to Crowthorne, ignored the signal, and said, "It could be argued that this was our fault, sir."

Crowthorne wheeled around and said, *"What?"*

Wood gulped and said, "Our fault, sir, it could be us who's held responsible for this."

"What the hell are you talking about?"

"Us, sir, we were the ones who put EM up to the break-in."

"And he deserved to be shot did he? And we come across a simple roadside break-in and find two murderous psychopaths waiting inside to shoot anybody who enters? *What the fuck are you talking about?!"*

Leo looked down and knew that it had been wrong of Wood to say anything like that to Crowthorne.

Wood said, "I'm sorry, sir, I was just saying..."

"Well don't! I don't want to hear another single word!" Crowthorne glared at Wood and then said, "Now get over there and wait by the side of the road." He pointed towards the grassy incline of the beck. He then turned to Leo and said, "You stay here."

He waited until the men had acknowledged his orders, and then walked up the road and onto the bridge. He placed both hands on the parapet wall, looked towards EM's body, and yelled, *"Fuck!"* He knew that he could be in serious trouble for planning the break-in, but that paled into insignificance compared to having to break the news of the driver's death to his family. He thought about EM, too, and knew that he had no family to mourn his passing, but that was beside the point.

He drew in a deep, exasperated breath and then felt a huge weight descend onto his heart. He closed his eyes and knew that for the rest of his life, he'd never be able to forgive himself for being responsible for the deaths of two good men who hadn't deserved to die the way they had.

Chapter 37

"*Fiat justitia, ruat coelum* – Let justice be done, though Heaven fall." The Latin proverb kept sweeping through Crowthorne's mind as he walked towards his office.

He'd spent the worst night of his life racking his brain and savaging his conscience about the previous night's events, and even when he'd attempted to sleep at 4:30 a.m., he'd found it impossible. He was an honest man through and through, and there was only one course of action open to him; to take full responsibility for what had happened and to submit his resignation. He'd put on his best uniform, and he'd decided that his first task was to see the Chief Constable.

"Sir, sir …"

Crowthorne turned and saw Inspector Milnes trying to catch up with him. He stopped and said, "Peter?"

Milnes walked up to Crowthorne and said, "It's a heads-up, sir, the Chief Constable's in your office, waiting for you."

"Good grief," said Crowthorne, "what's …" he stopped speaking as he guessed what the visit would be about.

"He didn't give a reason, sir, he just turned up unannounced."

"What time did he arrive?"

"Quarter of an hour ago, I gave him coffee and biscuits and told him that you weren't due in 'til ten."

Crowthorne nodded and said, "Okay, thank you, Peter."

"Shall I send a coffee for you too, sir?"

"No thanks," Crowthorne saw Milnes nod and walk back to the information room; he drew in a deep breath, and stepped into his office.

"Good morning, sir," he said as Chief Constable Barnaby Dane stood up and extended his hand, "it's good to see you again."

Dane said, "Bob," took Crowthorne's hand and shook it.

Crowthorne sat down at his desk, and said, "If this is about last night, sir, then please let me make things easy for you, I will ..."

"It is about last night," cut in Dane, "and I have no idea what's going on."

"Perhaps I should explain," said Crowthorne.

"No, hear me out first; you can say your piece afterwards."

Crowthorne nodded and said, "As you wish, sir."

"And cut out that 'sir' bullshit when it's just the two of us, I've always been Barney to you, and I always will be."

"All right – thanks, Barney."

"Right," said Dane, "what the hell were you doing taking a police car out of the pool without informing anybody about what you were doing?"

Crowthorne was shocked; he said, "What?"

"I repeat: what were you doing taking a car from the pool without at least informing the duty Inspector? And a high-vis traffic car to boot?"

Crowthorne couldn't believe his ears; he said, "What on earth are you talking about? I didn't take a car; I was driven to an old temperance hall on Hollin Lane near Keasden."

Dane looked into Crowthorne's eyes and said, "You are in the Greater Manchester force; what were you doing there?"

"I, I …" Crowthorne knew that he hadn't appraised the CC of the situation at Keasden, and felt on shaky ground.

"Well?" said Dane.

"I took Detective Inspector Wood and Detective Sergeant Chance to an old temperance hall there as part of an inter-force investigation into …"

"And you didn't think to inform me about this situation?"

"I …"

"Didn't think?"

Crowthorne wasn't often caught on the back foot; he looked down and then said, "Sorry, Barney."

"Go on,"

"And when we arrived, we found …"

"What time did you arrive?"

Crowthorne cast his mind back and said, "About 21:45."

"Hmm, and then what?"

"We discovered that the hall had been broken into and …"

"You called it in; I know. Only it hadn't had it?"

Crowthorne hesitated and looked at the stern face of his old friend, and saw him nod. At first he wasn't sure whether Dane had mixed up the sequence of events, or that he was cutting to the integral parts. He said, "It had, but it was more …"

"It hadn't."

Crowthorne stopped speaking and frowned; he saw Dane nod again. He said, "I don't understand?"

"Neither do we, Bob. First you take a car without permission, you drive out of our area, and then you report a hoax break-in."

Crowthorne was shocked; he said, "I did what?"

308

You reported a hoax break-in; and for your information, it wasn't at 21:45 it was …" Dane removed a piece of paper from his tunic pocket, looked at it, and then said, "… 23:23."

"23:23?"

"Correct; and our men arrived on scene at 23:45."

"What?" said a flabbergasted Crowthorne, "What on earth are you talking about?"

"Your supposed crime scene at Keasden, that's what."

Crowthorne's frown deepened; he said, *"Supposed crime scene?* What do you mean by that?"

"I mean exactly that. There was no crime scene."

Crowthorne's mouth fell open; he said, "Are you kidding me? What about the officers who attended, and Wood, and Chance? They were all there, they knew what had happened!"

"But that's just it," said Dane, "they weren't!"

Crowthorne looked at Dane in complete bewilderment; he wondered if he was being subjected to some sort of weird test or psychological mind game. It was irrational, preposterous, and ridiculous. He said, "What the hell are you talking about, Barney? Of course they were!" He paused and then said, "Get them in here and ask them."

"I've already spoken to the officers who attended the temperance hall, and they've confirmed that nothing was out of the ordinary."

"What?" said Crowthorne. "Now I know that you're joking!"

"Do I look like I'm joking? Do you think that I'd be here to play jokes on you?"

Crowthorne hesitated, and saw how serious Dane looked. He said, "No …"

"Then stop pissing me about, and tell me why you requested what you did!"

"Wait a minute," said Crowthorne, "are you seriously trying to tell me that the officer who drove me home last night, had no recollection of it?"

"Nobody drove you home last night!"

"Then how the hell did I get to my house from there?"

"In the car that you took from the pool – the same one that we collected from your house at 5:30 a.m. this morning."

Crowthorne gasped and said, "Am I dreaming this?"

"You tell me."

Crowthorne shook his head, frowned and then said, "Okay, what about the three officers who attended the scene, what did they say?"

"Two officers," said Dane.

"Three officers," reiterated Crowthorne.

"Two officers!"

Crowthorne realised that he was beginning to push the Chief Constable too far. He sat forwards and said, "Barney, I am not lying; nor am I going stupid, three officers attended last night."

"Two."

Crowthorne couldn't believe his ears; he stared at Dane for a second or two and said, "Fine – then what did they say about the scene?"

"They arrived at 23:45 and ..."

"Wait, wait" interrupted Crowthorne, "it was 22:45."

Dane glared at Crowthorne in an odd way and then said, "No – it was 23:45."

Crowthorne's bewilderment deepened; he cocked his head to one side and looked at Dane in a questioning fashion.

Dane stared back and then repeated, "Listen to me, Bob, and listen carefully, this is what happened last night. Do you understand me?"

Crowthorne said, "Go on."

"Last night you took an unmarked car from the pool, and for reasons unknown to me, you drove to the old temperance hall at Keasden. At 23:23 control received a call from you requesting scenes-of-crime. At 23:40 a car arrived on the scene. The officers examined the hall and surrounding area; they didn't find you, and they didn't find signs of any crime having been committed either. They reported their findings, or lack thereof, to control at 00:10 this morning, and then departed."

Crowthorne was shocked into silence. He had no idea how any of what he'd heard had occurred, and he didn't know how to respond.

"And that is what happened," said Dane.

Crowthorne said, "So if none of what I reported had happened, what was the point of me calling it in, in the first place?"

Dane leaned forwards and said, in a louder voice than normal, "That's what we'd like to know."

Crowthorne looked at his old friend's face and saw him nod towards his desk pad. He ripped a piece of paper off and pushed it, with a pencil towards him.

Dane scribbled something on the paper, and then pushed it back.

Crowthorne looked down and saw the words, 'don't argue'. He suddenly felt vulnerable. He looked at Dane and saw him nod at the paper again. He gathered his wits and said, "Look, I, er, I don't know what to say, Barney. I know that I've been working long hours lately, but if I've taken such leave of my senses that I don't know what I'm doing anymore, my stress levels must be more serious than I thought, and I'm sorry for my odd behaviour."

Dane put a serious expression on his face and said, "It's unacceptable from a man of your rank."

Crowthorne opened his mouth to respond, but saw Dane gesture for him to remain silent.

Dane continued, "And until all of this has been resolved, you are temporarily suspended from duty."

Crowthorne was shocked; he gasped and said, "Suspended? From when?"

"With immediate effect – now please hand over your Warrant Card."

Crowthorne handed his Warrant Card to a dispassionate-looking Dane, and heard him say, "You can leave your personal stuff in the office until a review board has concluded its findings."

Crowthorne said, "And when will that be?"

"Sometime within the next four weeks."

"And my pay?"

"You will remain on full pay. How did you get here?"

"In my car."

"Good, we'll give you thirty minutes to collect what you need to take home, and then you have to leave."

Crowthorne said, "One last question sir; where are DI Wood and DS Chance?"

"DI Wood is on his way back to London, and DS Chance has been assigned to another case."

Crowthorne frowned and was about to speak, but then saw Dane push the paper with 'don't argue' back under his nose. He nodded, and said, "Thank you, sir."

Thirty minutes later, a dismayed Crowthorne was driving home. He'd concluded from the meeting that the whole bizarre episode must have been some kind of MI5 whitewash, but he hadn't any idea of what had really happened to Wood and Leo. He looked down at his mobile, but didn't trust its security any longer. He decided that he needed to buy a new one.

He turned left off the main road and into the road heading to his house, but then changed his mind. He decided that since he was no longer on duty, there was no time like the present. He checked his mirror, indicated left, stopped, and let a grey saloon with two men inside pass him. He then executed a three-point-turn and headed back to the main road. He knew that there was a superstore less than half a mile away.

He drove to the store, bought a new tablet computer, a mobile phone, and a 'pay-as-you-go' sim card, and then returned to his car. He looked at the rugged packaging and decided to open them once he'd returned home.

He reversed out of his parking place, drove through the busy car park, and then turned right onto the main road. Having completed the manoeuvre, he checked his rear-view mirror, and saw a grey saloon with two men inside, turn out of the superstore car park, and fall in line three cars behind him.

Chapter 38

Eleanor Drake, still using the name Violet Burgess, parked her old Land Rover in the trees out of sight of the main gate. She checked the time and saw that it was 9:10 p.m. It had taken her three-quarters of an hour to get from her house to the site, and she'd told her daughters Val and Janet that she'd received an urgent call to go to work, but she'd lied. And she wasn't the only one lying either. Her husband Malory had told her that he was going to the local pub to play darts with his pal, but she knew otherwise.

From the cover of the trees she watched as Dave Gill, the last member of the weekend security staff, closed the gates and waved goodbye to his fellow guard. She knew that he'd started work at 4 p.m., and that he'd be accompanied until 9 p.m., but on Sunday nights alone, up until 6 a.m. Monday, he'd be alone.

It had been some bureaucrat's attempt at cutting staffing costs, but, it suited her, and it suited others from the Unit too. They all knew that Dave was a committed skiver, and that once he was alone, he'd lock up the gates and go to the bar at the end of the lane until closing time.

Her suspicions had first been raised about the St Mary Cross clandestine activities in the latter part of 1972, but she'd had no proof until one Friday night when she'd stayed late to finish a particular project.

She'd been working in Lab 2 using white mice and rabbits to test skin sensitivity with mild perfumes containing plant extracts. The test had involved shaving a tiny area of fur off their backs and dropping a miniscule amount of the liquid, from a pipette, onto it.

From a moral point of view, she was against using animals for research, but in the time that she'd been working there, she'd seen that each of the animals had been used just once. No chemicals had been placed in their eyes, and she knew that if any of them had been affected by the test, they'd been returned to good health, and then taken to the local pet shop to be sold as pets to loving boys and girls.

With that ethic, and the St Mary Cross 'Rules of Animal Care', she'd had no problem; until the night that she'd worked late.

It had been just after 10 p.m., and as far as she'd been aware, Malory and the girls had been at home. She'd been plagued by trying to modify a beautiful perfume that had persisted in remaining at an unacceptable PH level each time she'd tested it. She'd known that she'd been on the verge of solving the problem, and that she and her family had been due to start a week's holiday the next day, but she'd refused to give up. It had been her project from the outset, and she hadn't wanted anybody else involved in its development.

That night, she'd become tired and had removed her eye protectors; she'd sat back in her seat, stretched her arms high in the air – and then heard a scream that had made every hair on her body stand on end.

She'd leapt out of her chair, raced down to Lab 4 and tried the door handle, but it had been locked. She'd opened her mouth to shout, but then heard such a terrible commotion inside, that she'd stepped back in alarm. Screeches and yelps had erupted from within, men had begun shouting abuse and swearing as the screeching had increased. Then she'd heard furniture being strewn about, and the sound of breaking glass. She'd thought that her heart was going to beat out of her chest. She'd stared at the door in unadulterated fear in case whatever had been going crazy in there had got out. She'd started to back away, and then she'd heard a man say "hold the fucking thing still," followed by a bone-jarring smack and a dreadful squeal. Thereafter she'd heard more blows followed by more squeals and wails, until she'd been able to stand no more.

With a hammering heart she'd grabbed her coat from Lab 2, switched off the small desk light and had raced outside. She'd been convinced that she'd be stopped by security at the gates, but nobody had been there. She'd run across to her car, but then changed her mind in case anybody heard the engine. She'd then edged her way around the perimeter fence, slipped through the small picket gate in the main gate, and had started to half-run down the lane with the idea of calling for Malory from the phone box at the end. Her mind had been in turmoil and she hadn't thought that things could have got worse, but they had.

As she'd walked down the lane, she'd heard the sound of an approaching vehicle behind her. Her first instinct had been to flag it down, but then she'd realised that it might have come from the Unit. She'd run off the side of the road and hidden in the trees until the vehicle had driven past. And then she'd stayed rooted to the spot with her hand up to her mouth. The truck had been from Ormskirk Zoo, and the driver had been Malory.

Later that night she'd taken him to task and discovered that he'd been delivering a variety of animals from the zoo for testing, and that the head keeper there had been in on it, too. They'd argued, and he'd become evasive and angry, telling her that he'd only been doing it to earn extra cash for the family, but she'd gone on to tell him that if he'd carried on, she'd not only report him *and* the head keeper, but that she would leave him. Thereafter he'd promised to stop.

But as the months had passed, she'd realised that he hadn't. Furthermore, she'd begun to suspect that he'd been using the money to support an extra-marital fling with a local barmaid. The situation between them had deteriorated, but she'd remained silent and with him, until she'd been in a position to be able to do something about both problems.

With the aid of her closest friend, Christine, she'd managed to get copies of the full set of keys for the Unit, whilst Christine had plied an already-tipsy Dave Gill with increasing amounts of booze, in the local bar, one Sunday night.

She'd seen from her previous forays that once Dave had entered the pub on his Sunday night jaunts, that a watching man would make a call from the telephone box on the corner, and then get picked up by a car fifteen minutes later. They would then escort an unmarked truck, usually driven by Mallory, down to the Unit, where their latest animal specimens would be unloaded in the loading bay.

This she knew to be fact, but one last thing puzzled her.

She'd allowed Malory to believe that she'd accepted that he was no longer involved in the animal trafficking and that he played in a local darts league that toured northern pubs every third Friday and Saturday nights. She'd also gone along with his lie that the team met for practices each Sunday night. But the deception had served two purposes. It had made Malory careless and blasé and it had given her the freedom to investigate everything that had been going on.

Over time, she'd established that the animals had been taken to Lab 4 to be experimented upon, and she'd known that those experiments had only ever taken place on the third Friday and Saturday nights of the month, with the fresh animals arriving the Sunday before. But she had no idea where they'd been kept.

Her suspicions about a possible location had been aroused by her discovery of an unusual pipe below two of the lab benches. She hadn't spoken to anybody about it, but over several weeks, she'd established that it hadn't appeared to serve any useful purpose. It appeared at random in different cupboards and under the bench in Labs 2 and 3 on the same side of the central hall, but then it fed through the partition wall and into the loading bay. From there, she'd worked out that it was one of four pipes that ran over the bay at roof level until it reached the back wall to the right-hand side of the back office door.

There it had become confusing.

She'd seen the three pipes that entered the building from the outside, and that two of them ran up to the underside of the roof and back towards the labs. And that the third one appeared to go back outside. She'd checked the exterior and seen from its position that it must have run back out and into the back of the fuel container on the rear of the building.

In Lab 4, and when nobody had been watching her, she'd reached under the bench and felt the pipe for fluctuations in temperature, but she'd felt none. That indicated that it hadn't been used for water, or any cold, or inert gas. One time she'd even placed her ear against it when she'd pretended to have dropped her pencil under her bench, but she'd heard nothing either.

Then she'd had a minor stroke of luck.

During one morning tea break, she'd decided to go for a breath of fresh air. She'd walked down the central corridor to the loading bay with the intention of standing on the platform outside. On the way, she'd seen a maintenance engineer doing something up a ladder near the mystery pipe. She'd ambled over, tried to appear as casual as possible, and had asked if there'd been a problem. The engineer had smiled and said, "Nothing like that, Doctor, I'm just removing some old I.D. plates that had let the engineers who constructed the place know which pipe went where." She recalled the flush of excitement she'd felt as he'd unscrewed the plate above the mystery pipe and had said, "Here, catch!" She'd caught the small black plate and seen the inscription 'PL3' on it.

"Pipeline three, Doctor," said the smiling engineer, "if that makes any sense to you!" She'd handed it back to him, and told him that it hadn't; and had gone outside for her tea.

That night, she'd told her daughters about it.

Now here she was, on the verge of carrying out her next foray.

She heard the picket gate open and peered around the thick tree trunk concealing her. She watched Dave step through, lock it behind him, and then put the keys in his plastic shopping bag – the one that held his constant companion; his bottle of sweet sherry. He then strolled down the lane to the pub with a smile on his face, and without a care in the world.

She waited until he'd gone out of sight, and then stepped out of the trees. She listened for the sound of approaching vehicles, and heard none. She ran to the picket gate, let herself in, locked it behind her, and ran down to the research building. There, she let herself in to Entrance A, the first door on the left, at the front,

She locked the door and checked her watch. She estimated that she had twenty minutes before she needed to get out.

Being a thorough and efficient scientist by profession and by nature, she'd decided to eliminate every possibility before checking out the probability, so starting at the top of the building; she looked in every room; each office, laboratory, washroom, storeroom, mess room, rest room, and even the canteen. Next, she'd checked the ladies and gents toilets and even the broom cupboards, but as she'd suspected from the outset, she'd found nothing that could house, or conceal, any large animals.

She looked at her watch and saw that she had five minutes left. Everything had gone to plan. She now needed to get out and return at a later date to check out the loading area.

She started to walk back up the central hall towards Entrance A – and then she heard the door open and close behind her. She stopped walking and turned around. She stared at the person in front of her. Her mind went into sudden and violent turmoil and her mouth fell open. What she saw couldn't be. But then she saw that the person in front of her was looking at her in the same way.

She frowned, raised her right arm, and said, "You! How the hell…?"

Chapter 39

"Patience is bitter, but its fruit is sweet"
- French Proverb

For the first time in his life, Adrian Darke felt apprehensive and edgy. He looked around the sumptuous lounge and saw that his top men looked edgy, too. He'd never been in a position where he felt out of control, but the revelation delivered by his 'pet' policeman Mick Bryce had been shocking in the extreme. The only person who looked cool and untouched by the events was Ajax.

"That's Hayley, speared onto a metal fence, Dom shoved out of a tower block window, and now Garrett pushed in front of a train? That's bad, boss," said Leander Pike, "are none of us safe from this loony?"

Darke didn't know what to say; Hinchcliffe had been his top man since he'd started his various ventures, and it felt as though a huge hole had opened up next to him. He not only missed him as a top employee, but also as a good and true friend.

"Haven't you got any clues, Mick?" said Pike.

Bryce shook his head and said, "None: whoever's doing this is good. We haven't found a single piece of evidence linking any of these crimes to anybody or anything."

"That must tell you something then," said Constantin.

"Only that whoever's doing this is a professional," he turned to Ajax and said, "Do you agree?"

Ajax nodded.

Darke looked at Ajax and said, "Have you any ideas?"

Ajax didn't speak, he just shook his head.

"Well I don't like it," said Constantin, "and I think that we should do something about it."

"Like what?" said Bryce.

"Like disband this group and go our separate ways until all of this is over."

"Fucking eyeties!" said Bryce. "Typical!"

"And what do you mean by that?" said Constantin.

"What do you think I mean, you numpty?"

"I don't know 'mister fucking-bent-policeman' – enlighten me."

"All right, all right," said Darke, "enough, you two!" He looked at Bryce and said, "Deangelo's idea may not be such a bad one."

"You are kidding me aren't you?" said Bryce. "Do you seriously think that whoever's doing this will stop because you aren't in each other's company? Christ-on-a-bike – were you all together when he did the others?"

Nobody spoke.

"Right – this twat's picking you off when you're alone and vulnerable, so going your separate ways would be exactly what he, or she, would want!"

"*She?*" said Darke.

322

"Yeah – *she*," said Bryce, "how many women's husbands or boyfriends have you done or pissed off? Do you even know?"

Darke looked puzzled, but didn't respond.

"Exactly," said Bryce. "What about that fucking mare, Gillorton? Was she a dyke? And if so could her partner have thought that you'd ordered her death?"

"That's ridiculous!" said Darke.

"No it isn't," said Bryce. He looked around the room and was met by blank stares. "Until we find who, or why somebody is doing this, it could be for any number of reasons."

"And that's what I'm paying you for," said Darke beginning to tire of Bryce's arrogance and attitude, "so why haven't you come up with anything?"

Bryce heard the edge in Darke's voice and knew when to rein in his dictatorial ebullience. He said, "I'm working on it."

Darke expected more, and said, "And?"

Bryce looked around the room and said, "I wasn't going to mention this until I had more info, but I may have come up with a name."

Everybody turned to look at Bryce.

"Go on," said Darke.

"Anybody here heard of Fergus Rome?"

Nobody spoke.

"Right, he's an ex-SAS Captain who lives in Paris."

Darke frowned and said, "Fergus Rome? Who the hell is he, and why would he want to harm any of us?"

"Rome had a brother named Angus. He was an undercover cop working at your Crag Vale drug facility last year. He'd tried to save a woman you'd held hostage there, and he ended up being shot by one of your security guards."

Darke cast his mind back and said, "Yes, I remember him."

"Right," said Bryce, "according to my guy in Lancashire police, it seems that his brother Fergus had been sniffing around asking questions about his brother's death; but when he was questioned himself, he disappeared into thin air."

"And you think that it's Fergus Rome killing my people?" said Darke.

"He's the most likely guy."

"Do you know where he is right now?" said Constantin.

"I do," said Ajax.

Everybody turned and looked at the quiet figure in the corner of the room.

"You do?" said Darke.

"Yes, it's right here on this piece of paper." Ajax reached into the inside pocket of his jacket and pulled out a silenced handgun. Within seconds he'd shot Constantin and Pike in the head, and then Bryce in the left lung. He walked over to Bryce saw the pink frothy blood gurgling out of his mouth, and said, "You are a disgrace to your profession and to humanity." He lifted the gun again and shot Bryce through the forehead.

Darke was petrified: he stared at Ajax expecting to be shot at any second. He saw him walk across to him and raise the gun. "No! Please don't!" he begged.

"I'm not going to shoot you," said Ajax.

"Then what do you want? I have money, name your price."

"You can't give me what I want, because you took it away from me."

"What?" said Darke. "I don't understand."

"My brother, Angus."

Darke frowned and said, "What? You're Fergus Rome? I thought …"

"You thought that I was Ajax; but you hadn't ever seen him had you?"

"No, I …"

"No," said Rome, "but don't worry yourself – you'll be with him in no time at all." He then brought the butt of the pistol up, and smashed it down on top of Darke's head.

Darke wasn't sure what time he came to, but when he did, his head, his feet, and his wrists, hurt like hell. He tried to open his mouth, but it was gagged with duct tape. He opened his eyes, and his heart leapt into his mouth. He was upside-down and nothing was below him except one-hundred-and-fifty feet of fresh air. He craned his neck upwards and saw that he was dangling from below a window-cleaner's platform and suspended at the ankles by two thick, plastic cable ties. His arms had been folded and bound around his chest so that his hands were below his chin.

"Nice view up here isn't it?" said Rome.

Darke craned his head backwards and saw that Rome was standing on the balcony of his penthouse. He had been hauled up and faced outwards so that the back of his head was at face level with Rome. He tried to speak but a pathetic 'Hmming' sound was all he could manage.

"Yes, I agree," said Rome, "but as much as I'd like to, I can't stand here chatting all day." He then reached up with a pair of steel snippers and cut through the centimetre wide cable tie holding Darke's right foot.

Darke's body dropped and arced to the left as his full weight was taken up by the cable tie on his left ankle. He let out a terrified yelp and began to make mewing sounds.

"Unlike all those poor bastards whose death you ordered, including my brother Angus, I'm going to give you a choice," said Rome. "Down below you is a steel fence with vicious spikes on top, much like the one I dropped that objectionable woman of yours on with the aid of a JCB."

Darke looked down, but couldn't make out any detail.

"Oh yes, it's there alright, but now here's the dilemma. I'm going to snip halfway through the last cable tie and it's going to tear. I don't know how long it'll take, but I do know that the more you struggle, the quicker it will go. Then you'll fall.

"Now, will you go down head first and get speared through the face or brain, or will your body twist around in flight so that you become impaled though your belly or maybe your crutch or back?"

Darke started to cry and make whimpering sounds. He shook his head from side to side imploring Rome to spare his life.

"Yes, me too," said an ice-cold Rome, "I couldn't predict that either." He paused as he looked down and then back up. "But," he said, "I did promise you a choice." He removed the silenced handgun from his jacket pocket and held it in front of Darke's face. "This was Ajax's gun; I say 'was' because he is now an integral part of a motorway bridge in France." He waggled the gun a couple of times and said, "I know that it's ironic, but it's the same gun that he used to take the life of people on your orders, and I thought that it would be nice to offer it to you, to end yours." He paused to let the statement sink in, and then continued.

"In the chamber," he said, "is one bullet, and I've positioned your hands so that you'll be able to put the barrel in your mouth and blow your brains out. And please don't think about trying to shoot me with it, because it isn't going to happen."

He twisted Darke's body round, placed the gun in his right hand, and twisted him back. He then reached up and cut half of the cable tie.

Darke felt the action and squealed.

Rome looked at the tie and said, "Oh, dear, it appears to be tearing quicker than I thought." He reached up, patted Darke on the back and said, "Got to go old chap, things to do etcetera, so on behalf of me and my brother Angus, have a pleasant flight."

He stepped off the balcony and watched through the apartment window.

Darke panicked; the last thing that he wanted to do was to fall one-hundred-and-fifty feet and be impaled on a railing. With his breath coming in short gasps, he twisted the gun around, pushed the barrel in his mouth, and pulled the trigger.

Rome saw the back of Darke's head blow off, and then the cable tie part. As it did, Darke's body fell two feet, and was then arrested by the rope that he'd tied around his ankles.

As quick as a flash, he went outside, pinned a piece of paper onto Darke's jacket, and then disappeared forever.

On it was written *"veni vidi vici"* – "I came, I saw, I conquered".

Chapter 40

Crowthorne turned his car into the road leading to his house. For an hour he'd been driving to meaningless places, buying essentials that he hadn't needed, and going to the local park to take in air that he hadn't wanted to; and for all of that time, he'd been tailed by the two men in the grey Ford saloon.

He'd racked his brain about numerous things. Was he going to be discredited and forced to leave the police? Why were the men following him? What had happened to EM, the two assailants, and the dead police driver at Keasden? Was Wood actually on his way back to London, or had something happened to him? And Leo – assigned to a new duty – really?

All of these things worried him, but the most overriding was Naomi. She was the loose cannon, and he didn't know whether MI5 were onto her or not. He worried about her impetuosity, whether she would attempt to return to the Ascensis facility alone, which for certain, would alert MI5 to her activity. And, about her security if Leo had been despatched to somewhere else?

And the most frustrating thing was his uncertainty. He'd always been capable and decisive, but now, when he needed it the most, his ability to rationalise seemed to be at an all time low. He looked down at his new phone and tablet, and couldn't decide which course of action to take.

With an exasperated gasp he turned into his personal parking place, picked up his purchases, and got out of the car. Out of the corner of his eye he spotted the grey Ford parked further up the road. He was tempted to walk up to the car and confront the men, but his dratted indecision kicked in again, and instead, he made his way indoors.

In a state of high dudgeon he closed his front door, locked it, and then noticed a mobile phone lying on the carpet. He put down his shopping, picked up the phone, and turned it on. He scrolled through to the contacts and saw just one mobile number. He walked through to his living room, looked out of the window, and saw the grey Ford still in place. He was about to dial the number, but then wondered if his house had been bugged. He went up to his bathroom, turned the tap to his shower on, and then dialled the number.

He heard the phone connect, and then a familiar voice.

"Sir," said Leo, "I'll keep this brief. When this call is terminated, dispose of the phone, do you understand?"

"Yes."

"We've been subject to an MI5 whitewash. Wood's okay but he's had a strict OSA gagging order slapped on him, as have I. I'll fill you in on what happened at Keasden when we meet."

"When will that be?"

"Soon."

"Where are you?"

"Nearby – now listen carefully. Put on a raincoat, hat and trousers, not jeans. At 1400 walk into the gent's toilet in your local Tesco superstore and enter the third cubicle. It will say 'out of order' but push the door. Put on the clothes in the box, leave yours, and your car and house keys in there. Wait until somebody knocks on the door three times, and then come outside and get onto the rear of the black motorbike that will be waiting near the main entrance. Is that understood?"

Crowthorne wanted to say that he hadn't been on a motorcycle for years, but said, "Yes it is."

"Good," said Leo, "bring enough cash, not cards, to be able to stay away from home for two nights."

"Will do."

"Excellent; now terminate the call and dispose of this phone."

"Okay, bye."

Crowthorne's mind went into overdrive; he was intrigued, and excited at the same time. He hadn't done anything as impulsive as this before and he realised that his confidence and cold hard logic was back with him.

At 13:55 he walked towards the main entrance of his Tesco superstore dressed as Leo had instructed, and saw no motorbike. He collected a shopping trolley, and then feigned kneeling down to tie his shoelace. He saw the grey Ford pull into a parking bay, and one of the men step out. He stood up, walked into the store and went to the gent's toilet. He saw the 'out of order' notice on the third cubicle, waited until he was alone and then went inside. On the seat was a large cardboard box containing a leather motorbike jacket, leather pants, which he hoped he'd be able to get into, some leather boots, a pair of black leather gloves, and a white helmet. He stripped off his top clothes, put on the leather gear and waited. In what seemed like seconds, he heard three knocks on the door; he stepped out and saw a man dressed identically. They nodded towards each other; he waited for a couple of minutes, and then went outside.

Waiting by the front door was a large black 1400cc motorbike with a rider in the front seat. He nodded, climbed onto the rear, and then they drove away. He leaned his head to the right as they exited the Tesco car park, and saw that they weren't being followed.

Back at the Tesco superstore, DC Roger Walburn took off the motorbike leathers, put on Crowthorne's clothes and then kept far enough away from his follower, to succeed in duping him whilst he did a bit of shopping. He then drove back to Crowthorne's house, let himself in, and walked through to the lounge. From there he saw the grey Ford parked at the end of the approach road.

"So far, so good," thought Walburn. He then walked into the kitchen and hoped that Crowthorne had the same taste in coffee, as he.

Half an hour later, the motorbike pulled into one of the westbound service areas on the M62 motorway. The driver pulled into a parking bay, and they dismounted.

Crowthorne pulled off the helmet, waited to see who had been driving, and then saw that it was Leo. He smiled, shook Leo's hand, and said, "Wow! That was invigorating!"

Leo smiled and said, "I'm glad that you and DC Walburn were the same size, sir."

Crowthorne said, "Me too; and right now I'm suspended from duty, so it's plain old Bob."

"Thank you, Bob," said Leo, "but you'll have to forgive me if I forget and slip the odd 'sir' in now and again."

Crowthorne smiled and said, "No problem: let's get a coffee and you can bring me up to date."

The companions walked into the self-service restaurant, bought a coffee and sat at a table with nobody nearby.

Crowthorne took a sip, screwed up his face, and said, "This stuff doesn't get any better." He put the cup down, and said, "So what happened last night?"

"It was a very bizarre experience. Within ten minutes of you leaving, an unmarked, black car, and a black van arrived. The guys in the car were all dressed in jeans, leather jackets, open denim shirts and such, not a bit like I would have expected. The four guys in the van all wore black overalls. One of the men from the car asked who was in charge, and DI Wood said that he was the senior officer. The man informed him that he was a senior member of the Security Service, and that the whole scene had become their jurisdiction.

"Mr Wood started to object but was told that if he, or any of us, didn't comply, we'd be arrested under the Security Service Act 1989. DI Wood and I were driven to Bury in the MI5 car with the guy in charge, and the police officers who'd attended were driven to Rochdale in the police car, with another MI5 man.

"Once in Bury, DI Wood and I were put into separate rooms. I had to wait until about 1am, at which time, the Chief Constable no less, walked in and informed me that Mr Wood had been despatched back to London, and that I was to be put on another assignment with immediate effect. I objected, and attempted to tell the CC what had happened at Keasden, but he, too, said that if I spoke about it to anybody, including him, I would be charged under the same Security Service Act. I was flabbergasted, but kept my mouth shut.

"I was told to take the rest of the week off; I was ordered not to make contact with you or DI Wood, and not to say anything about what had happened at Keasden, and to report for duty next Monday."

Crowthorne shook his head and said, "What about the deceased driver and EM?"

"No idea sir – sorry, Bob."

"And the crime scene guys? Did they turn up?"

"No."

"Amazing," said Crowthorne, "a complete cover-up and no questions asked?"

"Yes."

Crowthorne pondered for a second or two as he sipped his coffee. He looked around to see if anybody appeared to be showing them any interest. He then turned back and said, "What about the crime scene?"

"I couldn't help it; at 7 a.m. this morning I jumped on the bike and drove up there. I slowed down as I passed the temperance hall but didn't stop in case anybody was watching."

"And what was it like?"

"Clean as a whistle; no blood, no tracks through the grass, no signs of a break-in, nothing."

"Good grief," said Crowthorne. He thought of something and said, "Do you think that if somebody was watching they got your bike registration number?"

Leo looked from left to right, and then said, "I unscrewed one off a boat trailer in the motorway car park, and put that on 'til I'd come off the moor at Slaidburn, sorry, sir."

Crowthorne raised his eyebrows and said, "Resourceful and understandable, but wrong."

Leo dropped his gaze, then looked up, and smiled. He said, "It's a good job that I'm confiding in my friend Bob then, and not my superior officer!"

Crowthorne smiled and said, "Okay, what's the plan?"

"We're going to lie low until tennish tonight, and then we're going into that Ascensis building. There's more to that place than meets the eye."

"Good God," said Crowthorne, "that's playing it close to the knuckle isn't it?"

"Maybe, sir – Bob – but it's the last place that they'd expect us to go now."

Crowthorne sat back in his chair and said, "I wouldn't be too sure of that; that was the first place MI5 warned us away from."

"No, sorry, Bob, they didn't. They told us that we weren't allowed to investigate anything to do with that site up to and including 1956. They never said anything about what we'll be doing."

"What, even though they're aware that we know about their K1 and K2 sites, are you serious?"

Leo pondered for a few seconds and then said, "Okay, you may be right, but can you think of anything else to do?"

"You do recall that we were warned off don't you?"

"And has that ever stopped you before, sir?"

Crowthorne's eyes narrowed; he leaned forwards and said, "No, I don't suppose it has: and it's not going to stop me now."

Chapter 41

Heav'n has no rage like love to hatred turn'd,
Nor hell a fury like a woman scorn'd.
- William Congreve 1670 - 1729

Eleanor stared in disbelief and said, "What are you doing here? And how did you get here?"

"I work here Doctor Drake," said Axel Klossner, "but more to the point, what are you doing here?"

"I thought that you were dead; that you'd been killed in an accident in 1937?"

"An elaborate ruse played out by me, a lorry driver, a fake doctor and a dead body which unfortunately, cost Ronnie Bowers his life."

Eleanor said, "I don't understand." She gestured around and said, "This is an animal research unit used for developing modern cosmetics, not a weapons research facility, so what exactly are you working on, and why haven't I seen you here before?"

Klossner stepped closer to Eleanor and marvelled at how young she still appeared to look. He said, "If you don't mind

335

me saying, you are looking very well Doctor Drake, considering that I thought you'd died in 1937, too."

Eleanor looked at Klossner and saw that his Teutonic face had become harder looking. His eyes looked cold and soulless, his once-full lips appeared to have disappeared leaving a down-turned, determined-looking slit of a mouth, and his black hair had given way to sparse grey strands over a balding head.

"The event of my death was a necessary ruse, too," said Eleanor trying to read Klossner's body language, "but I suspect for a very different reason than yours." She looked at his eyes and saw them darting about the place, as though he was trying to work out some logistical manoeuvre. She took half a step back and turned sideways on.

"I see that I make you uncomfortable, my dear, was it something I said?"

"You haven't answered my questions, Doctor Klossner; what are you working on, and why haven't I seen you here before?"

"Ah, yes," said Klossner stepping closer again, "what am I working on?" He paused and then said, "That, I cannot tell you, but I can show you. And why haven't you seen me before? Because I didn't want you to see me."

"What? You knew that *I* worked here?"

"No I didn't, as much of a pleasant surprise as that would have been, I meant that very few people know that I work here, and that is why I am not seen."

Eleanor frowned and said, "But this place is so small, and I've been working here for nearly three years."

"Then that is most gratifying. It shows how effective I've been at concealing myself and my department."

"Your department? What department's that?"

Klossner's slit of a mouth tightened for a second; he stared at Eleanor and then said, "Der Menschliche Abteilung."

"You'll forgive me, Herr Doctor," said Eleanor slowing, and emphasising her response, "aber meine deutsche Sprache ist nicht so gut. Was ist der Menschliche Abteilung?"

Klossner's eyes narrowed and he said, "Your German sounds okay to me, Doctor; are you toying with me?"

Eleanor suddenly realised where she was, and who she was with. A feeling of vulnerability spread over her and she regretted rubbing Klossner up the wrong way. She said, "My basic German is still okay, but I don't understand any technical terminology."

Klossner nodded, and then said, "In that case, der menschliche abteilung is the human department."

Eleanor swallowed hard; she said, "Human department? What human department?"

She saw a subtle shift in Klossner's demeanour as he stood looking at her without answering. She began to feel uneasy. She looked at her watch and realised that the truck with Malory and his co-conspirators would be getting close. She looked up and saw that Klossner had stepped closer.

"Are you expecting someone, my dear?"

"I, er, popped in to pick up some research papers, and my husband is waiting for me in the car park."

Klossner nodded and said, "And we both know that that is not true, don't we?"

Eleanor stepped back and looked at the door behind her. She didn't give it a second thought, and ran for it. She charged up the central hallway, got to Entrance A, and then plunged her hand into her coat pocket to retrieve her keys.

"Are you looking for these?"

Eleanor wheeled around and saw Klossner halfway down the hall, holding her keys in the air. He said, "You dropped them when you ran through the door."

She looked at the slim, but aged figure of Klossner, and considered running at him and tackling him if necessary, and then the door opened behind him, and a younger version of him stepped into the hallway.

Klossner didn't turn around. He waited until the other man was by his side and then said, "Helmut, let me introduce Doctor Eleanor Drake, formerly of the K1 Research Unit at Keasden Beck."

Helmut nodded but didn't speak.

"And Doctor Drake, this is Helmut, my son, he is also a talented research physicist – but his speciality is people."

Eleanor's heart rate accelerated; she nodded and said, "Nice, but I have to go."

Helmut leaned towards his father and whispered something in his ear.

Eleanor saw Klossner nod, and then the son retreat through door behind them.

"I told you, I have to go, my husband's waiting outside." It was a weak and pointless statement and she knew that Klossner didn't believe her. She said, "I'm going to London tomorrow, and I left a piece of research on my desk which I need for my trip."

"Yes, yes, of course," said Klossner, staying rooted to the spot.

Seconds later, the door behind him opened, and Helmut reappeared with the most vicious looking dog she'd ever seen. The instant it saw her it lunged forwards snapping and snarling, and straining at the lead. She stepped back in alarm, and then saw Helmut lean towards his father again. She saw

Klossner nod, and then watched in horror as Helmut reached for the dog's collar.

"Oi! What's going on, and who's she?"

Helmut stopped what he was doing, stood up, and looked over Eleanor's shoulder.

Eleanor wheeled around and saw a thickset man standing behind her. Two seconds later, she saw Malory enter the hall.

Malory was shocked. He said, "What are you doing here?"

"More to the point," said Eleanor, "what are *you* doing here?"

"Oi! Oi!" said the thickset man, "I repeat; who the fuck is she, and what's she doing here?"

Malory said, "She's my wife, Violet."

"Violet?" said Klossner. "*Violet?* I don't think so."

Malory looked at Klossner and said, "What do you mean, Axel?"

Eleanor couldn't believe that Malory knew Klossner well enough to call him by his Christian name.

Klossner looked at Eleanor and said, "Is that what you've been calling yourself all these years – Violet? Couldn't you think of a more classical English name than that?"

"Wait, wait," said Malory. "What do you mean, 'is that what you've been calling yourself all these years'?"

"Her name is Doctor Eleanor Drake. She and I had the pleasure of working together many years ago."

"Pleasure?" snapped back Eleanor. "You and Hallenbeck were criminals! No, animals! Cruel, heartless, cowardly animals! And what happened to all of those people? To my friends, and to your friends?"

Everybody was stunned into silence except the dog, which was barking incessantly.

The thickset man glared at Helmut and said, "Get that fucking thing out of here!"

Malory waited until Helmut had disappeared with the dog, and then he looked at Eleanor and said, "What people? What are you talking about?"

Eleanor glared at Klossner and said, "Go on tell him! I'd like to hear, too!"

Klossner's demeanour changed, his mouth turned into a snarl, and he said, "Bring her down to my lab."

"Wait," said Malory. He turned to Eleanor and said, "Is it true? Is your name Eleanor Drake?"

Eleanor nodded.

"Your name isn't Violet Burgess?"

"No."

Malory stared in disbelief. He said, "So when you married me all those years ago, you weren't who you said you were?"

"No," Eleanor was in no mood to explain anything to anybody, and she found it hard to believe that her own husband had been collaborating with one of the men she despised most in the world.

"So the children?" said Malory, "What does that make them?"

The thickset man had had enough. He said, "What is this, the fucking marriage counselling office? We've got work to do, so either stick her in your truck and make sure that she keeps her mouth shut, or give her to the doctor to play with."

Eleanor's mouth fell open in horror as she realised what the thickset man was implying. She turned and looked at Malory and saw an unusual expression on his face. She said, "Mal?"

Malory stared at whom he thought had been his wife, and didn't respond.

"Malory?" repeated Eleanor.

Malory looked at Klossner and saw his questioning look turn to cruel anticipation. He then looked back at Eleanor, and heard her say a third time, "Malory?" He looked back at Klossner, nodded, and said, "Take her away."

Eleanor couldn't believe her ears. She looked at her husband and said, "Why? Why are you doing this?"

Malory stared into Eleanor's eyes for several seconds, and then turned and walked away.

Eleanor shouted, *"Wait, can't we?"*

And then all went black.

Chapter 42

Crowthorne looked at his watch and said, "Today seems to be dragging past."

Leo stopped sipping the umpteenth coffee that they'd consumed as they killed the time. He said, "It does."

"And I have to admit," said Crowthorne leaning towards Leo, "that I feel a bit self-conscious in this leather gear."

Leo looked at Crowthorne's fit-looking, athletic figure, and said, "You look good in it though."

"Maybe, but give me good old-fashioned slacks and a blazer."

"That is old-fashioned, Bob!"

"I know, but I'm more of a golf club kind of guy than a biker."

Leo put down his cup and said, "I suppose we could have nipped to a store or something if you'd wanted to change, but you'd have still had to wear the leathers on the bike."

"Exactly," said Crowthorne, "which would have made the whole exercise pointless."

"Yes, I suppose so."

Crowthorne looked around the nondescript cafe interior, and then said, "Shall we head over …"

A noise came from Leo's phone; he looked at Crowthorne and said, "Only you and Rog Walburn have this number. He pressed the icon and said, "Hello?"

Crowthorne watched as Leo's face became more serious, and listened to his terse comments.

"When?"

"Oh, that's not good."

"Are you sure about that?"

"Yes, yes, *what?* You are joking? Okay, okay, I'll be in touch, bye."

He waited until Leo had put the phone down on the table and then said, "That sounded serious, what was it?"

"Adrian Darke and some of his cronies have been killed in a hotel in London."

Crowthorne was stunned. He said, "Good grief!"

"The Met police have identified Darke; his top bodyguard, Leander Pike, the guy believed to be responsible for launching that RPG at the Malaterre Estate last year, and one of their own number, a Detective Sergeant named Michael Bryce."

"Was it a police action?"

"No, it was reported in; the Met officers found Bryce shot through the chest and forehead with the others, leading them to believe that he was in Darke's pocket."

Crowthorne shook his head and said, "Damn – I hate corrupt cops."

"Me, too," said Leo. He paused and then said, "There was another guy there, too, but he hasn't been identified yet."

Still reeling from the enormity of what he'd heard, Crowthorne said, "And Darke, had he been shot, too?"

"Yes, but the crime scene guys think that he may have shot himself."

Crowthorne gasped in surprise.

Leo continued, "He was found hanging upside-down below a window-cleaner's platform, a hundred-and-fifty feet up in the air. From what the guys could make out, it looks as though the killer had rigged the situation to make Darke believe that he would die either by falling onto some railings below, or by blowing his own brains out. And it seems he took the second option."

"Good Lord in Heaven," said Crowthorne, "how the mighty have fallen." He sat back in his chair and said, "With all that's going on around us, I'd forgotten about him."

Leo didn't know how to proffer his next piece of info; he looked at Crowthorne and said, "We need to be careful with Naomi."

"Why?"

"Her protection has been removed."

"No, no, it couldn't just happen like that," said Crowthorne, "there are protocols to be followed."

"It already has."

Crowthorne said, "What? Impossible! Darke and his associates have only just been found. That doesn't mean that all the bets are off and contracts terminated. There'll be lots of people still unaware of his death!" He held his hand out and said, "Here, give me your phone, I need to make a call."

Leo shook his head and said, "No, you can't."

Crowthorne said, "Yes I can, give me the phone!"

"No – sorry, sir, you can't because it would make anybody you telephoned question how you got this info."

Crowthorne grunted and said, "This is ridiculous, when was her protection cancelled."

"At two o' clock this afternoon."

"Good God alive. Who the hell authorised it?"

"Inspector Milnes."

Crowthorne shook his head and said, "What? Peter Milnes? He should have known better; I'm surprised at him." He looked and said, "So now, nobody knows where she is?"

"No, sir."

"Right, then," Crowthorne was about to say something else, but saw an odd look on Leo's face. He said, "is there something else?"

Leo wasn't sure how Crowthorne would respond but said, "There is, yes, sir."

"Go on."

"Before the assassin left Darke's penthouse, he removed a pocket book from Bryce's jacket and ringed three telephone numbers and initials.

"All three numbers have been traced, and they all belong to serving policemen. Two are already known to have been corrupt associates of Bryce and are under investigation, the third was about to be investigated."

Crowthorne remained tight-lipped, but saw from the look on Leo's face that he wasn't going to like what was to come.

"He's from the Manchester force, and we may know him," said Leo.

Crowthorne gasped and said, "Who?"

"Inspector Milnes, sir."

Crowthorne was mortified. He said, "What? That's preposterous! Peter Milnes an associate of Adrian Darke? Never in a million years!" he hesitated and then said, "Wait, you said we *may* know him – we *do* know him."

Leo said, "It's the best guess so far. The initials that Bryce ringed were 'PM'."

"And that means nothing until it's verified. There could be other 'PM's at Bury."

"I don't know sir…"

"Well I do!" snapped Crowthorne, "It's balderdash, downright bloody balderdash!"

Leo frowned and said, "It *was* suspected that Darke had a contact in the force."

"Stop it! Stop it now!" said Crowthorne, "I won't have you thinking like that until we've established the truth behind this ridiculous assertion."

Leo looked down, and then straight back into Crowthorne's eyes. He said, "Sir – you are suspended – I am not. I have the authority of the crown here, not you. Now please listen to me. Whether Inspector Milnes is guilty of co-operating with Darke or not, is entirely beside the point right now, our immediate consideration has to be Naomi Wilkes because of the position that he has put her in."

Crowthorne's comfort level about Milnes dropped a notch when he realised that Milnes would have known that, too. He said, "Yes, yes, of course, you're right. What are you proposing?"

"That we find out where she is, and make sure that she's protected."

Crowthorne frowned. He knew that Milnes was aware that Darke was dead, and that any potential assassin wouldn't be paid, so what was his point of removing her protection so quickly? It didn't make sense – and he knew that he was missing something. He looked at his watch and saw that it was 6:45 p.m. He said, "It's too late to try her office, try her home number."

Leo nodded and dialled the number; he heard Carlton say, "Hello?"

"Carlton, it's Leo; where's Naomi?"

"She's gone out with Helen to some historic society meeting, why?"

"Which historic society?"

"I'm not sure; why, what's going on?"

Leo didn't want to alarm Carlton and said, "I need to talk to her urgently."

"About what?"

Leo hesitated and then said, "Carlton, please take my word for it, I need to know where Naomi is right now, it's …"

Crowthorne heard Leo's indecision and said, "Give me the phone."

Leo handed the phone over.

"Carlton," said Crowthorne, "it's Bob. Some very confusing and unusual circumstances have occurred over the last forty-eight hours and we think that Naomi may have got caught up in the tail-end of it. Her life could be in imminent danger, and we need to know where she is right now."

Carlton was horrified. He said, "I thought that you guys were watching her, so why are you asking *me* where she is?"

"It's complicated, and we're wasting time. Now do you know where she is or not?"

Carlton stopped and thought for a second; he recalled hearing a remark by Naomi as she spoke to Helen on her mobile. He said, "I heard her say something to Helen about how long it would take to get to Skelmersdale, so I guess that's where they've gone."

Crowthorne clasped his hand over the mobile phone and said to Leo, "They've gone to Ascensis." He then removed his hand and said, "Okay, Carlton, I think I know the place. Leave it with us and we'll be in touch."

Carlton said, "Don't you let anything happen to her Bob! We've been here before, and I'm trusting you."

"I won't, I promise," said Crowthorne. He terminated the call and then turned to Leo; he said, "We've got to go – *now!*"

As the companions walked out to the motorbike Crowthorne couldn't stop thinking about Peter Milnes. His decision to cancel her protection at such short notice made no sense at all, and he couldn't understand it.

For the first time, he dared to consider whether it may just be possible that Milnes had been Darke's mole in the Manchester force after all.

He followed Leo out into the car park whilst pulling on his leather gloves, and then walked smack into his back. He jumped back and said, "Whoa! Sorry."

Leo didn't respond; he just stood looking into the car park.

Crowthorne stepped to one side and then stopped too.

Parked either side of the motorbike were two cars, each containing two men, and looking straight at them.

The driver of one stepped out, walked across to Leo and Crowthorne, held up a Warrant Card and said, "Gentlemen, my name is Mackenzie Hudson and I'm a senior field operative with MI5. Perhaps you'd care to step into the back of the car, and tell us what you've done to wind up our bosses in London."

"I'm Superintendent Robert Crowthorne of Greater Manchester Police, and this is Detective Sergeant Brandon Chance," said Crowthorne.

"We know who you are, sir."

"Then how did you find us so quickly?" said Leo.

Hudson raised his eyebrows and said, "Really Sergeant? You need to ask?"

Leo shrugged and said, "Okay, but I'm not getting into the back of any car."

Hudson said, "I can accept that," he pointed towards the cafe and said, "will here be okay?"

"No it won't," said Crowthorne, "we think that a couple of colleagues of ours could be in grave danger, and we need to get to them quickly."

"You are suspended from duty, sir," said Hudson, "and you will answer our questions, or we will arrest you as a matter of national security."

"National security?" said Leo, "you've got to be joking! We haven't done anything to endanger national security."

"And I'll be the judge of that after we've asked the questions, or you will be arrested." Hudson pulled his leather blouson jacket to one side and revealed a holstered firearm. He then said, "Do we have an understanding, Sergeant?"

Crowthorne shot Leo a quick glance, and then turned to Hudson. He said, "All right, we'll answer your blasted questions, but if anything happens to our colleagues, we will hold you personally responsible."

Hudson nodded towards the two cars and another man walked over and joined them. He said, "This is my associate Mister Jones, and he will be accompanying us."

Crowthorne and Leo nodded at the implacable-looking 'Mister Jones' and then walked with Hudson, back into the cafe.

Chapter 43

Wood sat tapping his pencil on his desk; he couldn't concentrate, he didn't have the will to move on to his next job, and he couldn't put the events of the previous night out of his mind.

Everything, it seemed, had happened in a flash. The car and van had arrived within fifteen minutes of Crowthorne's departure; the men had identified themselves as MI5 operatives and he and Leo had been whisked away in the blink of an eye. Within the hour he'd been instructed by no lesser person than the Chief Constable of Greater Manchester Police himself, that he was to speak to no one about what had gone at the temperance hall in Keasden, and that if he did, he'd be arrested and charged under the Security Service Act of 1989. He'd then been placed on an express train, and sent to London in a First Class compartment, minus his confiscated mobile phone, but with two-hundred-and-fifty pounds in cash to buy a new one, and a meal for the journey.

He'd gone home, slept fitfully, and then returned to Hampstead Heath Police Station at 12 noon. There, it had become even more surreal. When he'd returned, it was as though he'd never been away; that he'd left the station after a previous day's work, and had come back, the following day.

Nobody had spoken to him about his trip up north, not even the Detective Chief Inspector in charge of his department, and he'd found himself looking at everybody as they went about their tasks, ignoring him, and keeping out of his way.

He drew in a deep breath, put the pencil down, and decided to have a hot drink. He walked up to the canteen deep in thought, and then ordered a mug of tea.

"Hey kid!"

Wood turned around and saw the lone figure of PC Frank Hawcroft sitting in the corner with a coffee.

Frank Hawcroft was a uniformed Constable who'd been with the force for thirty-three years. He was one year from retiring, and by the rank and file, was one of the station's most loved characters. On the other side of the coin, the senior ranks considered him impossible to control, devoid of any respect for authority, and a complete pain in the backside. He was a huge and imposing man with a massive chest and biceps, he was ruggedly handsome, and he was loved by dozens of the borough's single and married ladies, who'd all nicknamed him *Errol Flynn* because of his renowned sexual athleticism and apparent size in that department.

But because of his exemplary police record and his years of service, despite being in trouble time and again, the senior ranks had put up with him and his antics; some better than others.

Wood couldn't help smiling; he recalled the years of endless fun, watching Frank getting in and out of all sorts of scrapes, and the joy of working with him from being a young PC, to the position he was in now. And he knew that his rank of Detective Inspector meant nothing to him – that he was still just a mate, and that he'd still be called 'kid' by him.

"Hiya, Frank," he said, "What are you doing here on your own?"

"Grabbing a cuppa before I head back out."

"Have you made an arrest or something?"

Frank said, "No nothing like that – here, come and sit down."

Wood walked over to the table and was about to sit down, until Frank pushed his chair back, opened his legs, and pointed towards his crotch.

In his deep husky voice, Frank said, "Stick your hands over these."

"Over what?"

"My bollocks."

Wood half-smiled and said, "And why would I do that?"

"Feel how hot they are."

"Why? What's happened now?"

"I've just had them roasted by Splasher and the Super."

Wood knew that by 'Splasher', Frank had been referring to his Duty Inspector Carpenter, who had the reputation for over-salivating when he ate. He smiled and recalled how Frank had been hauled over the coals one day, when he'd laid newspaper all around Splasher's chair during one breakfast time when his salivation problem had gone into overdrive.

"Splasher *and* the Superintendent?" said Wood sitting down, "Why, what did you do?"

Frank leaned forwards and said, "Do you remember that old car of Gus Hall's?"

"Our Gus Hall, the drill instructor?"

"Yes."

"What, that ancient green, 1950s, Ford Popular?"

"Yes – and do you remember its wheels?"

"Yes, they were really thin, like fat bicycle wheels."

"That's it," said Frank.

Wood frowned and said, "What about it?"

"Last night I saw it parked in Hill Street and thought that I'd play a prank on him."

Wood sat back in his chair and said, "Go on, what did you do?"

"I stuck a ticket on it, and signed it so that he would know it was from me, informing him that his vehicle was going to be reported under the 1991 Road Traffic Act for having no visible means of support."

Wood burst out laughing and said, "For Christ's sake, Frank, only you would do a thing like that!"

"Yeah maybe, but then it went tits up."

Still smiling, Wood said, "Why, did Gus take umbrage or something?"

"No – he'd only gone and sold the fucking thing!"

Wood rocked back in his seat and laughed. He said, "*Sold it?* Priceless!"

"Yes, to some sour-faced old sod who was a Ford enthusiast, and he came in here this morning with a right old cob on!"

Wood burst out laughing again and said, "You crack me up, Frank, you really do."

Frank pointed to his crotch and said, "So now you know where to stick your bread if you want toast for the next couple of hours."

Wood finished his tea, and felt like a new man. He admired Frank's boundless enthusiasm for fun, for never staying put down, despite the odd 'roasting', and how he never took life too seriously. And by the time that Frank got up and announced, "Gotta go kid – Rosie in the butcher's shop has put some sausages aside for me," he'd made up his mind.

He stood up, patted Frank on the arm and said, "Take care, mate, and try to keep out of trouble!" He saw Frank wink, and then leave.

He went downstairs, walked back into the CID office and said, "Right, listen up everybody, unless any of you are working on who stole the Crown Jewels, I want you to stop, and come and see me."

Minutes later most of the duty staff was gathered around his desk. Taking a leaf out of Frank's 'say-it-like-it-is' book, he said, "I don't know what you've been told about me, but here's the 'SP' – last night I was given the bum's rush back here from North Yorkshire after stumbling upon a crime scene that had something to do with MI5. I won't go into details about it for the obvious reasons, but they wanted me out of the way quick time, and just when it had started to get interesting.

"Now, despite sticking a gagging order on me involving the Security Service Act of 1989, they didn't say that I had to stop investigating the peripherals." He paused and looked from interested face, to interested face. He then said, "So that's what we're going to do."

A voice from behind the gathering said, "Wait, one minute."

Everybody looked as Detective Chief Inspector Jim Abrams joined them.

Wood's heart sank as he thought that his plan was about to be scuppered.

"If we're going to do this, we need to be very careful not to alert any unwanted attention," said Abrams.

Wood could have jumped up and kissed him. He said, "We have your permission to do this do we, sir?"

Abrams said, "As long as we play it by the rules. I've had outsider's sticking their beaks into my investigations and putting the brakes on for no good reason, far too often before, so let's see if we can do this one on our own." He looked at the staff one-by-one and then said, "Right, that's all I wanted to say for now, so I'll leave you in Inspector Wood's hands," he then looked at Wood and said, "And you let me know if I can help."

"I will, thank you, sir," Wood smiled and waited until Abrams had departed. He looked at his watch and said, "It's four o' clock. I'm going to make a list of what I want done, and then I want a volunteer to drive me to Skelmersdale near Liverpool, in half an hour's time."

"I'll do that, Guv," said a fresh young face that had recently joined the CID.

Wood looked up, and saw a handsome, fit-looking, and enthusiastic young man looking at him. Something looked familiar about the twinkle in his eye, and the husky timbre of his voice. He said, "You're new to the department, and a bit of a fire-brand I've been told, what's your name?"

"Simon, Guv, Simon Hawcroft."

Wood frowned and said, "You're not related to Frank by any chance?"

"He's my dad."

Wood sat back in his seat and saw the same effervescent enthusiasm and suppressed humour in the young man's face, and wondered if he'd be making a rod for his own back. He looked at Simon for a few seconds, and then heard him say, "I'm a good driver, Guv, honest."

"All right," he said, "be ready with my car by four-thirty."

Seconds later he walked into Abrams office and said, "You know that you said to ask, if I needed your help, sir?"

Abrams looked up from his desk and said, "Yes?"

"Well, what I need, is a bit of inter-force agreement, which the other force might not necessarily know about …"

Chapter 44

Eleanor lay in bed with her eyes closed; she had no idea where she was or what day it was, but she guessed that it must have been the evening. Everywhere was warm and gloomy, but it was as quiet as the grave. She was locked in a nine feet by eight feet open-barred cell within a room whose walls had been painted black, and covered in spongy-looking cones. She'd surmised that they had been some kind of sound-proofing.

Inside her cell was a functional single bed with clean linen; a washbasin with soap and a towel, and there was a toilet behind a rudimentary curtain. A small CCTV camera had been positioned over her bed.

Since she'd first awakened with a sore head, she'd had one meal that she'd presumed had been dinner, followed hours later by an obvious breakfast, and then two others, leading her to believe that it was evening, but she'd guessed that if somebody had been playing mind-games with her, the order of food could have been adjusted, to make her believe that it had been evening, when it hadn't.

She hadn't been mistreated or maltreated, but she'd been undressed, and she'd been shocked to see that her normal length blonde, pubic hair had been trimmed making the external physical detail of her vagina more evident. She'd then been clothed in only, a knee-length, white cotton nightdress.

She'd seen that there was no apparent way that she could get out of the cell without the key, and that even if she had, she'd still be locked in the outer room. Her only visitor, Helmut Klossner, had two sets of keys, and she'd noted that he'd been careful to lock both doors before departing.

Her bright and intelligent mind had gone into overdrive calculating every possible scenario about the reason for her captivity instead of disposal, and her best guess had been that she was being kept in peak condition, until somebody, more than likely Axel Klossner, was ready for her. But what that entailed, she didn't care to speculate. His admission that he was running 'der menschliche abteilung' or 'human department' had been enough to get her planning, and an idea had formed when she'd seen Helmut looking at her legs as she'd bent over to get her empty lunchtime food tray.

She knew that despite her age, she had good legs and a good figure, and she'd been ready with the next part of her plan when Helmut had come to collect her dinner tray that night.

With her back to him, as he'd waited by the open cell door, she'd bent over, picked up the tray, and then knocked the plastic beaker off it, onto the floor. Then slowly, without bending her legs, she'd bent over further to pick up the vessel, knowing that the lower part of her bottom would have been seen by him.

And she'd known that she'd achieved the effect that she'd wanted when she'd turned around and looked at him. His mouth, which had been closed prior to her bending over, had come open.

Another part her plan had worked too. She'd seen the CCTV camera above her bed move when she'd pretended to

357

be too warm. She'd pushed her sheet down, and as it had gone down, so too had the camera. She'd lain still for several minutes, and then parted her shapely legs – but not too much – knowing that her nightdress had ridden up without exposing her. The camera had buzzed as the zoom had been operated.

With a satisfied feeling, she'd turned over and not moved thereafter, knowing that she'd got somebody, probably Helmut, hooked.

Wednesday 15th August 1973.

<u>*P.M.*</u>

Eleanor had completed another successful day. She hadn't been required to do anything other than stay in her cell, but she'd used the time well on two things, her thumbnails and Helmut.

Being a research physicist, she'd always preferred to have short nails, but because of an upcoming family event, her daughters had persuaded her otherwise, and she'd grown them more than a quarter of an inch in length. And since her captivity, she'd wasted no opportunity to file away at her thumbnails on whatever rough surface she could find whenever she'd been out of view of the camera.

And then there had been Helmut. She'd teased him with little flashes, until in the evening after dinner; she'd exposed more of her backside, and for a much longer time than before. She'd turned around and seen him stroking his semi-hard penis with his left forefinger. He'd looked flushed, but when he'd seen her looking, and kept on looking, he'd openly squeezed it, whilst staring into her face. He'd then swallowed hard, and departed.

Within minutes, she'd heard the CCTV camera moving.

She'd climbed on top of her bed, laid with her legs closed at first, but then she'd opened them, and being careful not to expose anything, she'd made one or two definite rubs with her right middle finger over the top of her clitoris.

The zoom on the camera had gone crazy for minutes afterwards.

Thursday 16th August 1973.

<u>*A.M.*</u>

Following her breakfast, Eleanor had heard her first terrified scream. It had sounded feminine, but it could have been a high-pitched male or young boy. Regardless, it had brought her back to reality. She'd almost lulled herself into believing that as long as she'd teased Helmut, she would be left alone. But all of that had changed.

Midway between her breakfast meal and her lunch, the door to the room had opened and Axel Klossner had stepped in. He'd stared at her for a few seconds, and he'd appeared to be about to speak, but then he'd been grabbed by the arm and pulled out of the room. Her understanding of German wasn't that good, but from the snatches that she'd heard, it had sounded as though Helmut had been asking his father to leave her alone. She'd heard an aggravated exchange, and then Axel say, *"Ordnung - aber nur eine Woche, verstanden?"*

She'd known what that had meant; *'Okay, but one week only, understand?'* The door to her room had then been closed, but not before she'd heard another agonised scream. That had meant that either the poor soul being tortured, or experimented upon, was being done so mechanically, or that there had been more personnel than just the Klossners, in the facility.

She knew then, that she had to act quickly.

An hour later, as Helmut had opened her cell door to give her, her lunchtime meal, she'd taken a huge chance. She'd walked across to him whilst squeezing both of her nipples through her nightdress, she'd looked him straight in the eyes and said, "I heard what you did for me earlier today, and tonight you won't regret it."

Helmut hadn't responded, but he'd swallowed hard. He'd felt his heart rate increase, and the familiar surge of blood in his penis as it responded to the implication.

He didn't know what it was about the English woman, but he wanted her. He'd always had a thing for older and more sophisticated women, but he'd never seen one in such good physical condition as Eleanor. And with every ounce of his being, he wanted to see her awake and naked; writhing in the throes of sexual abandonment, and to be caressing every glorious contour of her body.

With panting breath, he'd handed the tray through the door, he'd seen Eleanor raise her arms to take it, and then as she'd done so, her nightdress had lifted, and he'd seen her soft, blonde, pubic hair. The hair that he'd so relished trimming, without his father's knowledge.

He'd not been able to help himself. He'd reached out to touch her, but Eleanor had backed away, and whispered, "Be patient … come back tonight."

He'd nodded, departed, and gone back to his room. Once there, he'd locked his door, almost ripped his trousers and underpants off, and had masturbated until he'd ejaculated more sperm than he'd ever seen before.

P.M.

When he'd returned, Helmut had been ready.

He'd known that he'd be alone that night because his father had driven to Ormskirk Zoo. The same as he had on every other Thursday night, to view the animal specimens on offer there.

He'd prepared Eleanor a juicy steak meal, better than anything that she'd had before, complete with a glass of chilled Liebfraumilch, and a flower. He'd put on his best shirt and trousers, and he'd shaved and applied his best aftershave lotion, but he hadn't been stupid enough to realise that Eleanor may have only been teasing him, in order to effect some sort of escape plan.

On the other hand, he had heard that some captives had developed feelings for their captors, and as he'd turned the key to the cell room door, he'd hoped that that had been the case with her.

Whether she had, or had not however, and whether or not it meant having to resort to force, he had determined that that night, he was going to have her.

He stepped through the outer door, locked it, and then looked over to her cell. His heart rate leapt. He saw that she was stark naked, and that she looked magnificent. He felt his hands begin to shake, and the blood course through his temporal veins as she stood watching him with her left hand squeezing her left, pale pink, nipple, and her right hand stroking her beautiful, creamy-white thigh.

He went to the cell, held the dinner tray in his left hand, unlocked the door, and stepped through.

Eleanor remained where she was for a second, and then smiled and said, "Here, let me." She reached out and took the tray.

She turned her back on him, bent down to put the tray on her bed, and then turned and looked over her right shoulder. He was looking down at her shapely, naked backside.

She laid the tray on the bed, glanced at her razor sharp, pointed thumbnails, and then turned around to face him. She saw that he was transfixed by her nakedness. She walked over to him, took his right hand in her left, and guided it down between her legs. She then stepped closer and placed her hands either side of his face. She waited until she felt Helmut's middle finger slip between the outer lips of her vagina, and then she plunged both of her pointed thumbnails deep into his eyes, and slashed them down his cheeks.

Helmut screamed and staggered back, clawing at his agonised face.

With the speed of lightning, Eleanor snatched the steak knife off the tray, grabbed hold of the hair on Helmut's forehead, yanked it back, and then rammed the knife into his Adam's apple, and slashed across.

Blood spurted out across the room, Helmut dropped to his knees coughing and gurgling, and then fell face forwards on the floor.

The next thirty minutes were the most terrifying of her life. She snatched Helmut's top clothes off and put them on to the best of her ability, she then tore a strip of sheet off her bed and placed it around her neck like a scarf to cover the blood stains. Then with a deep breath, she let herself out of the cell room.

She found that she was in a large laboratory surrounded by bottles containing body parts soaked in formaldehyde. Everything was there, from hands and feet, to organs and foetuses. She saw vicious looking instruments laid out next to two porcelain post-mortem tables with blood channels and restraining straps. She shivered and didn't even want to contemplate what God-forsaken atrocities had been carried out there.

Then she heard a whimper. Within ten minutes she'd freed another four people, and they'd made their way out of the building via a long tunnel, and into a deep wood. She had no idea where she was, but she instructed the four captives to hide in a certain cluster of trees until she'd sent for help.

She walked through the wood following the North Star, and thanking God for the clear night, until she found a road. She then stopped and considered her situation.

She knew that MI5 wanted to silence her because of her knowledge of K1; she expected that Klossner and his associates would do everything in their power to recapture her to get revenge for his son, and to silence her about their sick activities, and she knew that she'd be wanted by the police for Helmut's killing.

She looked left and then right and wondered what to do. She sat down on the edge of the road, and then felt a lump in her back trouser pocket. It was Helmut's wallet, and it was stuffed with cash. She then had a brainwave, a lifeline that had been given to her thirty-six years earlier.

She turned left, and followed the lonely road until she realised that it was the one that led to the St Mary Cross Animal Research Unit. At the end she saw the familiar telephone box on the corner. She went inside, dialled a number, and hoped that somebody would answer.

Chapter 45

Helen was full of misgivings. She looked at the dark and forbidding woods either side of the approach road to the Ascensis facility and thanked Heaven that it was a full moon that night. She turned to Naomi and said, "I don't know about this, N, I think that we should have told somebody where we were going before coming here."

"And what would the point of that been?" said Naomi, "We wouldn't have had the carte blanche that we will now, and I'm determined to get to the bottom of this case if it's the last thing that we do."

"And that's what I'm worried about, I don't want it to be the last thing that we do."

"Oh come on," said Naomi, "that's a bit melodramatic isn't it?"

"No, I mean it."

Naomi turned and glanced at Helen and saw the worried look upon her face. She said, "I did offer to come alone, and if you're that worried now, I'll go back and drop you at that pub on the corner, and then come and pick you up after I've done."

"No way," said Helen, "I'm here now, and I'm not letting you out of my sight."

Naomi nodded and glanced down at the satnav in her car. It showed a chequered flag at the end of each destination, and she could see it now, on the small screen resolution.

"Half a mile to go," she said, "we'll get in, go straight to the loading bay, check that out, find out where that odd pipe went to from Lab 2, and then get out. Nobody will ever know we've been."

Helen looked at their black clothes and sturdy shoes and said, "Okay, I don't look good in all black."

Naomi turned and stared at her friend; she said, "What?"

Helen kept her gaze forwards and said, "It's just an observation, that's all."

"I don't believe you," said Naomi, "we're heading out to a remote site in the back of beyond, to a place where people have gone missing, and without anybody knowing but us two, and your biggest concern is that you don't look good in black?"

"I didn't say that it was my biggest concern," said Helen; she paused and then added, "it is *a* concern, but not my biggest."

Naomi smiled and said, "Priceless, H, you never fail to amaze me."

Helen didn't respond, she looked down at the drab clothing, shook her head in disdain, and then continued looking out of the windscreen.

Naomi said, "It's just round that bend up ahead. Get the keys out of my bag and it's the big silver ..." she stopped speaking, frowned, and then hit the brakes.

Helen, who'd, been reaching into the foot well for Naomi's bag, lurched forwards and then said, "Whoa, what the hell?"

Naomi pulled the car up on the side of the road and said, "There's a light on up there."

Helen stared along the gloomy road, and said, "Where?"

"Look up into the trees off to the right-hand side of the road."

Helen looked to where Naomi was pointing and said, "You're right," she thought about it for a second or two, and then said, "Maybe a rabbit activated a security light or something."

"Or maybe somebody."

A shiver ran down Helen's spine; she looked at Naomi, and saw for the first time, the difference between them. Naomi had a grim and determined expression on her face, and rather than looking put off by what they'd seen, she appeared to have gathered more resolve. She said, "We're not going to be taking any silly chances are we?"

Naomi remained silent for a second and then said, "Okay, here's what we'll do. We'll keep going down the road, drive straight past the gates, and see if we can see where the light's coming from. If it looks safe to stop and investigate, we will, if not, we'll keep on driving and stop another half mile up the road and consider our options."

Helen drew in a deep breath and said, "If you say so, but, I don't want us to get - well, you know."

"I know," said Naomi, "and I won't let anything happen to you."

Helen turned and looked her friend. She knew that she was the eldest, but Naomi appeared to have grown in stature and confidence and for the oddest reason, she did feel safe with her. She turned and looked up the road, and then said, "Right, let's do it."

Naomi put the car into gear, drove up the road, and was about to drive past the site without stopping, until she saw Carlton standing outside the brightly lit the gates.

"Bloody hell!" she said, hitting the brakes once more.

"Was that?"

"Carlton? Yes; what the hell is he doing here?" Naomi backed the car up, turned into the Ascensis driveway and pulled up next to Carlton. She wound the window down and said, "What are you doing here?"

"More to the point," said Carlton, "what are you doing here?"

"I'm, I'm …"

"You're doing it again, aren't you? Going off and taking silly chances without letting me know."

Naomi was flabbergasted; she said, "But how on earth did you know that …"

"That you were going to do something stupid tonight?"

"All right, all right, enough with the moralising," said Naomi, "I'm sorry I didn't tell you and …"

"And it won't ever happen again, do you hear me?"

Naomi caved, and said, "Yes okay, I promise, but what are you doing here?"

Carlton turned and pointed through the gates; he said, "I'm with them."

Naomi squinted into the abundance of bright lights and said, "Who?"

Carlton said, "Drive through the gates and park your car on the right-hand side of the path. You'll see when you get out."

Naomi did as she was instructed, parked her car and got out with Helen.

"I thought that you said we'd be alone," said Helen.

"I thought we would be."

"Only this is really annoying," said Helen.

"I know: but maybe it's for the best after all."

Helen turned and glared at Naomi; she said, "No it's not! I told you that I don't look good in all black!"

Naomi opened her mouth to respond, but then heard a voice behind her.

"Good evening, ladies, fancy seeing you two here."

Helen turned and saw Bob Crowthorne standing behind her, dressed in his leather gear; her heart leapt a beat when she saw how masculine and handsome he looked. She then looked down at her drab clothing, and shot Naomi a scathing glance.

Naomi said, "What?"

Helen widened her eyes and looked down at her clothing, and then looked back.

Naomi's mouth fell open; she looked at Helen, turned and looked at Crowthorne, and then turned back to Helen. She said, "Have you got the hots for Bob?"

Helen glared and said, *"Shush!"*

"Helen Milner, you have!"

"No I haven't, now shush!"

Naomi stared at the flustered-looking Helen with a half-smile on her face until she heard her say, "Stop gawking at me like that!"

Naomi nodded and said, "Okay, but when we get back to the office, we're going to have some serious heart-to-hearts!"

"Okay, whatever!"

Naomi turned, looked at Crowthorne, and said, "Hi Bob," she gestured around and said, "I don't get this; what are you and Carlton doing here?"

Crowthorne said, "Not just Carlton and me," he turned and pointed to a group of approaching men.

Naomi squinted into the bright arc lights that appeared to have been set up all around the building, and waited until more men came into view. She recognised Leo, smiled, and give him a quick hug, and then she saw another man approaching.

"This is my good friend Detective Inspector Maurice Finney of the Lancashire force here in Skelmersdale."

Naomi introduced herself and Helen and then said, "Now will somebody tell me what you are all doing here?"

"We're here because of you and your impetuosity," said Carlton as he caught up.

"And to try to sort out this mess once and for all," added Crowthorne.

Naomi turned and saw four more men in plain clothes, walking towards them.

"Naomi, Helen," said Crowthorne as the men approached, "this is Lieutenant Commander Mackenzie Hudson of MI5 – and his associate, known to us all as 'Mister Jones'."

Naomi nearly gagged, she said, "*MI5?* What the hell are MI5 doing here?"

Hudson and Jones shook Naomi's hand, and a serious-looking Hudson said, "We're assisting the police with their investigation, Madam."

"But why? And what have MI5 got to do with this?"

Crowthorne said, "It's complicated and it's protracted, perhaps we can explain later?"

Naomi raised her eyebrows and said, "Okay."

Crowthorne turned to the two other men and said, "And these two gentlemen are Detective Inspector Stuart Wood and Detective Constable Simon Hawcroft of the Metropolitan Police."

Naomi exclaimed, "The Metropolitan Police? From London? My God!"

Wood shook Naomi's hand and said, "The same, and it's nice to meet you."

Simon stepped forwards and offered his hand.

Naomi was instantly taken with Simon's good looks. She took hold of his hand and knew in an instant that he'd be a real ladies' man.

"Hello," said Simon, "it's a pleasure to meet you," he leaned his attractive-looking face towards Naomi's left ear and half-whispered, "but I'm not so sure about the gentleman thing though."

Naomi smiled, and stepped aside until the introductions had been completed, and then said, "Now, will one of you gentlemen ..." she cast a glance at Simon and saw him raise his eyebrows, "... please tell us what's going on, and why you are all here."

Crowthorne looked at Hudson and Wood, saw them both nod, and said, "Okay, as I said earlier, it's complicated, and because of the building's history, there are certain restrictions in what we can have access to."

Naomi frowned and said, "Then that makes coming here beside the point doesn't it?"

"Not at all," said Crowthorne, "I don't mean that we will be restricted about *where* we can search, I mean that ..." he turned and looked at Hudson, saw him nod, and then continued, "... we er, just can't have access to any construction plans."

Naomi didn't have any compunction about confronting Hudson. She turned to him and said, "Why not?"

"It's classified, Madam, and there's nothing that any of us can do about it."

"Poppycock!" said Naomi, "We're looking for potential missing persons here. You could walk away for half an hour and let us get on with our jobs."

Hudson looked down at the ground, and then back up again. He said, "Not to put too fine a point on it, Madam, why do you think that we're here trying to assist?"

Naomi realised that she may have overstepped the mark and said, "Oh, of course, sorry."

"The information regarding the building's history and construction are indeed classified, but even HM Government has a heart when it comes to missing people, and we will do all that we can to help our colleagues in the police, within the confines of our restrictions."

Naomi felt two inches tall, and repeated, "Yes, I'm sorry, Lieutenant Commander."

"Mackenzie will do fine," said Hudson.

"Thank you, Mackenzie; and I really am sorry, I didn't think," Naomi glanced at Carlton and saw him look at her with a 'that told you' expression upon his face. She turned back to Crowthorne and said, "Okay, so where do we go from here?"

Crowthorne said, "The history and the usage of this building has been the source of derision and wild speculation for years, but certain hitherto unknown things, have come to light," he glanced at Hudson, and said, "things that are not classified under the Official Secrets Act, such as the building's services."

"The services?" said Naomi. "What have they to do with any of this?"

"We don't know: but we do know that nobody appears to be supplying the building with any of its power, water, gas, and sewage services, and that as far as the Skelmersdale Council Tax Department is concerned, this place doesn't exist."

Naomi said, "That is odd," she turned to Hudson and said, "Were MI5 aware of this?"

Hudson considered his answer before replying, and then said, "In a nutshell, no. The classification restrictions are so stringent, that a very limited number of people have access to the files, and I'm not one of them."

"So you're just as much in the dark about here, as the rest of us?"

"One of the reasons for us being here."

Naomi turned to Wood and Simon and said, "And why are Met officers here?" She saw Wood look at Hudson before responding.

"We're here because there's a lot more to this place than meets the eye, it has links to London, and to Yorkshire as well, and we're all trying to solve what appears to be puzzles within puzzles."

Naomi shook her head and said, "So where do Helen and I fit into all of this?"

Crowthorne said, "We want you to lead us."

Naomi was astounded; she looked at all of the equipment and personnel and said, "*Us?*" She made a sweeping gesture with her left hand and said, "With all of this at your disposal you want *us* to lead you? What the hell can we do that you can't?"

Crowthorne said, "Were you and Helen planning to do this on your own tonight?"

"We er …"

"Be honest."

Naomi shot a guilty glance at Carlton, and then looked back at Crowthorne. She said, "Yes."

"Well," said Crowthorne, "that's all that we want you to do now. Consider us as back-up."

Naomi looked around: she saw Doberman Security vans, police vans and cars, two police dogs, plain clothes officers, two police women, the two Met police officers, two MI5 guys, Crowthorne, Leo, and Carlton. She said, "My God, I'll bet

Bush and Blair didn't have this much back-up before the first invasion of Iraq!"

Crowthorne raised his eyebrows and said, "Don't even get me started on that!" He stepped to one side and said, "We've opened the first door, and set up lighting inside, do you want to start in there?"

"We do, but it's the loading bay that interests us most."

"Us?" said Crowthorne. He turned, gave Helen a sweeping look up and down, and saw from her reaction which buttons to push. He said, "Do you mean you and Coco Chanel here?"

Naomi couldn't help grinning; she looked at Crowthorne's impish face, and said, "You bugger!"

Crowthorne smiled, stepped closer to Helen and half-whispered, "Choose those yourself did you?"

Helen glared at Crowthorne, and then at Naomi; she said, "Wait 'til I get you back to the office!"

Naomi grinned, winked at a still-smiling Crowthorne, and said, "Okay, let's go."

Chapter 46

Naomi walked into Entrance A of the building and was shocked to see what had been set up. Unlike her previous visit when everywhere had been bathed in natural daylight, the interior had been illuminated by high-intensity arc lamps creating an environment that highlighted every spider's web, scar, and blemish of the raggedy interior, making it brighter, but somehow, more spooky.

She walked straight to Lab 2, removed a powerful torch from her bag, and looked under the bench.

"You were looking at something under there the last time we were here," said Crowthorne, "what is it?"

Naomi looked up and said, "It's a pipe."

Crowthorne walked around to Naomi and crouched down. He looked under the bench and saw what Naomi was pointing at.

"It comes in or goes out at one end of the lab, and does the same at the other," said Naomi.

Crowthorne looked at her with a puzzled expression. He said, "And that's unusual because of what?"

"Two things: it appears to serve no useful purpose, and once it goes into the party wall…" she pointed towards Lab 4, "…it disappears altogether."

Crowthorne turned and looked at the wall opposite and said, "And that side?"

"It's a utility cupboard with several pipes running across at roof level. It could be any one of them."

Crowthorne stared at the wall for a second, and then turned and looked at the party wall to Lab 4. He said, "Am I missing something here?" He looked down at Naomi and said, "What's so intriguing – isn't it just a utility pipe?" He faltered as he said the word 'utility' and recalled that there were no records of any utilities going into the building. He frowned, swivelled around, looked at the wall next to the cupboard again, and then stood with a puzzled expression on his face. Seconds later he said, "I recall from our last visit that you were interested in this pipe, and that was before you knew that no utilities were recorded coming into the building; what interests you about it?"

"I told you; it appears to serve no useful purpose."

Crowthorne wasn't often stumped, but he felt stupid, and when he saw Wood and Hudson walk in with Helen, he didn't like it. He frowned and said, "Hey, how about you tell me what's on your mind."

Naomi stood up and said, "Why doesn't this pipe run through the lab at roof level like the others?"

Crowthorne was rendered speechless for a few seconds, and then when he attempted to speak, he was cut off.

"Val Lockyer told us that her mother had told her, to check out pipeline 'PL3'. She didn't tell Val what PL3 was, where it was located, or what it was for, but I wondered, because of the mysterious aspect of its placement, whether this could be it."

"Interesting," commented Wood. He got down on his haunches, looked at Hudson and said, "May I?"

Hudson said, "Be my guest."

Wood took hold of the mystery pipe and wrenched it down. Several retaining brackets popped off the underside of the bench exposing several feet of it. He saw that it was a ten foot length bonded to others with black-painted sleeves. He wrenched another section down, saw the line warp, but not break, and noted that all of it consisted of ten foot lengths.

Hudson, who'd knelt down too, felt the pipe, and then looked from end to end. He said, "This is steel, so given the age of the building, it's not a water pipe, otherwise it would have been made out of copper."

"What's this?"

Everybody turned and saw Naomi looking at her right hand. They walked over and saw a dark, sticky substance between her right forefinger and thumb on her protective gloves.

"Where did that come from?" said Crowthorne.

"It oozed out of one of the joints when Inspector Wood wrenched the second section of pipe down."

"It looks like oil," said Wood.

Naomi held her hand up to her nose and then recoiled at the smell. She said, "It isn't, it doesn't have that smell, and it stinks."

Crowthorne looked at the substance and said, "Is it affecting your glove?"

Naomi looked closer and said, "No."

Leo leaned over, looked, and frowned. He said, "May I?"

Naomi lifted her hand up to Leo's nose, saw him smell it, recoil, and then step back with a frown on his face.

Leo looked at Crowthorne and said, "I think it could be old blood."

Naomi was shocked, she looked at her hand and said, "Ooh!"

"Curiouser and curiouser …" Everybody turned and saw Wood staring at a joint in the pipeline.

"What?" said Crowthorne.

Wood elevated the section of pipe and said, "Unless I'm mistaken, these are masking sleeves."

"Meaning what?"

Wood looked up and said, "Meaning that it looks as though each end of these ten foot sections could have re-routed whatever it was carrying, to somewhere else." He looked at Naomi and said, "Can I borrow your torch for a minute?"

Naomi handed the torch over and watched as Wood worked his way along the pipe, from one end to the other.

A few minutes later he looked up and said, "There are corresponding holes running through the bench above each of the joints."

Helen looked at the work surfaces and said, "There are none on the bench tops."

"Then new tops must have been installed when the joints were capped."

"Indicating that whatever was routed through was no longer needed," offered Hudson.

"Or that it was re-routed to another lab," said the taciturn 'Mister Jones'.

Crowthorne felt that he needed to take control. He looked at Hudson and said, "If the substance is blood Commander, we need to get forensics here."

Hudson said, "I agree, but I need to make a call first." He then disappeared.

"It could be animal blood," suggested Naomi, "given the history of the place."

"And if it isn't?" asked Wood.

"Then it wouldn't bear thinking about," said Helen.

"And if it is animal blood, why pipe it in? Quantity?" said Wood.

"And maybe more to the point," said Crowthorne, "where was it being drawn from?" He became decisive and said, "Okay, I know that I'm supposed to be suspended, but I think that we should leave this room, now."

Nods of agreement were passed around and everybody began to shuffle into the central hall.

"Can we look in the loading bay, Bob?" said Helen.

Crowthorne was about to say, "Not yet," but then saw Hudson return with a determined look upon his face.

Hudson said, "Right, the Director has given us the green light to carry out an extensive search, but he's insistent that the classified info is to remain intact," he stopped, turned to Crowthorne, and added, "and your suspension has been lifted; you are now officially in charge of this investigation."

"Good," said a relieved Crowthorne, "thank you – I think!" He looked around the hallway and then said, "Right, let's adopt principles; Helen, Naomi, Leo, you come with Lieutenant Commander Hudson and me, and everybody else, please go back outside."

"May I come too, sir?" said Wood.

"You may." Crowthorne waited until everybody else had departed and then said, "If that is blood in the pipeline, this could turn out to be something nasty, so let's not screw up any evidence by being over-enthusiastic, okay?"

"Did you tell Bob about the extractor fan?" said Helen.

Crowthorne turned and said, "Extractor fan? No she didn't; what about it?"

Naomi said, "On my first visit here, I took a few unofficial photos. One was for fun more than anything else, because it showed a lone pigeon sitting on a security camera …" she didn't notice a furrow appear on Hudson's brow, and continued, "… and when Helen saw the photo, she pointed out that the fan below it appeared to be switched on."

"What gave you that impression?" said Wood.

"The blades were blurred."

"Couldn't that have been camera shake or the breeze?"

"No," said Helen, "because we could see other fans in the photo, and all of their blades were still."

"And an operating fan is not bad for a facility that's supposed to be shutdown, *and* have no electricity," added Naomi.

Crowthorne pondered and then said, "Okay, let's go to the loading bay."

"Wait a minute," said Hudson, he turned to Naomi and said, "Did you say that there was a security camera outside?"

"On the rear elevation, yes."

"Was it active?"

"I don't know – I don't recall seeing any red lights or anything."

Hudson frowned and then said, "Okay, thank you."

Minutes later, Crowthorne led everybody into the loading bay. He turned to Naomi and Helen and said, "Right, what interests you in here?"

Naomi didn't answer at first. She looked up and saw the two pipes running at roof level from the Labs to the rear wall. She followed their progress and saw that each exited the building behind the exterior fan array. She also noted the third pipe that came in from behind the array and then went back out again behind the fuel tank. A thought crossed her mind; she shivered and said, "Surely not?"

Crowthorne, who'd been looking up as well, looked down, and said, "What?"

The more that Naomi considered the thought, the less she liked it. Her expression changed as she turned to the rear elevation with a look of deep consternation on her face.

Helen saw and said, "N, what is it?"

Helen's question made Wood and Crowthorne look too.

Crowthorne said, "Naomi, what?"

Naomi said, "That cylindrical tank outside – I'd thought that it might have been used to contain fuel oil but now I'm not so sure."

Crowthorne said, "What are you driving at?"

Naomi looked up at the pipe entering and leaving the building. The thumb pushed down on her left shoulder; she reached up, rubbed it, and saw that the movement wasn't lost on Helen or Crowthorne.

"That's it my poppet," said the female voice in her head, *"now you see, don't you?"*

Once again Naomi followed the route of the pipes along the roof level, and then looked at the pipe that came in and went out.

"Naomi," said a frustrated Crowthorne, "talk to me please."

Naomi ignored the comment and pointed to the discarded wooden ladder lying on the floor next to the office. She said, "We need that."

"Why?"

"I want to examine that pipe," she pointed to the one that came in and went out.

"No, no," said Crowthorne, "I'm sorry; I can't allow that until forensics have finished."

Naomi felt thwarted; she said, "So this whole circus today, was for nothing?"

"No," responded Crowthorne with equal terseness, "it was your discovery in Lab 4 that brought me to this conclusion."

"And what about in here? You knew that this was the place that interested me most."

"N," said Helen, "You know that Bob's right; he has to examine each piece of evidence without fear of further contamination. If we go mucking about with those pipes we could ruin it."

An aggravated Naomi drew in a deep breath and said, "And what about the missing people? Are we supposed to leave them until forensics have finished the precious exam?"

"That's unfair," said Crowthorne, "you know that their safety is the prime consideration. We will be as quick as we can, but I don't want to spoil our chances of finding them by not being professional."

Two people were ignoring the exchange, and were deep in thought. Hudson couldn't get the idea of the outside security camera out of his mind, and Wood was thinking 'out-of-the-box'.

Wood came to a decision and looked at Naomi and Helen. He said, "Ladies, whilst we're waiting for forensics to complete ..."

"And I will instruct them to do in here first," added Crowthorne.

Wood nodded and then continued, "... and with the permission of your other halves, etcetera, I'd like you to come to London with me tomorrow. There are some people I'd like you to meet."

Chapter 47

The police car containing Naomi, Helen, Wood, and Simon pulled up outside of McCready House. Seconds later a second police car pulled up behind them, and an elegant, but older lady stepped out.

Wood turned to Naomi and Helen and said, "Ladies ..." and indicated for them to exit; he then turned to Simon and said, "You wait here."

Simon said, "Would you mind if I have a quick butcher's in that void before we leave guv?"

"No, but wait here until we've finished, then you can go in."

Simon smiled and said, "Thanks, Guv."

Helen waited until Wood had stepped out of the car, and then dug Naomi in the ribs; playfully, she said, "Bye Simon," she then looked at Naomi and whispered, *"I would!"*

Naomi's mouth fell open and she mouthed, *"Stop it!"*

Helen flashed a cheeky smile at Simon as she saw him grinning at her through the rear-view mirror.

Naomi said, "Hey, I thought you had a thing for Bob?"

Helen didn't take her eyes off Simon's sexy brown eyes and said out loud, "Doesn't stop me window-shopping though, does it?"

Wood opened the nearside rear door and said, "What are you two talking about?"

Naomi flashed a glance at Helen and said, "Nothing."

Helen smiled, looked at Simon and said, "I wouldn't say *nothing* exactly." She saw Simon looking at her through the rear-view mirror and nodding in a knowing-fashion.

Wood knew what was going on and said, "Then if you've finished your window-shopping, shall we go inside?"

Naomi and Helen giggled as they got out, and saw Simon grinning back at them.

Wood waited until the lady from the second car approached, and then said, "Naomi, Helen, let me introduce Miss Ulyana Vetochkin, she was one of the original members of a pre-war SIS monitoring station here at McCready House."

"SIS?" queried Helen.

"Secret Intelligence Service," said Wood, "the generic name for the security services including MI5 and MI6."

Naomi extended her hand and said, "Wow, it's a real pleasure to meet you."

"Inspector Wood has told me about you and your colleague, and it's an equal pleasure to meet you too, my dear," said Ulyana.

Helen shook hands and smiled.

Naomi stepped back, looked at the terraced facade of McCready House and said, "This place looks so innocuous and unassuming, you'd never guess that it had been so important." She turned and said, "Are you still in touch with other members of your unit?"

Wood said, "That's a good point Ulyana, when will we meet Miss Picard?"

"Soon, Inspector, I promise," Ulyana turned to Naomi and said, "And in answer to your question, we are all of a certain age, and I'm afraid that there are just three of us left. Me, a

French lady named Evelyn Picard, and the leader of our team, Lady Jocelyn Fitton-Kearns."

"And will they be joining us?" said Helen.

"Evelyn will, but Jocelyn won't; she lives in Bournemouth with her lady companion and doesn't travel much anymore."

Naomi, ever-mindful of opportunities, said, "Do you think that she'd be amenable to us visiting and asking her a few questions?"

Ulyana hesitated and then said, "I suppose that it would have to do with the questions."

"Of course," said Naomi, "and we wouldn't press her to answer anything that she didn't want to."

"My dear," said Ulyana, "please don't be under any misguided impressions about Lady Jocelyn; she may be older now, but she's still a formidable woman. There would be nothing you or anybody else could do to make her answer any questions if she didn't want to."

"She sounds formidable," said Helen.

"And she would not have been put in charge of a place like this, if she hadn't," added Ulyana.

"Then do you think that she would allow a couple of historic researchers the opportunity of asking her non-sensitive questions about her life in the unit?" said Naomi.

Ulyana pondered for a second or two and then said, "I think that she would enjoy that."

Naomi turned to Helen and said, "In that case, do you fancy a trip to the seaside before we go back home?"

"Whoa, whoa," said Wood, let's not put the cart before the horse. We need to conclude our business here first."

"Then we should go in," said Ulyana.

Minutes later Dan Lowe let them in and said, "It's as you left it Inspector; nobody's been allowed back in the void."

Wood said, "Crossed swords with the old dear next door lately?"

Dan said, "Don't! She's a pain in the …" he hesitated as he saw the three women and then said, "… backside. She never misses an opportunity to give me earache."

"Just earache?" said Wood.

"You know it," said Dan, "and the rest."

"Sounds interesting," said Ulyana, looking at Dan and smiling.

"Not the words I'd use."

Naomi and Helen saw Ulyana smiling some more and shot each other a questioning glance.

Wood saw the exchange and said, "I'll fill you in later."

They walked into the central hallway and Ulyana stopped. She looked around and said, "Even though everywhere is stripped out, I can still picture it as it was."

She gave everybody a quick run-down of where each office was, which were the private rooms, and the type of restrictions that they'd all been placed under. She then turned and pointed down the hall and said, "And that room was the monitoring station."

"I'll leave you guys to it," said Dan, "I'll be in the kitchen trying to figure out the most painful way to murder the old bat next door."

Wood smiled and said, "Okay, thanks."

Naomi and Helen were shocked; they looked at each other, and then at the retreating figure of Dan.

Naomi looked at the unperturbed Wood, and said, "Do people talk to you like that all the time?"

"No, but we'd make an exception for the old trout next door."

Naomi looked at Helen and then back at Wood, "I'd love to meet her if she's really that bad."

Wood said, "She really is, and you wouldn't."

With the statement hanging in the air, they walked down the hall and into the last room. Everybody looked around for a few seconds and then filed into the void.

Ulyana took everything in, and then said, "This really takes me back."

Naomi and Helen were fascinated by the micro-cosmic time capsule, but turned when they heard Wood say, "Will you show me the frame?"

"Frame?" repeated Naomi.

Ulyana looked at Wood and said, "How much have you told them?"

"Nothing, I'd harboured a hope that they could come here one day, and that you'd be able to explain all of this to them in person."

"Ah," said Ulyana. She turned to Naomi and Helen, and said, "All right, I have been given assurances that I am able to divulge certain aspects of our activities here, so I will tell you what I know about K1 and K2."

Naomi and Helen listened at first in amazement, and then with growing suspicion, as they heard about K1 being set up in Keasden to develop a special weapon for the armed forces, about its apparent excessive costs, and subsequent closure. And then the setting up of K2 in Skelmersdale to research the chemicals that could have been used in weapons by the Axis powers, and how they were to try to develop antidotes for them.

When Ulyana stopped talking, Naomi felt uncomfortable. She looked at the older, but astute lady in front of her, and wanted to say, *"And you believed that did you? You didn't question for one second whether the research was to develop a British weapon, rather than to treat the effects of a German one?"* but she was aware that things had been different in the

1930s and that people didn't question authority the same. She also knew that Germany had used chemical weapons in the First World War, and that more than one person at the top level of government and the armed forces had been aware of the dire warnings of German re-armament being voiced by Churchill.

She shot Helen a glance and saw the same suspicious expression on her face. She opted not to question Ulyana's loyalty to her department, and instead, said, "Can you tell us when the military moved out of K2?"

"The labs were shut down in 1952."

"And then it became the civilian St. Mary Cross Animal Research Unit?"

Ulyana hesitated and then said, "I can't answer that."

"Why?"

"Because the operations here at McCready House were closed down, and we had nothing more to do with it."

Naomi frowned and said, "That didn't really answer my question Miss Vetochkin."

Ulyana looked at the slight, but shrewd figure of Naomi and said, "But it is the answer that I am giving you, nevertheless."

An awkward silence descended on the room until Wood said, "Please don't forget that Ulyana is bound by the Official Secrets Act ladies."

Naomi looked at Ulyana; her eyes narrowed and she said, "Are you bound by the Official Secrets Act because of what went on in the 1930s or is there more?"

Ulyana cast a glance at Wood and saw the inquisitive look on his face too. She turned back to Naomi and said, "I can't answer that."

"So there is more?" said Helen.

"I can't answer that," repeated Ulyana. She then turned back to Wood and said, "But sometimes, actions speak louder than words …"

The penny dropped and Wood said, "The frame."

Ulyana nodded and said, "Yes." She turned around and lifted the picture of King George the Sixth off the wall and laid it face down on the desk.

Wood studied the back once more and couldn't see a single thing that could give away a sealed compartment.

Ulyana undid the knot on the length of twine that suspended the picture, and removed it from the eyehooks in the rear. She laid it to one side, turned the right eyehook three times to the right, and then pulled it out.

"Oh," said Wood, "I thought that you were tightening it, not undoing it."

Ulyana glanced at Wood and said, "A reverse thread." She then removed the backing board, print, and glass, and laid them on the desk next to the twine. Next, she positioned the whole frame upright with the right-hand side over the edge of the desk; she picked it up, and then brought it down with a sharp bang. Nothing happened. She picked up the frame, inspected the base, and said, "Does anybody have a knife?"

Naomi said, "I have a nail file if that's any good?"

Ulyana took the file off Naomi and scraped some of the dark brown varnish off the base of the frame; she then picked it up, and gave it another sharp bang on the desk. A circular section of wood shot out and landed on the floor.

Wood said, "Simple – simple but ingenious; and I didn't see any sign of it because of the varnish."

"Oftentimes, Inspector," said Ulyana, "the most effective things are the simplest, and the most successful way to hide anything, is to do it in plain sight." She bent down and picked up the ejected piece of frame.

It was approximately eight inches long and resembled a fat pencil that had a six-inch centre section hollowed out, giving it the appearance of a blunt-ended canoe.

In the recess lay a rolled up piece of paper.

Ulyana looked at everybody and said, "According to Jocelyn, this was the last secret of K2."

Naomi said, "Before you remove it, may I ask you a couple of questions?"

"You may."

"First, did Lady Jocelyn ever leave you with any information about K1?"

"No she didn't."

"Were you aware of what happened to it?"

"Only that it closed down in 1937."

"Did you ever know where it was?"

"I already told you, my dear; it was at Keasden in North Yorkshire."

Naomi frowned and said, "But I've spoken to the Superintendent in charge of this investigation in Manchester, and he has told me that neither he, nor anybody from the Yorkshire force, can find any trace of that old unit."

"That doesn't surprise me," said Ulyana, "the SIS was always meticulous when it came to removing anything that it didn't want others to find. All of it would have been destroyed."

"Then if it was so meticulously destroyed," said Naomi, "how come the red phone started bleeping again?"

A deathly silence fell on the room; Ulyana looked down at the piece of paper in the wooden section, and then back up at Naomi. She said, "Maybe this will give us some answers."

She removed it from the recess, unrolled it, read it, and then looked up with a frown on her face. She said, "This doesn't make sense."

389

Naomi said, "May I?"

Wood and Helen stood either side of Naomi. She read:

*"Valerie and Janet Burgess, I am sorry. What I had to do
was necessary.*

I love you.

M x"

Helen looked at Naomi and said, "Look at that surname."

Naomi stared at the paper with a frown on her face, and
racing thoughts.

"I'm sorry, Helen," said Ulyana, "I don't understand,
what do you mean, 'look at that surname'?"

Naomi turned to Ulyana, and said, "What did you expect
to be in here?"

Ulyana said, "I don't know – perhaps some long kept
secret, something about the two sites, maybe even the name of
the man who ran the K2 site, who was reputed to have been
recruited from K1 to run K2 …" she paused, looked down at
the paper and said, "… but that? I have no idea to what it is
referring."

Naomi looked at Helen and then turned back to Ulyana.
She said, "We might."

Ulyana frowned and said, "How could you? This was a
top secret military establishment sealed up years ago."

Naomi ignored Ulyana's question, turned to Helen and
said, "We need to go to Bournemouth now."

Before Helen could respond, they all heard a loud banging
on the front door. Seconds later they heard Dan say, "Hey!
Whoa, stop! *Face-ache, I said stop!*"

They then heard, "Up yours, monkey boy, I need to see
that copper."

Wood closed his eyes, looked at Naomi and said, "Looks like your wish has come true."

Bemused, the companions moved out of the void and waited until Dan appeared with Esme.

"This *'lady'*," said Dan, he turned, looked at Esme, and said, "as if ..." he then turned back to Wood and said, "... wants a word. But could you make it quick, we don't want the milk going off."

Esme grabbed Dan's arm, yanked him down, and said, "Piss off, dickhead, or I'll clobber you one!"

"Yeah?" said Dan, "you want some now do you?"

Naomi and Helen couldn't believe their ears; they stood looking in shocked silence.

"Stop, stop!" said Wood, he looked at Dan first, and then at Esme and said, "How can I help you, Mrs Pilchard."

Ulyana burst out laughing. She looked at Esme and said, "Pilchard? A little fish? That's hilarious!"

Naomi, Helen, Wood, and Dan, were amazed at Ulyana. They couldn't believe that she'd been so rude. They watched in shocked silence until Ulyana walked over to Esme and took her arm.

"Everybody," said Ulyana, "I'd like you to meet my very good, and long-time friend Miss Evelyn Picard."

Dan and Wood were stunned.

Wood said, "This is Evelyn Picard?"

Esme stepped forwards, and in a completely different tone of voice, and accent, said, *"C'est vrai Inspector, je suis Evelyn Picard."*

Ulyana saw Dan frown and said, "My friend said, *'It's true Inspector, I am Evelyn Picard'.*"

Chapter 48

A stunned Dan sat with everybody in the kitchen of McCready House and listened to Ulyana and Evelyn, whom he still thought of as Esme, talk about some of their experiences monitoring the phones and emergency signals from K1 and K2 in Yorkshire and Lancashire, and from anybody issued with a special card. He heard about how they were in contact with members of the Special Operations Executive based in Claughton, Lancashire, and how they could activate a deadly response if necessary. Every-now-and-then, he looked at Evelyn and recalled all of the foul-mouthed exchanges, and he would never have believed that she could have been such an important member of MI5.

Evelyn turned and looked at Dan. She said, "Why do you keep looking at me like that?"

Dan said, "I can't help it; one minute you're the foul-mouthed old trout from next door, next you're Evelyn Picard, an MI5 agent."

"In that case I'd say that I'd done a good job of allaying curiosity about my identity; wouldn't you?"

"Too right," said Dan. He looked at his watch, and said, "Blimey, I've got to get on – I'll leave you guys to it." He got up from the table and was about to walk away when he saw

Evelyn gesture to him to come to her. He frowned, walked around the table, and was then pulled down so that his left ear was close to Evelyn's mouth.

Evelyn whispered, "Don't think it's over between us monkey-boy ..."

Dan stood up, smiled, and said, "That's more like it!" and exited the room.

Wood looked at Ulyana and said, "So Evelyn's presence next door was another example of hiding something in plain sight."

"We were well-trained, Inspector."

Naomi took hold of the reins. She looked at Evelyn and said, "Now that we've heard the outline of your duties, can I ask you something more detailed?"

Evelyn shot a glance at Ulyana, and then said, "You can ask."

"Did you ever visit K1 or K2?"

"No."

"Did you ever meet anybody who had?"

"Yes."

Naomi waited for more, but then realised that if she didn't ask the question, she wouldn't get the answer. She said, "Did he or she know about the existence of K1?"

"No."

Naomi's heart sank: she said, "So it was K2?"

Evelyn didn't answer, she raised her eyebrows.

"Sorry," said Naomi, "silly question. Was the person you knew a member of MI5, too?"

"Yes."

Naomi paused before delivering the big one, and then said, "And to the best of your knowledge, when did that person last visit K2?"

"In 1972."

Naomi was stunned, she hadn't expected to receive such an answer, but she had, and it was out in the open. She wasn't the only one surprised by Evelyn's answer either, she saw Ulyana staring at her with a shocked expression on her face.

Wood said, *"1972?* I thought that the military moved out of K2 in 1952?"

Before Evelyn could respond, Helen said, "That's one year before Violet Burgess disappeared."

Ulyana turned to Helen and said, "Burgess? That's the surname in the frame compartment, but they were Valerie and Janet, who was Violet?"

"She was a research physicist working at the St Mary Cross Animal Research Unit in 1973."

Evelyn looked at Ulyana and said, "You opened the frame?"

Ulyana nodded and said, "I didn't see what harm it would do after all these years," she handed the note to Evelyn.

Evelyn read it and said, "Who were Valerie and Janet?"

Naomi said, "They were Violet's daughters, why?"

"Because I've heard their names before."

"Wait, wait," said Wood, "Before you answer that, I want to hear about K2." He turned to Evelyn and said, "Now, are you sure that the military were still there in 1972?"

Ulyana said, "That is not what Evelyn said Inspector. Naomi asked her *when* the last time somebody from MI5 visited K2, and Evelyn replied, 'In 1972'. That does not imply that the military was still there, nor does it imply that the person from MI5 was visiting any military personnel at the K2 site."

"Then what does it imply?" said Wood.

"Nothing," said Ulyana.

Naomi was surprised at how sharp Ulyana had become and realised that she hadn't lost any of her quick-wittedness.

"Nothing?" repeated Wood.

"Yes," said Ulyana.

"Of course it does," said an aggravated Wood, "It implies at least that somebody from MI5 visited the K2 site in 1972."

Ulyana paused, looked at Wood, and said, "That was not an implication, Inspector, that was a statement."

"And that was splitting hairs," snapped back Wood.

"Whether it was, or was not, is of no importance, because we already informed you that military activity ceased there in 1952." Ulyana finished the sentence and then turned and looked at Evelyn.

"Were you Evelyn's superior when the unit was active?" said Naomi.

Ulyana said, "What has that to do with anything?"

"Nothing," said Naomi, "it was just an observation." She turned to Evelyn and said, "Let's just cut straight to the chase shall we? Were you aware of any military involvement at K2 in 1972?"

"No I wasn't, and it wasn't named K2 then either."

"Okay, you said that you knew the person who visited the St Mary Cross Animal Research Unit in 1972, will you tell us who it was?"

"No."

"Then will you tell us *why* the MI5 person went to the St Mary Cross Animal Research Unit in 1972?"

For the first time, Evelyn faltered; she looked at Ulyana and saw her frown. She turned to Naomi and said, "I'm sorry, but I can't answer that."

"Perfect," said Naomi, "then there was still a military presence there." She saw Evelyn's mouth fall open, but then close again. "Now," she said, "we have to find out why it was still there when it was supposed to have ceased activity in 1952."

395

"No, no, no," said Ulyana, "that's a ridiculous assumption. The MI5 person could have been going there for any number of reasons, including investigating something associated with the old site."

Naomi had the bit between her teeth and knew that the two ladies were hiding something. She could feel the growing hostility in Ulyana and didn't want to antagonise her any further, but she didn't know how to proceed without doing so. She looked from face to face, opened her mouth to speak, and then felt the thumb press down on her shoulder. She hesitated, reached up to massage it with her right hand and then heard the lady's voice say, *"Where did Mary go?"* She frowned, and then heard it again. The voice said, *"Ask, 'where did Mary go?'"* She looked at Evelyn, it didn't feel right; she turned to Ulyana and then said, "Where did Mary go?"

Ulyana didn't register at first, but then she sat with an astonished expression on her face. She stared at Naomi and said, "What did you say?"

"I said, where did Mary go?"

Ulyana frowned and said, "Mary who?"

Naomi heard the voice, and then said, "Chambers."

Ulyana and Evelyn looked at one-another in stunned silence.

Wood said, "Who was Mary Chambers?"

Ulyana said, "Mary Chambers was an ex-member of our unit who disappeared whilst on holiday in Blackpool in …" she hesitated when she realised that two and two were beginning to make a horrible four. She said, "… in 1972."

Helen cut in and said, "Did she go missing before, or after, the MI5 person went to the St Mary Cross Animal Research Unit?"

Ulyana looked at Evelyn, then looked back at Helen, and said, "Before."

"And was she ever found?"

"No."

A silence dropped on the room. Naomi. Helen, and Wood were filled with a plethora of questions. Ulyana and Evelyn were exchanging glances and wrestling with their consciences.

Wood was the first to speak. He said, "Can we go back a couple of steps?" He waited until he had Evelyn's attention and then said, "A few minutes ago, you said that you'd heard the names Valerie and Janet; where did you hear them?"

Evelyn pondered for a few seconds and then said, "It was from Jeanie Henderson, Jocelyn's lady companion. We'd all gone to Harrods's for afternoon tea."

"We?" said Wood.

"Yes, Jocelyn, Ulyana, Jeanie, and me; Jocelyn and Ulyana had gone to the ladies powder room, and Jeanie and I had told them that we'd meet them by the front entrance. As we walked down, we walked through the confectionary department and saw all manner of wonderful things. Sweets, chocolates, lollipops, candy canes and such, and out of the blue, Jeanie said, 'Valerie and Janet would have loved it here.' I asked her who Valerie and Janet were, and she told me that they were a couple of children that she'd known in her past. I asked her if she was still in touch, and she told me that she wasn't.

"A few minutes later we were joined by Jocelyn and Ulyana, and nothing more was said about them."

Wood turned to Ulyana and said, "Did Jeanie ever mention them to you?"

"No."

"So to sum up," said Wood, "we have Lady Jocelyn Fitton-Kearns and Jeanie Henderson living in Bournemouth. Jocelyn was in charge of this unit here ..." he looked at Ulyana and said, "... and she told you about the secret

397

compartment in the picture frame …" he saw her nod, and then said, "… and inside the compartment we have an apology to Valerie and Janet Burgess signed by somebody with the initial 'M'." He turned to Evelyn and said, "Some years earlier you had heard Jeanie mention that she knew two girls from her past named Valerie and Janet?"

Evelyn nodded.

"Then up in Skelmersdale, we had one Violet Burgess, an ex-employee of the St Mary Cross Animal Research Unit go missing in 1973. Now," said Wood, "do either of you two ladies know when Jeanie Henderson first became Lady Jocelyn's personal companion?"

Ulyana felt the hair on her head lift. She looked at Wood and said, "Yes – it was in September 1973."

"Are you sure about that?"

"I'm positive, it was my fifty-fifth birthday and we three had planned to celebrate it together, then Jocelyn turned up with Jeanie," she looked at Evelyn and said, "Remember?"

Evelyn nodded.

"But the note in the frame was initialled 'M', not 'J'," said Wood.

"Could it have been 'M' for mum or mother?" said Naomi.

Helen couldn't help herself; she said, "Oh come on guys, what are we waiting for?" she looked at Wood and said, "We've got to go to Bournemouth." She looked at her watch and saw that it was 3:50 p.m. She said, "We could even go now."

"No, wait," said Naomi, "I've got a better idea," she turned to Wood and said, "but it may take a bit of string-pulling by you."

Chapter 49

At 10:25 a.m., two police cars pulled up outside of an impressive-looking apartment block. The drivers remained where they were, the others got out. They took the lift up to the top floor, and rang Lady Jocelyn's doorbell. The door opened, and they were confronted by a small, slim, well-dressed lady.

Wood said, "Lady Jocelyn?"

Jocelyn looked up and said, "And you must be Detective Inspector Wood?"

"I am."

Jocelyn extended her hand and said, "Then, how do you do?"

Wood shook hands and said, "I'm very well thank you Lady…"

"Oh please do call me Jocelyn; I'm not one for too much formality." Jocelyn saw more people behind Wood and said, "And please ask your friends to come in too."

One-by-one, Naomi, Helen, and the uniformed Crowthorne, who'd met the companions in London the previous day, Ulyana, and then Evelyn entered.

As soon as Jocelyn saw Ulyana and Evelyn her eyes lit up. She hugged each one and said, "My word, it's good to see you two again! It's been far too long." She then turned and made sure that everybody was seated in her spacious and tasteful lounge. She said, "Before we start, can I get you all a drink, tea or coffee, maybe?"

Following nods all round, she looked at Ulyana and said, "Maybe you and Evelyn can help me?"

Ulyana said, "Where's Jeanie?"

"She had to go to Devon to visit a friend who'd contracted an awful chest infection."

Naomi's heart sank; she shot a glance at Helen, saw her raise her eyebrows, and heard her expel a frustrated breath.

Jocelyn led her two friends into her kitchen and said, "What's this all about girls – has something gone wrong somewhere?"

Ulyana explained as much as she knew whilst the drinks were being prepared, and by the time that they were seated in the lounge again, she'd managed to acquaint Jocelyn with most of what had been going on.

Jocelyn looked at her guests, and said, "All right – Inspector Wood, I know who you are; who are these two ladies?"

Naomi took up the reins and said, "I am Naomi Wilkes and this is Helen Milner; we are professional historic researchers, working in conjunction with the Greater Manchester, Lancashire, Yorkshire, and Metropolitan Police forces."

"And why have you come to see me?"

"We hoped that you might be able to give us some information that may help us with our investigation."

"What kind of help?"

Crowthorne felt that he should be the one asking questions and said, "Naomi, Helen, may I …?"

Jocelyn looked at Crowthorne, "And you are?"

"I am Superintendent Robert Crowthorne of Greater Manchester Police, and I am in charge of this investigation."

"Ah, I see now," said Jocelyn, "then fire away, I haven't enjoyed a good grilling for a long time."

Crowthorne smiled an awkward smile and then said, "Detective Inspector Wood and I had been working on two separate cases; he had been investigating why the red telephone had started bleeping again at McCready House ..."

Naomi noted an immediate but subtle response in Jocelyn and watched her eyes like a hawk.

"... and I," continued Crowthorne, "had been investigating the disappearance of two people at the old Ascensis facility in Skelmersdale."

"Ascensis facility?" queried Jocelyn.

"You would know it better as either the K2 site or the St Mary Cross Animal Research Unit."

"Yes, of course: and when did these people go missing Superintendent?"

"One, a lady, went missing in November last year, and the other, a man, went missing eight days' ago."

Jocelyn was shocked. She said, "Last November, and eight days' ago, surely that cannot be?"

Crowthorne wanted to ask 'why?' but instead, went for a softer approach. He said, "It's true, and their disappearance is what's brought us here today." He expected an immediate response from Jocelyn, but nothing happened. He sat in puzzled silence as she appeared to stare at a point above his head. He opened his mouth to say something, but then saw Ulyana gesture to him to keep quiet.

Jocelyn's mind was racing; for the first time in years, she felt exhilarated. She recalled the gesture of signing the Official Secrets Act, and the replacement of the original note in the picture frame. She remembered the years of trying to keep the red phone at McCready House live, and how devastated she'd felt when she'd been informed that the power to it was being cut, and that its life, and therefore its lifeline, was being terminated forever. And now here she was being told that it had started bleeping again. It seemed implausible, but she couldn't allay a feeling that the past was calling out to her again.

She found it difficult to imagine that two more people had gone missing near K2, especially when she was under the impression that it could never happen again. It was shocking and worrying, and it had her wrestling like crazy with her rusty logic.

She arrived at her decision. She thought about it for a few seconds longer, considered the ramifications, the threat of arrest by the security services, and then she picked up a telephone handset from her nearby coffee table and pushed a button. She waited until somebody answered, and then said, "Would you come in here please? – Thank you," and put the phone down.

At the same time, the mobile phone in Crowthorne's tunic pocket buzzed. He retrieved it, excused himself, and went out of the lounge. He said, "Crowthorne."

"Good morning, sir, it's Milnes."

"Good morning Peter, how can I help?"

"We've just received the toxicology report about the black substance in the pipes at the Ascensis facility."

"Go on …"

"It's human blood."

Crowthorne didn't often give way to expletives, but said, "Good God, that doesn't bear thinking about does it?"

"No, sir, it doesn't, but that wasn't all the lab boys found. They discovered that the blood contained traces of naphthenic acid, palmitic acid, and gasoline gel."

Crowthorne said, "Should that mean something to me?"

"No, sir," said Milnes, "but it did to the lab boys. Those substances were used to make napalm."

"Napalm? What the hell was napalm doing in the blood?"

"They're not sure yet, but they are working on a theory which they'll share with us when they know more."

Crowthorne said, "All right, but I have to say, I don't like the sound of that."

"I agree, sir," said Milnes. He paused and then added, "The lab boys have promised to give us a full report by the end of next week, but I thought that you should hear their initial findings as soon as possible."

"You were right, Peter, thank you." He was about to say goodbye, but then remembered something. He said, "I've been meaning to ask you, why did you cancel Naomi Wilkes's personal protection when you did?"

"I didn't, sir, it was a ruse. I let it be known to all and sundry that I had in an attempt to flush out any of Darke's nasties before word got out about his death, but in reality, she was being protected at all times."

Crowthorne expelled a long and relieved breath. He said, "Good man, Peter, and a good move."

"Thank you, sir."

Crowthorne said goodbye and walked back to the lounge. He recalled that Milnes's, or somebody else's initials had still been circled by Darke's assassin, but he put it to the back of his mind until he could give it more consideration. He also cringed at the thought of what might have gone on at Skelmersdale, but he knew that he'd have to wait until the blood had been dated before he could ascribe any of it to either, K2, St Mary Cross, or Ascensis.

He gathered his wits and walked into the lounge. Sitting beside Jocelyn was another older lady that he hadn't seen before.

"Superintendent Crowthorne," said Jocelyn, "this is my companion and good friend, Jeanie Henderson. She has something to tell you."

Crowthorne frowned but held his tongue. He saw that the lady wore stylish clothes and shoes, and that she was young-looking for her advanced years. She had blonde, well-coiffured hair, and a trim figure.

"Before I speak," said the lady, "I must have all of your assurances that what I am about to reveal will stay a secret, and will not be disclosed to anyone outside of this room."

Looks were passed around and everybody nodded in agreement.

"Okay, then first I should tell you that my name is not Jeanie Henderson ..."

Helen shot a glance at Naomi, and waited for the lady to announce that her name was Valerie Burgess.

"... it is Eleanor Jayne Drake."

Naomi was shocked, and she saw that Helen was too.

Eleanor said, "I am the last remaining research physicist who was attached to the K1 Weapons Research Unit based in Keasden, North Yorkshire."

You could have heard a pin drop.

"Every other member of the Unit was killed."

Everybody wanted to speak at once, but Crowthorne prevailed. He said, "I have a question er ..."

"Eleanor is just fine."

"...thank you," said Crowthorne. "Were the other members of your unit killed by the weapon that they'd been working on?"

"No they weren't. All but two of us were killed by members of a mercenary unit attached to the Armed Forces, who then wiped out all traces of the facility itself."

"Good God," said a shocked Helen, "Our own men killed our own people?"

"Correct, but I repeat, they were mercenaries, not regular soldiers."

"How many people were killed?" said Crowthorne.

"Seventy-two."

Naomi was stunned, she said, "Why? Why would they do that?"

"I cannot answer you with certainty, but the members of my unit had been working on a dreadful weapon named *The Halo* and it's my belief that something went wrong with it during its second test. Thereafter, I presume that orders had been issued to expunge all traces of it, the personnel, and then the facility itself."

"Good grief, said Helen, "that's unbelievable."

"But true," said Eleanor.

"Eleanor," said Wood, "I am Detective Inspector Wood of the Metropolitan Police. How did you and the other person survive?"

Eleanor pondered for a few seconds, and then came to the decision that now was the time to get all of the old secrets out into the open. She said, "Four of us survived the initial op. I was with two girlfriends from the unit and we should have been on site at the time, but our car had broken down. We'd set off walking up the brow to K1, but then saw some soldiers chase a man across the moor and shoot him. At first, we thought that we'd been seeing things, but then the soldier walked up to the prone man, and shot him again. I told my friends to hide in a nearby shed whilst I went for help, but then I fell onto my back in a deep, wet ditch. While I was lying there, I heard a scream and two more shots, and I never saw my friends again."

Naomi clasped her hand up to her mouth and said, "How horrific! How did you survive?"

"I lay in the water, not daring to move, until I passed out with hypothermia, but then I was rescued by a local farmer whose dog found me, He and his wife looked after me until they were able to take me to the local railway station. I then made my escape and never returned."

"What about your car?" said Helen.

"It had disappeared."

"You said that you were one of four who'd escaped the initial cull," said Crowthorne, "who was the other person?"

Eleanor looked at Jocelyn and saw her give an assuring nod. She turned to Crowthorne and said, "His name was Klossner, Axel Klossner, a German Jew who'd been given sanctuary in the UK in return for his expertise in developing the weapon with the leader of our unit, Doctor Karl Hallenbeck.

"Everybody had thought that he'd been killed in a motor vehicle accident, but it turned out that the accident had been faked by members of the SIS, so that he could secretly open up a second unit codenamed K2, to develop chemical weapons."

"In Skelmersdale?" said Helen.

"Correct."

"And you met him again?" said Naomi.

"I did."

"Is he still alive?"

"No he isn't," said Eleanor, "I killed him."

A deathly hush fell on the room.

"Him, and his moronic son, Helmut."

406

Wood looked at Crowthorne and didn't know what to say. He'd never had anybody admit to the murder of two people so openly before.

Crowthorne said, "That's a serious admission; perhaps you'd better explain."

Eleanor told everybody about her employment at the St Mary Cross Animal Research Unit, and how over time, she'd discovered the clandestine activity there. She related how she'd been caught one night trying to uncover details of the activities; how she'd been held captive with her husband's knowledge that she'd not survive, and how, in the end, she'd escaped.

Crowthorne looked down at the floor and considered his options. He then looked back up and said, "You say that you'd discovered some clandestine activity there; what kind of activity?"

"A depraved, horrific, and barbaric kind," said Eleanor. She paused, looked at the faces of the newcomers and then said, "Klossner told me that he'd been working on a project named the *'Blut Bombe'* programme, and that I would not be allowed to interfere in his life any longer."

"Blut Bombe?" repeated Helen.

"Blood bomb programme," said Eleanor.

Crowthorne frowned as he recalled the phone message from Milnes.

"He'd been injecting napalm into human blood and then trying to ignite it by exposing it to oxygen."

"So he was capturing people for their blood?" said a horrified Helen.

"Yes, but not only that; he was also injecting the napalm into their blood streams and trying to ignite it inside them."

Wood was mortified, he said, "Holy Christ."

Eleanor turned and said, "Neither Christ nor anything else Christian had anything to do with those unspeakable animals Inspector."

Everybody was stunned into silence until Naomi said, "How could Klossner and his people expose the napalm to oxygen if it had been injected into people?"

"By hacking open several of their arteries," Eleanor lapsed into silence as she recalled what she'd been told, and then said, "And do I mean hacking."

Everybody sat with horrified expressions on their faces until Naomi said, "In God's name, why?"

Eleanor said, "I didn't ask their motives, I ended them."

Crowthorne made his mind up, but remained silent.

Naomi pulled herself out of her horrific thoughts and said, "And where did the other victims come from?"

"They were tramps, vagrants, young people who'd been kidnapped, and anybody else they could lay their sick hands on."

"And what happened to them?"

"I freed the ones who were still alive?"

"And didn't they report the activity, too?" said Wood.

"If they did, I never heard about it." Eleanor turned and looked at Jocelyn and added, "Maybe courtesy of MI5."

"You're not hinting that they had anything to do with this are you?" said Crowthorne.

"I don't know, I contacted Jocelyn, and then disappeared from public view."

"And at this time, you'd changed your name hadn't you?" said Naomi.

Eleanor said, "I'd had to. Until I took up lodging with Jocelyn, my life had been in constant danger."

Naomi looked at Helen, and then turned back to Eleanor. She said, "You became Violet Burgess didn't you?"

It was Eleanor's turn to be surprised. She frowned and said, "Yes I did, how did you know?"

"Deduction," said Naomi, she paused and then said, "There's …"

"Wait a minute," said Crowthorne to Naomi, "before we go any further," he turned to Eleanor and said, "you say that you killed Axel and Helmut Klossner, were they together when you did this?"

"No they weren't: I killed Helmut whilst making my escape, and then I returned to the St. Mary Cross Animal Research Unit one night, and killed Axel too."

"Was he alone?" said Crowthorne.

Eleanor hesitated and then said, "No, he wasn't he was with two other sub-human morons who enjoyed the work as much as he did, so I killed them too. They were like the UK's Doctor Mengele and his brutal SS assistants, they enjoyed watching, and listening to the excruciating suffering they'd been causing, and because they didn't appear to exist, there was nobody else to stop them but me."

"And me," said Ulyana.

"And me," said Evelyn.

"And me," said Jocelyn.

Crowthorne, Wood, Naomi, and Helen were stunned. They looked from aged face to aged face, and couldn't believe their ears.

Jocelyn said, "Apart from our monitoring duties at McCready House, Ulyana, Evelyn, and I were undercover SOE assassins planted to eliminate breaches of security to foreign powers. When we learned of Eleanor's intentions, we lent assistance."

"*Lent assistance?*" said Crowthorne, "by God, I've heard it called many things before, but never, 'lent assistance'."

The four old ladies remained impassive and unmoved.

409

Crowthorne sat with his hands up to his mouth. He looked at each old lady in turn and said, "What am I to do with you? You are jointly responsible for four murders."

"And the cessation of all the atrocious activity at Skelmersdale until you came here today, and told us that more people had gone missing in the last few weeks."

Naomi turned to Eleanor and said, "One of whom is your granddaughter, Denise."

Chapter 50

As the police car pulled up outside of 'Entrance A', Eleanor looked out of the window and shivered. She recalled the last time that she'd gone through the door and the look of surprise on Klossner's face as she'd entered.

She, Ulyana, Evelyn, Jocelyn, and another member of their special SOE team named Trixie Hoath, had cut their way through the perimeter fences, and had entered one night, following weeks of monitoring Klossner and his associates.

Evelyn and Jocelyn had moved to the rear of the building, whilst Ulyana had placed a small explosive charge on the door. As soon as it had detonated she, Ulyana and Trixie had moved into the main building and found it deserted. Ulyana had taken the rooms and labs on the right-hand side, whilst Trixie had taken those on the left. She had entered the loading bay area.

Standing with a pistol in one hand, and a large, glass flask in his other, Klossner had been waiting. He'd said, "I knew that you'd come back." She remembered that she hadn't questioned why she'd found him in the loading bay, but she did recall seeing an unusual movement on the wall above his head.

411

"You took away all that was left of my family you murdering bitch," Klossner had said, "and if it hadn't had been for you, my boy and all of those people at K1 would still have been alive."

She hadn't answered: but she'd seen him approach with the gun trained on her. He'd told her about his *blut bombe programme* and how she was going to be his favourite patient. He'd then held up the flask and told her that it contained sulphuric acid, and that he was going to enjoy pouring it into her eyes – slowly, and one at a time. He'd then informed her that he'd seen her two other companions position themselves at the rear of the building, and that they wouldn't be able to save her, but he hadn't mentioned seeing Ulyana and Trixie.

She'd slowly backed up until she was against the plastic doors, and then with a hammering heart, she'd ducked, turned, and slammed through the doors back into the central hall.

Ulyana and Trixie had been listening and waiting with their backs against the inside wall, knowing that she'd make a break for it.

As Klossner had followed, Trixie had snatched the flask out of his hand, and Ulyana had tripped him up. In an instant they'd had him bound and gagged. Ulyana had shot him through the right hand, and ordered him to lead them to the underground labs. There they'd dispatched two other depraved members of Klossner's staff, and had freed his new, terrified hostages.

With hearts of pure ice, they'd secured Klossner to one of the post-mortem tables with the flask of sulphuric acid balanced on his chest. She'd then taken Trixie's gun, waited until her two companions had exited, and shot him in the left lung through the flask.

Now here she was again. She'd hoped that she'd never have to return, but once she'd learned that her granddaughter had gone missing, wild horses couldn't have kept her away.

"Are you ready?" said Crowthorne.

Eleanor looked at Crowthorne in the front seat, and then at Naomi next to her. She said, "As ready as I'll ever be." She got out of the car, and then waited until the others including Helen and Leo, had joined them from another police vehicle.

Once the introductions had been made Eleanor turned to Crowthorne and said, "Now – Superintendent; first things first; have you got the other exit covered?"

Crowthorne frowned and said, "Other exit? Do you mean the other doors?"

"No, I mean the other exit." Eleanor saw the lack of understanding on Crowthorne's face and said, "The exit in the trees through there," she pointed towards the opposite end of the building.

"I wasn't aware that there was another exit," said Crowthorne.

"I thought that you said your men had carried out an extensive search?"

"Only within the bounds of the perimeter fence, are you saying that it extends beyond there?"

"Yes."

Crowthorne turned and looked at the opposite end of the site and said, "How far beyond?"

"It's a long time ago now," said Eleanor thinking back, "but I'd estimate at least one hundred yards."

Crowthorne signalled for two uniformed officers to approach. He said, "You and two others go to where Miss Drake tells you, and stay there until you hear from me, got it?"

The two officers nodded and said, "Yes, sir."

Crowthorne turned to Eleanor and said, "What should they look for?"

Eleanor cast her mind back to the night in the 1970s and said, "It's similar to a rusty-looking metal inspection hatch that you could see on any road or footpath," she hesitated and realised that she hadn't seen it for over thirty years, and that it may have become overgrown. She hesitated and then said, "I think that I'd better go with the men. It'll be difficult to locate now, but I can still recall the tree formation where I asked the others to wait."

Crowthorne nodded and said, "If you think so, but it might look different after all these years."

Eleanor said, "Maybe."

"Do you mind if I tag along?"

Eleanor and Crowthorne saw Naomi standing with an inquisitive look on her face.

"It's okay with me if it is with the Superintendent," said Eleanor.

Crowthorne knew that it would be pointless to argue with Naomi. He shrugged and said, "Yes, okay."

Five minutes later, Eleanor, Naomi, and the four officers had made their way around the exterior of the perimeter fence until they were at a point that Eleanor thought right. They spread out and walked in a straight line, scanning the ground for any sign of a hatch.

Foot-by-foot they edged forwards until Eleanor said, "Stop." She looked at the nearby trees and saw that they looked familiar. She cast her mind back to the night that she'd escaped, and tried to visualise the scene again. She then looked back at the trees, factored in thirty-plus years of growth, and said, "It's somewhere near here."

One-by-one the officers commenced looking around; occasionally scraping away soil and leaves with their boots until they heard a series of loud cracks in the undergrowth to the side. They looked and saw Naomi snap the twigs off a hefty-looking branch, and then ram the narrow end into the soft soil.

Naomi glanced up, saw the policemen staring, and said, "Woman's logic guys – if it's metal, I'll hear it with this."

Ten minutes later, and with everybody ramming branches into the ground they found it. The men cleared away the detritus, and exposed what appeared to be a circular drain cover set into concrete.

One of the officers kneeled down, looked at the cover, and said, "It doesn't look as though this has been opened for years."

"Which," said Eleanor, "could be the impression that some smarty-pants is trying to have us believe."

"True," said the officer, "but if you two ladies would like to return to the Superintendent, we'll keep this place covered until we receive word."

Eleanor and Naomi rejoined Crowthorne at Entrance A, and then made their way inside.

Eleanor ignored the labs and led everybody straight into the loading bay; she stopped, looked around and then turned to Crowthorne. In a quiet voice she said, "Did anybody notice anything unusual in here?"

"The police dog picked up an unusual scent in the room over there." Crowthorne pointed to the small office in the corner.

"In what way unusual?"

"There was no start or end to the trail; it went around the room in a continuous square, without leading in or out."

Eleanor pondered and then said, "Anything else?"

Naomi waited until she realised that nobody else was going to speak. She said, "I saw something that got me puzzling." She pointed up to the odd pipe that appeared to come in from the rear elevation, drop down three feet, and then exit again. She said, "That pipe there – it doesn't seem to make sense."

"Ah!" said Eleanor, "And what about the marks?"

Naomi frowned and said, "What marks?"

Eleanor said, "Come with me." She led everybody to a point below the pipes and then pointed to the floor. She said, "Those marks."

Everybody looked down and saw two distinct scuff marks approximately four inches long by two inches wide; a foot apart.

"A ladder," said Crowthorne.

Naomi could have kicked herself. She turned to her left and saw the old wooden ladder lying against the wall in the same position as the last time she'd seen it. Looking closer this time, she estimated its length, then looked from the scuff marks to the wall and saw that they would have terminated just below the three pipes. She said, "Bugger."

Eleanor said, "Precisely …" she turned to Crowthorne and said, "… perhaps one of your young men could oblige?"

Crowthorne ordered two men to fetch the ladder, and within seconds it was in place below the pipes.

"And now?" said Crowthorne.

"Watch," said Eleanor. She started to climb the ladder, but was stopped.

Crowthorne said, "Whoa, please stop. I don't doubt that you could make it up there, but I would be much happier if you'd let one of my men."

Eleanor agreed and waited until one of Crowthorne's men had reached the top.

The constable turned and said, "Yes sir?"

Eleanor said, "Take hold of the pipe that comes in and goes out, and pull it towards you."

The constable turned around, took hold of the pipe, and pulled.

To everybody's amazement, the centre pipe slid out of the wall six inches. It was followed by the sound of whirring mechanism, and seconds later, an eight feet high, by three feet wide, section of the brick wall retreated back, and then sank below floor level, exposing a metal door in the back of what everybody had thought was the cylindrical fuel container.

"My God," exclaimed Naomi.

Eleanor turned to Crowthorne and said, "You need to be quick now, alarms may have gone off inside there."

Crowthorne turned to Leo and said, "You wait here with the ladies," he turned to his men and said, "Okay in you go." He grabbed the door handle, yanked the door open and stepped aside, expecting to see his men rush in. Instead, they stopped dead.

"What the hell?" said the first policeman.

Crowthorne turned, looked through the door, and saw that it was jet black inside. He frowned, pushed past the first man, and walked into the doorway. He looked in all directions, but the only thing that he could see, was that he appeared to be standing on the top landing of a metal fire escape. He stepped forwards one pace, and listened. For several seconds he strained his ears in the dark, but heard nothing. He turned to Eleanor and said, "Was it like this when you came here?"

"No it wasn't, it was well lit."

Crowthorne looked down into the stygian darkness and said, "How far does this go down?"

"About thirty feet."

"Thirty feet?" repeated Crowthorne.

417

"Yes, and it leads directly into the central lab," Eleanor frowned and said; "can't you hear anything?"

Crowthorne turned and stepped back onto the landing. He indicated for everybody to stand still and keep quiet. For several seconds he listened, but heard nothing. He stepped back out of the metal door, looked at Naomi, and said, "Your ears are younger than mine, see if you can hear anything."

Naomi nodded, stepped onto the landing, and in an instant, the door slammed shut behind her.

In the loading bay, Crowthorne jumped back in alarm as the door slammed, and the wall slid back into place. He said, "What the hell?" turned to one of his officers and said, "Quick, get up that ladder and open the door again!"

The young PC almost sprinted up the ladder and yanked on the pipes, but nothing happened.

"Shit" said Crowthorne. *"Shit!"*

On the other side of the door Naomi was petrified. She grabbed her torch out of her pocket, and switched it on. She shone it down and said, *"Hello?"* but received no reply. She then said, "I don't mean you any harm, but you have to cooperate with me." She heard nothing. She waited for a few seconds longer and then attempted to look around.

It was weird – the light from the beam didn't reflect off anything. It was as though she had gone to her back door on a moonless night, and shone the light into space.

She stayed rooted to the spot, aiming the beam left, then right, and then up. It was the same. She saw nothing. She then aimed the light down and attempted to see how far the steps went down, but then she became more puzzled when she couldn't see.

A pressure started on her left shoulder and she knew that something wasn't right. Her breathing became more rapid and she began to be gripped by a sudden desire not be there.

She quietly said, "Stop it, get a hold!" and then shone the torch straight up to see if she could see any part of a ceiling – but nothing was there. She frowned and wondered if she *was* looking into space, and then switched the torch off to see if she could see any stars. It was pure jet black.

And then she heard it – breathing – below her. Every hair on her body stood on end and her eyes widened in fear. She heard the soft pad of something step onto the metal staircase below.

She panicked and tried to switch on her torch, but in doing so, dropped it. She tried to catch it, but instead, sent it flying into space. In the breathless, petrified silence that followed, she expected to hear it hit something below, but no sound came at all.

And then she heard whatever it was, breathe again, and start climbing up the steps …

Outside, in the loading bay, Crowthorne was going frantic. He turned to a nearby PC and said, "Contact the men at the other end of the tunnel and see if they can gain entry there." He then looked at the man up the ladder and said, "Don't just stand there! Keep on trying."

The hapless PC yanked at the pipes again, but as before, nothing happened.

Inside the door Naomi began to panic. As the breathing got closer she became convinced that it was a dog coming up the steps. She groped around in the pitch dark trying to find something that she could use as a weapon, but nothing came to hand. She thought about her shoes, but they were useless, they were leather, and soft-soled. She dismissed her car keys, and then remembered the one item that Carlton had insisted she carry – a mace spray. She plunged her hand into her small leather shoulder bag, rummaged about, and then located it.

She heard the panting animal reach the steps below her and then stop. Her heart rate increased – she knew that it was close, but she still couldn't see it. A deep guttural growl started and she backed into the farthest corner straining her eyes for the faintest sign of movement.

A thought crossed her mind. Maybe, just maybe, she thought, if she couldn't see it, it couldn't see her.

Instead of backing into the corner, she walked to the edge of the top step, dropped into a kneeling position, and aimed the spray at arm's length down in front of her. She waited until the creature was at the bottom of her flight of stairs, and then stopped breathing.

The dog hesitated until it heard Naomi move, then it ran up the final stairs, snapping and snarling like something possessed.

Naomi waited until the dog was almost upon her and then pressed the button on the top of the canister. The effect was immediate.

The dog howled in agony as the spray went into its wide-open eyes. In wild and frantic frenzy it snapped at everything it touched, running around in circles, and banging into the metal sides of the fire escape. Then in blind panic, it lost its footing and cascaded sideways down the first landing. Like a slavering demon it scrambled to its feet and launched itself back up the stairs.

Naomi was petrified; she pressed the button on top of the spray can but nothing happened. She threw the empty can at the approaching dog, and then stood up and lashed out with her right foot, catching it on the side of its jaw. She thought that her heart was going to burst with fear.

Out of the blue, everywhere was suddenly filled with light. A shot rang out, and the dog fell back down the stairs. It writhed and shuddered in a final death spasm, and then lay still.

Leo rushed forwards, grabbed Naomi and pulled her into his arms. He said, "It's okay, it's okay, I've got you now."

Naomi burst into tears and sobbed on Leo's shoulder. She was aware of police rushing past her, but she was way beyond being able to take any of it in.

Chapter 51

"If I should meet thee
After long years,
How should I greet thee? –
With silence and tears."
Lord Byron 1788 – 1824.

Naomi wasn't sure how long she remained in Leo's arms. She was aware that policemen were all over the place and that everywhere was now bathed in light, but it wasn't until she saw a man being led past in handcuffs, that she felt safe. She extracted herself from Leo's arms and looked into his eyes. She said, "Thank you, I feel better now."

"Are you sure?" Leo looked down at the dead dog and said, "That would have put the willies up me, and I had a gun."

Naomi looked at the dead animal and recalled Sugg, the horrendous and ghostly dog from Whitewall Farm. She said, "I've experienced worse."

Leo looked at the dog once more and said, "Well rather you than me!"

Crowthorne walked up the fire escape and onto the top landing. He said, "You had us worried there; we weren't aware that the door would close automatically and that it took a while before the opening mechanism repositioned itself."

"Trust me, I was worried, too," said Naomi.

Crowthorne looked down at the large, mean-looking, dog and shuddered. He hated them, and the thought of coming up against one in total darkness was horrific to him. He drew in a deep breath and said, "I'll bet you were." He then looked around and said, "At least now we have light, and we've got the person responsible for all of this."

Naomi looked over the fire escape and saw that uniformed officers were everywhere. She said, "Where's Helen?"

"She's waiting in the loading bay until we're sure that it's safe."

"Have you found the missing people or what made that awful noise?"

"No," said Crowthorne, "and apart from a door leading to the other escape route, we haven't found any other rooms."

Naomi's heart sank; she hated the thought that they were too late. She said, "Didn't the man say anything when you arrested him?"

"Nothing of any consequence."

"Do you know who he is?"

"He is known to us, yes. He was sectioned under the Mental Health Act a couple of years ago, and he's known to be a resourceful recluse, but this surpasses anything he's ever done before."

"And the dog?"

"His by all accounts; and his most outspoken words were swearing at us because we'd shot it."

Naomi looked over the fire escape and saw that the police appeared to be checking every nook and cranny. She felt the thumb press down on her shoulder and heard the lady's voice say, *"Ask Ellie, she knows."* She reached up, put her right hand on her left shoulder and said out loud, "Who's Ellie?"

"I am."

Everybody turned and looked.

Eleanor was standing behind them. She said, "Where did you hear that name?"

Naomi looked at Crowthorne, and saw him shrug. She turned to Eleanor and said, "I experience things."

"Psychic things?" said Eleanor.

"Yes."

Eleanor hesitated and then said, "Only one other person ever called me Ellie, and she was a lady named Sandi Schmidt."

Naomi looked at Eleanor and said, "I take it that you know …"

"That she's no longer with us? Yes. She was one of my two girlfriends who were shot on Turnerford Brow."

"My God," said Naomi. She paused and then asked, "Where's Turnerford Brow?"

"It's near Keasden Beck in Yorkshire and I'll tell you more about it later. Now, what did Sandi say?"

"She said, 'Ask Ellie, she knows'."

Eleanor turned to Crowthorne and said, "Have you found the hostages?"

"No, our men have been looking, but they haven't found any other rooms or labs, apart from the escape route to the trees."

Eleanor looked down into the laboratory and said, "You need to come with me." She walked down the fire escape and across to the two post-mortem tables. On the left-hand side of each was a stainless steel wheel that appeared to be used to alter the angle of the table to assist with the flow of liquids.

She reached down to the one on the right-hand table and began to rotate it anti-clockwise. After two full revolutions, the whole table slid to the right and revealed a staircase. She attempted to go down but was stopped again.

"Eleanor, please, no," said Crowthorne, "let my men go first."

Eleanor drew in a deep breath and said, "Okay, but tell your men that there's a light switch on the right as they go down."

A few minutes later, everybody heard a call, *"Sir, you need to get down here."*

Crowthorne descended the steps followed by Leo, Eleanor, and then Naomi. As he reached the bottom he saw that he was in a dimly-lit, sparse-looking corridor similar to that of a seedy hotel. To the left and right were three doors each side, with policemen standing by each one.

"All right," he said in a hushed tone, "on this occasion we go in quietly, understood?" He saw nods of agreement and then added, "Be aware that there may be people or animals in those rooms."

"Not rooms," said Eleanor, "they're cells."

"Okay, cells," said Crowthorne, "so keep vigilant and remember that if anybody's in there, they may be traumatised enough." Once again he saw nods all round, "Right," he said, "in you go."

At first one, and then another voice called, *"In here, sir."*

Crowthorne shot a glance at Eleanor and said, "Don't get your hopes up."

Eleanor nodded, but didn't reply. She followed Crowthorne into the first room, and saw a naked young man through the bars of an internal cage.

"Rod!" said Naomi. She pushed past everybody and said, "Thank God: are you okay?"

Rod attempted to cover up his nakedness and said, "I am now."

"Are you hurt, or have you been contaminated with anything dangerous?" said Crowthorne.

"No," said Rod, "that loony didn't do anything to us. He just liked to look at us naked while he tossed himself off." He noticed the old lady standing behind Naomi and said, "I'm sorry …"

"No need to apologise," said Eleanor, "I've dealt with wankers all my life."

"Us?" cut in Leo. "You said, 'us'?"

"Yes, me and the girl."

Eleanor turned and charged into the other room. She saw a naked young woman holding her right hand over her pubic region, and her left arm across her breasts. She walked up to the bars, and realised, that for the first time in her life, she was afraid. She drew in a deep breath and said, "Is your name Denise?"

The young woman said, "Yes it is, Denise Lockyer. Who are you?"

Eleanor smiled, exhaled a deep, relieved breath, and said, "I'm your grandmother."

Chapter 52

Monday 12th February 2007.
Bury Divisional Police HQ

Three days after the dramatic rescue Crowthorne looked around the table in the corner of the canteen and saw Naomi, Helen, DI Wood, Mackenzie Hudson of MI5, Leo, Eleanor Drake, Val and Denise Lockyer, and Rod Carroll. He said, "Thank you all for coming, some further than others. I thought that it would be a worthwhile venture to bring some closure to a trying and puzzling case and to bring you up to date with the latest findings and events." He looked at Hudson and said, "And thanks to Lieutenant Commander Hudson here, to inform you that the ex-K2, St Mary Cross Animal Research Unit, or Ascensis Facility, whichever way you care to remember that place, is to be demolished."

"Hallelujah to that," said Eleanor reaching out and squeezing first Val's and then Denise's hand." She looked at her daughter Val, and could still see the look of shock, disbelief, and then relief on her face as she had arrived with Denise at her house, three days earlier.

Crowthorne acknowledged Eleanor's statement and then said, "But I do have to inform you that a lot about this case is still classified under the Official Secrets Act, and as much as you would like to grill Commander Hudson, he will be restricted in what he can say."

427

"May I ask him a few questions first?" said Eleanor.

Hudson said, "You may."

Eleanor said, "First, can you confirm that none of the ladies will be prosecuted by the Government or the police as a result of this case and its revelations?"

Hudson looked at Crowthorne, saw him nod, and then turned back to Eleanor. He said, "Only one person will be prosecuted; the man who was arrested on site last Monday. Everybody else is immune."

Eleanor nodded and said, "Okay, now, after all of these years, can you at last, tell me what happened to the K1 facility?"

Hudson looked down and considered his answer. He then looked back up and said, "The furthest that I can go, is to inform you that all evidence of K1 and its activities, were expunged in the 1930s."

"And apart from me and Axel Klossner," said Eleanor, "so were its personnel."

An awkward silence fell on the room until Hudson said, "I really am sorry, but I cannot comment on that." He saw Eleanor open her mouth to say something, but cut her off and added, "Times are vastly different now, and actions that may have been put into practice before the war, notwithstanding whether they could be construed as detrimental to the security of the nation or not, would not happen now."

Crowthorne recalled what had happened at the temperance hall, and raised an eyebrow. He looked at Hudson, opened his mouth to differ, but then thought better of it.

Eleanor said, "I'm pleased that you seem so certain about that Commander; I on the other hand have seen first-hand what our government is capable of."

Crowthorne looked at Hudson's face and saw that it remained impassive.

Eleanor paused and then said, "And can you tell us anything more about K2?"

Hudson pondered for a second or two and then came to a decision. He said, "Given all of the, er, extraordinary activities that occurred at K2, I think it best to remain silent and let it sink into historical oblivion," he looked straight into Eleanor's eyes and said, "Don't you?"

Eleanor recalled a valuable piece of advice that had been given to her by a senior member of MI5 when she'd been training in her younger days. He'd said, "Never waste a good opportunity to keep your mouth shut."

She looked at Hudson and nodded.

"I have a question for you, sir," said Wood to Crowthorne, "who did you arrest at Skelmersdale, and what was he doing down there?"

"His name was Christopher Manns; an inventive but unstable character who'd been detained under the Mental Health Act on previous occasions. He'd broken into the deserted facility some months earlier with the intention of finding anything to steal, and during an attempt to strip away some pipe work, he'd found the underground lab."

"And why had he taken Denise and Rod captive?"

"For no other reason than he'd found them." Crowthorne looked at Denise and Rod, saw them nod, and then turned to Wood. He said, "Apart from keeping them naked for his own sexual gratification, he didn't do them any harm; he fed them, on takeaways mostly, gave them showering facilities and a certain amount of freedom within the concealed lab, but they weren't allowed to leave, in case they gave away his hiding place. It was as simple as that."

Wood turned to Denise and said, "Didn't you try to escape?"

429

"No, he had that awful dog, and he'd told us that he'd electrified the exits, and that even if we'd overpowered him, we'd never be able to find out how to disable it. He also promised us that if we didn't cause him any grief; we'd be freed, unharmed within a few more weeks."

"And you believed him?"

"We didn't think we had a choice, we had no weapons and we were kept locked up in the buff," said Rod.

Eleanor recalled how she had escaped in similar circumstances, but kept quiet.

Naomi turned to Denise and said, "Was it you who screamed and banged into the wall of the central lab a couple of weeks ago?"

Denise said, "Screamed?"

"Yes, it was the scream …" Naomi hesitated and then said, "… or more of a screech, that first alerted us to somebody being held captive in there."

Denise frowned and said, "I'm sorry; I can't remember anybody screaming or screeching in there."

Naomi looked at Leo and said, "We both heard it."

Leo nodded and said, "True."

Denise shook her head and said, "I'm sorry guys – I can't help you with that, and it certainly wasn't me."

Naomi and Leo exchanged puzzled glances but didn't say anymore.

Wood broke the silence. He looked at Rod and said, "And are you okay now?"

Rod said, "It was unnerving and creepy, but like the Superintendent said, we never felt as though our lives were in danger."

"Neither of us believed that we'd be harmed," said Denise, "In a strange sort of way, when you got to know Chris, apart from his weird masturbating thing, he was a harmless sort of guy who could chat for hours over a huge range of interesting topics."

Crowthorne sat back in his seat and glanced at Naomi. He recalled the Stockholm Syndrome effect where hostages developed a connection with their captors, but he opted not to comment.

Denise then turned and looked at Eleanor; she took hold of her hand, and said, "What I can't get over is that I went to Skelmersdale to look for evidence of my grandmother's disappearance, and that in the end, she came and rescued me!"

Eleanor squeezed Denise's hand, and said, "And it was my pleasure darling."

Naomi looked at Crowthorne and said, "And I can't get over hearing about my old adversary Adrian Darke."

Eleanor looked at Naomi and said, "You have an adversary? After all that you've done for me and my family, if there's anything that the girls and I can do to help you with that, just …"

Crowthorne, Hudson, and Wood all said in unison, *"No!"* and looked at one another in near panic.

Hudson took the initiative and said, "I do believe that the Metropolitan, Greater Manchester, Lancashire, and Yorkshire police forces, *and* MI5, would all rest easier knowing that you and your 'grannies-from-hell' unit had finally ceased all of its clandestine activities!"

"I'll endorse that," said Crowthorne.

"Me, too," said Wood.

"And my old adversary was found dead last week anyway …" Naomi's words trailed off as a weird possibility shot through her mind. She looked at Eleanor and said, "It wasn't? – You and the girls didn't …?"

Eleanor smiled and said, "No, dear, we didn't."

Crowthorne and Hudson looked at one another, and experienced a palpable sense of relief.

Leo said, "A fascinating case all round." He looked at Wood and said, "You investigating why a red phone began to ring in a concealed void in London, us asking Naomi and Helen to assist Val in finding her daughter Denise, and all of this coming together with the discovery of two pre-war secret research facilities, a secret cell of lady assassins, the arrest of a wanted man, and the final release of the hostages." He looked around the room, and then said, "A satisfactory conclusion maybe, but we're still no wiser about the screech at K2, and what went on at K1 to cause such secrecy after all these years."

Hudson looked at Eleanor and said, "And as long as nobody ever reveals any of those long-past activities, no further action will be taken against anybody," he paused, looked around the table and concluded, "and this case will be closed, and I hope, in time forgotten."

"Closed maybe," said Eleanor, "but as long as I am around, neither it, nor the people who worked at K1, will ever be forgotten."

A silence fell onto the room until she said, "One last thing, Commander, is there any possibility that the red phone will ever ring again at McCready House?"

Hudson said, "No: the power to it has been cut and the lines have been removed; there will be no possibility of it ever ringing again."

"And what about the void?"

Wood said, "I've been in touch with James Garrison of Garrison-Lane, and he's informed me that it will be resealed after it has been put back the way that Lady Jocelyn originally left it."

Eleanor sat in silence for a few seconds and then said, "Commander, when you say that the power to the red phone, and the lines were cut, which did lines did you mean?"

Hudson frowned and was hesitant about answering. He said, "There was only one line, and it was removed two days ago."

Eleanor sat back in her seat and remembered something that Hallenbeck had once told her. About a second escape tunnel that he and Klossner had had constructed at K1 without the knowledge of MI5 in case something disastrous had happened, and how another link had been set up to the red phone in McCready House.

She sat back in her seat, looked at Hudson and said, "If you say so Commander, if you say so ..."

Epilogue

Sunday 14th June 2009

Young friends Callum Parker and Jamie Shaw sat in the inflatable two-man dinghy at the northwest portal of the nine-hundred-and-twenty-four feet long tunnel, and stared into the pitch dark.

Jamie said, "It looks a bit … well …"

"Don't be so bloody nesh," said Callum, "at least we've got torches and the outboard. The poor sods that went through here in the old days had to lie on their backs and walk their feet across the roof to get to the other side."

Jamie looked into the gloom and heard the distant plip-plopping of water as it dripped off the damp, lichen-covered roof, and half-wondered what kind of hellish-sized spiders and creepy-crawlies could be falling onto them. He looked down at the five-speed electric outboard motor and said, "Are you positive that the battery and spare are fully charged?"

"Course I am," said Callum, "now stop pissing about and let's get on with it. You get to the front with the torch, and I'll steer."

Jamie pulled his baseball cap tighter on his head, fastened the top button of his prized Manchester United football shirt, and said, "Okay."

He was about to take his place when he saw an impact wave emanate from the centre of the canal and spread out to both banks. He looked ahead and saw the same wave spreading out in both directions as far as he could see. He said, "Did you see that?"

Callum looked up and said, "What?"

"A weird wave just spread out from the centre of the canal and hit the banks on each side."

"Course it did you plank," said Callum, "that was because you were moving about in the boat."

"But …"

"But nothing, stop fucking about and let's go!"

Jamie pursed his lips, and then took his place in the bow. He checked that the torch was switched on, and then said, "Okay, ready."

Callum engaged first gear and the dinghy edged forwards. He waited until it had reached optimum speed, and then engaged second gear. As the boat gathered momentum he said, "Watch out for weed and crap in the water. We don't want a plastic bag wrapping itself around the prop and stopping us half way."

Jamie kept staring into the torch light and said, "Right."

In almost total darkness, and four hundred feet into the tunnel, something seemed to shudder around them. The dinghy moved in an unusual and involuntary way, as though they'd just gone over a wave.

"What was that?" said Jamie.

"Dunno," said Callum, "did we just hit something?"

Their voices echoed down the dark tunnel lending an even more eerie aspect to the claustrophobic proximity of the walls and roof.

"Like what?" said Jamie.

"I dunno – like a body or something?"

Jamie was horrified. He said, "Thanks, that made me feel much better." He paused and said, "Is the motor still okay?"

Callum wiggled the tiller from side to side and said, "Yeah."

A second shudder emanated below them and the whole tunnel grunted like an ancient, rock giant.

"Fucking hell," said Callum, "I didn't like that."

"Neither did I," said Jamie, "let's get out of here."

The boys looked in both directions and saw that the tiny arcs of light at each end appeared to be the same size.

The tunnel shuddered and grunted again, but this time pieces of brick and mortar showered down onto their heads.

Callum's heart rate leapt. He said, "Shit – I don't like this, I don't like this one bit," he looked behind and said, "Hold on, we're going back." He pushed the tiller as far away from him as it would go and jammed the motor straight into third gear. The boat turned right and collided with the tunnel wall. He then pulled the tiller back and engaged full speed reverse. The boat shot back as far he would dare, and then he pushed the tiller over and engaged third once more.

The boat surged forwards, almost made the turn, and then hit the tunnel wall again. It scraped along for a few feet, and then stopped.

Callum yanked the tiller back and engaged reverse gear, but nothing happened. He turned and looked into the water, but he couldn't see a thing in the dark. He engaged forward drive again, but as before, the boat remained stationary. He tried different gears but nothing happened.

"Come on!" said a panic-stricken Jamie, "Stop fucking about and let's get out of here!"

"I can't," said Callum, "there's …" He stopped talking as a distant rumble began to grow in intensity behind him. It sounded like a huge roaring lion, racing up the tunnel towards them.

Both boys turned around and saw that the light had gone from the opposite end. They stared in silence, and then abject terror, as the tunnel collapsed foot-by-foot in the torchlight, until it finally engulfed them.

Up above, David Blackhurst was returning to his farm, towing a small trailer with his brand new tractor.

Without warning, a gigantic hole opened up behind him and began to spread out in all directions. He whipped around, saw what was happening, and yanked the accelerator handle down. The tractor surged forwards, but it was too late. The hole continued to open up at an alarming rate until the trailer started to fall backwards over the edge.

David leapt off the seat, got his head down, and ran as fast as his legs would carry him …

If you enjoyed this novel, look out for the next in the series:

'The Monkshead Conspiracy'

Other novels by Stephen F. Clegg:

'Maria's Papers'

'The Matthew Chance Legacy'

'The Emergence of Malaterre'

'The Fire of Mars'

www.stephenfclegg.com